Rough Cut

Also by Anna Smith

The Rosie Gilmour series

The Dead Won't Sleep
To Tell the Truth
Screams in the Dark
Betrayed
A Cold Killing

Anna Smith

Rough Cut

Quercus

First published in Great Britain in 2016 by

Quercus Publishing Ltd
Carmelite House
50 Victoria Embankment
London EC4Y 0DZ

An Hachette UK company

A CIP catalogue record for this book is available
from the British Library

PB ISBN 978 1 84866 432 6
EBOOK ISBN 978 1 78429 314 7

10 9 8 7 6 5 4 3 2 1

Typeset by Jouve (UK), Milton Keynes

Printed and bound in Great Britain by Clays Ltd, St Ives plc

Glasgow, January 2000

Nikki stood staring down at him in disbelief, paralysed with fear, willing him to utter a noise – any noise that would mean he wasn't stone cold dead. She scanned his naked, lifeless body slumped on the floor where he'd keeled over. His fleshy mouth hung open as though in mid-sentence, and bubbles of saliva formed at the side of bloated jowls. The belt was still rigid around his neck, and purple welts began to appear there, creeping up towards his ears. One arm was raised above his head, the other draped across his thigh where a streak of fresh semen glistened under the harsh ceiling light. It crossed Nikki's mind to reach down and loosen the belt. Maybe he'd come round and splutter back to life. She took a step closer, then stopped. No. This was really happening. This bastard was dead. Her whole body jerked at the sudden, shrill ringing of her mobile, and she stumbled as she clambered around the body and across to the double bed where she'd placed her handbag when she came in. She snatched the phone out of the bag, but it flew out of her hands onto the floor, still ringing. Jesus! She dropped to her knees and picked it up, clutching it with both hands. It was Julie.

'Hey, Nikki. You about finished yet? Or are you doing a bit of overtime?' Julie's twenty-fags-a-day voice rasped.

Nikki opened her mouth to speak, but nothing came out.

'You there, Nikki? Everything alright?'

'Ju-ulie,' she managed to squeak. 'This guy's dead . . . Oh Christ, Julie!'

Silence. Nikki pressed the phone to her ear and could hear her own blood pounding in her head. Her legs wobbled and she began to sit down on the bed, but stood up again. Better not touch anything.

'What . . . What do you mean, dead?'

'Fuck's sake, Julie! What do you think I mean? I mean dead . . . as in not breathing. Oh Jesus! I-I think I've killed him!'

'What?'

Nikki tried to breathe, her chest tight with panic.

'I didn't mean it . . . He . . . He wanted me to do this thing with a belt round his neck . . . and . . . I had to pull it harder. He kept saying, "Tighter, tighter". Then . . . then . . .' She burst into tears. 'I didn't know what I was doing . . . I must have pulled the belt too hard. I . . .' Her voice trailed off in muffled sobs.

'Oh fuck!' Julie whispered.

Silence. Nikki heard Julie take a deep breath and clear her throat.

'Right. Calm down.' Her tone was suddenly firm, in charge. 'Just stay where you are. I'm on my way. Don't answer the door, unless it's me. What room you in?'

Nikki couldn't remember. Her mind was a blur. She pictured herself coming in through the crowded hotel foyer less than an hour ago, taking the lift and walking along a quiet corridor. Then it came to her.

'Room three-two-four. Hurry! Please!'

She stepped backwards towards the bathroom, her eyes still fixed on his body, watching for any movement. There was none. Her bare feet on the cold tiled floor made her look down, then up again. When she caught sight of herself in the bathroom mirror, her hand automatically went to her mouth as she gasped. Tears and smudged mascara blurred her reflection. She glanced over her plumpish body, breasts pushing over the black lace bra, its thin straps too tight for her beefy upper arms. The black suspenders held up fishnet stockings, and tripey mounds of fake-tanned flesh at the top of her thighs spilled over like blancmange.

'Christ! Look at you!' she whispered, shaking her head slowly. 'You're disgusting! What the fuck were you thinking?'

How could she have been stupid enough to allow Julie to

talk her into this? She'd convinced her they'd both make a few extra quid – a lot more on some weekends. And nobody would be any the wiser. Why the hell had she agreed? But it was too late now to ask stupid questions, too late for moral high ground reproaches. She broke down in sobs, slumped against the wall, as the sordid little scene five minutes ago ran through her mind like a low-budget porn flick.

It had only been her third time as an escort. In fact, calling herself an escort was an exaggeration, because that implied some kind of social interaction before you ended up on your back in a hotel bedroom with some random guy grunting on top of you. But at least it had been normal enough sex and not too unpleasant. Her second punter a few days ago had given her an extra thirty quid because she listened patiently for half an hour to his sad bastard life story before he asked her to climb on top of him. But this guy tonight was clear from the start about what he wanted. He'd been pleasant enough when he'd opened the hotel bedroom door to her – a fat, Asian bloke, Pakistani she assumed, with a northern accent. He'd said he was from Bradford and was up on a bit of business, but that was it. He then asked her to strip off, and she stood in front of him in her underwear, feeling a self-conscious flush in her chest. Whatever he'd been expecting, he didn't seem disappointed. He told her to keep her underwear on, then he took the belt off his trousers and stripped naked, already aroused. For a fleeting moment, Nikki thought he was some psycho who was going to use the belt on her. But he just drew his lips back in a smile, then knelt down with his back to her and put the belt around his neck. He told her to get behind him and rub herself against his back while he masturbated. Pull the belt tight, he told her. Don't stop till I tell you. When she protested, he got angry. 'Just pull the fucking belt tighter!' She did. 'Tighter', he kept saying, groaning, his breath coming in gasps. 'Tighter', he repeated, gasping 'yes, yes'. Nikki could see the colour rise on the back of his neck but he still wanted it tighter, calling her a bitch. 'Just pull the belt', he gasped. So she did. Then suddenly, he fell over. She let go of the belt, waiting for him to turn around. But he didn't.

The loud knocking on the bedroom door startled her back to the present, and she dashed out of the bathroom, bumping into the door as she stumbled.

'It's me, Nikki. Open up.'

She unlocked the door and Julie burst in.

'Christ! What's happened?'

She saw the body on the floor.

'Aw Jesus!'

Julie dashed over and dropped to her knees beside him, checking his neck for a pulse. She looked up at Nikki.

'He's fucked, Nikki.'

Nikki's hands went up to her face.

'Oh Julie! What are we going to do? Oh my God!'

Julie jumped to her feet and grabbed Nikki by the shoulders, prising her hands from her face. She looked her square in the eyes.

'Right! Listen! Enough of that! Just quit it! We need to get out of here – fast.'

'But . . . he's lying there dead—'

'Fuck that! It's nobody's fault. Kinky bastard anyway. What is it with these guys? I mean, what happened to an old-fashioned blowjob? No. There's always some prick wants to do something stupid. Well, fuck him! He's dead! At least he died happy.' She looked at Nikki, her ruby-red lips curling a little.

Nikki looked around the room.

'But what we going to do?'

Julie turned towards the body again, then went over to where his suit jacket was lying on the bed.

'Let's see who he is.'

Nikki watched, open-mouthed, as she went through his pockets and brought out a wallet. She opened it and held it in front of her, fat with wads of cash.

'Christ, he's loaded.'

She stuffed the wallet into her bag.

'What you doing, for Christ's sake? Stealing his wallet? Jesus, Julie.'

'Yep. I am. And his mobile.' She took his phone out of his trouser pocket and shoved it in her bag.

There was a holdall on the floor, and she rummaged

through it. It was only some clothes. Her eyes flicked around the room, and fell on a small hard shell silver attaché case.

'What's that?' She turned to Nikki.

'Don't know,' Nikki was confused. It was all happening so quickly. 'It must have been here when I came in. It must be his.'

Julie crossed the room and lifted the case. It was light. She tried to open it, but it was locked. She shook it and it made a rattling noise.

'It's not clothes, whatever it is.'

She walked towards Nikki with the case in her hand.

'Right. Listen, and listen good.'

Nikki nodded, swallowing.

'In about thirty seconds, we're going to walk right out of here, as if we were a couple of hotel guests on our way to a night out.'

'What? J-Just leave him?'

'Well, we can hardly call the bloody cops.'

'But we can't leave him lying there!'

'He's dead. There's nothing we can do for him. There's no crime been committed here. It's his own fucking fault.'

'B-But . . . You're taking his phone and his wallet. That's a crime.'

'I'm buying us some time, Nikki. If he's got no documents or ID on him, then when some wee chambermaid comes in tomorrow morning and finds him lying stiff, they'll take ages to find out who he is. He'll have used a false name for the room – that gives us time to work out some kind of plan.'

'But the case?'

'Just take it. Leave the holdall with the clothes. You never know what's in the case. Trust me. Okay? That's all you have to do.'

Nikki didn't answer.

Julie gently moved her towards the bed.

'C'mon. Get dressed. Let's move it. The place is mobbed down there in the foyer. Seems to be some kind of party going on, so nobody will even notice us leaving.'

Nikki pulled on her dress over her head and shoved her feet into her boots.

'I'm scared, Julie,' she sniffed.

'Stop it! You'll be a lot more scared if somebody walks in here and we're caught with a dead body on the floor.'

'But taking the case – what if he's a drug dealer or something?'

'Never mind what he is. I don't give a shit. I'm taking everything that will identify him for now. We can chuck the case in the river once we manage to open it. You never know, it might be full of money.'

She grabbed hold of Nikki by the elbow and pushed her towards the door.

'C'mon. Let's go.'

CHAPTER ONE

Rosie's shoes made a scrunching sound as she crossed the frozen grass, her breath steaming in the crisp, cold air. She climbed the wide steps of the three-storey sandstone villa and gazed up at the top floor windows, wondering which one the young Pakistani bride had tumbled from to her death. She shivered a little at the thought of the girl's final moments, that split second when the window had been flung open and she would have felt the blast of cold on her face for the last time. She wished morbid pictures wouldn't flood her head, but it was always the same on a death knock – though this was no ordinary death knock. What brought Rosie to the place they called Little Karachi, a five minute drive from Glasgow's city centre, was whether she fell or was pushed. A Pakistani girl had committed suicide, the police had concluded, in the absence of any evidence to the contrary.

The problem with poking around a place like Little

Karachi was that you had to tread carefully. Once home to generations of Scottish industrialists and merchants, Pollokshields, with its rows of two- and three-storey detached houses, was now the dominion of hundreds of Pakistani families – most of whom were business people, intermarried within their own communities. Of course, there was a bit of mystery about the way they led their lives, how they arranged their marriages, the strict rules and regulations – but they'd become part of Scottish culture. Nobody asked questions ... until recently. A couple of years ago a gang of Pakistani yobs had kidnapped and beaten a local white boy, burning him alive and abandoning him in waste ground, where he died in agony. It had sparked outrage outside the community, and plenty of anger within. Then, another story about a young woman who'd apparently set fire to herself in a house up around Maryhill. There were whisperings of some kind of honour killing. Police couldn't prove any foul play, and put it down to suicide. But a whiff of mistrust hung over the community now. People, probably racist deep down to begin with, started to question the way the Asians lived. The Asians shrank into themselves, but they were no longer left to their own devices. People asked questions and felt strongly that to do so was their divine right. Rosie's Pakistani contact had told her there was something dodgy about the latest young bride's death. Omar, a born and bred Glaswegian, might attend Friday prayers at the mosque, but he was as much a wide boy as any street smart punter from the East End, and had his finger in every Asian pie. He was her only link into their closed world, and he would never throw her a line like that if there wasn't something in it.

She could see shadows in the bay window of the big living room, where a few women seemed to be scurrying around. As she peered through the big stained glass door on the porch, someone was coming down the hall. More than one person. The door opened just a little, on a chain. Rosie put on her most understanding face.

'Hello. Sorry to trouble you at this time. My name is Rosie Gilmour. I'm from the *Post*. It's about the bride . . . Rabia—'

The door closed again. Rosie glanced over her shoulder to the car, where the photographer, Matt, was sitting looking up at her. She'd told him to stay where he was, as she thought it best to hit the door by herself. She shrugged at Matt. Then more shadows at the door, and this time it opened fully. A tall man in a traditional Pakistani tunic stood looking down at her, his pockmarked cheeks half covered by a bushy beard. She was ready with her pitch again, when to her surprise he took a step back.

'You can come in,' he beckoned her. 'I am Rashid Shah. Rabia was my son's wife.' His accent was Glaswegian but laced with Pakistani tones.

Rosie stepped into the large, gloomy hallway, her eyes drawn to walls festooned with tapestries of what looked like ancient Asian rituals or legends. Big porcelain jardinières with plant pots and plastic flowers framed the wide, spiral staircase, where a crimson carpet swept up to a landing, then around another staircase. A couple of children peeked out of a bedroom on the landing, then closed the door again. The pungent aroma of Asian cooking wafted from the kitchen at the end of the hall, and Rosie glanced over to see three woman coming out of an adjoining room, each of them dressed in full traditional clothes, bright oranges and reds. How many lived here? she wondered. Certainly more than one family, which wouldn't be unusual. Many Pakistani families shared their homes with their offspring even after they married, and the mother of a young husband was often the matriarchal figure who welcomed, and if need be, scolded the new bride into their ways. The father and the men were the breadwinners. There was a status that came with growing old, unlike the mentality around the corner, where white feral youths ran riot and did what they wanted to their fathers and insulted their mothers. You didn't get that in the Asian households. Their community had family and respect at its core, even if many of their ways seemed alien to outsiders.

'Would you like some tea?' the man asked as he led her down the hall, where a door opened into a large room.

'Yes,' Rosie replied, a little surprised at the hospitality. In a lot of death knocks you got huckled out smartish. 'Thanks. Some black tea would be great.'

The man barked something loudly in Urdu in the direction of the kitchen, and a young woman in striking yellow traditional dress with her head covered, came out and more or less bowed. She made brief eye contact with Rosie. It was only a second, but it was enough. There was something there, something in the dark shadows under her eyes, which darted from Rosie to the ground. She was very pretty and probably in her early twenties; clearly cowed by the older man, she kept her eyes downcast as she nodded, then turned and went quickly back into the kitchen.

Rosie was a little taken aback when she was led into one of the large rooms off the hallway. She glanced quickly around the three big sofas and chairs, where at least eight men sat in a circle as though in a meeting. They were all dressed traditionally, a few of them rattling prayer beads in their hands, talking in hushed tones. They stopped instantly and turned towards her. Silence.

'Hello,' she said, not really knowing what else to say.

'Please. Take a seat.' Shah motioned her to an upright chair, and she could feel all the eyes following her as she sat down, as though it was she who had been summoned.

'This my family. Brothers and cousins. And –' he pointed to a lean-faced, handsome young man with thin lips, who looked up from the floor, then back down – 'this my son, Farooq. The husband of the bride. His heart is broken.'

The widower nodded and looked away from her, clasping his hands on his lap. Rosie could see his white knuckles. She glanced at his fingers, heavy with gold rings, a chunky bracelet on his wrist. A huge diamond ring, too big to be anything other than a fake, glistened on his pinkie. What was it with these guys and their bling? Don't judge, she told herself. Listen to what they say. There were people in the newsroom who would make their minds up straight away, but Rosie wasn't one of them. She did feel a little claustrophobic from the sheer presence of all these men, though, sitting looking at her, waiting. She swallowed back a little panicky feeling. Just get this over with, she told herself.

'I'm sorry for your loss, Farooq.' She looked directly at the widower, and waited at least four beats.

He raised his head in acknowledgement, but said nothing. Two out of five for the heartbroken widower impression, Rosie noted.

'My son is too upset to speak. It's been a very big shock. They were only married three months ago.'

'Yes,' Rosie said, and gave a sympathetic shake of her head. 'I read it in the police statement.' She took a breath and looked at Shah. 'I understand they met in Pakistan just a few months ago?'

She was trying to choose her words carefully. Arranged marriages were a way of life in the Pakistani culture, and it was difficult for others to understand.

'I take it the marriage was arranged in the normal way?' Rosie glanced around the room, stony faces staring back at her, and then turned to Shah.

'What do you mean – in the usual way?'

There was a little flick of resentment in Shah's tone. A couple of the men shifted in their seats and puffed. Rosie had to rescue this, but she also had to stand her ground.

'By that I mean, in the usual way within your culture, where people tend to meet their future husband or wife through family and connections.' Rosie looked around at the men who stared back at her. She let the silence hang, the air cranking up with tension. She wasn't going to shift on this. 'I understand Rabia was in the UK for the first time for the wedding. She must have found it very different from back home.'

Nobody was answering. Christ!

'What I'm trying to say is, Mr Shah, do you think perhaps she was homesick and it all got too much for her?' Rosie turned to the groom. 'Did she say anything, Farooq, about being depressed? Show any signs? Missing home? Understandable, really.'

Farooq glanced at his father but made no reply.

Shah took a deep breath and exhaled slowly.

'Yes. I think she may have been a little depressed. It happens with the young girls sometimes, because they are in a strange city, far from their families. But really, it just takes time to settle.'

'So there was no indication of how depressed she actually was?'

'I wish there was,' he said and looked at the others, whose faces were like flint.

Rosie said nothing. Her Strathclyde detective pal, Don, had tipped her off that the girl had marks on her wrist, consistent with self-harming, or someone else harming her. But the family couldn't throw any light on it, and Rosie got the distinct feeling that bringing it up right now was not a good idea. Police had ruled it was a straightforward suicide and the body had been buried within forty-eight hours, so it was really too late to do anything about it anyway. This was going nowhere. But something in her gut told her they were lying, or at the very least, hiding something.

The door opened, and the young girl from earlier came in carrying a small tray with a glass of tea and a plate of small pastries. She placed it down on the coffee table in front of Rosie and as she did, Rosie noticed welts and bruising on her wrists. The girl backed away, but was close enough to clock Rosie the moment she'd glanced at her wrists. She nodded in thanks for the tea and lifted the glass to her lips, hoping she had said enough with her eyes to acknowledge the girl's distressed look, before she backed away and left the room.

'She is the bride's sister, Sabiha,' Shah said. 'It has been difficult for her.'

'I see,' Rosie said. 'Has she been here for a long time?'

'Yes. Four years. Married to Farooq's cousin. They have two children.' He sat back. 'It takes time to settle down into the life.'

Rosie changed the subject.

'Its a very large house, Mr Shah. It must be good to have all the family together. To be honest, I think that's a great part of your culture, that family is at the heart of it.'

Rosie hoped to draw him out, but the notion of living with several families under the same roof would be her ideal of hell. She drank the lukewarm sweet tea.

He nodded.

'Of course. We all work very hard for each other. We have three families living here. My own wife and our two sons and their children. Often Sabiha and her children come to stay. It is very comfortable. You like to see? I show you around?'

Rosie wasn't sure what to do. He stood up. It didn't seem to be an invitation. They left the room and she followed him along the hall and upstairs. He showed her what he called the playroom, where two boys sat with toys on the floor and another two girls were drawing with crayons. They climbed the creaking stairs to the top floor.

'Did Rabia live on the top floor here with her husband?'

'Yes. In the room at the end. But we won't go there. It's too upsetting.'

Rosie glanced down the hall, where the light faded, and a sudden chill ran through her. At the very top of the door was a bolt with a looped latch, a crude effort, not even straight. Her eyes flicked to the bottom where there was another, similar lock. She looked away and said nothing. She'd seen enough. Whether Rabia had been homesick, they would never know. But she'd been locked in. Rosie suddenly wanted to get out of this house as fast as possible. She looked at her watch.

'Thanks for your time, Mr Shah. I do know how difficult it has been, and I appreciate you explaining your loss and the background, and giving me this time. I will go now and leave you in peace.'

'You will say what a good girl she was? That it is just a sad thing that has happened?'

'Yes, of course.' Rosie knew she had no intention of writing a story.

As the front door closed behind her, she took in a lungful of frosty air. The late afternoon sky was growing dark, the houses in the distance beginning to look like silhouettes along the skyline. She went down towards her car, where Matt sat up quickly and started the engine. As she approached, she turned around and could see the young girl in the yellow dress at the window. She was staring at her. Rosie thought her lips moved, but then she disappeared and the curtain was drawn.

'How did it go?' Matt said. 'Did they give you any food? No doggy bag with a couple of samosas or anything?'

Rosie suppressed a laugh.

'Christ! You never change.'

'I'm starving. But how was it?'

'Place gave me the bloody creeps. Come on. Let's get out of here.'

CHAPTER TWO

Nikki stared out of the taxi window, her mind re-running the scene they'd left, the body on the hotel room floor. Julie had warned her it was crucial that they looked just like any other guests. Once the body was discovered – no doubt by a chambermaid in the morning – the cops would be all over the place, she'd said. The Albany had been a decent enough city centre hotel in its day, but it wasn't top-drawer now, and was the kind of place random couples often booked into for the night if they'd got lucky at a club. Nikki had taken one last look over her shoulder at the naked body of her punter as Julie gently prodded her towards the bedroom door. They'd strolled down the long corridor in silence and stepped into the empty lift. When the lift doors opened she was glad that the foyer leading to the bar area was crowded. It looked like some kind of organised reception, and guests were being handed a glass of champagne on arrival. They'd made their way through the throng, and Nikki couldn't believe the cheek when Julie took a champagne flute from a waiter's tray and knocked it back, leaving her empty glass on a table close to the exit. They'd jumped into one of the waiting taxis, and as it pulled out of the car park Nikki started crying.

'Right. Calm down, you.' Julie handed Nikki a tissue. 'It's alright. Nothing's going to happen.'

Nikki sniffed and wiped her nose with trembling hands.

'Christ! I'm shaking like a leaf.'

'Come on now,' Julie squeezed her arm. 'You'll be fine when you get a stiff drink.' Julie leaned forward to the glass partition and spoke to the back of the driver's head. 'Cranhill, pal.'

'Have you got drink in the house?' Nikki asked.

'Are you kidding me?' Julie replied with a sarcastic grin. 'See. You'll be fine, Nikki. Just stop panicking.' She lowered her voice to a whisper, and continued. 'What we're going to do is convince ourselves that shit back there didn't happen. Okay, we've got the case, but who is ever going to know that? As far as any punter lying stiff on the floor, forget it. It didn't happen – okay?'

'Easier said than done,' Nikki sniffed.

In the driving sleet, the black Hackney weaved its way through the city centre and briefly on to the motorway before taking a slip road into Cranhill, a sprawling housing scheme in the city's East End. Julie told the taxi to pull up at the last house on the corner of a row of drab council maisonettes.

'Home, sweet home.' Julie gestured to Nikki to get out of the car as she paid the driver. Then she climbed out, clutching the attaché case, and slammed the car door shut.

The white Christmas that had seen the city clothed in six inches of snow had turned to brown slush in the constant icy rain. The dawn of the new millennium had been so exciting just twelve days ago, when Glasgow and the rest of the world hailed its arrival amid a spree of wild partying and hopes for a new beginning. Right now, all of that seemed a long time ago, as Nikki and Julie carefully trod over the slush and puddles, the freezing sleet slapping their faces. A blue carryout plastic bag swirled through air and attached itself to a naked tree where it fluttered like a flag. Two of the street lamps were out, and only the occasional chink of light from windows in the six-storey block guided their way up the steps and into the dark entrance.

'Fucking streetlights have been like this since the start of December. It's like the blackout. If it was posh Bearsden, the council would have been out smartish, but they don't give a shit about people up here.'

'I know.' Nikki picked her way up the steps, through the debris and discarded lager cans. 'I'm bloody freezing.'

Julie flicked a light switch when they stepped inside her hallway, then strode on ahead to the living room, switching on lamps and a gas fire. It immediately began to glow over imitation coals and the room came to life, as welcoming as a warm hug on a miserable night like this.

'There. That's better. All cosy now. The central heating came on two hours ago.' She put the attaché case down and turned to Julie, standing in the doorway. 'Come on. Let's get a bloody drink. G and T alright?'

'Thanks. It's nice and warm in here,' Nikki said, following her into the kitchen: marble worktops and top-of-the range units. 'Your house is really great, Jules. I think that every time I come here. Must have cost you a packet.' She smiled.

'Yeah. Would have done, but as you know, most of it was blagged.'

She took out a bottle of gin from the cupboard and two heavy crystal glasses, then a block of ice cubes from the freezer. Nikki watched as the ice cracked when Julie poured two good glugs of gin into the glasses, and the bubbles hissed and danced as she added the tonic.

She handed Nikki a glass. 'Sorry, we're right out of limes, pet,' Julie said. 'That bloody butler's getting fired in the morning.'

They both burst out laughing and clinked glasses.

'To us,' Julie said. Then she looked at Nikki wistfully and nodded. 'To friends forever.'

'Friends forever,' Nikki said, biting her lip to hold back the tears, suddenly remembering the first time they'd got drunk together, fifteen year olds before the school disco. It seemed a lifetime ago, and look at them now. She swallowed hard and smiled.

'God, I needed that,' Nikki said, taking another gulp, enjoying the alcohol warming her all the way down her gut. 'I wish I could be as calm as you. I keep seeing that guy lying dead on the carpet.'

Julie handed her a cigarette and they both took their drinks into the living room and plonked themselves onto the sofa. Next to the comforting hiss of the fire and the warmth of the room, they could have been two old mates relaxing after a hard day's work. If only, Nikki thought. Life would never be the same after tonight.

'So,' Nikki said. 'This is lovely, Julie. But . . . but we can't really just pretend that shit an hour ago didn't happen. There's a guy lying dead on the floor of the Albany.'

'I know there is. And he'll still be dead in the morning. We'll think of something.'

'What's going to happen once they discover him?'

'What do you mean? Is it going to lead back to us?'

'It won't. Unless that arsehole Georgie at the agency spills her guts. Like I said, the guy would have booked his escort under a different name than the name he gave at the hotel. Most punters do that. At least, let's hope so. I mean there's no evidence that a girl was in the room with him. It looks like one of these sexual things guys sometimes do themselves, when they're having a hand shandy. It's dangerous, but apparently that's part of the thrill. Whatever floats your boat, I suppose.' Julie shrugged, then looked at Nikki. 'I hope you didn't drop anything out of your bag, or anything like that.'

'No,' Nikki said, 'I don't think so.' She tried to remember her movements in the room, in case she'd left anything behind. Don't even go there, she told herself.

The alcohol was helping to calm her down and they sat staring at the flames for a long moment.

'Anyway, I'm sure you'll not be doing too many jobs like that in a hurry.'

'I don't think I'll be doing any more at all, Julie. I'm just no good at it.'

'Nonsense. Look how much you made last weekend. The old guy loved you. Left you an extra thirty quid for nothing. Some guys . . . they phone for an escort for the evening and nine times out of ten it's sex they want, and even if it is, most of them are just ordinary guys, but some are just lonely and want a woman to talk to. It's a matter of getting used to it. There's seldom a problem, think of it as a job and don't get all hung up about it. It has to beat the shit out of stacking shelves in the supermarket, or working in the old people's home as a skivvy.'

Nikki nodded, but her gaze fell on the attaché case. Julie gave her a mischievous grin.

'Will we open it?'

Nikki let out a sigh.

'Might as well.'

Julie brought it across the room, then knelt down and

fiddled with the lock, pressing the clips. Nothing. Then she fished around in her handbag and came out with two small keys on a ring. She held them up.

'I forgot about these. In his wallet.' She brought out a mobile phone. 'And this.' She handed it to Nikki. 'Here. Have a look through it. See if there's any numbers we recognise.'

'How do you mean? The agency? That'll be on it. But not my number. My number won't be on it, will it?'

'Just kidding. Lighten up, woman.'

She fiddled with the lock and key, and one lock snapped open. The other followed, and Julie lifted the lid. There were a couple of new white shirts, still in cellophane, and two pairs of underpants. She rummaged around, pushing them to the side.

'Looks like it's got a false bottom.'

Nikki got onto the floor, pulled herself closer and sat cross-legged, watching as Julie unzipped the false bottom and opened it. They both looked at the contents, and then at each other.

'Passports?' Julie screwed up her eyes, rumbling around in the case. 'Jesus!' Then her hand emerged, holding a thick wedge of money in an elastic band. 'Look. A late Christmas present!'

She flicked through the money, fifty-pound notes and twenties.

'There must be over three grand here. Jesus! I bloody knew he was dodgy.'

Nikki picked up a few passports. There were eight or nine of them, and she squinted at the Pakistani national crest on their fronts. She opened them up. The photos inside were mostly of men, but a couple of them were women; young faces.

'What the fuck is this all about?' Julie leafed through one or two of them, then tossed them on the floor. 'They must be fake or something. Guy was obviously in some kind of racket.'

Julie's eyes turned to two little black velvet padded pouches, each tied with red ribbon. She picked one up and held it in her hand.

'What's this? She opened it and pushed her fingers in, feeling around. She pulled out a couple of roundish, rough stones.

'Stones?' Nikki asked.

'Maybe it was a sting or something and they were suppose to leave the jewels they'd stolen, but what the guy left is a bag of driveway chips. I think somebody's been humped up the arse.'

'Let me see one.' Nikki took one. It was grainy-feeling. She got up and went into the kitchen and took a small knife from the cutlery drawer. Then she came back in and sat down, gently scraping the stone. She stopped as it suddenly glinted like glass in the light. They looked at each other, eyes wide.

'Fuck! Are you thinking what I'm thinking?'

Nikki kept scraping until the glass was almost clear on one side.

'Diamonds! Jesus Christ, Julie! I think that's a rough diamond. Holy fucking mother of God! We've stolen some bastard's diamonds.' She slumped back against the sofa and took another gulp of her drink.

Julie emptied the contents onto the carpet. Ten stones about the size of grapes. Then she took the other pouch and emptied them out. 'Diamonds? Oh Christ!' She picked two up and stared at them lying in the palm of her hand.

The mobile rang and they both jumped at the same time.

'Shit!' Nikki looked at it ringing and shuddering on the carpet, then at Julie.

'Leave it,' Julie said. 'Let it ring.'

They could see the name Khan on the screen. Then it rang off.

'Do you think they've left a message?' Nikki whispered.

'Leave it for a minute, then we'll check.'

The phone vibrated with a message alert and Julie picked it up and scrolled through it.

'It's a voice message.'

She put it on to loudspeaker. It was an Asian accent mixed with a rough northern England lilt.

'Ahmed. Where the fuck are you? You're not answering your phone. I need to talk to you about the meet tomorrow.'

Nikki's hand went to her mouth.

'Jesus, Jules! This is serious!'

'I know.'

For the first time all evening, Julie looked nervous. They both jumped again as the mobile rang, and watched in silence until it stopped.

CHAPTER THREE

From her seat at the cafe's window, Rosie watched the newsagent's across the street. She'd been outside the Shah house, sat in the dark, since before seven this morning, watching the comings and goings, hoping for a glimpse of the girl. Mostly it was men leaving early, probably going to work. At one stage the widower came out, got into his silver BMW and roared out of the street. Eventually, two women came out with kids in school uniforms and coats, wrapped up against the bitter wind, and they walked in the direction of the primary school at the end of the road. Then nothing. After another half hour, she saw the girl leave and head up the street towards the shops. Rosie followed at a very discreet distance. When she saw her going into the newsagent and not coming out after a few minutes, she assumed she must be working there. Perhaps it was part of the family business. Rosie and Declan had run a check on them, establishing that the Shah family owned a textile-importing business, a cash and carry and three Indian takeaways, as well as a string of corner shops. It was always difficult within the Asian community to figure out who actually owned what as business premises were often rented and the businesses run by extended families. Rosie knew she couldn't risk going into the newsagent in case she bumped into someone from the house yesterday. She wanted to get Sabiha alone. So she waited, ordered another cup of tea, and worked out her next move.

In McGuire's office yesterday afternoon, he was, as usual, strident as she'd told him of her visit to the Shah house.

'I just don't trust them,' he declared.

'You can't make sweeping statements like that, Mick. Not out loud anyway. It sounds racist.'

'I'm not racist. Not in the least. And I don't care whether it's Catholic, Protestant, Hindu, or born again fucking Christian. I don't like the way these people treat their women. They've obviously locked that poor girl in her room. Maybe she was forced into a marriage she didn't want, or brought over here against her will. I don't care what religion that is. It's just wrong. Stuff anyone who calls me racist.' He stood up. 'And don't forget, Gilmour. It was this paper that exposed the real racist bastards who were terrorising voters when that Pakistani MP was running for election. We put them in jail for what they did, and I'm proud of that. But I'll be asking questions whenever I want, about whoever I want. That's how I do business.'

Rosie smiled to herself, recalling his outrage when a Ku Klux Klan-style fiery cross was stuck in the Pakistani MP's garden days after he was elected to the House of Commons. The *Post* had gone all out on the investigation and tracked down the sick bunch of right-wing thugs to a flat in Glasgow. They'd found out that a couple of them were wealthy white businessmen.

'So, how we going to tackle this?' He sat down in the chair opposite her. 'I'm not putting some sob story in the paper about them all sitting round there weeping over the girl, if there is any hint that their actions, or inaction, played a part in her death. And that fucking lock on the outside of the door tells me enough. What are the cops saying?'

'Not a lot. I think there's a feeling they aren't getting the real story from the family. But they have no evidence whatsoever of a crime. Okay, the girl had recent slash marks on her wrist, and also marks that looked like she'd been restrained. But the family say that was self-inflicted, that she self-harmed. The cops have no way of proving any different.'

'But you saw the younger girl in the house with marks on her wrist?'

'Yeah. And that's where I want to start. If I could get Sabiha on her own, maybe I could get through to her. I felt like she looked yesterday as though she wanted to speak. But she'll be terrified. I might be wrong, but it's worth a try.'

McGuire's phone rang on his desk and he looked at his watch.

'I've got a conference call in five minutes. Get yourself out to that house in the morning early doors and see what you can see. But you have to be careful, or they'll start throwing accusations of racism at us.'

Rosie watched as one of the men from the house, whom she'd seen leave the shop a few minutes after the girl, returned. Then shortly afterwards, the door opened and the girl came out. Rosie leapt to her feet, left three pound coins on the counter and went out of the cafe. She got into her car and drove past the girl, then pulled in to the kerb a few yards up the road. Sabiha seemed to be going back to the house, so she would only have one quick shot at this. She watched from her rear-view mirror as the girl got closer to the car. Then, as she was almost there, Rosie got out and stood leaning on the passenger side of the car. The girl had her head down as she walked along the pavement, and looked up, startled, when she saw her.

'Excuse me, Sabiha?' Rosie took a step towards her.

The girl stopped in her tracks, her eyes darting around and over her shoulder. She took a step as though trying to pass Rosie.

'Wait! Please!' Rosie said. 'Sorry. But can I have one moment to talk to you?'

Sabiha stopped and shook her head quickly, her eyes full of fear.

'No. Please. No.' She sidestepped Rosie and went beyond her, walking briskly.

'Okay, I'm sorry.' Rosie quickened her step behind her. 'Sabiha, I wanted to talk to you about your sister Rabia . . . I think someone is not telling the truth. I . . . I saw the lock on the bedroom door. I think someone harmed your sister.'

It worked. Sabiha stopped rigid, and half turned, but then immediately turned away and kept walking.

'Listen, Sabiha. I have a feeling something very bad is going on. Don't be afraid. Just . . . please, take my card.'

Sabiha stopped again and this time turned fully around to face Rosie, and she could see the dark smudges under her eyes.

'Go away!' Her trembling fingers went to her lips. 'You'll get me into trouble talking to me. Go away! Don't you see? You can't help! Go away!'

Rosie resisted the urge to reach out and touch her arm.

'But maybe I *can* help,' she looked her in the eye. 'I can only help if someone talks to me. Sabiha. You have been here for four years. You must know what goes on. What was troubling your sister so much that she took her own life?'

The girl's lip quivered. She shook her head.

'No! Rabia did not kill herself.'

Rosie was nearly in. She opened her mouth to speak, but the girl put her hand up.

'Please. I must go home. I have my children. That is all that matters now.'

As Sabiha turned to walk away, Rosie stepped forward and thrust her card towards her.

'Here. Please take it. If you get a chance and feel you want to talk, then call me. Any time. No one will know. I promise.'

Sabiha shook her head, then she was gone, moving swiftly up the road, her steps quickening.

Rosie stepped on to the editorial floor of the *Post* as the various executives spilled out of the morning conference, each carrying their schedule for features, news and sport for tomorrow's paper. As she approached her desk, Declan, one of the paper's rising young stars, was putting on his jacket and stuffing his notebook and tape recorder into his pocket.

'I was going to phone you in a minute, Rosie.'

'What's up? Where you off to?'

'The Albany. Guy found dead in a hotel bedroom. I got a tip from one of my cop pals. A chambermaid found some guy naked on the floor with a belt round his neck.'

'Why are the cops into that? I'm surprised they're not

just saying it looks like suicide, or one of those kinky sex jobs. Do they think someone's done him in?'

'Dunno yet. But I'm going to take a run up, and see what's going on. I'll give you a shout once I get a handle on it.'

Rosie was already punching a phone number into her mobile: Don, a detective sergeant in the Serious Crime Squad, who'd been her close friend and police inside source for years.

'Don. Howsit going?'

'Rosie. The very woman. I was going to buzz you to see if you fancied a drink later.'

'Good idea. What about the dead body on the floor at the Albany. Did somebody bump him off?'

'Don't know yet. But it's who he is that's of interest to us.'

'Who is he?'

'Ever hear of a Pakistani gangster by the name of Ahmed Malik?'

'Nope. From around here?'

'Initially, Glasgow. But moved down south years ago. Manchester or Bradford. He's a major racketeer now, involved in fake passports, identity cards. And, wait for it, we're hearing from the boys down at Scotland Yard that he's been dabbling in diamond smuggling.'

'Diamond smuggling? Pakistanis? That's a new one on me. We looked at a guy a few years ago who was making fake passports for illegal immigrants he was bringing in to work in restaurants. I'd have thought that was the level of stuff they did. But diamonds?'

'Word is that there's a bigshot Pakistani boss down in Manchester – his name is Sahid Khan – and this guy was working for him. Malik was a glorified delivery man.'

'So what was he doing up here?'

'That's what we're trying to find out. Tell you what, Rosie. It's too early to get any real picture here. Why don't I meet you later at O'Brien's and maybe I'll have some more.'

'Great. We've got a young reporter up at the Albany anyway, sniffing around.'

'Okay. See you later.' Don hung up.

Rosie sat down at her desk and checked her screen for anything on the wires about the dead body. Nothing so far. She picked up her mobile and punched in a number.

'Omar. What you up to, pal? I need to pick your brains on a couple of things. Do you fancy a coffee? I'll come up to the West End if you can take afford to some time out from your empire.'

'For you, Rosie, anything. See you in fifteen minutes.'

She hung up and headed back down the stairs.

CHAPTER FOUR

'Right. Run that past me again, Nikki . . . You got the call from Julie that you both had punters to meet . . . She went to see hers at the Thistle, and you went to the Albany.'

'That's right, Gordy.'

Nikki's mouth was so dry she could barely get the words out. This was the first time she'd met big Gordy MacLean in person, but his reputation was enough to scare the shit out of her. Nobody ever crossed him and lived to brag about it. Anyone who did was usually found face down in the Clyde, or trussed up and buried in a shallow grave out in the country – and, rumour had it, they weren't always dead when it happened. He looked like a mean bastard too, his eyes piercing her as though he could see she was lying through her teeth. She could feel her face redden. She chanced a glance at Julie sitting next to her, who gave her as reassuring a look as she dared. Nikki cleared her throat. She took a breath, hoping the story she and

Julie had concocted this morning would be believable. It had to be.

'Yeah. That's it. The guy didn't talk much at all, just wanted straight sex. He seemed alright and was keen enough, if you know what I mean, when he took his clothes off. But when he tried to have sex with me, he couldn't manage it. So, after a couple of attempts – and I mean, I was doing everything I could for him – he just said sorry and asked me to leave. I wasn't sure if he'd pay. I'm new to this, so I wasn't sure what the set-up was. But then he took a wad of notes out of his jacket pocket and gave me the money. He looked more embarrassed than anything. So I put my clothes on and left.'

'You left. Just like that?' Gordy sat back on his office chair and linked his fingers over his pot belly. 'Can you remember what was in the room, any bags or anything?'

'Bags?'

'Aye. Luggage. Like a suitcase or anything?'

Nikki narrowed her eyes, hoping she looked as though she was racking her brains.

'I think there was a holdall on the floor.'

'You didn't see an aluminium suitcase? Like one of them attaché cases you see businessmen carrying?'

She shook her head.

'Nope. Nothing like that. I mean, I wasn't looking for anything. To be honest, I wasn't paying much attention to what was in the room. Do other girls notice everything in rooms when they go to a punter? I'm only looking at the punter. He's the one who's paying for me, so that's all I'm interested in.'

Gordy picked up his mobile phone and held it up.

'You didn't see a mobile?'

Nikki shook her head.

Gordy said nothing and let the silence settle over them as he stared at Nikki for so long she could feel sweat trickling down her back. Her heart was thumping.

'So what is the situation, Gordy?' Julie broke the silence. 'This guy's dead. We know that much. And Georgie told us she heard he was naked on the floor with a belt around his neck. Is that right?'

'Aye.'

'So he either did it to himself or somebody's done him in. Who is he anyway, Gordy?'

Gordy glowered at her.

'Doesn't matter to you who the fuck he is. And, until I got a phone call putting a rocket up my arse about two hours ago, it didn't matter a fuck to me either. But now it does. Because now I've got someone breathing down my neck, asking where this Paki cunt's attaché case is. Because there were fucking rough diamonds in that case. Smuggled diamonds. And the last person to see him alive was you.' He turned his icy glare to Nikki.

'Well, he was alive when I left. That's all I can say. What else do you want me to say?' Tears welled up. 'The poor guy's dead. Who knows if he committed suicide, maybe because he couldn't have sex? I feel guilty. If I could have done something more for him to have sex with me, then maybe he wouldn't have done himself in, if that's what happened.'

'Fuck's sake!' Gordy shook his head and looked perplexedly at Julie. 'What you doing bringing somebody into this game with a fucking conscience?' He turned to Nikki. 'Listen, darlin', this isn't a social service we provide here. Some punter wants a ride, then we supply it and move on to the next customer. Anything else is of no consequence to us. But this guy was apparently carrying a case with a lot of valuable stuff in it. He was making a delivery down south, and decided to take a bit of down time before his meeting the next day. But suddenly he's found brown bread on the hotel floor. And his last point of contact was Discreet Escorts.'

'How do you know that, Gordy? Is he a regular?' Julie asked.

'No, he's not. First time. But he got one of the guys he knows up here to give him our number, and he called us himself. So, all of a sudden, every fucker is doing a postmortem trying to work out what happened. And somebody has told his boss that he was meeting one of our girls.' He looked at Nikki. 'That's you . . . and you were the last person to see him!'

'But maybe I wasn't,' Nikki protested, sniffing. 'Anything

could have happened after I left. But I didn't do a thing. Honest, Gordy. I've told you everything. You're looking at me as if I did something, and I didn't.' She broke down in sobs.

'Jesus wept!' Gordy said, as Julie handed Nikki a tissue. 'Who is she? Mary fucking Poppins?'

'I'm sorry,' Nikki sniffed. 'I'm just not used to it yet. He was only my third punter.'

'Aye, right.' He almost smiled. 'Well, don't get too attached to them.' Gordy stood up. 'Okay. The two of you can go now. I've got work to do. But don't be going on any holidays. I might need to talk to you again. The shite's all over the walls here – at least so far the cops haven't figured out that this fucker was with one of our birds, but they probably will. So keep your heads down, and talk to nobody.' He looked from one to the other. 'Am I clear about that?'

''Course,' Nikki said.

Julie nodded and they headed for the door. They didn't speak till they were out of the building and on the street.

'You were bloody dynamite in there, Nikki.' Julie nudged her. 'What a performance. You should get an Oscar – tears and everything! You didn't even flinch when he mentioned the diamonds.'

'The tears were real. I was shitting myself. Do you think he believed me?'

'I don't know. But he must be getting his arse felt by whoever belongs to the case.'

'But do you think he believed me?' Nikki insisted.

'Don't know. Let's hope so.'

As Julie waved down a cab, Nikki tugged her arm.

'This isn't over yet, Julie, is it?'

'No,' Julie shook her head as she climbed into the taxi. 'Come on. Let's go back to your flat and work out what we're going to do.'

An hour later, the two of them sat on the sofa in Nikki's flat, drinking coffee.

'Not a bad job is it? You can't tell it's been moved,' Julie said as they looked at the fake, wooden fire surround. 'And anyway, even if it got to the stage that somebody came searching, who's going to go behind the fireplace? That's one of your better ideas, Nikki. Is that where you keep all your money?'

'Yeah, right. I wish I had money to hide.' She sighed. 'But I actually had to hide all the endowments and savings accounts behind there before that useless bastard finally left. Otherwise I'd have lost the lot.'

Nikki's mind flashed back to the worst days before her gambling addict husband Paul finally left her, wrecking everything on his way out, pulling cupboards apart as he searched, desperate for anything he could turn into cash to punt at the bookies. A wave of depression washed over her, remembering how they had lost everything as Paul schemed and spent and stole from her, emptying their joint bank account for the bookies, and the threats from the moneylenders who were chasing him. He left her with nothing but the few sticks of furniture she had. But all of that had paled into insignificance when weeks later she lost the baby she was carrying six months into her pregnancy. It had taken her two years to get back to anything that would resemble the woman she was before, but she knew she could never have that old her entirely back. *She* was gone forever. Nikki still couldn't hold down a proper job, and bouts of depression still swept her down into the same dark alley. It was Julie who had helped pull her out of it, refusing to let her sink. It was Julie who had called in unannounced to find that she'd taken an overdose of pills when she didn't want to live another day. Julie stayed with her every day, pushed her to get better, or as good as she was going to get. She would have to make do with what was left of herself. She felt her eyes fill up.

'Sorry, Nikki,' Julie said quickly. 'I didn't mean to bring back any shit. I was only trying to lighten things up a bit. '

'It's okay. But I did keep stuff back there. It was the only place he hadn't turned upside down.'

'Bampot!' Julie said. 'You heard anything from him recently?'

'No. Not for a month. That's the longest he's been out of my hair. He's such a bastard. He left a message on my phone, after I ignored his calls. It said all he wanted to tell me was that he's moved in with some bird and was very happy. Good bloody luck to him. He must have found out she's got a bank account. Thieving, robbing bastard that he is.'

'You're well rid of him.'

'I know.'

They fell into silence, drinking their coffee and staring at the fire.

'So, what do you think has happened? That dead guy, whoever he was, must have had some serious business here. Do you think Gordy knows more than he's letting on?'

'Not sure how much he knows. He's not going to tell us, anyway.'

'Do you think he'll do anything to us?'

Julie shrugged.

'Hard to say, but we can't lose sleep thinking about that. He's a bad bastard, but I don't think he would actually go out of his way to do anything – unless he could benefit from it. I've known him a couple of years now and he's always been okay as long as nobody crosses him. There's absolutely nothing to suggest that we've done anything – and that's how it will stay. Especially now that he's confirmed that it's diamonds.'

'Anyway, Julie,' Nikki said. 'I'm not sure I'm cut out for this kind of escort stuff.'

'Christ's sake, Nikki!' Julie raised her eyebrows sympathetically. 'Do you think anyone is cut out for it? Nobody does it as a vocation. People do it because they have to, or because if you can separate yourself from what you're actually doing, it's quite an easy way of making money. I gave up all that feeling of being grubby and used a long time ago, and talked myself into it being a job just like any other. We provide a service and get paid. Simple as that.'

'I know, but I still feel awful with that guy dying on me. I've hardly slept for two nights. I keep seeing him turning blue.'

'It's normal to feel like that. You just have to go with it for the moment. But I think it would be a bad idea for you to suddenly tell Gordy you don't want to go back. It would look suspicious.'

'Would it not just look like I'm freaked out because of what happened?'

'It might. But we can't risk it, Nikki. We can't have him thinking that we are anything other than whiter than white here. So we just carry on as normal.'

Nikki sighed. 'We shouldn't have taken the case. That makes it even more dangerous. Somebody heavy is obviously looking for it. And Christ knows where that could end.'

'Just try to put all the anxiety stuff out of your mind and give it a couple of days. I've told Georgie I'm off for a day anyway and I won't be available till tomorrow night. She asked about you, and I said you'd be the same, maybe even an extra day. So just take some time to think about it.'

'Okay. I will.'

Julie looked at her watch. 'I'm going home to have an early night. I'd suggest you do the same. You want to come over or do you want to be on your own?'

'I'll stay here, thanks. I'm really tired.'

Julie stood up and picked up her bag, then Nikki walked her to the door. They had a long hug, but didn't speak, and Julie opened the door and left. At the sound of the main door to the building banging shut, Nikki felt a wave of loneliness wash over her.

CHAPTER FIVE

Rosie was glad to get out of the icy rain and into the warmth of O'Brien's, with its soft lights and polished elegance. She loved this place, its old stained glass windows and the anonymity of its green leather booths. Especially at this time of the afternoon, when all the lunchtime stragglers had finally sloped off and the waiters and staff quietly moved around the restaurant at the far end of the bar, preparing it for the evening. However depressing it was outside, with the rain coming down in sheets across the city, in here you could blot it out, sitting at the bar reading a copy of one of the posher broadsheets. You would never get a copy of a red-top tabloid like the *Post* in O'Brien's – a point which Rosie continued to make to the silver-haired Donegal barman, who usually gave her a sympathetic but ever so slightly condescending smile. The management don't think the customers would like it, he'd say. Then you should tell the management that plenty of the well-heeled punters who moved around in this place wouldn't know their way around a broadsheet newspaper, other than the fact that you got two fires out of it for kindling, she'd say. But it never changed, and she had to laugh at their double standards. It was well known that in O'Brien's, as well as the lawyers and top-drawer customers, there were always a few thugs who were just out of jail, or were lucky they hadn't been found out yet. She sipped from a glass of over-priced Spanish red wine, relishing the smoothness and reflected on her conversation an hour ago with Omar.

It didn't come as much of a surprise to her that Omar already knew the name of the dead Pakistani in the Albany, and his background. Rosie was glad that he'd confirmed what Don had told her – that Ahmed Malik was a racketeer involved in fake passports. Omar said the passports were used for the usual fraudulent activities – running up bills, obtaining credit and opening accounts all over the place. Banks and credit companies were throwing money at people these days, and if you could provide details over the phone, the money was in your account overnight. It was that easy. Fake passports could give a new identity for bank accounts to be opened and dirty money laundered. Omar didn't know Malik was into diamond smuggling, but he said it was easy.

'I've done it myself,' he said, looking a little smug.

Rosie knew Omar liked to shock her with his revelations.

She was intrigued by how well informed this elusive figure was, with no visible means of support, yet who drove a big car and lived in one of the city's more prosperous streets in the West End. He had also hinted over the years, that he had another life in the north of England, with another wife and two children. It was allowed, he'd declared, as long as you could support them. Rosie didn't judge.

'You actually smuggled diamonds?' Rosie looked at him in disbelief.

'Yes. I'm serious. I went to Africa – to Angola – and came back through Dubai and the Arab Emirates with a pocket full of stones. Rough diamonds. I was doing a run for a mate. Got well paid for it. It's much easier if you look like me than somebody like you, for example. You know what I mean. A white face. You don't get too many white faces along the way out there.'

'How difficult is it?'

'Rosie. It's like Sauchiehall Street over there. Everyone's doing it. We look at diamonds in jewellery shops and we know very little about them. If we know anything, it's probably that it's a very controlled, legalised trade, so that all the diamonds are authentic and every diamond in a ring can be traced back to the original stone. That's what we're led to believe, but a lot of that is crap. Diamond smuggling is big business. One of my contacts here asked me to do it for one of his contacts down in London. The money was great, so I thought, why not? I was amazed that once you get into Africa, crooked diamond merchants are all over the place.'

'I'd love to hear more of this story, but where does Malik fit in, as far as you know?'

'He's the guy – probably not the only one – who supplies the passports and delivers the rough stones. As far as I know he works all over the UK, but he's connected to one of the biggest, baddest guys in the country. A Pakistani from Karachi who works out of Manchester. His name is Sahid Khan. He stayed here a few years ago, but moved away. Really mental guy. Ahmed Malik works for him . . . or did. If he's been found dead in the hotel, then he must have crossed the big man. What are the cops telling you?'

'Nothing much,' Rosie replied. 'Officially, nothing except the fact that a Pakistani man was found with a belt around his neck. But one of my detective contacts told me the name, and also Khan's name. So, you're well informed.'

'I'm always well informed.' Omar drained his coffee cup. 'Somebody must have done Malik in.' He looked at his watch. 'Listen, I've got to meet someone now for a wee bit of business, but I'll keep my ear to the ground. I'll wait till I hear anything, but when I get it, you'll get it first.' He stood up and kissed Rosie on the cheek. 'You're my favourite woman. In fact, if you'd become a Muslim, I'd make you one of my wives.' He grinned, and turned on his heels.

*

Rosie waved as Don came into the bar.

'Hi, handsome,' Rosie planted a kiss on his cheek as he climbed onto a stool beside her. 'Let me buy you a drink.'

The barman pushed a pint of Stella Artois across to him, before subtly moving down the bar a bit to give them privacy. He knew Don was a cop and they were unlikely to be meeting socially.

'Here's to you, Gilmour.' Don took a long drink, then another sip before placing the glass back on the bar. 'I needed that.'

'Busy day with the Pakistani guy?'

'Yeah, mental. But I'll come to that in a minute.' He loosened his tie and ran a hand over his stubbly jaw. 'You know the girl who jumped out of the window?'

'Rabia Shah,' Rosie said.

'Yeah. Well, I did tell you that we were suspicious about marks on her wrists, and some other things we saw, but there was nothing really to open a proper case on it. So we had to release the body as they wanted to bury her within a couple of days – it's their custom.'

'So what's the problem?'

'A lot of flak coming from some rabble rousers in the Asian community, saying we were putting them under pressure with our questions. The family said we more or less accused them of harming the girl – which is total shit – even if I think they did.'

'Did you take part in the questioning?' Rosie knew Don was not known for his diplomacy.

'Aye. Me and the DCI. But we got nowhere. We did question them closely about the lock on the outside of the door. In fact, yeah, I did suggest to them that maybe they had locked her in. I have a gut feeling about it. Something isn't right.'

'Yeah. I know the feeling. I was there myself today, but I have nothing concrete to go on, so there is no way we can write any kind of story suggesting any wrongdoing. If we did, we'd be accused of racism.'

'Well, that's what's happened to the cops. The family filed a complaint of racism and now we have to get pulled in for an internal investigation. Pile of shite, but it has to be done.'

'For what it's worth, the family never mentioned anything about racist cops to me. If they had done, I'd have let you know.'

'Cheers, pal. That's something. I don't know what their game is though, making wild allegations. I still think they harmed the girl.'

'Me too.' Rosie didn't want to tell him that she had approached the sister. She changed the subject.

'So what about the Pakistani stiff, Ahmed Malik? What's the lowdown?'

Don sighed, offering Rosie a cigarette, which she declined. He lit one and inhaled deeply, swallowing the smoke.

'Forensics were in the hotel room half the day. They just

got back to us. The belt around his neck has other finger-prints on it – not just his.'

'Really? So somebody did him in?'

'It's looking like it. But we've got nothing so far. The prints didn't come up anywhere, so it could be anyone. But put it this way, if my trouser belt went in for forensic examination right now, the only fingerprints that would be on it would be mine.' He gave Rosie a mischievous grin. 'Unfortunately nobody has been rapidly unbuckling my belt to get into my pants of late.'

'I'm sorry to hear that, pet,' Rosie chuckled. 'But you're not home yet.'

'You don't need to throw yourself at me like a floozy.'

'Yeah, in your dreams, pal. But you never know who might walk in here looking for a macho detective with a lived-in face and a great line in patter.'

Don shrugged. 'Sure. I won't hold my breath. But any-way, back to the facts. Somebody had their hands on the belt. And –' he grimaced at Rosie – 'I don't want to put you off your drink, but tests on his penis show saliva. So unless he was also in the circus, then said saliva belongs to another person.'

Rosie chortled.

'Fascinating. And I take it you've no idea who?'

'Nope. And fat chance of us finding it either, unless we did swab tests of half the population in Glasgow – women *and* men.'

'I suppose he might have got a hooker or rent boy?'

'That's what we're working on. But it could be anyone. And why kill him? The other thing is . . . bags. There's nothing in his room – no wallet, no mobile. Only a holdall with a few things in it. But the hotel receptionist who checked him in says she remembers him carrying an aluminium case. So we're trawling through CCTV at the moment to see if we can see somebody with that.'

'Good story, Don. I hope you'll give me a shout if you get anything from CCTV.'

'The problem is the CCTV is only in the foyer area, and not in the corridors to the rooms, so we can't see who went in and out of his room.'

'That would have made it too easy,' Rosie said. 'It's all about nitty-gritty detective work – at least it is in the movies. So why are you involved? The Serious Crime Squad?'

'Because of the diamond smuggling. And who he is. Malik was a racketeer, well known for supplying fake passports, mostly to restaurant workers who came over here illegally. He was a real slippery character. Left Glasgow around six years ago but is mixed up with some joker down south – Sahid Khan. Big-time Pakistani dealer of everything from supplying people to work in restaurants to fake documents. And, of course, heroin. But these days, he's also a figure in the diamond smuggling industry. I don't know much about it, though I once did spend nearly a grand on an engagement ring for my ex-wife. Money wasted!'

Rosie smiled.

'I like the diamond-smuggling angle – makes it more exotic. I'm going to be speaking to an expert myself in the next couple of days. But when are the police going to officially issue a bit more on who Malik was?'

'Not for twenty-four hours – so you can break it yourself before the press release.' He winked. 'Don't say I'm not good to you. But Rosie, I want you to keep me in the loop if you hear anything. I know you have people you talk to on the ground that I don't get to, so I'd appreciate it.'

'Goes without saying.'

CHAPTER SIX

Nikki had only agreed to go on tonight's job because Julie said it would look suspicious if she knocked it back. Better to keep up a bold front for the next few weeks then gradually just phase yourself out. Fine, Nikki thought. I can just about live with that. But getting all kitted out in her working gear was the last thing she felt like doing right now. Her heart was still going like an engine half an hour after she'd slammed the phone down on Paul.

It had started off as a civilised conversation, when he'd called her out of the blue to ask if she'd received his text message that he was moving on with his life.

'Yes, I got it. Good luck to you.'

She hoped she sounded as uninterested as she was. She was surprised at how much she actually despised him now. Even the sound of his voice made her burn with rage. He had ruined her life. She lost the baby she'd longed for because of this selfish bastard. As far as she was concerned, he was already dead. Nikki put the finishing touches to her make up and looked at herself in the mirror while she listened to him. There were a few more lines around her eyes over the past eighteen months, and her face had lost a lot of its glow. When she was six months pregnant, she had just begun to put on a bit of weight around her middle and her face was fresh and full of hope. People talked about how vital she looked, and she loved it. Paul didn't even seem to notice – he was already lost in his gambling addiction, secretly emptying their bank account. She sighed, studying her face in the bathroom light, half listening to him. With her make up heavier on the eyes and blusher on her cheekbones, her features were more pronounced and she looked well. She hoped she wasn't too tarty – though that was what she was. Nobody was more aware of it than her. But it was only for a few more weeks. Paul was still droning on.

'Can you hear me, Nikki? I'm really doing well now.'

'Great. I said, good luck to you. Listen, Paul. I'm busy right now. I'm going out.'

'Oh aye. It's all about you, isn't it? Never mind me, and the fact that I've turned my life around. It's all about you. It always was.'

'Look. I don't need this. I haven't needed it for a long time, so can you just piss off and get on with your life and let me get on with mine?'

'Your new life.' Paul's voice was a snarl. 'Out every night. Some mother you'd have made anyway.'

'Piss off, Paul, you useless bastard,' she snapped. 'How dare you say that?'

'No! *You* fucking listen. I know where you go at night. You and that big fucking tart, Julie. You're whoring it.' He sniggered. 'A bit fucking past it if you ask me, the two of you. You must be offering discounts.'

She could see the red in her chest rise up her neck to her face, and the rage made her breath catch. How the hell did he know? She couldn't risk saying a word, because she knew her voice would quiver.

'Aye. You're quiet now, alright.' His voice dripped with sarcasm. 'You think because I'm not around the scheme I can't see what you're up to? I know what you're up to, you wee slut. I know who you work for and where you go.'

'I'm hanging up, Paul. You're talking a load of crap and I've not time to listen to you. Don't call me again. If you do, I'm going to get the cops to you. I'll get a fucking restraining order, you twisted bastard.'

'Yeah, right. Go to the cops then. Tell them you've got a new job. You think they'll listen to a fucking word you say.' He paused. 'I'm watching you. Don't you forget it.'

The phone clicked off and Nikki stood staring at herself in the mirror, her lip trembling. She swallowed. 'I won't let him do this to me,' she said out loud. 'I can do this. He won't beat me.'

In the taxi into the city centre, Nikki didn't mention Paul's phone call to Julie. When Julie asked her why she was so quiet, she said she was tired and hadn't slept much last night. She wanted to get this over and get back to the house. It was a hotel outside the city they were going to, Julie had told her. They were being picked up by Alex − Gordy's right-hand man − which was unusual in itself, as it was normally Davey, a pervy little creep, who drove them on jobs if they were out of Glasgow. He was waiting for them at the top of Renfield Street, and they got out of the taxi and into the car.

'So where is this hotel?' Julie asked.

'Just outside Paisley,' Alex said. 'I've got to get some petrol first on the way down.' He turned around to face Julie. 'But there's been a change of plan, darlin'. Did you get a phone call?'

'No.' Julie gave him a surprised look. 'What change?'

'You're to go up to the Thistle Hotel for a punter. Room two-six-seven. One of the birds had been booked earlier on, but she's called off. The babysitter didn't turn up or was pished or something. So she can't come. You've to go. So I'll drop you and I'll take Nikki to her punter.'

'But I didn't get a call. Usually, Georgie would call me.' She took her mobile out of her bag and scrolled down her call list.

'She's off tonight. It was Denny who phoned me. He said I'd to tell you. Do you want to phone him? He'll not be happy. He was just about to sit down to dinner with his wife when he phoned me.'

Julie sighed. Denny was one of Gordy's hardmen who occasionally worked at the agency if Georgie was off. She glanced at Nikki's worried look.

'So am I just to go on my own down to Paisley?' Nikki asked, looking from the driver to Julie.

'I'm taking you,' Alex said, indignant. 'Did I not just say that? I'm dropping you and I'll wait outside for you.'

Nikki looked at Julie.

'It'll be alright,' Julie said. She prodded Alex in the shoulder. 'Make sure you wait for her.'

'Fuck off,' Alex said, pulling the car up outside the Thistle Hotel. 'Your punter will be waiting for you.'

'I'll phone you,' Julie said, opening the back door. 'You'll be alright. I'll call you in about an hour. And any problems, you phone me.' She reached across and squeezed Nikki's shoulder, then got out of the car and tottered across in her high heels to the hotel entrance.

Alex drove out of the city and onto the motorway towards Paisley. A few miles along the M8, he took a slip road and headed for a service station. When the car pulled in, Nikki suddenly became aware that the petrol station was deserted, with no outside lights and the car park in darkness.

Suddenly two figures appeared from the shadows, moving towards the car.

'What is this?' She turned to Alex.

Her words were barely out when she glimpsed one of the men getting to her side of the car and grabbing the door.

'What the fuck? Oh, please, Alex! What's going on? Please!'

The car door was yanked and a hand dragged her out by the hair. She grasped at Alex's arm, trying to hold on.

'Don't do this! What's wrong?' She pleaded. 'What *is* this?'

'Fucking shut up!' Alex spat, jerking her hand away from him.

Nikki stumbled as she was pulled out of the car, but was hauled to her feet by the hair. Her face was slapped so hard she felt blood spout from her nose. Then she heard the flick of a knife, and saw the shine of the blade as he held it to her throat and dragged her across the darkened car park before bundling her into a car.

'Move one fucking muscle and I'll cut your throat.'

The voice wasn't Scottish. She glanced at his face, the sallow skin. He looked Pakistani or Indian. The accent was from Manchester or somewhere in the north of England.

He switched on the lights and screeched off, driving with one hand and holding the knife.

'Now just shut the fuck up.'

Nikki nodded, sniffing and wiping tears and blood from her face.

He drove out of the car park and onto the M8 towards Paisley. After a few minutes he turned off the motorway and into a slip road leading to a deserted industrial estate. He stopped the car and switched off the headlights. Nikki looked out of the windscreen at the total blackness, her head swimming with panic.

He turned to her, the knife at her throat. 'Where's the case?'

'What?' For a second Nikki had no idea what he was talking about.

'The fucking case you took, you bitch.'

She froze. She could feel her legs trembling uncontrollably and she swallowed the urge to throw up.

'Please don't hurt me! I don't know what you're talking about. What case? I told Gordy everything.'

'The case you took from the Albany. From your punter's room. We know you took it.'

She shook her head. How could they know that? She could hear her teeth chattering. This was it. She was going to die here in the middle of nowhere. She glanced down at the handle on the door. Suddenly, a mobile rang on the dashboard, distracting him, and in the moment it took for him to check the screen Nikki's hand had slipped down to the handle, opened the door and she had rolled out. She clambered to her feet and started to run in her high heels, going over on her ankle and kicking them off, then running barefoot in the rain and slush. In the distance she could see headlights from cars on the motorway, and she headed towards the lights, running so hard she could hardly breathe. His heavy footsteps pounded behind her, and she heard him curse and wheeze. Closer and closer. If she could just make it to the motorway, wave a car down. Then suddenly, she felt a thud on the back of her neck and everything turned black. On the ground, she opened her eyes, and he was on top of her, punching her hard on the face. She could feel the wet icy slush on her back and thighs and was on the verge of passing out again. But suddenly, something was hacking or burning at her leg and she screamed in pain with a voice she didn't even recognise. She could feel her flesh being torn. She opened her eyes and saw a crazed look on his face. He was kneeling behind her, and she saw the glint of what looked like a machete above his head. When it hit her arm just below her elbow, there was a moment of searing hot pain, and she opened her mouth to scream but nothing came out. Everything swayed above her. Somewhere she could hear the sound of hacking. She thought she must be dreaming because there was no pain any more. Then her head fell to the side, and she thought she saw part of her arm lying on the brown slush like a piece of meat.

CHAPTER SEVEN

Rosie was keying in the numbers on her burglar alarm as she prepared to leave her flat, when her mobile rang. She cursed under her breath, fumbling around in her bag for the phone while trying make it out of the door before the alarm went off. She found it and saw Don's number on the screen. It wasn't even nine in the morning, so if he was calling now, it must be important. She pushed the reset button on the alarm and went back into the apartment, answering the phone as she dumped her bag on the sofa.

'You not at your work yet?' Don joked. 'I thought you'd have had half a shift in by this time.'

'I'm always working, pal,' Rosie said in mock indignation. 'I'm just not always in the office.'

'Where are you?'

'I was on my way out the door of my flat, so now I'm back in. What's up? It's very early, even for Her Majesty's finest to be this switched on.' She crossed the room and stood by her terrace window, gazing out at the gloomy sky across the city and the traffic below.

'I'm giving you a heads up, Rosie. An attack on a woman last night. Really horrible – some psycho chopped half her arm off.'

'What? Is she dead?'

'Amazingly, she's hanging in there up at the Royal Infirmary. But she's in some nick. Lost a lot of blood, poor bastard. Hacked at her legs as well. What a mess.'

'What happened? Any ideas yet?'

'Well, she's unconscious, so we've got nothing from her. But she was found lying on a grass verge on a slip road off the M8, down towards Paisley. Christ knows how she's alive. She could have frozen to death, never mind her injuries and the blood loss.'

Rosie tried to get her head around it. There were plenty of psychos out there capable of all sorts of torture, but chopping arms off took gruesome to a whole new level.

'So who is she?'

'We know who she is from her purse and credit cards. We think she's a hooker. Nikki Russell. Thirty-something. We've got cops all over her street trying to build up a picture of her background. She's from the East End, so what the fuck was she doing out in Paisley in the dead of night?'

'It doesn't mean she's a hooker just because she was ten miles from her home. Christ's sake, man, she might have been visiting someone. Or it could have been a domestic.'

Rosie objected to police jumping to the hooker conclusion. She'd seen some brutal domestics, and sat through court cases where husbands did horrible things to their wives, and vice versa. But she had to admit to herself that a woman alone in this kind of situation did tick plenty of the vice girl boxes.

'So if – *if* – she is a hooker, did some punter pick her up and turn out to be a psycho?'

'We think so. That's the danger for these birds, but they just don't listen. We tell them not to get into cars with people because there are a lot of weird bastards out there, but they don't listen. Usually they're just working to get enough for their next fix.'

'Who found her?'

'A young couple taking the slip road noticed a shoe and then they saw her legs. But when they got out of the car they just about keeled over – her arm had been hacked clean off at the elbow. It was lying there in the snow.'

'Jesus, Don. That's awful. What kind of twisted bastard does that?'

'That's what we're trying to find out.'

'Did they . . . I mean, were doctors able to save her arm?'

'Nope. They tried, there was a five-hour operation to stitch it back on, but nothing doing. She'd lost too much blood. She's lucky to be alive – though when the poor bird wakes up she might not see it that way.'

'Christ!'

An image of Mags Gillick, the junkie prostitute who had her throat cut because she was helping Rosie expose police corruption, flashed across her mind. Nobody gave a shit about these girls, no matter how much lip service was paid to trying to clean up the streets and provide drop-in centres. Even if the police and social services did have some success, it wouldn't stop them. Most of the women who went out to sell their bodies for sex were risking everything for their next heroin hit.

'So do you actually know if she's a prostitute? Or a drug addict?'

'Well, not in the classic sense. Oddly enough, the word is there's no sign of drugs in her system. It's very early doors and they're doing tests, but we've had a nod from the hospital that she's not a user.'

'So she might not be a prostitute.'

'Well, maybe not. Though she could be an escort. Who knows? If I were a betting man, I'd say the good money is on her having been picked up by a punter who turned out to be a complete monster. And worryingly, he's still out there. The boys are going through CCTV footage of the motorway and homing in on that slip road, but that's going to take forever. We will find the fucker, though, mark my words.'

'I hope you do. And soon. What's happening re: press releases and stuff? Is there a press conference?'

'No press conference today. I think the bosses want to play it very tight for the first twenty-four hours, to see if she wakes up and can give them any information. According to the young couple, she was drifting in and out of consciousness when the ambulance came and she was calling out for Julie, whoever she is. We've been through her mobile and found a number for Julie – but it's ringing out. We're on the case, big time.'

'So are you putting anything out at all?'

'Yeah. There was a basic press release an hour ago, and in the next hour there will be more for the lunchtime news appeal, but it won't be as detailed I'm telling you, so be careful how you write this.'

'Sure.' Rosie picked up her bag and headed again for the front door. 'I'm going down to the office now, so I'll give you a shout later. You never know. We might get a call from a punter or friend who knows her.'

'Fair enough.'

He hung up.

Rosie met Declan on the stairs as she made her way up to the editorial floor. She'd already called Marion to arrange a quick meeting with the editor before he disappeared into the conference.

'Declan. That's some stuff about the girl on the motorway. What have the cops put out?' Rosie asked, stopping on the stairs.

'Not much. Just that her arm was hacked off and that she's in hospital. They're doing a bit more soon, I'm told.'

He shook his head. 'Unbelievable. Barbaric. No name yet. They're hinting that she was a hooker. Have you heard the same?'

'Yes.' Rosie jerked her head in the direction of the editor's office. 'I'm going in to see McGuire. You see what you can dig up from police, or any address. They'll have to put a bit more out in their next press release if they're making an appeal. I'm still working on the Pakistani bride death, so you'll have to take care of the day-to-day story on the girl. I'll feed you anything I get.'

Declan nodded, and Rosie walked briskly upstairs and across the floor to the editor's office. She knocked on the open door, but didn't wait for an answer before she went in.

'Come in,' McGuire said, glancing up from his screen. He motioned her towards the chair opposite his desk and she sat down. 'What the hell's going on, Gilmour? I mean, who chops a woman's arm off?' He narrowed his eyes. 'I hope you're going to tell me something I can put on my front page tomorrow.'

'Well, it's early doors yet, Mick. The cops are keeping everything tight and hoping to speak to the girl when she comes round.'

'Any chance of us getting in?'

Rosie gave him a look.

'No way.' She sat forward. 'A press interview will be the last thing on the police agenda.'

'So, what's the score?'

'Well, my cop pal tells me the thinking is she's a hooker, but no drugs have shown up positive, so if she is, then either she works on her own or with an escort agency. Police are all over that. But these escort agencies and girls working from flats are all so difficult to pin down. It's not as though they clock in.'

'So what else?'

'CCTV. Cops are going through the cameras on the M8 to see if they can get a sighting of the car that took her there.'

McGuire sat back and sighed.

'This is not good. We need to get into the hospital, or the cops have to give us something more. This is one of the most brutal attacks we've ever seen in this country, so they need to get their arses in gear and give us something good to latch on to. We already want to get a piece together on hookers and the dangers out there. I'll get Features to do that – speak to all these do-gooders and welfare workers who deal with them. Maybe we can get a couple of women on the game who'll talk anonymously? But the main thing is to build up a picture of who this girl is.'

'My police contact said the couple who found her have told them she kept calling out for Julie. They found her number on her mobile, but can't get through. No answer. So we have to find Julie, hopefully before the cops do.'

'Well, let me know if you need a hand.'

Rosie looked at him.

'Is that supposed to be funny?'

'What?' McGuire looked bemused, then half smiled. 'Oh, the hand!' He chuckled. 'Actually, no. I didn't even think of it – but you know what I mean.'

'Yeah.' Rosie stood up, ready to leave. 'By the way, I got hold of the girl I was staking out on the Pakistani bride story.'

McGuire perked up.

'Really? Did she talk?'

'Not really. She was terrified. Her name's Sabiha, and she's the bride's sister. She's been here for four years and has two kids. I took it as far as I could with her, following her up the road as she was trying to get away from me. I finally put it to her that I didn't think Rabia committed suicide. She stopped at that point, turned and I could see she was on the verge of tears. She said no way would Rabia kill herself. But she wouldn't speak to me.' Rosie sighed. 'So I'm not sure where I go with that. I tried to give her my card, but she wouldn't take it. But all I can do is hope for the best that she'll find my number and get in touch. I'm not really expecting her to contact me. Living in that house with all the family members, she's scared out of her wits. So I have to find another way. I'm working on it.'

McGuire pursed his lips.

'You haven't told me anything good yet, Gilmour.'

'I know, Mick. You'll be the first to know if I've got anything good to tell.' She stood up. 'But look on the bright side . . . At least you can clap your hands.'

Rosie headed for the door.

CHAPTER EIGHT

It was risky to pursue the girl again when the knockback had been so emphatic. But there was something about Sabiha's eyes, the desperation, the very fact that she had agreed that Rabia hadn't committed suicide. All Rosie's instincts were telling her that she was bursting to talk but was too terrified. McGuire's words kept coming back to her – that she hadn't told him anything good yet. It wasn't that she was under pressure, but she was acutely aware that she wasn't the only one who was impatient that nothing was moving on her stories. She was as desperate as the editor to get a handle on the background to Rabia's death, but these days, with the press trying to regulate itself so that they didn't step over the line, it was dodgy keeping on going back to someone if they'd already said they didn't want to talk. If they were a criminal you just waded in, regardless of the rules, as long as you were satisfied you could expose them all over the front page for what they were. But Sabiha was innocent, young and clearly damaged from whatever was going on in her life. Rosie knew it would only take the girl breaking down and blabbing to one of the elders in her family that she was being harassed by a newspaper reporter for lawyers' letters to start flying all over the shop. You had to tread carefully – even more so with ethnic minorities. I shouldn't even be here, Rosie thought, draining her coffee cup, keeping a close eye on the newsagent's across the street. Then she saw Sabiha coming out of the shop. One last shot, Rosie thought. One last shot.

She jumped up, left money on the counter and dashed out of the door and into her car, which was parked just a few yards away. To her surprise, the girl did not turn the corner to take the long straight road up to her house, but she crossed the street and went in the opposite direction. Rosie switched on her engine, turned the car and followed her slowly along the road. She kept well behind her, but could see her cross at the traffic lights, then walk towards the gates of the massive Queen's Park. Rosie pulled her car in to the side of the road and got out, following a long way behind her but keeping her in sight. She watched as Sabiha went into the park and walked towards the benches around the boating pond. From what she could make out, there was someone on the bench who stood up when approached. A young girl dressed in traditional Pakistani garb embraced Sabiha as she approached. Rosie glanced around the park, looking for somewhere to watch for a few moments without being noticed. A couple of joggers came up behind her and padded past her down towards the girls. Beyond where they sat, the park was quiet, except for one man walking his dog in the distance and two women pushing prams. Rosie walked on to the grass away from the girls, but where she could still see, and stood under a tree, watching. But she felt edgy. In a place like this you looked conspicuous if you just stood around under a tree. She had to make up her mind, fast. She strained her eyes and could see that the younger girl was crying, her head in her hands. Sabiha put her arm around her shoulder and leaned into her, comforting her. Rosie automatically found her feet taking her towards them. Just do it, she told herself. As she softly approached the bench, the girls glanced up at her and a flash of fear registered in Sabiha's eyes.

'Please, don't be afraid,' Rosie held out her hands in a calming gesture. 'Just, please, hear me out. Listen, I can see something is upsetting you. I know you are frightened, and I apologise for barging in. But please let me talk for a moment.'

The girl who had been crying suddenly stopped, looking bewildered, and turned from Rosie to Sabiha. She said something in Urdu, and Sabiha squeezed her arm as though she was reassuring her.

'What are you doing following me like this? Please. Can you not see we are upset? We are frightened. Can you leave us?'

'But perhaps I can help you,' Rosie chanced, because they made no attempt to stand up or run away from her. 'Is this your friend?' She gestured towards the bewildered girl. 'What's the matter?'

'She is my cousin.'

'What's wrong? I promise you can trust me.' Rosie looked the young girl in the eye, holding her gaze for a moment.

The younger girl again spoke in Urdu to Sabiha and she replied, glancing at Rosie as though explaining who she was.

'Please, tell your cousin not to be afraid, that I may be able to help. But I can only help if you talk to me.'

'I did already tell her who you were a couple of days ago. We have talked about you.'

Something was beginning to give. Rosie's gut did a little flip. She was nearly in. She took a breath, stepped a little closer.

'What's the matter with your cousin? Look, I don't know her name, or anything else about the two of you, so I promise, I'm not here to write a story or say anything to your family or anything else that would get you into trouble. I am just trying to get to the bottom of something that all of my instincts tell me is wrong. About Rabia's death. Can you understand that?'

The younger girl looked up through tear-stained eyes, and Rosie saw the dark under-eye circles of someone who hadn't slept in a while. Her skin was blotchy from crying, and she pushed back her headscarf, exposing lush, black hair. She turned to Sabiha and sniffed, wiping her nose with a tissue. Then, to Rosie's surprise, she spoke in a broad Glasgow accent.

'Maybe we can talk to her, Sabiha,' she said, her eyes pleading. 'Maybe we can find someone to trust. I don't want to go to Pakistan. I can't. I'll kill myself if they make me go.'

For a long moment, nobody spoke and Rosie held her breath. She was in. She glanced over her shoulder. The park was almost deserted.

'Can we talk for a few minutes?' Rosie asked. 'May I sit down?'

The two girls shuffled up together to make room for her on the bench. She looked straight at Sabiha.

'What's wrong, Sabiha? Why don't you just start at the beginning? I think your cousin is right. You need to talk to someone, and I may be able to help.'

Sabiha sat for a moment in silence, then glanced at her cousin, who reached out and squeezed her hand. Rosie looked at both of them, desperation and helplessness written all over their faces. It brought a lump to her throat.

'My sister.' Sabiha began. 'I know my sister didn't kill herself.' She swallowed. 'We will never know the truth – if she jumped from the window or was pushed. But all I know is that her husband and his father were in the room with her at the time, so if they saw her about to jump, then why didn't they stop her? They drove her to her death. They locked her in the room. Punished her.'

'Have you told this to the police?'

'No . . . No way. I haven't even been interviewed by the police.'

'But wasn't everyone in the house interviewed? Everyone who lives there?'

'No. They must have told the police that I don't live there. Maybe I'm not registered as living there. I don't even know. I can't ask questions. If I ask any questions they . . . they . . .' She broke down. 'They beat me, the way they beat my sister.'

She held out her arms and pulled back her sleeve to expose the red welts on both wrists.

Rosie looked at them and her heart sank.

'What happened?'

'It was after Rabia died. The day after. I was crying and screaming that it was their fault, and I said I was going to run away and take my children with me. They dragged me to the bedroom and beat me up, then tied me to the table so I couldn't move for hours.'

'Who did this?' Rosie asked.

'Farooq's uncle. And my mother-in-law.'

'They beat you like that?'

Sabiha nodded, wiping her tears.

'It's what happens if you disobey. It's normal. But I was so upset at my sister's death. I know in my heart she did not kill herself. She was very unhappy. She just wanted to be back home, but it wasn't allowed. She was here now and that was the agreement between the families. Nothing we could do about it.'

Rosie watched as the younger girl linked her fingers through Sabiha's.

'So, who are you married to?'

'I am married to the cousin of Farooq, but he is not here a lot of the time.' She dropped her eyes to the ground. 'He has another wife in Bradford, and he spends time there. For business as well. I cannot ask. Is not my place.'

'I understand,' Rosie said, even though she didn't. She didn't understand any of it – not the multiple nor the arranged marriages or the culture of fear – where young women had no say in their lives or their future, even within their own families. But you couldn't say that out loud in Glasgow or anywhere else without being accused of racism. The truth was that in most people's everyday lives you just let everyone else get on with it, as it was none of your business how anyone lived. But these girls were miserable, terrified and vulnerable.

'So,' Rosie turned to the other girl, 'why are you crying? Why do you not want to go to Pakistan?'

'Why do you think?' the girl answered.

'I can make a guess,' Rosie said. 'Are you to be married over there?'

The girl nodded.

'Yes. To a man I have not even met. I am fourteen years old and he is forty-eight. Old enough to be my grandfather.' She bit her lip. 'I'm to go with my uncle to Peshawar later in the month, the wedding will take place immediately and then our families will be linked in marriage and in business.'

Rosie didn't know what to say.

'Do you want to tell me your name?'

'My name is Laila. I've been here all my life. I go to school here. I'm studying to go to university and I want to be a doctor.'

'Do you want to get married? I mean, in the traditional Pakistani way?'

The girl shrugged and stared into the middle distance.

'Who knows? I'm fourteen. I don't even think about things like that. I just know I don't want to go there and be married to some old man right now.' She bit her lips tight.

'It's not just about the marriage,' Sabiha suddenly said. 'It's the whole criminal thing.' She paused, glancing at the younger girl. 'They are part of . . . of something dodgy. People go missing and their passports are used by criminals.'

'What do you mean? What criminals?' Rosie screwed up her eyes.

'I have heard they use people for smuggling and then they kill them over there. But they keep their passports, then they use them and doctor them so they are fakes for other people. But I have only heard it, so I don't know any more.'

'That's unbelievable,' Rosie said. 'How do you know this?'

'I don't know for sure. But I overheard them talking.'

'But is it organised? Who is in charge?'

Sabiha shook her head.

'I don't know who does this and that, but I know that my husband is part of it and that is one of the reasons he is down south a lot of the time. They are all criminals.'

'Smuggling what?'

Sabiha looked at her cousin, who seemed to give her the slightest nod of her head. Then Sabiha glanced up at Rosie.

'Diamonds.'

Rosie looked straight at both of them for any sign that they were lying in their eyes. There was none.

Rosie got into her car and sat back, shaking her head, still aghast at what Sabiha had said and wondering how McGuire would react. As she switched on the engine, her mobile rang in her bag. It was Don.

'Hey, Rosie. What you up to?'

'Actually, I've just been walking in the park.'

'Must be nice to be idle, strolling around all day, listening to the birds.'

'Yeah, sure. I was meeting someone.'

'I didn't know you were into dogging.'

'I'd bet that you know more about dogging than me, pet.'

She could hear him chuckling.

'Tell you what . . . I'm going to make your day.'

'That would be great. I'm all ears.'

'You see the dead Pakistani in the Albany? Remember I told you we were looking at CCTV from the foyer?'

'I do.'

'Well, wait till you hear this . . . We've homed in on two girls coming out of the hotel, one of them carrying a case. The place was really busy with some kind of function, but these girls kind of stood out. And guess what . . .'

'Oh, come on, Don. I'm dying of curiosity here.'

'The bird who's along with the one carrying the case is the same bird who's lying in the Royal Infirmary, minus part of her arm.'

'You have to be kidding me.'

'I'm not. We still know very little about her, but she bears an uncanny resemblance to the girl in the hotel. And the other one – we don't know who she is yet. But I'd say they're both hookers, and taking the theory further, maybe they'd just been with the Asian guy.'

'Why lump them together? If they were hookers at the hotel, they could have been to anyone's room, couldn't they? What's the link?'

'The case.'

'What case?'

'The attaché case the bird was carrying. Are you not listening?'

'Sorry. I forgot about that. My head's all over the place.'

'The word on the street is that this Malik punter had a case full of money and whatever other shit he was dealing with – he was up here on a drop. We think he had diamonds, but we're not sure. And the case was definitely not with him when the cops went to the room.'

'So you're thinking the girls, who you believe are hookers, went into the room, bumped him off and took his case? It's a bit far-fetched, is it not? They wouldn't even know what was in the case, would they?'

'Nobody is saying they bumped him off. Maybe he died during a sex game. The pathologist is looking at that too.'

'So during the sex game he croaks and the birds steal his case? That about it?'

'Well, it's certainly a credible theory. Especially if one of them ends up with her arm cut off and the other disappears.'

'And the case?'

'The case is nowhere to be seen.'

'I like the sound of this,' Rosie said. 'When are you talking to the girl in hospital?'

'We're hoping, this afternoon.'

'So, when she wakes up and realises she's lost her arm, she's going to see your face and discover she's in a shitload of trouble?'

'Something like that. But hey – I don't make these things happen, Rosie. I just catch the bad guys.'

'Sure. I wish I could talk to the girl.'

'Yeah. I know you do, but unless you're dressed as a doctor, I'd say that's highly unlikely.'

'But she's not a suspect, is she?'

'Not on paper. But she's a suspect alright, until we establish more on Malik's death.'

Rosie had to keep quiet about her conversation with Sabiha and Laila.

'Okay. If you get a word with her, it would be great to get a line, Don. One line would do it – nothing that would screw up your investigation, but just a line to keep it in the paper. This is beginning to sound like it's all irresistibly linked.'

'I like it when you're excited, Gilmour.'

'Yeah. Talk later.' Rosie hung up.

CHAPTER NINE

Somewhere in Nikki's head, a voice was softly saying her name. Then it would fade, echoing as it drifted away before she could answer. Was she dreaming? She didn't know. She could feel the sun, warm on her body. She would open her eyes, she thought, to see the bright blue sky. She could sense her eyelids flickering, but they wouldn't open. She was so tired. Then she was gone again, sleeping to the sound of the sea and the voice whispering her name. For a moment she thought she heard someone say 'Julie'. Who's Julie? Nikki's mind drifted again. The heat was rising on the beach, and she could feel her chest getting hot. She could see a face behind her eyes as she heard the name. 'Julie.' She tried to move her lips but they were stuck together, and her tongue was dry like paper on the roof of her mouth. Then she tried again to repeat the name. 'Julie.' Her lips were moving, but she couldn't hear the sound. Someone's soft fingers were on her forehead. It felt good and cool in the heat. 'Nikki. Nikki,' the voice said. She prised her eyes open, trying to focus. She could see a ceiling with tiles. She closed her eyes again. No beach. No sky. Where was she? She rolled her head to the side and saw what looked like a machine, with lights green and luminous. And wires. 'Nikki.' The voice again. 'It's me, Julie.' She opened her eyes and now someone was standing over her. She struggled to focus on the blur in front of her. Julie. She felt a smile on her lips. But where were they? Where was she? Julie was smiling. They must be on holiday.

'Nikki, it's me, Julie. Can you hear me?'

'Julie.' Nikki's lips moved but the sound didn't come out.

'It's okay, Nikki. Everything's going to be fine.'

Nikki's mind drifted. Fine. Why fine? Then she turned her head and saw the wires more sharply. She was in a hospital, but why? As she opened her eyes a fear ran through her and she focused on Julie.

'What's happ . . . Am I in a hospital or something? Am I sick? What's happened?'

She felt Julie stroke her forehead.

'You're fine, Nikki. It's going to be fine.'

Nikki was afraid, and her body began to feel cold. She closed her eyes to blink away a sudden picture. Dark night. Blackness. Snow and slush on the ground. Then the sound of hacking, and suddenly she saw herself lying on the ground. What kind of nightmare was this? Her eyes opened wide and she looked at Julie, who must have been able to see the fear in her eyes, because now *she* was crying. Nikki glanced down and could see a bandage. A heavy, thick, white bandage. Where was her hand? Her wrist? She couldn't feel it. Where were her fingers? She glanced at her other hand, hooked up to the machine, needles and drips and a bag of stuff on a tall steel trolley. Where were her fingers?

'My hand, Julie. Where's my hand?'

Julie was crying now, tears running down her face and streaming off her chin.

'Oh, Nikki, I'm sorry. Listen, It's going to be okay. You're alive. You pulled through. They didn't think you would make it. I . . . I thought I'd lost you, pal.'

'Make it? Where's my hand, Julie? My arm.'

'Ssshh, Nikki. They cut it. You lost it. I'm so sorry. But you're going to be alright, Nikki. I'm going to look after you. I'm here for you. Right here.'

She was sobbing now, and Nikki looked at her, confused. Her arm wasn't there. She couldn't feel her fingers. They cut it. Who cut it? Then she remembered again. The snow, the blood. The blind fear. She could feel her heart beating fast and the machine at her side was making buzzing noises. She saw the man's crazed face and the glint of the blade. She saw Julie through blurred eyes, then she drifted away again.

*

Julie sat in her car, with no idea what she was going to do, but she knew that time was running out. She had listened to the messages on her mobile, and they were more threatening each time. Big Gordy was onto them, he warned. And worse still, the Asian guys down south were onto them. They were coming to get her the way they had got Nikki. In their culture, you steal something, they chop your fucking hand off as a lesson. She was next. She'd better turn up somewhere, or get on the phone and arrange to give that fucking case back. Julie knew it was only a matter of time till they found her. She'd been into Nikki's house early in the morning to make sure the case was still there and took it. Then she'd hired a car for the week and took off with everything she had, staying in a small hotel out in the Stirling area, sure they'd never look for her out there. She used the money from the dead Pakistani's wallet and what was in the case to finance her. There was a lot of money. She'd counted it last night in the hotel room. Four grand and a few twenties and fifties. Enough for a while. Enough if she wanted to seriously disappear and reinvent herself abroad. But she couldn't do that, not with Nikki up in the Royal with her arm cut off. She thought of her lying there, the shock on her face when she realised what had happened. And how she had had to make herself scarce in case the nurses or the cops arrived. They would be there to interview her now that she was coming round. She knew she had taken a risk the two times she'd visited in the last few days, but what else could she do? Guilt seared through her. It was all her fault. She had talked Nikki into this bloody escort business. She knew she needed the money after that bastard Paul left her up to her arse in debt and suicidal with depression. It was only to be for a few weeks till she got on her feet again. And now this. Nikki could have died. Christ! What was she going to do now? She could go to the cops and tell them everything she knew – but she would be a dead woman, and so would Nikki, the moment she got out of hospital. Big Gordy would hunt them down, because the bastard had obviously lost face, sending one of his punters to get laid, providing birds who had stiffed him for the money and killed him. That's how they'd view it. Even if they thought he died from a sex game, they still knew they had stolen the case. They hadn't stopped to ask questions, as Nikki had found out. Why didn't he kill her that night? Why not kill Julie too? Maybe they had other plans. A car hooted and she nearly jumped out of her skin. She had to think. She had to get someone to talk to. A copy of the *Post* was on the passenger seat. She knew the office was close to where she was sitting, but what would be the point of talking to the papers? They'd only get the cops. How could you trust these people? Her mobile rang again. She didn't answer, but listened to the message. It sent a shiver through her

'We know where you are. We're going to get you, Julie. You're dead.'

She picked up the newspaper and looked at the story of

the horrific attack on the girl whose arm had been severed. Shit! She hadn't thought this through. Any of it. Not from the time they took the suitcase. But things were desperate now. Before she could stop herself, she dialled the number at the back of the newspaper and asked for the name that was on the story – Rosie Gilmour.

CHAPTER TEN

Rosie was in McGuire's office, midway through relating her encounter with Sabiha and her cousin in the park, when her mobile rang in her bag. McGuire tutted, irritated at the interruption, as she fished it out. There was a private number calling.

'I'd better take this, Mick. It could be anybody.' She put the phone to her ear.

McGuire leant back, folding his arms.

'Hello?'

Rosie never said her name when a call came in she didn't recognise. She preferred to find out who it was first.

Silence.

'Hello?' she repeated, rolling her eyes at Mick.

'Is that Rosie Gilmour?' the voice said.

'Yes, it is. Your name didn't come up. Who's this, please?'

'I . . . I've got something to tell you. I think you'll be interested. About that dead guy in the hotel. The Pakistani guy.'

'I'd like to hear about that.'

Rosie was suddenly firing on all cylinders. She automatically walked out of the editor's office. She needed to be alone to concentrate on this.

Silence.

'Are you still there?' Rosie said, walking towards a quiet corner of the editorial floor.

'Yes. I'm here . . .' The woman's voice was shaky. She could hear her take a short breath and sniff. Rosie wondered if it might be a junkie hooker who wanted to cash in on some information she'd picked up on the grapevine. It happened. 'Listen. I know about that guy . . . And other things . . . I'm scared.'

'How do you know about it?' Rosie said quietly.

It was risky getting straight to the point on the phone with a complete stranger, who was edgy and might just hang up. But it was better to find out now if she was a nutter than go chasing all over the city after her.

'Listen. Please, believe me. I know. I was there. I saw him.' She paused. 'I can't talk on the phone. Can I meet you?'

'Sure,' Rosie said. 'Now if you want? Where are you?'

'Near your office. In a car park.'

Rosie could feel her heart quicken as she walked back to McGuire's office. He looked up from his desk, but she put a finger to her lips and grabbed her bag. As she headed for the door, she caught his don't-mind-me-I'm-only-the-editor look of bewildered resignation as he shook his head.

'Which car park? Don't you want to meet in one of the pubs nearby?'

'No. The car park. The one behind the old tile place. I don't want anybody to see me. I'm scared. I told you that! . . . Fuck's sake!' The shaky voice went up an octave.

'Okay. No problem.' Rosie sensed her panic. 'I know where you are. I'll be there in two minutes. What kind of car?'

'I'm the only car here. The place is derelict.'

'I'm on my way.'

It was early afternoon, but the bleak January sky was already dark grey under the heavy downpour. Rosie pulled up the collar of her coat and tucked in her scarf against the biting wind as she walked to her car. She drove along the Broomielaw towards the turn off, her mind firing off a dozen scenarios, some of which she had to swiftly push away. Since the recent attacks on her in Spain and in Glasgow, she was careful not to meet anyone unless it was in a public place. What if she was being set up? A woman calling for a meeting would seem a safer prospect than some guy asking to meet her on his own. But Rosie was ever-paranoid and eyed everyone with suspicion these days. She breathed deeply to calm herself. The Broomielaw was busy with end-of-the-day traffic heading to the motorway or along the Clydeside, but the little side street was deserted apart from a few parked cars. Rosie drove towards the car park behind the tile suppliers, and she could see a red Ford

Fiesta. She drove in, kept her engine running and lowered her window. The woman's window slid down too and she could see her. Rosie quickly glanced in the back of the woman's car and over her shoulder again to see if there was anyone nearby. There wasn't.

'Rosie?'

'Yep. How you doing? You want to come into my car?'

There was no way Rosie was getting into a stranger's car – even a woman's – and run the risk of being driven off at speed. Christ! She really *was* paranoid.

The woman's eyes narrowed.

'Have you phoned the police?'

'Of course not. What kind of reporter would that make me, if I phoned the cops at every turn?' She gave her a trust-me smile. 'Don't be daft. Come on into my car and we'll have a chat. Don't worry.'

Rosie had to be calm, in control. That's what people expected. She leaned across and opened the passenger door. The woman hesitated for a long moment. Then she nodded, switched off her engine and got out. Rosie watched her coming around the front of the car. She looked on the rough side, late thirties or maybe forty, with hair dyed jet black that she might have got away with fifteen years ago. But this was a face where carefree youth was only a dim recollection, and a hard life had left her with deep creases around the eyes and the wrinkles of a twenty-a-day habit around the mouth. As she planked her hefty thighs down on the passenger seat, her black leather skirt rode up a little and she shifted her body and tugged at it, trying and failing to make it longer. Maybe try a bigger size, Rosie thought, glancing at her glittery, too-tight top, which made her look like a refugee on the walk of shame from a Christmas night out. She had 'hooker' stamped all over her. Not the kind that Rosie was used to meeting in sticky-floored pubs and cafes, or in the homeless units where they got a bed at night as long as they weren't smacked out of their head when they turned up. This dame was more the working-from-home type, where prostitution had spread to in recent years and people operated in a freelance or small-time way. Probably no different than it had been for women generations ago, only it was less well known then. Or she could be an escort. The escort agencies had grown up around the movie that sold the ridiculous idea that prostitutes looked like the *Pretty Woman* character, and could end up with a handsome millionaire promising them the earth. The reality was a world away. Of course, there were always one or two around a hotel bar when the rich people were having a meeting or hoping to pick up a random bird for the night. But nine times out of ten, if you were a punter and phoned an escort agency, it was like ordering a take-away dinner – if you were lucky you got their best dish, but more often than not you got whatever re-heated meat they threw into the bag and you made the best of it. It was a shitty way for women to earn their money, but that's how it was. Rosie's heart sank a little, knowing that whatever sensational claim she was probably about to make, it was coming from the lips of a hooker – and that would be her first problem. But here she was. Rosie stuck out her hand and looked her square in the eye.

'Rosie Gilmour.'

The woman clasped it, looking back at her with liquid brown eyes that had little bloodshot streaks from booze or lack of sleep.

'You can't use my name or anything.' She seemed to struggle for breath. 'I'm scared even to say my name.' She shook her head. 'Christ! What a mess! What a fucking mess!'

Then she suddenly started to cry, her face crumpling, making her look even older. Rosie heart was sinking further.

'Hey, come on. It's okay.' Rosie squeezed her arm gently. 'Look . . . I'm not about to go blasting your name all over the papers, or going to the cops. It was you who called me, so you have to trust me. Alright?' Rosie spoke softly as the woman dabbed her eyes with a rolled-up tissue. She was glad when she seemed to compose herself.

'Julie,' she said, offering Rosie a cold, damp hand.

Rosie hoped her face didn't show any flash from the little explosion that had just gone off in her head. Julie was the name that Don had told her the girl with the severed hand had been calling out. The girl the cops had been continually calling on Nikki's mobile. Surely, this was too good to be true?

'Good to meet you, Julie.' Rosie gave her a firm handshake. 'I hope you know that you can trust me.'

Julie sighed and shook her head, gazing out of the windscreen. She wiped her face with the palm of her hand.

'Right now I don't know if I'm coming or going. I don't know who I can trust. I'm scared to death.'

'I know.' Rosie nodded. 'Why don't we just have a chat? You can tell me, in your own time, what's happened. Tell me about the guy in the hotel you mentioned on the phone . . . and anything else.'

Julie nodded slowly, and examined the back of her hand, picking at the skin around her chewed fingernails.

'Okay. Well. I saw your name on the two stories – of the dead guy in the hotel, and the woman with her arm cut off.' She turned her face towards Rosie. 'They're both connected. Er . . . Nikki . . . Nikki's my best pal.' Her lip began to tremble a little, but she swallowed and managed to hold herself together. 'Sorry. It's . . . It's been awful. I still can't believe it.'

Rosie listened, barely breathing as Julie told her story. Julie said she'd been friends with Nikki since they were twelve years old, growing up in Easterhouse, living in one of the most deprived housing schemes in Glasgow, along with all the shit that threw at you. Long before the drugs took hold of the scheme, most people were all about honest graft, even if there were sometimes long periods out of work. Julie's marriage failed and she went into a downward spiral. She drank too much, did stupid things and ended up almost getting thrown out of her house. When she reached rock bottom, there was nowhere else to go. She turned to an escort agency to earn some money and it had worked fine for the past eighteen months. Her friend Nikki, whose husband was a complete arsehole, then got involved after he'd left her with a mountain of debt from his gambling habit.

'Nikki never wanted to do it.' She shook her head. 'That's why this is all my fault. I told her it would be fine, and look at what's happened. I'm such a stupid bastard. Everything's my fault.'

'What happened with the Pakistani guy?'

Rosie wanted to tease the facts out of her, because she could see she was getting more and more agitated and wanted to get the story out before she blew a gasket.

'He was Nikki's punter. So she went to the hotel . . . the Albany. This guy starts asking her to choke him.' She glanced at Rosie. 'You know that kinky sex stuff, where the guy gets a better buzz if they nearly pass out while they're wanking?'

Rosie nodded.

'I get the picture.'

'Well, he keels over while she's doing this. I mean Nikki's clueless about a lot of stuff – in fact, I wouldn't know much about that kinky shit myself. But she's totally new to this game, and her punters so far have been straightforward. But suddenly, this guy's dead on the floor.'

'Christ!' Rosie said. 'Then what?'

'She calls me. I'd finished with my punter, and went straight there. Sure enough, there he was. So that's when I made all the fucking wrong decisions.' She shook her head. 'When I think of it now . . . But of course it's too fucking late.'

'What did you do? What happened?' Rosie's heart was going like an engine. She hoped her tape recorder was getting all this, but even if it didn't, she wasn't about to forget a single word.

'I took his money. His wallet and his phone.'

'Oh,' Rosie said, raising her eyebrows a little.

'Yeah. Fucking stupid, I know. But was I supposed to call the cops? I mean, we work for an escort agency owned by big Gordy MacLean. You know him?'

'I do. Well, I know of him. Not to be messed with.'

'Exactly. So we couldn't spill our guts to the police. I decided we'd take anything that would ID the guy and get the hell out of the place. And that's what we did. Except . . .'

'What? Except what?'

'There was a small attaché case. A wee aluminium thing. I decided to take that too. Nikki didn't want to, but I thought, let's just take every fucking thing and leave the holdall with a couple of shirts in it. So we took it and walked out of the hotel bold as brass – even though our legs were like jelly.'

Rosie looked at her then out of the windscreen, thinking of Don's earlier chat about the girls walking out with the case. This story was screaming legally-in-the-shit all over it. But she had to get it – all of it.

'So what did you do with the case?'

'We took it to Nikki's and opened it. And inside it was lot of money and passports.'

'Passports?'

'Yeah. Maybe fake, or something. But all with Pakistani or Asian-looking fuckers on the pictures.'

'Incredible.' Another bell went off in Rosie's head, recalling Sabiha's claims about the passports.

'But that's not all. There were a couple of bags, pouches, with a load of stones in them. We emptied them out, they looked like little driveway chips or something somebody had taken from a beach. Who knows what kind of crap people collect? But now we know what they are.'

'What are they?' Rosie asked, but she already knew the answer.

'Diamonds. Rough diamonds.'

Rosie could feel her eyes widen.

'How do you know that?'

'Because we got pulled in by the boss – Gordy MacLean – and he's asking did we see the case. It was him who said he'd been told there were rough diamonds in it. We had already denied we took the case, and would never admit it, but once he said diamonds, we knew we had to deny it forever.' She paused. 'How much do you know about big Gordy?'

'I just know of him. Dangerous bastard, by all accounts. I take it he didn't believe you.'

'No. And that's why Nikki got done over. I don't know what the Christ this is all about or who's behind it, but apparently its some big Pakistani gang from down south, and they're all related to gangsters down there, who deal with people up here. So maybe the guy was up here on the drop.'

Rosie looked at her. This was confirming what Don had told her. She tried to contain her excitement.

'Drop to who?' she said.

'No idea, that's just what we've been told. I don't even know if that's all a load of fanny coming from big Gordy.'

'So what happened then? I mean that night when Nikki was attacked? How did it happen?'

'We got word to go see a couple of punters, and when we got there, she had to go on her own in the car with the driver, Alex. He's Gordy's best mate, and he doesn't normally do the driving, but that night he did. When Nikki went into the car with him and they sent me away, that's . . . that's the last I heard of her until it was on the news that she'd been attacked. . . . It's sick! So sick! And it's my fault. The bastard sliced half her fucking arm off.'

'Who? Alex?'

'I don't know. It was Alex who took her, but maybe he was meeting somebody. I don't think he's that kind of guy who would chop someone's arm off. He's an arsehole, but not like that.'

'What a mess, Julie. But you shouldn't blame yourself.'

'It was me who insisted we take the case.'

'Well. That's done now – you can't undo it. What you need to do is be here for Nikki and you really need to think about talking to the cops.'

'What? And get both of us killed? No fucking way.'

'So where's the case now?'

Julie was silent for a few moments, and Rosie waited, her heart thumping.

'In the boot of my car.'

'Fuck me!' Rosie murmured under her breath.

Every instinct was screaming at Rosie to call McGuire, get the cops involved and get the hell out of here. But nothing screamed more than the absolute kamikaze need to see the attaché case. Totally crazy and wrong on so many levels, because once she'd seen it and not done anything about it, she was part of the crime.

'Can I see it?' She couldn't stop herself.

'Wait here.'

Julie got out of Rosie's car and quickly pinged open the boot of hers. Rosie took out her mobile, then put it back in her bag and switched it off in case anyone phoned. Julie came back around the car and slid into the seat with the attaché case on her lap. She clicked it open. Inside were several passports – all Pakistani. Rosie was dying to pick them up and have a look, but just watched as Julie did it.

'You shouldn't be touching any of this, Julie. Your fingerprints are all over the place.'

'I know. But it's too late for that.'

Rosie glanced over her shoulder to make sure the car park was still empty as Julie fingered through the passports. There were nine in total, and as Julie opened each one of them, a Pakistani face looked out from the passport picture and Rosie looked at the name under each one. Most were men, but there were two women. They looked authentic, but could just as easily have been fakes, and sold or stolen by gangsters and then intricately doctored. Then, as Julie randomly flicked through them, a name caught her eye. Rabia.

'Hold on. Can you just go back to that picture again?'

'This one?' Julie held it up.

'Yeah. I want to see it again.'

The name was Rabia Sahid but the picture wasn't of the bride who'd jumped out of the window in Pollokshields. Julie flicked to the opening page and the date of birth and Rosie went through her notebook till she found the start of her notes on the story. The date of birth was the same. This was no coincidence. She took down the number and as much detail as she could, asking Julie to open all the pages where it had been stamped. The UK stamp was there and roughly matched the date when Rabia had come here for her wedding. She'd have to check the specifics when she got back. Julie went through the rest of them, and then laid the passports back in the case. Then she lifted out the wads of cash. Then the bag containing the stones. She emptied three out onto her palm.

'Jesus, Julie. This is crazy. I think they are rough diamonds. But obviously someone very dangerous is looking for these, if they're prepared to chop Nikki's arm off. And every second you have them in your possession, your life is in danger. You have to do something, fast.'

'What the fuck am I going to do? I'm not going to the cops.'

'You have to.'

'I can't. I won't. No way.'

Rosie didn't know what to say to her. She needed time. She wanted to talk to McGuire, but could nearly hear him screaming at the thought of her sitting in a car with a cache of smuggled diamonds and stolen or faked passports. But most of all she had to keep Julie onside.

'Where are you staying?'

'I'm not at home as they've been looking for me. I'm out in Stirling. At a small hotel on the edge of the town.'

'Good. I need some time to think. I've got to talk to my editor.'

'You can't put this in the paper.'

'No. Of course not. Not yet anyway, and I wouldn't do that without your consent. But I have to decide how to make a start. See where I can go with it.' She switched on her phone. 'Listen. I'm going to call a colleague I work closely with – you can trust him. I need him to get a picture of this stuff before we do anything, before we make any move whatsoever.'

'I don't know if that's a good idea. Maybe I should just fuck off now. Are you going to the cops? You are, aren't you?'

Julie was agitated now.

'No, of course not. I promise you. We'll talk about our next move. I want to make sure you're safe.'

'Okay.'

Rosie switched on her phone and punched in Matt's number.

'Matt, where are you? Okay, good. Can you jump down to the Broomielaw to the car park of the old tile place. I need a pic taken quickly and discreetly. Don't tell anyone where you're going.'

CHAPTER ELEVEN

Despite the icy-cold early evening, Rosie walked from her flat at St George's Cross down to the nearby bar off Elmbank Street to meet Don. So much had gone on in the last few hours, she wanted to use the five-minute walk to clear her head and try to think straight. How the hell was she going to tell McGuire she'd just been sitting in a car with a handful of rough diamonds? He would have to be scraped off the ceiling. She didn't want to tell Julie that she knew for sure they were diamonds, but she'd known exactly what they were from the moment Julie had put the pouch in her hand. Nine months ago, Rosie had been working on a story involving the smuggling of diamonds from Nigeria as part of a UK-wide feature, and had been given good access by police to see what rough diamonds actually looked like. She even had a few of them put in her hand at the two-day Scotland Yard seminar in London that the editor had sent her on. So she was as sure as she could be of what she was dealing with. The deadly trade of blood diamonds stretched beyond the dusty mines of Nigeria, and it was a safe bet that whoever was involved in this little cache wouldn't hesitate to murder to get it back. It was bad enough that Julie took the dead guy's case, his money and his passports, but now she had his diamonds. This was not good, on any level – especially now that Rosie had actually had them in her hand. Still, at least they had a photograph of them, which Matt was sworn to secrecy about. She knew she'd be in trouble when she had to spill all this out to McGuire in the morning. But, for now, she had to concentrate on whatever Don was about to tell her. If he mentioned anything more about diamonds, she'd have to keep her face poker straight.

'What a hoor of a night,' Don cursed as he came into the bar, his hair soaked, red-faced from the cold.

'I know. I just made it in before that heavy shower. You look freezing. Where are your gloves?' Rosie motioned him to sit down in the wall seating, where she'd found a space in front of the flickering coal fire. 'It's cosy in here. I love this place. Old-fashioned. Nothing's changed for generations.'

Don rubbed his hands together vigorously and held them in front of the fire.

'Gloves are for poofs.'

Rosie smiled and stood up.

'Pint?'

'Aye. Dying for one.'

Rosie returned with a lager for Don and her first glass of red wine of the evening.

He went into the inside pocket of his coat and pulled out a piece of A4 paper

'Wait till you see this,' he said, triumphantly unfolding it and placing it on the table, smoothing it out. He glanced over his shoulder, but the bar was almost empty, apart from two old punters playing dominoes.

Rosie leaned forward and immediately recognised Julie in the grainy CCTV picture. She hoped her face was impassive.

'Is this from the Albany?'

'Yep. From the foyer.'

'It's packed. Must have been some kind of do on.' She pretended she was peering through the crowd.

'Yeah. A sales conference. Loads of reps were gathered in the foyer for the champagne reception. But look closely at the two girls walking through that throng around the podium, going towards the exit. See them?'

He made a ring with his finger around the women. Rosie kept up the pretence, narrowing her eyes.

'Yeah. I see them now. One of them's carrying a case. Is that the girls you think were in the room?'

'Well, we don't know that. But one of them, the more hefty-looking girl, the one who isn't carrying the case . . .

That's the girl who's lying up in the Royal with her arm mutilated. That much we can be sure of.'

'Christ! You're positive?'

'Sure enough to be hovering around the ward waiting for the consultant to give us the go-ahead to speak to her.'

'What about the other girl? Is she the friend from the phone you were telling me about?'

'We think so. But we don't know for definite. We're busting our arses trying to find her.'

Rosie looked beyond him. She felt a twinge of guilt that she was keeping up the charade, but what else could she do? She couldn't tell Don that she'd just been sitting with this very girl in a car down at the Broomielaw. She took a large gulp of her wine and swallowed, feeling it burn all the way down.

'Do you have a cigarette?' Rosie asked.

'Sure.' Don scanned her face. 'Stressed out?'

'Yeah, a bit.' Rosie sucked in the smoke as Don flicked the lighter. 'So, are you any closer to finding what this is all about?'

'A bit. Number one, we've been told that some heavy people are going apeshit over the missing case. The word on the grapevine is that there were passports in it. Probably faked.' He leaned closer. 'But, listen ... The tip that there were diamonds is growing; we're as sure as we can be that he was delivering rough diamonds. Smuggled diamonds.'

'What?' Rosie sounded surprised enough to convince

herself that she actually *was* surprised. 'Rough diamonds? Up here? But who wants rough diamonds up in Glasgow? It's hardly the gem capital of the world! Are you sure about that?'

'Well, we can't be sure. It's coming from our mates down south at Scotland Yard that this guy was used by some crowd who are smuggling diamonds in from Africa. A Pakistani crew, apparently. It's part of an international smuggling ring. The cops are on the case down south, but they know they're not making great headway – they've made some seizures along the line and stuff, over the years, but nobody's really cracked it.'

'I did that seminar on diamond smuggling down at the Met a while ago and I remember the background. But what I can't understand is why Glasgow? Normally they go to dealers down in London and then to Antwerp, where the diamonds would be cut and polished. There's all sorts of required licences that can apparently trace every diamond back to its origin. It's quite complicated. So how come they got under the radar? And what would the rough diamonds be doing here?'

'That's what we don't know. But one theory is that this guy, Malik, was flying to Glasgow, maybe coming through Amsterdam or something and it was less risky to fly to Glasgow than Heathrow or Gatwick, and was maybe going to go down south on the train. Or maybe it's that diamonds are the new black in Glasgow.' Don rubbed his face. 'We just don't know. The dead Pakistani is from Bradford, but we don't know anyone here who's involved in it, so we haven't a clue why he'd be in Glasgow.'

Rosie was also trying to figure out what he was doing in Glasgow, but from a different perspective. She already knew from the limited conversation with Sabiha that someone within the Pakistani community was involved in smuggling, so maybe it was a reward, or whatever, for the provision of passports or bodies.

'So are the cops going to release the line about the women and the suitcase? And how about the ID of the woman with the severed arm? The dogs in the street are barking her name. We could have used it last night, but the editor decided not to. It was stupid of you guys not to confirm.'

'I know. New detective superintendent. He's a bit of a nutjob and hates the press.'

'Terrific,' Rosie said, knowing if the new superintendent had an inkling of where she'd just been she'd already be on her way to the cells, awaiting the custody court in the morning. 'Well, he'll need to get his act together. This is a big story, Don.'

'Tell me about it. Let's just say the assistant chief constable has had a word in his shell-like.'

'What about the Pakistani jumper – the bride who took the swan dive?' Rosie asked. 'Anything new?'

'Nothing.' he sighed. 'But we know it stinks. They're

up to something, but we can't go harassing or sitting on them, especially when they're already throwing racism allegations around.' He turned to Rosie. 'You hearing anything?'

Rosie sighed and shook her head. She hated holding out on Don like this, especially when he was being so forthcoming. She wished she could tell him just a hint of what Sabiha and her cousin had told her, but she couldn't risk it. Once she'd handed over the information, she'd be handing over the girls as witnesses. It was too risky for them. The wine, on top of the adrenalin-pumping day it had been, made her suddenly tired. She was looking forward to going home to sit in a hot bath till she had made some sense of all of this. She needed to work out what her next move would be. McGuire would have to be told everything, and she wasn't looking forward to that.

'I have to go after this, Don. I'm knackered, and I've got a couple of calls to make before I call it a day.'

Don drained his glass.

'Me too. We've been doing overtime every night this week with all this shit that's going on, so I'm pretty done in myself. Early one for me too.'

When they finished their drinks, they stepped outside into the sleet, the traffic thinning out as they were two streets away from Charing Cross.

'Will I walk you up the road?' Don asked, glancing around at the deserted streets.

'No, don't worry. Sure, who'd be out on a night like this, only whores and polis.' Rosie smiled.

Don chuckled as he leaned in and she felt the warmth of his lips as he kissed her on the cheek. 'Well, sweetheart, what does that make you?'

'Touché.' She gave him a hug, and watched as he turned and went in the opposite direction.

Rosie stood for a few seconds, gazing up at the rows of dismal tenements and feeling the sleet on her face. An unexpected image took her by surprise – of the night she and TJ stood in the downpour outside the restaurant after they had been on the brink of ending their relationship, but somehow couldn't bring themselves to do it. A heavy loneliness swept over her, and she suddenly wished she could be back there, in the warmth of his arms that night on the pavement in the deluge. But so much had happened in the long time apart while he was in New York. It was months since she'd heard from him, and it was only recently that she had stopped picturing his life every day, wondering where he was at certain times, if he was thinking about her. But she still pined for him. Sometimes she thought TJ played more of a part in her psyche in his absence than he did when he was here. How screwed up was that? But she couldn't help feeling the emptiness now that she was starting to move on, becoming less obsessed with him. He'd probably have moved on too, no doubt presuming she had. She'd convinced herself she had moved on, until moments like this. The sudden tears on her cheeks felt warm against the cold of the night, and she sniffed and pulled up her collar against the wind. Get a grip, woman, she told herself, as she walked up the road in the direction of St George's Cross. The traffic was quiet and she walked briskly, blinking away tears. As she was about to cross the road, she became vaguely aware of someone in a shop doorway, but when she looked over her shoulder there was nobody there. She crossed the road, quiet, with little traffic and made her way along the deserted street and towards the car park which adjoined her block of flats. She looked over her shoulder again, uneasy, and thought she heard footsteps, but there was nothing. A little wave of anxiety punched her gut and she quickened her step. Maybe it wasn't over yet with the UVF, or with Tam Dunn's mob from the arms smuggling. No, she told herself, they were all in jail, and nobody would be mopping up after them. Thugs and gangsters just moved in like vultures when their leader was captured. No honour in them, they surrounded the spoils like hyenas, tearing it up for themselves. Nobody gave a damn about a journalist. But she walked quickly anyway. She'd be glad when she was in and safely inside the six-bar-locked fortress that her flat had become.

As she walked across the car park, she suddenly became aware of a bin moving. Then, in a second, someone was on her. She was grabbed from behind and dragged to the side of the building into the darkness, away from the lights on top of the building and out of view of the CCTV cameras. Weirdly, her first thought was that McGuire would go nuts. He'd warned her so many times never to go home at night unless she was in a taxi right to the front door. But now, she felt a strong arm pull her back and her legs went weak as she felt the coldness of the steel on her neck. Christ! Outside my own house. How fucking stupid is that? She tried to speak, afraid to as much as move her hands. She could feel the knife and the pulse in her neck.

'Please. What do you want? Take my bag. I've got money.'

Even like this, desperate and vulnerable, Rosie hated the sound of her begging, when all of her instincts were telling her to kick backwards between his legs. But she was too terrified to move.

'Keep away from my family. You hear me?'

The Pakistani accent was crystal-clear, rasping in anger, and she could feel his hot breath on her hair. She was rigid with fear, waiting to have her throat sliced.

'Keep away from my family or I'll cut your head off, you bitch.'

The blade seared into her flesh, but she didn't feel pain. Just warm blood running down her neck. He released his grip and shoved the back of her head hard. Her face hit the brick wall as she slumped to the ground, her hand clutching her neck. She could hear his footsteps running away and she slowly got to her feet and staggered to the doorway, her bloodstained fingers trembling with fear as she pushed the key into the lock. As she stepped inside the door, she turned to see the hooded figure running out of the car park and jumping into a waiting car. Rosie closed the door and stumbled up the stairs to her flat, fumbling with the lock, one hand on her neck to stem the blood running through her fingers. She rushed into the bathroom and slammed on the light with her free hand, still clutching her neck with the other. In the mirror, her shocked, ashen face stared back at her with terrified eyes, one side of her cheek grazed and bleeding from the roughcast wall. Blood was dripping through her fingers and onto the basin. She rinsed a facecloth in cold water and pressed it tight to her neck, barely breathing, her legs feeling like jelly. After a few seconds she took her hand away and could see the gash. It wasn't much. A line of about three inches, though deep enough to bleed heavily. Jesus! She wasn't even sure where the jugular vein was, but she would be bleeding much more if it had been hit. But what if the knife had nicked some little vein next to it? She rinsed the cloth and pressed it to her neck again, then slumped onto the toilet seat, feeling lightheaded. Calm down, she told herself. You're not going to bleed to death. It's only a flesh wound. She rested her head back on her shoulders, hoping that would stem the blood flow, and closed her eyes. The shrill ring of her mobile startled her, and she fished it out of her coat pocket. No name. She pushed the answer button, trying to compose herself.

'Rosie! Rosie! It's me. Sabiha!'

'Sabiha! Are you alright?'

'No. I can't talk. Listen to me, please, Rosie. I don't have much time. It's Laila. She's gone! They've taken her!'

'Gone? Where?' For a moment Rosie was confused, her head swimming.

'To Pakistan! They took her! To the north – the Swat Valley! Please help! I can't talk to you again. Please!'

'Have they hurt you?'

'Yes!' Sabiha was crying. 'Please keep away from me. I'm sorry. Help my cousin! Please help us!'

'Where are you?'

'I can't talk. I will try to get a message to you. Don't contact me again. They saw us in the park. They beat me! They won't let me see my babies!' She broke into sobs.

'I'm so sorry, Sabiha.' Rosie felt suddenly nauseous. 'I'm so sorry.'

The line went dead. Rosie stood up and looked in the mirror, her face crumpling as the floodgates opened and tears ran down her face. Stop it, she told herself. You cannot lose it. She gingerly took the cloth off her neck and watched the drops of blood mixed with her tears rinse away.

CHAPTER TWELVE

It had been a sleepless night after Rosie finally went to bed, lying flat on her back, careful not to move a muscle for fear of opening the wound. She'd decided the cut wasn't bad enough to merit a trip to the Accident and Emergency unit. She'd delicately cleaned it and used a couple of butterfly stitches she had dug out from an old First Aid bag that the *Post's* in-house medical department had given her for one of her foreign trips. It seemed to hold it in place. She'd forced herself to drink a brandy for the shock and went to bed. When she eventually drifted off, her nightmares were full of shadowy figures chasing her with knives and dragging her up dark alleys, and finally she woke to the same ringing of the phone in her head that she'd been waking up to for most of her life. And again her eyes were wet, as the final, garish image that brought her screaming out of her fevered sleep was that of her mother hanging on the end of a rope. Rosie lay still for a few moments, wiping her eyes with the palms of her hands and sniffing. Crying in her sleep again. Always the same when she was stressed, and sometimes even when she wasn't. She was fine, she told herself. It could have been worse. Her finger lightly brushed the wound. It stung, but at least it was holding up. She let out a long sigh, staring at the ceiling. If she didn't get out of bed right now, she never would. 'Come on, Gilmour,' she said aloud. 'Get on with it.' She swung her legs onto the floor.

'What the fuck—' McGuire's mouth dropped open as Rosie walked into his office. He slammed his pen onto the desk and sat back. 'What the fuck happened to you, Gilmour?'

Rosie put her hand up in a calming gesture. She knew the bruise and grazing on her face were raw.

'I'm fine, Mick. It's not as bad as it looks.' She didn't need sympathy or she'd go to pieces right here in front of him. 'I got attacked last night.'

'What? Christ almighty! Where? Who?' McGuire was on his feet and coming out from behind his desk. 'Come on, sit down.' He took her arm and led her to the sofa. 'Tell me.' He sat opposite her. 'Are you okay?'

'Yeah,' Rosie said, through gritted teeth. 'I'm fine. Don't fuss.'

'Where did it happen?'

Rosie shifted in her seat and pushed out a sigh.

'Er . . . Outside my flat. In the car park.'

'Aw, for fuck's sake, Rosie! How many fucking times have I told you? Fucking hell!'

'Christ, Mick,' Rosie could feel her lip trembling. 'Give me a break, I got bloody cut.' She bit her lip to stop the tremor.

McGuire's voice suddenly softened as he put both hands up.

'Okay, I'm sorry.' His eyes rolled to the ceiling. 'It's . . . It's . . . Well . . . you know, Gilmour, how much I live in dread of something like this fucking happening to you.'

His eyes met Rosie's and for a poignant moment there was no need for words.

'I'm well touched, Mick. And they say you're a right hard bastard too. It's just not true.' Rosie shot him a little tongue-in-cheek smile. She had to do something. A spat she could cope with, but a tender moment would have her blubbing all over his office.

'Yeah, right.' He smiled back. 'I am a hard bastard when people like you don't do what they're bloody told – as if you ever would. But I just don't want you getting killed, okay?' He cleared his throat and folded his arms. 'So, what the Christ happened?'

'I was coming into the car park after having a glass of wine with a cop contact, then just as I'm getting towards the front door, suddenly some bastard grabs me from behind and holds a knife to my throat.' Rosie eased down the zipper in her high-neck sweater, revealing the wound.

'Aw, for fuck's sake! Why didn't you phone me last night? You should have gone to Casualty.'

Rosie shook her head.

'No point, Mick. Once I got into the house and I could see it was only a flesh wound, I dealt with it. I honestly didn't want to involve anyone. You go to Casualty, they have to tell the cops, then I have to deal with a lot of questions I don't want to answer.' McGuire nodded in agreement.

'So who was the bastard? How did you get out of it? Your face looks sore.'

'I know. He pushed me hard against the wall when he let me go – once he'd cut me. Then he just ran away. I got into the house in time to get a quick look and saw this guy in a hooded jacket running towards a car. He climbed in and they roared off.'

'Bastard!'

'He was a Pakistani.'

'A Pakistani?'

'Yep. Didn't see his face, but I knew from the voice. And he said to me, "Stay away from my family or I'll cut your head off." Nice guy.'

'Shit! We should tell the cops.'

'No. No. Definitely not, Mick. Not right now. I've got a lot to tell you. We need to talk – the bastard last night must be attached to the Shah family. It has to be one of them.'

'But why? I mean it's not as if we've done anything yet. We haven't even written a proper story.'

'I know, I didn't get a chance to tell you last night, but I talked to the Pakistani girl – Sabiha. Remember the one I told you about who was giving me the eyes that day, but wouldn't talk?'

'Yeah.' McGuire nodded. 'How did you get to her?'

'I went back down to the shop where she worked and waited for her to come out. She went to the park and I followed her.'

McGuire let out a little chuckle, shaking his head.

'Despite the fact we were supposed to be taking a step back in case we were accused of racism and harassment?'

Rosie shrugged, half smiling.

'Well, I thought I'd give it one last shot. And hey, I'm glad I did, because she spilled her guts. Plus there was another girl with her. A lovely little Glasgow girl, born and bred here, only fourteen, and she told me she was getting shipped off to Pakistan to get married to some old bastard. The kid was really upset. I honestly couldn't believe my ears when they just started talking, Mick. What a result!'

'So, tell me everything.'

He got up and buzzed Marion to bring some tea in, then sat back down, rubbing his eyes.

Rosie relayed chapter and verse what the girls had told her. About the passports and what they believed happened to people. She watched his eyes almost pop when she told him what Sabiha had said about the diamond smuggling.

'But the thing is,' Rosie continued, 'after I saw them

yesterday, I got attacked last night outside my home. Plus . . . they rumbled poor Sabiha and gave her a right hiding.'

'Jesus! How do you know?'

'Because when I got into the house and was trying to compose myself, with blood pouring out my neck, the mobile rang and it was her. She was terrified and sobbing. Told me not to get in touch with her again, that they'd beaten her up and won't let her see her babies. Someone had seen us talking in the park.' Rosie shook her head. 'Christ! I can't believe these bastards.'

'Shocking.' McGuire shook his head.

'Sabiha was pleading with me to help her and her cousin – they've already taken the young girl away to Pakistan. They must have just stormed in there after seeing me with them yesterday and more or less kidnapped the poor girl. It's outrageous, Mick. It really is. They shouldn't be allowed to do this with kids. It's just wrong. '

The door opened and Marion came in with a tray and set it down on the coffee table. McGuire poured, handed a cup of black tea to Rosie, and then sat back, cup in hand, his feet on the table.

'I know it's wrong,' he sighed. 'But it's not for us to judge. It's how they do business.'

'Yeah, that's what I mean. And nine times out of ten it *is* business. These arranged marriages. Much of it is to link families' wealth together.'

'We can't say that, Gilmour. We'll get fucking hanged.'

'I know we can't say it. And of course it's their culture to arrange marriages, and I can see why they want to keep to themselves and work within their own community – given that there are plenty of racist bastards out there who wouldn't give them jobs otherwise. It was the same when the Irish came generations ago, they had to look after each other, intermarry and all that crap, so that they could take care of their community. It's the same for the Asians, and of course I respect that. But you can't be taking fifteen-year-old girls out of the country against their will – the country they've been born and raised in – and shunting them to Pakistan to some village to marry a middle-aged bastard. It's just wrong.'

McGuire nodded, rubbing his chin.

'I know. That's a good point. The kid is probably as Scottish as any teenager in Glasgow. It's not fair. But we need to tread carefully. I'm not sure what we can do on this. But there must be a public interest defence we could make if we published it and were taken to task by lawyers or courts.'

They sat in silence for a long moment.

'I don't think we should be publishing anything right now Mick.'

'Why?'

'We should go and find the girl. Bring her back.'

He looked at her, incredulous.

'Aye. Fine. I'll do the jokes, Gilmour.'

'I'm serious. She's a British citizen – and a minor – and she's been kidnapped. She told me herself yesterday what was going to happen. She was crying.' Rosie rumbled around in her bag. 'I've got it on tape, Mick. Everything she said.'

'You have that on tape?'

'Yes. And the other stuff Sabiha said about Rabia and the fake passports. It's all on tape. We have to find a way to use it.' Rosie paused for a breath. 'But listen, what a scoop it would be if we could go over there and bring that kid back!'

McGuire was silent for a moment, and Rosie could almost see his brain ticking over.

'It would cause a riot within the Asian community.'

'Maybe not. You might find she's not the only woman who's been treated like that. But forget that for the moment. We should concentrate on what we can do for her. She's the one whose life is going to be in ruins. And she's just a kid.'

'And how in the name of Christ do you propose to bring her home? Are you just going to waltz into some remote village in Pakistan like the cavalry and tell them, "Sorry, guys, the wedding's off, the bride has a pressing engagement in the House of Fraser?" You'd get lynched.' He shook his head, slowly and put his cup down. 'No chance, Gilmour. I've been there before with you. But this would be right off the scale. It's Pakistan, not the Costa del Sol. That whole area is a hotbed of Islamist fanatics since the Taliban started marching around Afghanistan, stringing everyone up. You could disappear into the middle of nowhere and nobody would even know where to begin to look for you.'

'I could take somebody with me.'

'Oh yeah! Sure. Matt would be perfect . . . Shitting himself in the hills of Pakistan.' He looked her square in the eye. 'No chance, Gilmour. Are you reading my lips?'

Rosie looked at him defiantly.

'I've got a friend . . . A Pakistani guy, a contact I've used for years. He's already helping me on this. He knows a lot of stuff and is a real Glasgow wide boy. He'd be our man on the ground, and if anyone can get this girl out, then it's him. Omar.'

'Omar? Omar fucking Sharif?' McGuire chuckled in disbelief.

Rosie couldn't help but smile.

'Yes. Omar. He's good. A bit of a crook, but he knows his stuff. And he knows Pakistan like the back of his chapati.'

Mick shook his head and said nothing. Rosie could see he was at least considering the option.

'There's something else, Mick.'

He looked at her, puzzled.

'What?'

'Well. Again, it was something that happened yesterday. A lot happened yesterday . . . Er . . . A lot.'

He folded his arms and looked up at the ceiling.

'What the fuck happened yesterday?' he said slowly.

'I met the girl who's the best pal of the woman who got half her arm cut off.'

'Now you *are* kidding me.'

'Nope. She phoned me. Out of the blue. Her name is Julie. I met her yesterday afternoon, that's why the day became such a blur. She told me everything. Honest to God, Mick, you won't believe this shit. I can hardly believe it myself . . .'

McGuire shook his head and sighed as he got up and went to his desk. He went into his drawer and took out a foil packet of pills.

'I'm going to need one of these.' He held it up. 'My ulcer's starting to niggle.'

'I think you should definitely take one,' Rosie said, dreading how he would react.

He popped a pill and perched on his desk, looking down at Rosie. 'Go on. Get on with it.' His brows knitted.

'It's all connected,' Rosie said. 'At least I think it is. The diamonds, the attaché case, the girl with the mutilated arm. I haven't worked it out yet, but I think it's all part of one big story.' She waited as he turned the information over in his head. 'There's something else. Now I don't want you to go nuts when I tell you this . . . just hear me out. Julie and the other girl, Nikki. They took the attaché case from the hotel room.'

'What attaché case? This is the first I've heard of this.'

'Oh . . . right. I forgot to tell you. But there's this attaché case that belongs to some dangerous people connected to the dead Pakistani guy. It was in the hotel room at the Albany, and now it's missing. The bad guys want it back. It contained a lot of money, fake passports . . . and diamonds. Rough diamonds.'

'Is this a fairy story this Julie bird has spun? How much money is she after?'

'None. She's shitting herself, because *she* has the case and knows they're after her. And it's not a fairy story. My cop contact told me.'

'Are you seriously telling me that this Julie bird has the missing case? The case that may be linked to all this, and therefore is linked to at least one, possibly four crimes? One of them being a girl whose arm was taken off?' McGuire covered his face with his hands. 'Gilmour, please tell me you didn't see this case. Please tell me you didn't.'

'Well . . .'

'Aw fuck! You did. You handled the case. Christ almighty!' Rosie put her hands up.

'I know, I know. It was a spur-of-the-moment thing, Mick, she had it in her car. She opened it and I saw inside. What was I supposed to do? Phone the cops?'

'Well . . . That's one thing you could have done, given that half of Strathclyde's finest are hunting for her.'

'I know, but I didn't. It's an amazing story. There are passports and money in the case . . . and diamonds!'

His eyes widened. 'Did you touch them? Did you touch anything?'

Rosie said nothing.

'Fuck. You did, didn't you?'

Rosie nodded.

'Well, just the diamonds. I had to. I had to see them for myself.'

'Aw, Jesus wept! We're in trouble. This bird will be next for shaving, and the cops will get a hold of this bloody attaché case. We're fucked.'

'No we're not. We just have to find a way around it.'

'What bloody way around it?'

'I don't know that yet. That's why I'm telling you, Mick, let's think about it.'

McGuire's phone rang and he looked at his watch.

'Christ! I've got conference in five minutes. Come in after lunch and we'll talk . . . That's unless this bird is found dead before then.'

Rosie stood up and headed for the door.

'What about Pakistan? We should go.'

McGuire rubbed his eyes and pinched the bridge of his nose with his thumb and forefinger. Then he shook his head and gave her an exasperated look. 'Get me a costing . . . You, Matt and this Omar Sharif character. Have it on my desk in the morning and I'll make a decision.'

Rosie tried hard not to smile as she swiftly left before he changed his mind.

CHAPTER THIRTEEN

Nikki sank back in the pillows, gazing out at the raindrops making tiny rivulets through the grime on the high-arched, steel windows. Glasgow's famous Royal Infirmary looked a daunting enough building from the outside, with its old Victorian towers dominating the skyline at the edge of the city centre. Inside, though much had been modernised, Nikki still felt like a prisoner of some dark age. Her nightmares in the first few days after the attack had left her screaming and confused. And now, even though they'd stopped the morphine, the heavy painkillers made her spaced out and drowsy. So it had been hard to concentrate when the police had finally been allowed to interview her. They'd been waiting several days, they told her, as they placed the plastic chairs either side of her bed. The big cop had introduced himself as a detective inspector, but she couldn't remember his name now, or the female detective sergeant. Nikki reflected on their questions and her answers and hoped she'd got away with it. They'd been very gentle with their probing, unlike the police she'd witnessed many times in Cranhill or Easterhouse when they battered down someone's door in the middle of the night, and dragged a hoodlum from their bed. With her, they'd been more like counsellors, gently telling her that they know she's in trouble, and that some very dangerous people are after her. Cheers, pal, she almost said – you don't need to tell me they're after me, I'm the one who'll never be able to do a handstand again. But she'd kept her face straight, and said as little as possible. Her shock when they told her that she was recorded on CCTV coming out of the Albany Hotel was genuine. They'd even shown her the picture, and she could see Julie carrying the case. Her insides rattled like an engine, and only the sedative effect of the drugs made her calm enough to keep her mouth shut. Am I under arrest? she'd asked them. No, they told her: enquiries are ongoing. But they didn't suspect that she had played any part in the killing of the Asian man in the hotel room. They swallowed her story that the dead man had been her punter, that she'd fled the room when he'd kept urging her to pull the belt tighter during a sex act. She told them he was alive when she left him. The only conclusion she could come to was that he did it himself after she left. What about the attaché case that's clearly in the picture, they asked? She insisted she didn't know anything about it. She couldn't even recall if Julie was carrying anything, but if

she was, then it was probably her own case, because sometimes she took a change of clothes with her when they
were working. Julie had concocted the story last evening
during visiting, on the off chance they had CCTV. She'd
schooled Nikki so well that she was beginning to believe it
herself. Now that the detectives had gone, she was
exhausted and wanted to sleep. She closed her eyes, but as
she was drifting off, she could hear a familiar voice in the
corridor outside.

'Thanks, Sister. I won't stay too long . . . I understand.'

Christ! It was Paul. What the hell did he want? Nikki
opened her eyes to see him coming in the door, a sheepish
look on his face and a bunch of petrol station flowers in his
hand. With her good arm, she shifted in the bed and pulled
herself up a little on the pillow.

'Let me get that for you, Nikki.' Paul took a step towards
the bed and puffed up the pillow behind her, so that she
was more upright. 'There. That okay, darlin'?'

He smiled, and Nikki met his bloodshot eyes and caught
a whiff of fags on his breath.

'Don't call me darlin',' Nikki snapped, her stomach ten-
sing up. 'I'm not your darlin'. What are you doing here,
Paul?'

Paul's face fell. He glanced away from her, then back, and
his gaze fell on the bandaged stump. His lip trembled.

'I'm your husband, Nikki. I want to help you . . . Look
after you.'

'Piss off, Paul,' Nikki snarled. 'Seriously? My husband? You should have thought about that when you blew our life savings at the bookies. You ruined everything . . . Everything.' She turned away.

'I'm so sorry,' Paul's lip twitched. 'I . . . just want to look after you.'

For a few seconds Nikki was so choked she couldn't speak. She'd heard all this before, the contrite weeping and promises he would change. No more, she told herself. She pulled her stump away as he reached out.

'Don't, Paul. I . . . I can't do this right now. Can't you see the state I'm in? . . . I've lost my bloody arm. My life will never be the same again.'

Paul placed the flowers on the bed, and she felt his hand brush across her foot and rest on her ankle. She wished he would just go, but the touch of him, the sheer feel of human contact was a comfort, even though everything in her body told her it was wrong. She had to find the strength. She jerked her feet away.

'Don't. It's no good.'

They stayed silent, and Nikki turned her face away, but could see Paul wiping his tears from the corner of her eye.

'Did you speak to the cops? What are they saying? Have they got the bastard for this yet?' he muttered.

Nikki shook her head but kept her face turned away.

'No. Probably never will.'

'It's been in the papers.'

Nikki nodded, staring out of the window at the after-noon sky turning dark.

'They hinted that you were a prostitute. And that this was some kind of punishment. That you might have robbed a punter.'

Nikki said nothing, but kept gazing out of the window.

'Is it true?'

Nikki pushed out a breath.

'How the fuck do I know what they're saying? Listen. I don't want to talk, can you not understand?'

Silence. Paul walked around to the other side of the bed and wiped away the condensation on the window with his jacket sleeve.

'There's a lot of talk in the street as well. Something about a Pakistani guy – some guy who was found dead in the Albany Hotel. They're saying he was a gangster . . . that somebody stole his money.'

Nikki ignored his unspoken question and reached across to the cabinet to the glass of lukewarm water. She sipped from it and placed it back down.

'I don't know anything, Paul. Okay? I . . . I'm shattered. All I know is that my life is in a mess. I've lost part of my arm, and I don't know what's going to happen to me next . . .' She looked up at Paul, who was crying again.

'I never wanted this to happen,' he whimpered.

For a second, Nikki wasn't sure what he meant. Paranoia kicked in. Was he a part of this? Had he handed her over to them, helped set her up in some way? Knowing him, he'd do anything for money. Maybe that's why the bastard was in here now . . . on a fishing expedition. But he just stood there, face in his hands, snivelling. Could he really do that? He looked so upset.

'I'm so sorry . . . I just want you back.'

Nikki had heard enough.

'I want you to go, Paul. I'm tired. I need to rest.'

'What about Julie? Have you seen her?'

That was it. The bastard *was* fishing, she thought.

'What do you care about Julie? You can't bloody stand her.'

'I . . . I only want to know that you'll have someone to look after you when you get out . . . if you don't want me. Listen. I'll do anything for you. Anything at all. I've stopped gambling.'

'Aye. Sure you have.'

'Well . . . I'm going to. I can get a job, make a new life for us.'

She turned to face him.

'Paul. I need to rest. I'm not well.'

'Okay, I'll go. But think about it. When are you getting out?'

'Christ! Why all the questions? I don't even know myself. A few days, they said, if they get everything stabilised. But my life is different now. It's over between us. Please go.'

Nikki turned her head away, easing herself down on the

bed, turning her body to face the window. She was barely breathing, and she could feel the warmth of his fingers, and the gentleness of his touch on the top of her arm where the bandage stopped.

'Okay, Nikki. I'm going. I'm sorry. So . . . so sorry.'

She didn't turn around, but heard his footsteps as he left.

CHAPTER FOURTEEN

It was baking hot. In the back of the taxi, Rosie squinted through the clouds of dust at the mayhem that was downtown Peshawar, Pakistan. The culture shock of suddenly being thrust into the midst of this nearly took the feet from her. The stench wafting in from an open sewer at side of the road turned her stomach. She closed the window and wiped sweat from her brow. The streets were teeming with people. There seemed to be no traffic laws – cars and trucks barging their way through the gaps between rickety carts pulled by hulking oxen. Tiny rickshaws buzzed like wasps alongside the cars, all honking horns continuously and fighting for space among the potholes.

'Christ!' Rosie fanned herself with her notebook. 'Why is everyone rushing all over the place?' She tapped Omar on the shoulder. 'They're driving like maniacs. What's with the mad rush? Is there something I should know?'

'It's always like this.' Omar half turned, flashing a smile.

'At this time of day, everyone's hungry, and they're all frantically dashing home for the evening meal. It's pretty mental. People get all aggressive when they're hungry.'

'I know the feeling,' Rosie sank back. 'I'm starving. Are we nearly at the hotel?'

'A few more minutes.'

She took in the scene across the busy road, where people swarmed around the throng of market stalls, selling everything from pots and pans to rusty car wheels and tyres, alongside mountains of fruit and vegetables. Nearby, children poked around a rubbish dump, collecting plastic bottles and tin cans and shoving them into sacks. Two men argued and pushed each other over a market stall, then fell into a fight, sending everything flying as they grappled on the ground. She closed her eyes and rested her head back. She'd be glad to get to the hotel. Minutes later, the car braked suddenly and screeched on a roundabout, knocking over a cyclist with a wooden cage full of live chickens perched on his handlebars. The taxi drove on, and Rosie caught a glimpse of the teenager on the ground, the bike on top of him and the chickens fluttering furiously, two of them escaping through some broken spars in the cage.

'We just hit that guy! Shouldn't we stop?' Rosie asked.

The driver sped up and cursed, turning to Omar and shaking his head. They spoke in Urdu, chuckling.

'He'll be fine, Rosie. It happens all the time.'

Matt turned to look out of the rear window.

'A couple of happy chickens just made it off death row.'

'They'll not get very far.' Omar rolled down his window and stuck his head out for a look. 'So, guys, what do you think of Peshawar?'

Rosie puffed. She'd only seen the north-west frontier city that bordered Afghanistan on television and in newspaper coverage of the Afghan war with the Russians back in the eighties, while she was cutting her teeth as a reporter. She hadn't been there, but the chaos on the streets reminded her of places in war-torn Africa where she'd later reported from, all of them lawless and edgy. As always, the nervous churning in her stomach when she knew she was in a foreign land and things were out of her control had started. Anything could happen in a place like this. She should feel safe with Omar, she reminded herself. He was more or less a local, he'd told her before they left Glasgow.

Once McGuire had agreed to the trip, demanding to be phoned from Pakistan several times a day, Rosie and Matt had spent most of the afternoon and evening with Omar before they left, discussing plans. In theory it sounded plausible, and so far, so good. They'd made it to Peshawar, and were on their way to a hotel. How hard can it be? Matt had said, nudging her as they'd gone through customs and immigration without a hitch. Their cover story was that they were here to report on Afghan refugees, who were stranded in camps in the Pakistan border because their country was still too unstable to go home. Omar knew the ground well, and he'd described to them how he had relatives in Peshawar and all along the border. Most of them weren't blood relatives, but they were all brothers.

'I'm not going to lie to you,' Omar had spoken frankly, 'There's an element of danger. Inside Peshawar itself, but especially outside. Some of these Afghan border towns are bandit country, so it's not always safe. But I think we'll be fine.'

Rosie hadn't relayed the 'I think we'll be fine' part to McGuire. She'd been so surprised and pleased that he had decided to give the mission the green light that, as usual, she hadn't given too much consideration to safety. She could only think of the plan. If all went well, they'd be in and out in a few days, hopefully with Laila and a couple of front-page splashes and spreads. She hadn't heard from Sabiha – apart from the panicked phone call a couple of days ago – and she didn't want to risk going anywhere near the house. Probably best that Sabiha didn't know she was out here anyway. The less anyone knew, the better.

The taxi pulled off the main road and into the sweeping driveway of the Pearl Continental Hotel, a lavish white four-storey building, like an oasis in the midst of the swirling, dusty desert. A doorman kitted out like an extra from a film about the old Raj stood like a sentry, complete with crimson tunic coat, shiny buttons, fez headgear and a waxed moustache. When the car stopped he approached, bowing and scraping as he opened the door.

'Welcome, Mem Sahib.'

Rosie managed to keep her face straight, not quite knowing how to reply, then turned to Matt.

'Just bear that in mind, pet. Refer to me as Mem Sahib from now on.'

'Aye, right.' Matt went to the boot as it clunked open and unloaded his gear, slinging his camera bag over his shoulder, and his laptop bag on the other.

'This is rather plush,' Rosie said.

'Believe me,' Omar said. 'You don't want to go downmarket in Peshawar. Some of the budget hotels . . . well, you don't know what you're going to wake up beside.'

Rosie made a mental note to bring Marion back a present for pushing the budget to the limit. She felt edgy enough in the streets, so the safety of a big international hotel was like a comfort blanket. But she knew it wouldn't stay like that. In the next couple of hours they would meet Omar's cousin, a Pakistani Glaswegian doctor who had married over here. Hopefully, he would give them the lowdown on Laila. Then it would be up to them how they played it. Rosie was impressed by how much Omar had gleaned of the area where Laila was apparently staying and what the set-up was. The Pakistani community was so tight-knit. In Glasgow, Pakistani people would more often than not know what was going on in their old homeland village, whether it was illegal or not, but they would never discuss it. That was the problem police always said they had with them – everyone who wasn't Pakistani was an outsider. It was rare when a journalist like her could strike up a friendship with a character like Omar, and it was always the only chance anyone had of getting a glimpse behind the veil drawn over life in Pakistan.

'So, we have a fair idea of where Laila is. Nothing concrete yet, but I have eyes and ears who are keeping me informed.'

Ismal spoke with an educated Glasgow accent – the product, Omar had told Rosie, of the city's best private school, where wealthy Asians sent their sons to be turned into accountants, lawyers, surgeons – fulfilling the aspirations they had had for themselves, but could never have achieved as penniless immigrants a generation ago. Omar's parents had never made enough money to send him to private school, but he always joked that he made more cash living on his wits than most professionals. Knowing Omar, he probably did. But if Omar was the market trader who could convince you to buy something you absolutely didn't need, Ismal was the studious pragmatist, who exuded an air of calm and maturity beyond his thirty years. Over dinner in the hotel's swish restaurant, Rosie had allowed the two cousins to run the show, content to listen to their stories of growing up in Glasgow, of the racism and the camaraderie among the group of Muslim mates who all stuck together. In his Western clothes and with a trendy haircut, Ismal looked too young to be a doctor and to be working in the kind of difficult environment he had described, in the Afghan refugee camp deep in Pakistan's famous Swat Valley. As Rosie watched the two of them in discussion, she also didn't object to the fact that they would slip into their own language when they were talking about something they did not want her to hear. It rankled a little, but now was not the time to deal with it. She'd come all the way over here to get Laila, and she needed them, Ismal especially, onside. Finally, over coffee, the conversation was turning to the business in hand.

'So, how much do you know about where Laila is?' Rosie looked inquiringly at Ismal. 'Is she here in Peshawar?'

Ismal put down his cup and clasped his hands in front of him on the table, in the kind of pose he probably used for doctor–patient chats. He nodded slowly.

'Here's the situation.' He glanced at Omar. 'I've already told Omar what I know, but we should go over it together now, so that we can make a plan.'

'Of course.' Rosie nodded.

'Laila was brought here by one of her uncles – she arrived a few days ago – and she is staying with his family. They have a lot of connections in Peshawar, in the textile industry. You know that Laila's father has a textile warehouse in Glasgow. The family are merchants who have been here for generations and they supply a lot of stores and factories within the city, but they have ambitions to branch out to the outlying areas and Islamabad. There is a larger, more successful textile firm in Islamabad, and that is run by this guy by the name of Gashood Maan. He is recently widowed and is, I think, forty-eight years old.' He paused, glancing from Rosie to Omar. 'An agreement was reached between the two families – a business agreement – that they would work together, create bigger profits for both of them, spread the firms further afield. You know how these things work.' He paused again as they nodded. 'But Gashood wants a young wife.'

'And that's where Laila comes in,' Rosie said, knowing she looked disgusted.

Ismal raised his eyebrows and made a resigned face.

'It happens,' he sighed. 'A lot. Too often for my liking. It's not right. Laila's only a child, barely two years older than one of Gashood's oldest kids . . . and he has four children in all. So Laila will be a skivvy for him and his children.' He shook his head. 'And, what will be really tough for a young girl like Laila, born and bred in Glasgow, is that she will have to live here. Probably in Islamabad, where she won't know anyone, and where she'll have to adhere to the strict regime of the family pecking order.'

'Jesus,' Rosie said, catching Matt's eye. 'So she'll be more or less a prisoner?'

'Yes. No other way to put it.'

'So unfair.'

'I know.' He nodded to Omar. 'We both know how these things are, don't we, cuz?'

Omar shrugged and looked down at the table.

'Sure. That's why I turned down any offers I had from my parents trying to match me off with women. It just wasn't not for me, and it caused me a lot of problems in my family. Some people don't even speak to me. But I'm my own man, and I won't change. I made my own choice of wives.'

Rosie and Matt exchanged glances and managed to keep their faces straight at his 'wives' remark.

'You're married, Ismal, aren't you?'

'Yes, I am. But not the way my family wanted. I came here a couple of years after I qualified and had worked in Glasgow hospitals. I decided I wanted to take a year or so out to work with the refugees. I came with an aid agency, and that's where I met my wife – Asima. She's Pakistani and a nurse. It was one of these things, a blessing to meet someone who became a friend, and it developed from there. I couldn't have wished for anything more. My parents were trying to marry me off –' he snorted and shook his head – 'more or less to the highest bidder. Trying to find me a wife from Pakistan or Scotland, because as a doctor I'd be considered a good catch.'

'But I'm better-looking,' Omar chipped in, grinning.

'No you're not.' Ismal gave him a playful dig across the table. 'But seriously. That's how it was. Who knows what would have happened? Would I have resisted my parents' wishes forever? I don't know. But they know I'm strong-willed, and in the end I think they were just glad I married a Muslim girl. Asima is from Peshawar, and she knows Laila's family. That's why I'm so well informed. She wants to help us too.'

They sat in silence for a few moments and Rosie waited for Ismal to take the lead.

'So,' Ismal said. 'By tomorrow, I will know for sure where they have taken her. Her uncles have family up along the Swat Valley, and they are going there while they make preparations for the wedding.'

'The wedding?' Rosie felt her mouth drop open. 'They'll marry her off that quick?'

'Oh, yes, absolutely. She'll be married within the next couple of weeks. Plans are already underway. Once the agreement is made by the family, nothing will break it.'

'Except us,' Omar said with a Glasgow swagger.

'That's the plan.' Ismal looked at his watch. 'So I think we should be looking at heading up to Swat tomorrow, early. I'll organise the transport, and Omar will take you two in the morning and get you kitted out. You can't turn up in any of these areas with jeans and a T-shirt on. You'll have to get the full traditional shalwar kameez gear, and you, Rosie, must keep your head covered at all times – your face also, when we drive through bandit country.'

'Bandit country?' Rosie said. 'Omar did mention something about that.'

'Yeah. I always have an armed guard with me when I'm going up to the camps, when I drive through certain areas. Swat is lawless. It's run by gangsters who will do anything for money – kidnap, robbing, murder.'

'Just like Glasgow, then.' Matt shrugged.

They all laughed, but Rosie felt her stomach knot.

'Yeah. Just like Glasgow, Matt. Only worse – there's no drink! These days, there's also the Taliban, and that's another story.'

Ismal's smile faded as he got to his feet. He glanced furtively around the hotel foyer, where a few businessmen sat in corners, and Rosie watched them, wondering if they were selling textiles, or daughters.

'Be careful who you talk to around here,' Ismal said softly. 'Walls have ears. All sorts of people come here for business meetings, so you never know who's sitting opposite you, and don't think for a moment you're safe speaking English. Nine times out of ten, people will understand what you're saying. And half of them probably live in Bradford or London. So don't be fooled by appearances. Things are changing here . . . and not for the better.' He looked at Rosie. 'Just be careful. Omar has told me about you and Matt and the scrapes you've been in. You've had some lucky escapes, so I don't want anything to happen to you on my watch.'

'I'll second that,' Rosie said.

And with that he was gone.

CHAPTER FIFTEEN

Big Gordy MacLean's arse was twitching. As if things weren't fucking difficult enough, having to put fires out all over the housing schemes, with these turf wars in the East End spilling over into his side in the north of the city, he now had a posse of fucking Pakis digging his ribs. Pakis? Who knew they were into anything other than sneaking a few bodies in to give them cheap labour in their restaurants and shops? Nothing wrong with that, but diamond smuggling? This was a new one on him. In fact, in the beginning, when they'd found that creepy cunt lying stiff in the Albany Hotel with a belt around his neck, Gordy hadn't even given it a second thought. Even when it turned out that he was a punter, and one of his escort birds had been the last to see him before she bailed out, he still didn't think it was a big deal. Shit happens – as long as everybody keeps their mouth zipped. But within twenty-four hours, he was getting grief from the boys in Manchester and London, telling him he'd better come up with some answers. Some big shot in the Pakistani crew who ran heroin out of Asia and supplied a lot of the market back in the UK was royally pissed off because his attaché case had gone missing. So Gordy had better find out what had happened, and quick.

That was two weeks ago, and if the threat didn't exactly freak him out then, it sure as Christ did now. Because in the space of a fortnight, he'd been instructed to look the other way when the Paki mob sent one of their boys up to deal with the bird. Part of him felt a bit sorry for that daft Nikki when the word came back that they'd chopped her fucking arm off. I mean, who does that, these days? Plus the fact he was pissed off that they did it on his turf. But worse than anything, wee Alex, his trusted mate, who'd been with him since they were teenagers slashing their way across Glasgow, had been murdered two days ago. Shot once between his eyes at point-blank range, in his own car – and for what? Gordy had screamed at the big man down in Manchester, after he'd seen seen his mate lying on a mortuary slab. Because Alex had driven the car with the bird in it that night she got the chop, and he'd set her up. Just in case he talked. They couldn't take any risks. Swallow it, he was told. And now this. He was getting a visit from the big man himself. Johnny Vanner had phoned this morning to say he was on his way up from Manchester and he was bringing some big shot called Sahid Khan. Just be ready, he was told.

Gordy sipped a glass of mineral water in his office and looked at his watch. He was already nervous that he'd been told to send everyone home so that he was completely alone before Johnny and this Khan character arrived. It was important there was nobody who could clock a face. It had the reek of a hit all over it, and although Johnny had given him assurances that he wouldn't come to harm, Gordy was still shitting himself. It wouldn't be the first time he'd used that line himself on somebody whose brains he'd blown out later. It wouldn't be the first guy he'd knowingly sent to his death, with an arrangement that they'd hook up for lunch with him the following day. Christ! This shit was getting harder every fucking year. Part of him wished he could just sell up, take the money and run. He was already worth a fortune in property in the Costa del Sol and Glasgow. He could survive on what he'd made so far. His da would have been proud if he'd been here to see how well he'd done. Given that Gordy and his ma had been left with shag-all after his father was murdered, it had been a long haul punching his way through the ranks to take over the north side, but he and Alex had been tough bastards and nobody messed with them. Being Gavin MacLean's son had helped a little, as his father's reputation was feared. But he'd still had to fight like a tiger to get where he'd got to. Gordy had reaped rewards for having no fear. For the last couple of years he and Alex stayed away from the drugs and were content to run the birds and the escort agencies and saunas, as well as their lap-dancing club – El Paradiso. They'd made a deal with the East End boys that's how it would be, and let them run the coke and the heroin. It was shitty stuff anyway. Running whores had never been easier, especially now they were being shipped in from all over the world. Cheap as chips, and beautiful too. Nobody gave a blow job like a Ukrainian teenager who was shit scared it would be her last. That was how he kept them. But things were about to change. He opened his desk drawer and brushed his fingers over his gun. It was loaded and ready, but Johnny would expect that anyway. His eyes fell on his glass rosary beads, the ones his ma had given him when she came back from Lourdes four years ago. He swallowed hard at the thought of his wee ma. He'd cried for a whole year after she died and his life would never be the same again. He'd made her happy after his da's shooting fifteen years ago, and that's what drove him on to be the best. Nobody, but nobody would ever hurt him or his ma again. He was untouchable. Or so he thought. The front door intercom buzzed and the hair stood on the back of his neck. Fuck's sake, man, calm down. He pressed the buzzer.

'Aye?'

'It's me. Alright?'

Gordy recognised the voice. It was Johnny Vanner.

'In you come, man,' he said, trying to sound as though he was taking all this in his stride.

Gordy stood up as Johnny Vanner walked into the office

and held the door open for the Pakistani man coming in behind him.

'Howsit going, lad.'

It was a statement more than a question, and the 'lad' part was always thrown in by Vanner to let Gordy know that whoever he thought he was in Glasgow, he was shag-all outside of the city. In fact, Vanner had once actually told him that, in a friendly but firm way, during a boozy night in Glasgow when he'd been there on business. Gordy was in no doubt who was running the show here, and he hoped the hand he reached across to Vanner wasn't like a wet dish cloth.

'Not bad, Johnny.' Gordy glanced at the Pakistani's poker face. 'Well . . . It was okay till all this shit started to hit the fan.'

'This is Sahid Khan.' Vanner nodded in the Pakistani's direction. 'He's a good mate. We do a lot of business together, so, as I was saying to you on the phone, somebody fucks with Khan's lads, they fuck with me.'

Gordy stretched out his hand to the big Pakistani who looked uncomfortable in his pinstriped suit, the jacket buttons stretched over a pot belly. His fleshy cheeks were pockmarked and the stubble on his chin had flecks of grey. He said nothing as he shook Gordy's hand and held on for a few beats, looking right through him. Gordy motioned them to sit down, and he watched as Johnny smoothed out his lapels of his jacket and checked the creases in his trousers, tilting his head to the side to admire the shine on his black brogues. Then he sniffed and looked up to Gordy.

'So. What's the fucking score, lad? You found this case yet?'

Gordy put both hands up.

'I'm on it, Johnny. I've got my people all over the place. If this guy had a case with him in the hotel room, then the only person who could have taken it must have been that bird, Nikki.' He shot Khan an angry look. 'The one whose arm you got chopped off.' A surge of rage bit at Gordy's gut as he eyed the Pakistani, and the words were out before he could stop himself. 'And by the way, Khan, with all respect, I think your guys went a bit far there. I mean, chopping half the bird's fucking arm off!'

Khan stared back at him, unblinking.

'It was only supposed to be her hand. But my boy fucked up.'

'Oh,' Gordy said, surprised at the sarcasm in his voice. 'So that makes it alright then? You come up here, and chop up one of my girls, and I'm supposed to swallow it. Well, let me tell you, pal, I don't know how you do business down in your neck of the woods, but you don't do that here.' He paused, glancing at Johnny, whose face was impassive. 'This is my fucking turf. I run it. You have no say here.'

The silence hung in the air and Gordy could feel his breath shallow and the anger rise up, tightening his throat. Calm the fuck down, he told himself. He knew Johnny would let him go so far, a bit of respect on another man's turf, but he had to watch his step. He waited for a reaction. So far, there had been no mention of diamonds from Khan, and he wasn't about to bring it up. Khan had obviously been told by Vanner that Gordy was some kind of gofer up here and he didn't need to be told all the details. Resentment tore at his insides. Eventually, it was Khan who sat forward.

'Okay . . . I hear what you're saying, Gordy, but this was my stuff. The guy in the hotel was dropping something for me, and it cost me a lot of money because now I can't deliver. Where I come from, you steal something, you lose your hand.'

'You don't even fucking *know* if she stole it.'

'Well, we think she did.'

'You *think*?' Gordy heard his voice go up an octave with indignation. 'It's not enough to chop someone's bastard arm off because you *think* she stole it. I assumed she was only going to get a bit roughed up, or I wouldn't have co-operated.' He glanced at Johnny. 'And that's the truth, Johnny. It's not right.'

'I want my case.'

'Okay.' Johnny broke in. 'Listen. The bottom line here, Gordy, is that this case has some valuable stuff in it. I told you about the diamonds.' He looked at Khan, who nodded his approval. 'Rough diamonds. Worth a lot of money.'

Gordy's eyebrows went up. He felt a little better that he was in the loop.

'Yeah. I know that. But what the fuck were your diamonds doing up here? Who's dealing in diamonds?'

Gordy was more curious that he was missing a trick on diamond smuggling than he was about the suitcase. The only diamonds he ever moved on were ones that were ripped off people's fingers and wrists. Usually when they were bound and gagged – or dead. But rough diamonds? What the fuck was this all about?

'They weren't staying here. The guy was making an overnight stop and coming down the next day. He made some flight paths so he wouldn't be detected. Came all the way from Sierra Leone – through Germany and Amsterdam. Came to Glasgow instead of coming to Heathrow as the checks are not so strict here. He was supposed to come down on the train the next day.'

'I see.'

'Right. So what have you got?'

Gordy looked at Johnny. He wasn't going to address this fucking Paki. He didn't like the look of him. Guys like him, all dressed up in their pinstriped suits. Who the fuck did he think he was? It's working in a warehouse or a corner shop he should be, not mixing with the big boys.

'Johnny, I'm doing what I can. I've got people searching for Nikki's pal. She was with her earlier that night and they do everything together. If they took the case out of the room that night, then Julie will know about it, but she's disappeared off the face of the earth.' He glanced at the Pakistani, then back at Vanner. 'So that either makes her guilty, or scared because of what Ali fucking Baba here did to her mate.'

Khan stood up and reached over the desk, grabbing Gordy by the collar, shouting, his face puce with rage.

'Don't you fuck with me, you racist cunt. You think I'm just some Paki boy who you can push around? You don't know me, do you? Even after I cut your bird's hand off you try to fuck with me? I'll cut your fucking throat!'

Johnny leapt to his feet and came between them.

'Right, right, okay, guys. Just calm the fuck down.' He poked his finger at Gordy. 'Listen, lad, and listen good. You don't go talking like that to a guest I brought up here, never mind someone who has lost something, when it was one of your birds who was the last to see the guy. That implicates you. So don't think for a moment it hasn't crossed Khan's mind that you're in on this. Stop fucking about and let's get a plan here so we can get this case back and then we all go back to doing what we do best.'

'How the fuck can I get it if I don't know where it is?' Gordy said, frustrated.

'Yeah, so you say,' snorted Khan. 'All we have is your word, you Scottish cunt.'

Gordy was on his feet again.

'Look, you! Don't fucking take me on on my own turf!'

'Lads! For fuck's sake!'

'Right, okay,' Gordy said. 'Let's just calm down. I've got people looking for Julie. I've got one guy who's been to see Nikki and done a bit of fishing. It might take a bit of time, but if your case is somewhere here, I'll get it for you. What more do you want me to say?' He looked at Johnny pleadingly. 'Big man. You know me. I'm giving you my word. I'll find it if it can be found, but I'm not dancing to this cunt's tune, let's be clear about that.'

Khan's mouth curled in a snarl. Then his mobile rang in his pocket as he was about to speak. He pulled it out and looked at the screen.

'I must take this call. Excuse me, Johnny.' He didn't look at Gordy as he left the room.

As soon as he'd closed the door, Johnny leaned across the desk and lowered his voice.

'Listen, you stupid Scottish cunt, play the fucking game here. That's all I'm telling you. Play the game. If you think for one minute that this Paki bastard is getting his case back, you're thicker than I thought you were.'

Gordy looked at him, confused for a second, and then the penny dropped. He felt relief flood through him and his face almost broke into a smile.

'Fuck! You serious?'

'Just get the fucking case and we'll split it. Okay? So in the meantime, play along with this prick.'

'Got you, Johnny. Don't worry. I'm all singing, all dancing . . . But what's all the passport shit about?'

'Never mind. I'll phone you later and explain. Here's this arsehole coming back.'

The door opened and Khan came back in and sat down.

Gordy took a deep breath and put on his game face as he opened his hands in a pleading gesture.

'Look, Khan, mate. I think we got off on the wrong foot.'

'I'm not your mate.'

'No. Well. Okay, I realise that. Listen . . . Johnny's just reminded me that we're all in this together, and it's for the good of the working relationship we all need to have so we can function. I . . . Well, I just got a bit short-tempered there, because that bird got her arm chopped off. I only met her once, and she seemed like an innocent, stupid little fucker who was in the wrong job. I don't think she deserved that. So let's put it behind us. If she's got your case, or her mate has got it, then I'll bust my arse to get it for you. I know it's of value to you, so once I get it, you'll get it. Just trust me on that.'

Khan looked at Johnny, seeming surprised at this sudden change of demeanour. Johnny nodded reassuringly.

'No sweat, Khan. I think we can go back down the road now. We've made the situation clear here.' He stood up. 'Come on, mate. Let's go.'

Gordy stood up and came out from behind his desk. He walked with them to the door, and out along the corridor to the exit.

'Okay, Johnny. Good to see you, big man. I'll be in touch as soon as I get anything.'

He put his hand out to Khan, who shook it and nodded, but remained stony-faced and silent.

Gordy opened the door and watched them go down the steps and into the waiting Mercedes. He waved them off and then stepped back inside and closed the door, standing with his back to it, breathing a huge sigh.

'Fuck me!'

He took his mobile out of his trouser pocket and punched in a number.

'Paul. Where are you, ya wee prick? You were supposed to call me when you saw that fuckwit wife of yours. Now get your arse in here, pronto.'

CHAPTER SIXTEEN

Rosie was feeling ropey – a mixture of nerves and the movement of the bulky 4x4 as it wound its way through tight mountain roads, deep into the Swat Valley. She'd been awake half the night with a sense of dread of going into the unknown, even more so than she'd felt before. There was something about the vastness of this land that made her feel isolated and acutely anxious that they could quite easily disappear here, and nobody would ever find them.

When Ismal had left the hotel last night, Omar had given her and Matt some hard facts about the kind of area they were about to go into. Since the Russians pulled out of Afghanistan twelve years ago, after a long and bloody war, the country had been taken over by the Taliban Islamic fundamentalists, who ruled the country with their medieval sharia law. Omar explained that the ruthless Taliban had now spread across the Pakistan border and into the Swat Valley, and that people lived in terror. As they drove through remote villages, Rosie and Matt were in the back seat of the 4x4, kitted out in traditional clothes, squeezed up beside the Pakistani bodyguard who sat with his Kalashnikov between his knees, a blank expression on his weathered face. For over an hour they'd been behind a trundling bus, and she watched in disbelief the people clinging to the roof and sides as the old vehicle belched fumes, inching its way round narrow, precarious cliff edges with sheer drops on either side. Rosie didn't even chance looking down, but gazed straight ahead at the breathtaking scenery, dotted with the occasional local trudging on mountain passes. In the distance two old women were bent double, carrying a load of sticks on their backs and negotiating a suspended rope bridge stretched across a colossal ravine. Just looking at it made her dizzy.

Ismal's mobile rang and he picked it up from the dashboard, one hand on the steering wheel, as he drove too close to the edge of a cliff for Rosie's nerves. Matt was trying his best to put on a brave face but he was getting paler by the minute. They could hear Ismal talking in Urdu, then Omar turned around from the passenger seat and gave them a thumbs up. Ismal put the phone back on the dash, and Rosie caught his eye in the rear-view mirror as he spoke.

'That was Asima. She's found out where Laila is staying. She's with an uncle up in Behrain, which is around another hour's drive from the town we are heading towards now.

She's going to find a way to make contact. She doesn't know the family well, but knows who they are, and they know that she's a nurse. She will make some excuse to get close enough to people who know the family, and she hopes to get a message to Laila telling her our plan. We have a house there – it's been in Asima's family for generations. We use it when we have a few days' holiday so we can go hiking in the Swat Valley. The area is very beautiful, though not so safe now.'

'But won't Asima be placing herself in danger?'

He shrugged.

'People respect her as a nurse, and she has sometimes worked in the district, so it will be alright. She's hoping she can get someone who knows the family to bring Laila to the market tomorrow, then Asima can make it look like she's met them by chance. There are people in this area who think the way we do about the Taliban, and about children being forced into marriages, but they dare not say it. We are lucky in many respects because of our professions and education, but many ordinary people here have no escape from the terror that goes on every day.'

'But it's still dangerous for Asima?' Rosie asked.

'Yes . . .' Ismal's eyes locked with hers in the rear-view mirror. 'But she feels very strongly about these things. Especially about what is happening in the Swat Valley now with the Taliban. They are turning it into an Islamic fundamentalist hellhole in the same way they've done to

Afghanistan, which was once a beautiful country with incredible people. It's terrible.'

The traffic slowed and Rosie rolled down the window and stuck her head out to see what the hold-up was. She felt hot and uncomfortable with so many clothes on, covered up to her wrists. A trickle of sweat ran down the back of her neck, and she yanked up her hair to let some air in. There was none.

'What's going on?' Rosie asked.

'I don't know,' Ismal replied, peering through the windscreen. 'We are approaching Mingora, the biggest town in Swat, but something must be happening. Maybe an accident.' He stuck his head out of the window and looked at the long line of traffic. 'Uh oh,' he said suddenly. 'Look, Omar, one of the Taliban nutters is coming this way.'

Rosie's heartbeat quickened.

'What? Will they ask us anything?'

'Don't know.' Ismal sounded concerned. 'They seem to be directing the traffic into the town, but *we* don't want to go to the town, we want to keep to the main road. Here he comes. Just sit tight back there, Rosie. Keep your head down and don't make eye contact. Cover your hands, as they are very pale. Same for you, Matt. Just keep your head down.'

Rosie felt claustrophobic, and tried to breathe slowly as the man in the black turban approached them, carrying a Kalashnikov. She glanced at their guard, whose small eyes stared straight ahead. She stole a fleeting glance at the

Taliban soldier and saw his piercing green eyes narrowing as he stood at Ismal's rolled down window. Clenching her fists under her sleeves, she looked down at the floor, barely breathing. Ismal nodded when the Taliban soldier spoke and pointed them in the direction of the rest of the traffic. When he walked away, Ismal turned around.

'Okay, guys . . . Here's the bad news. We're going to have to go with the flow here. The bastard Taliban have requested we go and attend a stoning in the centre of the town. It's more of a command than a request, so we'll have to go with it.'

'A stoning?' Rosie heard her voice go up. 'Like a stoning to death?'

'Yes, Rosie. I'm afraid so. It's a public execution.'

'Fuck me!' Matt glanced at Rosie in disbelief.

'Who's getting stoned to death? What's it all about?' Rosie asked, as Ismal edged his way along the road and took the narrow dirt track up into the town.

'A woman. She's been convicted of adultery.'

'Christ almighty! And they're going to stone her to death?'

'Yes. Not only that, they convicted her in their sharia court, which consists of Taliban elders. She might not even have done anything. There doesn't need to be evidence – merely the hint that she *may* have committed adultery – like if she was seen with a man who wasn't her husband.'

'That's barbaric!'

'I know. We don't have to watch, but we're going to have to be among the crowd. We don't want to arouse suspicion by refusing to go. We'll stay in the car though. We can park at the top of the road a few yards away from the crowd.'

As they drove up the hill, they could see the crowd gathering below. A sea of people, excited chatter – a carnival atmosphere. Women and children milled around, but it was mostly men who jostled for position at the front. Ismal parked the car and they had a vantage point to look down from and see the circle that was being formed like an arena. Rosie spotted a pile of white stones, and a deep hole dug in the ground.

'What's the hole for? Don't tell me they're going to put the woman in that hole?'

'Yes,' Ismal sighed. 'It's awful. Closing your eyes is maybe the best thing, Rosie.'

'I need to get a picture.' Matt rummaged around in his bag. 'I've got to capture this.'

Rosie shot him a dismayed glance.

'Matt. If they see you taking pictures, we could be in all sorts of shit.'

'They won't see me. Don't worry.' He fiddled with a long lens and put it under his tunic. 'Right, you shift over to my side, so I can get a better view.'

'I don't believe this,' Rosie muttered as she slid across while he climbed over for an uninterrupted view.

'It happens all the time,' Omar said. 'Honestly. These guys are fanatics, and it's only going to get worse. They're spreading everywhere.'

Rosie said nothing, transfixed by the people scrambling down the hill to join the mob. She could still see through the gap below Matt's arm where his camera rested on the window. Then, suddenly, a cheer went up, as three or four men in black turbans dragged a woman out of a corrugated tin shack. She was struggling with them, but they pinned her arms and dragged her across the dirt. Rosie saw one of her shoes come off. Someone from the crowd picked it up and threw it at her, striking her. Everyone cheered. Rosie felt sick. The men roughly shoved the woman into the hole and she stumbled, trying to get to her feet. She was up to her waist. There was a low murmur of conversation among the crowd, then a heavy, dreadful silence. Rosie looked as the first stone was lifted and thrown at the woman, hitting her on the shoulder. She slumped forward. The crowd erupted, and there was a sickening screeching of burka-clad women ululating in celebration. Rosie looked away in a cold sweat. Then another man picked up a rock, and another. Suddenly rocks were raining down on the woman.

'Fucking hell,' Matt said, the camera whirring as he fired off several shots. 'This is from the Dark Ages. They're murdering that poor woman.'

'My God!' Rosie murmured, her hand to her mouth.

Ismal and Omar sat staring out of the windscreen, and

the guard was like a statue beside them, only his eyes moving, scanning across the horizon, watching for trouble. The clunking sound of the stones on flesh sent shivers through Rosie, and she took one last fleeting glance at the woman slumped over the top of the hole, her robes soaked in blood. Finally, the stoning stopped and the baying mob cheered. Then they filtered away.

'I feel like throwing up.' Rosie's throat was choked with emotion. 'Never in my life did I think I would witness something like that.'

'Let's get the hell out of here.' Ismal switched on the engine and eased the car out of the tight area and down the hill onto the main road.

They drove the rest of the journey in silence.

CHAPTER SEVENTEEN

The sweltering heat woke Rosie from a fitful sleep. Through the gaps in the wooden shutters she watched a tiny green lizard sneak in and race up the wall, where it lodged itself in the cornice, staring nervously down at her. Inside the mosquito net her view was fuzzy and she lay back on the bed, hypnotised by the wooden ceiling fan slowly rotating the thick humid air around the small room. She put her hand on the back of her neck and her hair was soaked with sweat. She pulled off the damp cotton vest she'd slept in and lay naked, her body clammy on the cotton sheets. She hoped she hadn't been screaming in the night from the suffocating dream that she was being buried alive, stoned to death by men in black turbans. Christ! She blinked to erase the image of boulders striking the poor woman. She tried a deep breath, but her chest felt tight. Somewhere in the house, she could hear activity, crockery and cutlery rattling, and the aroma of Asian herbs and cooking drifted into her room. She glanced at her watch. It was just gone seven. She pulled back the mosquito net and swung her feet onto the stone floor. As she opened the shutters, the sun streaming in brightened the room, and she was just in time to see a massive cockroach scurry to the far corner and disappear. She shuddered, wondering where it had been all night. Don't even think about it, she told herself, as she went into the bathroom and turned on the shower, watching it spurt out lukewarm water.

Ismal and Omar were already at the massive wooden table when Rosie came through to the kitchen. Asima stirred a frying pan full of vegetables on the cooker and looked over her shoulder, a friendly smile spreading across her face. The scene could have been a tourist bed and breakfast in any mountain resort in a far-flung land, Rosie thought. Yet outside, people lived in fear of being stoned to death if they put a foot wrong. The first lash of tension slapped across her stomach. It was going to be a tough day.

'Morning, Rosie. You're looking chilled.' Omar quipped as he folded a piece of flat bread filled with vegetables.

'Yeah, but below this steely exterior is a woman who's basically shitting her pants about the day ahead.' That was the truth, but it sounded better if she made light of it. It wouldn't do to wimp out in this kind of company.

Ismal gave her a sympathetic smile.

'Don't worry too much. It should be fine.' He motioned

for Rosie to sit. 'We're on, by the way. I've had a phone call this morning, so we have a definite plan. Sit and we can discuss it.' He looked up at Asima as she put fresh flatbread on the table. 'And you must taste my Asima's wonderful breakfast vegetables and bread. She spoils me with her cooking.'

Matt came shuffling in, his blond hair messed up.

'Hey, Matt. You look wrecked, man. Your hair's like a burst couch. Did you hit the night club last night?' Omar said.

'Oh yeah. Just got home.' He sniffed and plonked himself onto a chair. 'Couldn't sleep a wink. So bloody hot.'

'Have some coffee and breakfast, then we'll be on our way. It's going to be a stormer of a day,' Omar said.

Rosie followed Omar's example and spooned some vegetables onto the flat bread and folded it. She bit into it.

'This is wonderful, Asima. Thanks,' she said, then looked at Ismal. 'But I might need to wear a bin liner, eating this kind of stuff for breakfast. There's not exactly a loo on every corner.'

'There is,' Omar grinned. 'It's called the side of the road.'

'Cheers for that, Omar. I might just overdose on the Imodium before we leave.' Rosie smiled and swallowed a mouthful of coffee. What the heck, just bung everything up with medication and worry about your guts when you get home.

*

An hour later they were packing everything into the 4x4, the guard standing by the car drinking coffee, greeting them with what passed for a nod. They piled into the vehicle. Ismal had told them the plan was to go to the market place and walk around like travellers, shopping and buying some trinkets and vegetables. He'd been told that Laila would be taken there by a relative, and they were going to try to make contact with her, to pass the information on for the escape plan later in the day. It sounded good around the table, but Rosie was jittery as the car wound its way out of the narrow track from Ismal and Asima's cabin and on to the road towards the village. Asima was staying at home, preparing the plans for later.

Ismal pulled the car up on a layby at the side of the road, then shifted so he could see Rosie and Matt in the back seat. She looked out at the crowded market nearby.

'Okay, guys. As you can see, the bazaar is heaving with people buying and selling all sorts of stuff. It's always mobbed at this time of the day, which is good for us, as we'll just be in there browsing or buying a few things, melting into the crowd. It can be quite a suffocating atmosphere in this place, so we need to stick together at all times, okay? Don't go wandering off on your own.'

Fat chance of wandering, Rosie thought, as she and Matt exchanged glances. Her eyes scanned the bazaar, instinctively looking for an escape route. But there were only two endless rows of shacks and huts that made up the village

main street, and tiny alleys leading off them to the foot-
hills surrounding the village.

Ismal drank from a plastic bottle of water and wiped
beads of sweat from his top lip.

'Hopefully, Laila will turn up in the market quite soon.
The woman she is with knows me by sight. She's a friend of
Asima, so she knows what we're doing, and she's on our
side. When I spot her and Laila, I'll give you a signal.' He
turned to Rosie. 'Rosie. Have you got a good enough relationship with her to let her know it's you underneath all
that garb?'

Rosie nodded.

'I think so. It was Laila who was the most outspoken
when I talked to her and her cousin, Sabiha. I think she's
the one who's driving this, and it was she who urged Sabiha
to talk to me. So I'm okay with approaching her. As long as
she's not too shocked or does anything that might attract
attention.'

'She won't be. The note I will slip to her will tell her
you're here, and that she must stay calm. You alright with
that?'

'Sure,' Rosie said. She swallowed a ball of dryness and
rummaged through her rucksack for some water. Sweat
trickled down the back of her legs. She pinched her lips
together to stop the little tremor that would give away
how terrified she was.

'Right. Let's do this,' Ismal said.

Rosie pulled her headscarf tight over her mouth so that all that was showing were her dark glasses. Apparently some tourists and travellers still ventured this far into the valley, and Rosie scanned the crowd in the hope she could see any others. But there was nothing but a sea of burkas and men with pashtun caps, or the dreaded black turbans.

'Watch out for the guys with black turbans. They're Taliban,' Ismal said. 'Some of them are just parading around looking for a reason to arrest someone. They'll all be carrying Kalashnikovs. Whatever you do, don't make eye contact or engage them in any way.' He turned to Matt. 'And it goes without saying – no pictures, Matt.'

Matt slung his rucksack over his shoulder and nodded. He and Rosie had decided late last night to take a risk and rig him up with a secret video camera. Ismal had said that although tourists did come here and take the odd picture, it could complicate things. You couldn't just take a snap of a Muslim in the street as if you were on a jaunt to the Greek islands. You had to ask permission, and in this tense climate it wasn't a good idea to draw attention to themselves. But Matt had pleaded with Rosie that he needed a record of where they were for the full story, and she realised that as much as he did. Eventually, she agreed. Discretion, as he'd kept telling her over the years, was his middle name.

They walked together towards the bazaar, Ismal pointing things out as though they were visitors. They kept close to each other.

'Is the camera working?' Rosie murmured to Matt.

'It was when I got out of the car,' he whispered.

They strolled past stalls with garishly embroidered shawls and table covers, and others with wood carvings and hand-made jewellery. Rosie looked around the busy little streets off the market area where there were shacks and workshops, and wondered if these were also people's homes or if they lived further out in the country.

'I see my friend,' Ismal said suddenly. 'Follow me, slowly.'

Rosie peered through the crowd at the woman and girl browsing at the jewellery stall. The girl was trying on some bracelets. She was covered from head to toe, and only her eyes and nose were showing. Rosie couldn't be sure, but once they got a little closer, the lady spotted Ismal and turned around, nodding discreetly. Ismal approached very carefully and nudged the girl, who turned, a little startled. Rosie barely saw him hand her the note and watched as she glanced at the woman, who nodded her approval. It was hard to see if she was confused. But she opened the small palm-sized piece of paper in her hand, and suddenly she stood rigid, her eyes anxiously scanning the crowd. Rosie watched her, moved a little closer, and then the girl turned and she saw a flash of recognition in her frightened eyes, the shadows even darker than now than when she'd seen her in the park. Rosie reached out a hand and squeezed her arm. She didn't dare speak, but only nodded. Laila nodded back, her soft brown eyes full of hope and relief. Then she turned to the woman who was with her, and went back to browsing the jewellery. A wave of sadness choked Rosie at the sight of this Glasgow kid in the midst of all this land that was alien to her, a prisoner in the bloody mountains, so far from home and all she knew.

Then, suddenly, all hell broke loose. Rapid gunfire – three or four shots – echoed around the bazaar and everyone stopped in their tracks. It was all happening in a blur. The roar of a motorbike racing down the dirt track in the middle of the bazaar sent people stumbling into stalls out of the way. It was being chased by another motorbike, with a man with a black turban on it, shooting wildly. People dived to the ground as another motorbike raced through, knocking everything flying. Some people scurried up side streets. Rosie jumped out of the way of a motorbike heading straight at her, and it clipped a stall as it passed, which collapsed on top of her. In the mayhem she tried to scramble from beneath pots and pans and bits of tin sheeting piled on top of her. When she sat up, people climbed all over her and rushed up a side street. Where was Ismal? Matt? Where the Christ were they? Her scarf had come off and she hurriedly pulled it back on, covering her face. She moved over and crouched, but spotted a man across the street looking straight at her. She pulled herself to her knees, then got to her feet. As she steadied herself, dizzy with panic, she was swept along by the wave of the crowd until she was suddenly up an alleyway, away from the bazaar. She tried to catch her breath, pushing past people to head back to the bazaar. But they were shouting and pushing her, and still the sound of gunfire echoed in the distance. Everyone seemed to be going in the opposite direction. Then towards the middle of the alley, people dispersed into tighter dirt roads that forked off into a warren of shacks. She was in the heart of the village, and terror swept through her. She staggered around, trying to find a way out, stumbling towards what looked like the end of the road, praying it would lead her back. But when she reached the end, there was a crowd of men all frantically shouting at each other. She stumbled into a busy cafe. Suddenly, all the men turned to her and began shouting angrily. Wherever the hell she was, she was the only woman, and clearly shouldn't be here. They surrounded her, and began pushing and shoving. She had to get out of here. She had to run. She turned to try to move, when suddenly a hand grabbed her by the hair, and an irate voice shouted in her ear. Then she was being dragged into a side alley towards a shack, a door was pushed open and she was thrown inside. She stumbled and fell onto the dirt in the darkness, tasting earth in her mouth. She was afraid to turn and look up. When she did, there was a woman standing over her and two children with dark, haunted looks on their faces. The small girl smiled, with perfect white teeth, and poked at Rosie's bare arm, which had become uncovered in the struggle. The other child poked and scraped at her white arms, and they both giggled. The woman shouted something at them, and they stopped. Rosie looked up at her, and the woman looked back, unblinking. Rosie swallowed and sniffed, trying to hold back the tears. Then the door burst open, and two men in black turbans came in. Her heart thumped like a drum against her ribs.

CHAPTER EIGHTEEN

Rosie could smell the acrid sweat from the Taliban soldier as he circled her, leaning close, prodding her with the butt of his rifle. She shifted her position so her back was to the wall of the small, musty room. The children weren't smiling any more, and the woman busied herself at the far side of the room with her back turned. The soldier came close to Rosie again, and her body jerked as he barked something into her face. She shook her head, raising her hands submissively. Make a gesture, she told herself, any gesture, that will make this bullying bastard understand she was lost and terrified, and no threat to him. He fixed her with dark eyes full of anger and contempt. She looked away, choking back the whimper rising in her throat. Don't, she told herself. Man up. Not one word of bloody Urdu did she have to communicate. Nothing.

'Ismal!' she finally managed to whisper. 'Doctor!'

She gestured, with hands on her chest that she was with

Ismal, hoping they would know him, but it didn't seem to register with him as he stared through her.

'Ismal,' she repeated. 'Doctor.' Then, the name of the border refugee camp suddenly flashed into her mind. 'Dangam! Ismal. Me . . .'

Nothing. Then, behind him, the man who had dragged her into the house suddenly spoke. She thought she caught the name Asima, but she was too afraid to risk speaking. The rage seemed to slip from the Taliban's face and he immediately turned and left the room.

Rosie broke down, covering her face with her hands. The children eyed her, bewildered, as their mother came over to her and put her finger to her lips.

'Ssssh.' She reached out and gently touched her arm. Then she crossed the room and brought back a small glass with what looked like tea in it. She handed it to Rosie and smiled.

Rosie gratefully sipped the warm, sweet mint tea.

'Asima,' the woman whispered.

'Asima?' Rosie said, hopefully. 'She's your friend.' She wished she had a gesture for friend.

The woman nodded.

Then she pulled up a small wooden stool and beckoned Rosie over to sit. She brushed her finger on Rosie's cheek, wiping away a tear, and Rosie struggled not to start blubbing again.

Rosie stiffened as she heard raised voices outside. The

woman moved swiftly to the other side of the room, gathering the children around her. The door was thrown open and Rosie braced herself. To her relief, Ismal came in, behind two Taliban soldiers and two other men. He was speaking in Urdu all the time with an air of confidence and the men stood back as he looked at Rosie.

'It's okay.'

She suppressed the urge to throw her arms around him.

'Thank Christ you're here, Ismal. I thought . . . I thought . . . Jesus. I don't know what I thought. I was terrified.'

'I know. When all the crap happened at the bazaar, we looked around and you were gone.'

'A stall fell on top of me – pots and pans. When I got up, there was nobody there. And then I got swept away in the deluge of people.'

Ismal smiled.

'Don't worry. It's all okay now. The problem is, I'm told you wandered around on your own and went into one of their cafes. That's just about a hanging offence here, a woman walking into a place full of men. You're not in Byres Road now, pal.'

'What would have happened if you hadn't found me?'

Ismal shrugged.

'Don't know. Maybe nothing, maybe something bad. It depends on which headcase you come up against, and what he's trying to prove to others. But put it this way, you don't want to be at the mercy of these guys. Come on, let's get out of here. The lads are in the car.'

He turned to the Taliban and shook all of their hands, totally ignoring the woman who was standing with her back to the stove. Rosie glanced over her shoulder, and the woman was still looking at her.

'We heard you were getting stoned to death.' Matt grinned as Rosie climbed into the back seat behind him. 'In fact we were just finishing our lunch before going up to get a ring-side seat.'

'Yeah, very bloody funny, you.' Rosie couldn't help but smile. She was glad Matt hadn't given her a sympathetic look or she might have completely lost it. 'I was bloody terrified.'

'Where were you?'

'Where was I? Christ! I stumbled into some men's afternoon domino session and got banjaxed by the Taliban.' Rosie shook her head and rolled down the window. 'Honestly, Matt, I thought I was a goner.'

He turned close to her, and peered at her face.

'You've got dirt all over your face.' He rubbed it with his thumb.

'I fell, or rather I was thrown, into someone's house. I'll tell you about it later.'

'Okay, guys, all safe and well. Let's go.' Ismal switched on the engine and headed down the hill.

Omar turned around to face Rosie, a big smile on his face.

'I reckon, with the right negotiations, we could get good money marrying you off to some Taliban bloke. I mean, you're white as a sheet – that's got to count for something if they want to widen the gene pool up here.'

'Yeah, right. Everyone's a bloody comedian.' Rosie smiled back at him, glad of the banter.

Over lunch back at the house, Ismal and Omar set out the plan for early evening, when they would pick up Laila, and, all being well, head for Islamabad.

'I'm friends with a Scottish couple at the British Embassy in Islamabad,' Ismal said. 'I met them at one of these charity functions for the Afghan refugee camps. They're good people – very much onside with our sentiments over forced marriages.'

'Really?'

'Yes. We got on well and we've had dinner once. Asima told them about the work she does with the group she's involved with to help young girls. I talked to them the day before you arrived, actually, and told them the situation. So, they've agreed to help.'

'But what can they do?'

'Well, once we leave here, we're very much on the run until we get flights sorted for tomorrow.' He glanced at Rosie. 'Listen. I'm confident this is going to work. Once we get out of Swat, we just hammer it to Islamabad, so you should get your office to book you, Matt and Omar on a flight out of there tomorrow morning. I'll sort out Laila's flight – but not till the very last minute. We don't want to alert anyone, especially if we get followed once we've picked her up.'

Rosie nodded slowly, a blur of images flashing through her mind of getting collared at the airport and flung into a jail cell.

'So, how will the Scottish couple help?'

'We stay with them tonight. Their house is on British Embassy grounds, so once we're in there, nobody can touch us. And they have diplomatic plates on their car. So Gerry – that's the husband – will drive us to the airport in the morning. That way, we go right through to security. Just a quick check of your bags – it makes things quicker and gets you off the main concourse of the airport. It's how the diplomats travel.'

'But how is, er, Gerry able to do this?' Rosie asked, puzzled. 'Will he have to tell people in the embassy to get the authority, or can he just go ahead and do it?'

Ismal shook his head.

'He doesn't have to explain everything he does to the embassy officials. He's quite senior, so he can take decisions. Call it one of the perks of being a diplomat.'

'Sounds too good to be true.' Rosie was relieved.

She'd never been involved in anything like this before.

The last time she was being pursued to an airport was in Malaga after Adrian had had to shoot their way out of a jam – leaving their fixer, Javier, in a car park bleeding from gunshot wounds. Diplomatic plates that could take you almost to the departure gate made her feel a lot more comfortable.

'Do you think Laila will be able to go through with this? What if she bottles it?' Matt asked.

Everyone looked at Rosie.

'She won't. She's a plucky girl, and angry that she's where she is. I'd be surprised if she's not ready and waiting for us right now.'

'I think so too,' Ismal said.

They sat quietly for a moment, and Rosie watched Asima clear plates away and work around the kitchen.

'What about you, Asima? Do you ever worry that someone will inform on you for the work you do to help these girls?'

Asima stood with her back to the sink, drying her hands on a towel.

'Not really.' She shook her head. 'People are very good at keeping secrets in this part of the world. Especially women. We've had to. But in recent years, there has been a growing sense of resentment, and even though women don't dare to voice this in public, we can talk amongst ourselves. That is where our movement found its roots.' She sighed. 'We can't help everyone. The truth is, we help very few – maybe only two girls a year – while hundreds are married off against their will. But it's a start.'

Rosie said nothing. Asima's courage, fighting her ground in a hostile country, made her feel a little ashamed of the nerves in her stomach at the prospect of the evening ahead.

CHAPTER NINETEEN

They left Ismal's home and made their way in the direction of the village where Laila was being held. Asima was in the car in front, driven by a young medic friend of Ismal's who was trusted enough to be in on the operation. The sun was slowly sinking behind the mountains, bathing the sky and the landscape in the amber glow of early evening. Ismal hung back a little as Asima turned into the village, and Rosie shuddered, recalling her panic and terror while trapped among the Taliban earlier. Now, the village main street that had been bustling with market traders was empty and tranquil. Ismal had chosen this time of the day because almost everyone would be home eating, or would have just finished and be relaxing for the night. They drove down to the foot of the hill and Ismal pulled off the road and up a tight, hidden path where he could watch for Asima approaching.

'So, now we wait.' Ismal switched off the engine and sat back.

'How long do you think you'll stay in Pakistan, Ismal?' Rosie asked. 'Do you want to raise a family here, or will you come back home?'

He let out a weary sigh.

'In the beginning, I wanted to come back to my roots here, put something back into the country which my parents had left so they could give me a better life. I was full of all these ideals. But, now that I see what is happening, how it's being ruined, I don't think Asima and I will stay. Actually, we are looking at possibly working in America. We both have relatives who moved there and settled a few years ago. I had an offer from a hospital a few months ago, but didn't take it up. Now, I've had another offer and I feel differently. I'm going to talk to them next week.'

'You should leave sooner rather than later,' Omar said, ruffling his cousin's hair affectionately. 'It's four years since I've been here, and it's no place for people like us to live any more. You should leave them to their own devices. There's only so much you can do for people. I don't think it's safe to have the kind of mentality and beliefs you have here, Ismal. Sooner or later, they will come after you.'

Ismal nodded.

'I know.'

'And another thing,' Omar said. 'Now, don't take this the wrong way.' He spread his hands. 'You're a brilliant doctor and a great guy, but tell you what, we're going to need some crazy driving here in case anything happens, so I think you should move over and let me take the wheel.' He paused and Ismal looked at him, saying nothing. 'Trust me.' Omar grinned. 'I'm a Paki.'

Ismal smiled back, shaking his head.

'Okay, big potatoes,' he said, opening the driver's door and getting out. 'But just don't get us all killed, alright?'

'No chance.' Omar jumped across to the driver's seat.

In the distance, clouds of dust swirled as a bus appeared and they watched as it rolled past them, half empty. The dust settled for a moment, then suddenly more clouds appeared, and Omar sat forward, peering out of the windscreen. He switched on the engine.

'I see Asima's car. Here they come! Game on!'

Rosie strained her eyes as the dust cleared and the car came closer. She could see what looked like two people in the front seats.

'Can you make out how many are in the car?'

'I only see two,' Omar said. 'But Laila may be lying flat in the back so they can get out unnoticed.'

'Whatever,' Ismal said. 'We'll know soon enough. Let's go.'

As Omar drove down the hill, Ismal's mobile rang, and he pressed it to his ear.

'Great.' He looked in his rear-view mirror and Rosie could see the smile on his face.

'We're on!' Ismal said. 'They got Laila!' He slid on his

seatbelt. 'Now strap yourselves in, folks, because something tells me this is going to be a bit of a white-knuckle ride. We have to get away from here as fast as possible.'

Omar allowed Asima's car to speed past them, then followed.

Rosie and Matt bounced in the back seat as the car zipped down the mountain roads. In a couple of minutes they could see the bus beyond Asima's car. But she sped up and overtook it on a long straight stretch. In seconds they were behind the bus, but on a mountain path, hurtling towards a blind bend with a sheer drop. Suddenly, Omar put his foot down. Rosie glanced at Matt and closed her eyes. The bus honked angrily as Omar overtook on the tightest part of the bend, leaving clouds of dust in his wake.

'Don't tell me you didn't enjoy that, guys,' Omar joked. 'You okay in the back there, Rosie?'

'Oh, yeah,' Rosie replied. 'You should have given us blindfolds.'

They picked up speed and sat behind Asima's car all the way down the mountain and towards the main road. At the foot of the hill, they could see two pickup trucks and men in black turbans.

'Shit! They're flagging Asima down,' Ismal said.

Rosie and Matt exchanged perplexed glances.

'What do you think, Ismal?'

'Asima will just play it by ear. My young trainee is good

too. As long as these guys don't want to make trouble, it should be okay.'

'I hope they've had their dinner.' Matt tried to lighten the tension. 'Or they'll be grizzly as fuck.'

Omar chuckled in the front seat, but Rosie sensed it was more from tension than anything else. He drove slowly, hanging back a little as the Taliban soldier leaned in through the passenger window to talk to the medic. Rosie could see the figure in the back seat, covered from head to toe, now. The Taliban soldier went to the back of the car and opened the door. Asima and the medic protested, but he reached in and dragged Laila out. He pushed her to the side and towards the other Taliban soldier, who grabbed hold of her by the hair, her headscarf slipping. Then the other one went to the driver's door and pulled the medic out. Asima got out of the other side and came around to the front. The first Taliban soldier lined all three of them up, and seemed to speak to the other one, who was on his mobile.

'Shit,' Ismal said. 'This is bad. Someone must have got word to them that Laila's got out.'

'Bastards!' Omar grunted.

'Maybe we should go down and see if I can talk to them,' Ismal said.

'No way.' Omar grabbed hold of his arm. 'Listen, mate. We're going to have to do *something*, but these guys don't negotiate. So . . . just leave it to me.'

'What do you mean?' Rosie knew Omar was a Glasgow wide boy, but he was not the type to pick a fight.

'Don't worry, Rosie. We need to take a risk here. Just keep calm, whatever happens.'

'Jesus,' Rosie muttered to Matt.

Omar said something in Urdu to the security guard in the car with them, and he answered, uttering a few words, then shifted a little in his seat. His hands gripped the rifle and he brought it up, flicking off the safety catch. Rosie looked at Matt, then at Ismal, his face grim as he looked out through the windscreen to see the other Taliban man slapping Asima hard on the face. The medic protested and was hit by the butt of the second soldier's rifle.

'Right, troops. Are you strapped in?'

Before they had the chance to answer, the wheels span, and the 4x4 took off down the hill and swerved onto the road, picking up speed as they approached. He'll slam on the brakes now, Rosie thought. Any minute. He has to. Instead, Omar picked up speed and the truck got closer and closer. Christ! He was going to ram them. Hearing the engine, the Taliban soldier turned in disbelief as Omar drove straight at him. But before he could move, Omar had driven into him and rammed him up against the truck, his body buckling. Asima had jumped away and the medic threw her to the ground, diving on top of her to protect her. In the confusion, Laila broke free as the other Taliban soldier aimed his rifle at Omar's windscreen. Then the gunshot. Rosie wondered why their windscreen hadn't shattered, then she saw the Taliban soldier drop to the ground. Ismal jumped out and grabbed Asima. The medic got hold of Laila, and they all piled quickly into the car.

'Let's go!' Omar was looking in the rear-view mirror. 'I can see the other one getting up. I thought I'd done him in, but the bastard's on his feet, limping.'

From nowhere another Taliban soldier came up, pulled the shot man to his feet and pushed him into the pickup, along with the other one.

'They're behind us, Omar. And they're catching up,' Ismal said.

'Fuck!' Omar pushed his foot to the floor.

In the back, everyone was almost on top of each other. Asima's cheek was red and swollen from the slap. Laila lay on Matt's shoulder, whimpering. The guard wound down the window and leaned out, firing off a couple of shots at the truck. They could hear glass shattering, then more gunshots and a thud. The guard slumped back, blood pouring out of his shoulder.

'Oh Jesus, Omar! He's been shot,' Rosie said.

Omar said something in Urdu, and the guard grimaced and touched the wound, his hand covered in blood. Then he pulled himself up and leaned out of the window again. Omar sped around the last of the mountain path, the car skidding, and Rosie eyed the drop, wondering if it was better to get shot or captured, or just go over the cliff. If it's going to happen, make it quick. She turned in time to see the security guard let off one more shot, and the Taliban truck swerve wildly all over the road. It was out of control, and she watched as it skidded over the cliff, soaring through the air, its wheels still spinning.

'Bullseye!' Omar said, keeping his boot down.

'Fucking beauty!' Matt said, as the guard came back in and almost passed out on his shoulder.

Asima climbed across.

'Let me have a look.' She tore at the guard's tunic and opened it up to see the hole in his shoulder gushing with blood. Then she pulled off her headscarf and told Matt to press it hard against the wound. 'He's bleeding badly, Ismal. We have to get somewhere fast.'

'It's less than two hours to Islamabad. We need to keep going. Look in the back there. My bag. Get something we can use to stop the blood and see if you can fix him up.'

Rosie watched, squeezed up against the door, as Asima rummaged in the bag, then expertly wrapped a bandage around the guard's wound, taping it to his chest.

'Will he make it?' Rosie asked.

'I hope so. I can't do anything more now.'

'He'll be fine. He's a tough guy,' Omar said. 'Hasn't spoken a word all week, but when the chips were down, he was there. He saved us. I won't let him die. Once we get out of this valley and onto the main road, we can drive like the wind.'

Rosie sat back and breathed let out a long sigh. She suddenly felt Laila's hand reach out and clasp hers tight.

'You're okay, Laila. It's going to be fine. It's over now,' she whispered.

Rosie's mobile rang and she saw McGuire's name come up. She flashed it towards Matt, who snorted.

'Good luck with that one,' he said.

'Hi, Mick.'

'Fuck's sake, Gilmour! I said to call me at least a couple of times a day – you're there two days and I haven't heard a cheep. What's going on?'

'Oh, I know, Mick. Sorry. I was going to call you last night, but there was no signal . . . You see, I'm up in the mountains here, in Swat Valley. Hellish place.'

'I can smell bullshit,' McGuire barked.

'Well, it might not actually be *bull*shit,' Rosie joked. 'Listen, Mick. Everything's okay.'

'What do you mean okay? What about the girl?'

'We got her.'

'You did? Brilliant! Is she alright? Are you alright? Are you in any danger? Listen, Gilmour, I want you out of there pronto if you've got the girl. Like tonight if possible, or tomorrow at the latest.'

'We're flying tomorrow, Mick. With Laila. We're just on our way down to Islamabad now. I'm going to phone Marion when I get there.'

'Great. I can breathe easily. So was there any trouble?'

Rosie let it hang two beats.

'A bit. But hey, we're just about there. So we got away with it.'

'That sounds suspiciously like a body count. Are you sure that big Bosnian isn't with you?'

'No,' Rosie smiled at the sudden thought of Adrian. 'No. He's not here. There was a bit of aggro though, but I'll tell you all about it tomorrow. Have to go now.'

'Right. Okay. But I'm planning to make a real issue of this kid and the forced marriage story. So I hope she's all singing, all dancing.'

'Er . . . Yeah . . . I'm sure we'll be alright. Have to go.' Rosie hung up.

She hadn't even spoken to Laila about going public with the story yet. They were too busy trying to stay alive. She would have Laila all sewn up before she got home, because as soon as it hit the *Post*, the media, and not just in Scotland, would be all over it.

'Is that your editor?' Laila asked.

'Yeah. He's a bit of a livewire.' Rosie looked at her. 'We'll have a talk between tonight and tomorrow to plan what we do.'

'I overheard what he said.'

Rosie gave her a guilty look.

'I want to tell my story,' Laila said, a determined look in her eye.

'We will,' Rosie was relieved. Music to her ears. 'Look,'

she nudged Omar. 'A sign for Islamabad. And the road ahead is getting more populated.'

'Halle-fucking-lujah!' Matt rested his head back and closed his eyes.

On the outskirts of Islamabad, the tall buildings and monuments cast shadows in the setting sun. Rosie was delighted to see traffic lights and normality – just the sense that they were in any big capital in the world, where there was some kind of order, as opposed to the lawless area they'd escaped from. They dropped the medic off at his mother's home in the city. He wasn't planning to go back to Swat any time in the future. Omar drove past houses and along tree-lined avenues, past houses and gated compounds. The remnants of British colonial rule, where houses would have been owned by merchants or diplomats, had left their marks. Signs in English for tennis clubs, private schools, Catholic and Episcopalian churches.

Ismal punched in a number to his phone and spoke.

'We are ten minutes away, Gerry. So far, so good. But there was trouble. Our armed guard has a gunshot wound. I should be able to treat him once I get a good look. Sure. Thanks.'

Along the avenue where the British Embassy was, they drove towards a gated complex. A security guard approached and Omar wound down his window. Ismal leaned across and spoke, and the guard walked across and pulled open the tall iron gates. Rosie rolled down her window, taking in the scene – lush green gardens and a few villas dotted along the avenue. Somewhere in the distance she could hear the thwack of what sounded like a tennis ball striking a racket. Behind the tall trees she glimpsed a green wooden clubhouse and people sitting in the garden sipping tall drinks. In one of the trees, two exotic red-and-yellow birds squawked as they took off into the evening sky. It was mesmerising, given where they'd been.

'God almighty! It's like something out of that movie, *White Mischief*. What's going on?' Rosie asked.

'That's the tennis club in the embassy grounds,' Ismal said. 'Only for diplomats and invited guests, such as businessmen who are working out here. It's where people can get out of the dust of Pakistan and feel very British. All rather old Raj.'

'Yeah,' Matt said. 'To hell with all that Taliban shite up the road, I was made for places like this.'

'Sure.' Rosie smiled, feeling the tension evaporate from her body. 'You could fit into this very well.'

They pulled the car up on a red-brick driveway and the front door opened. A silver-haired man dressed in white linen shorts and a polo shirt stood there, bronzed and handsome. Behind him was an attractive blonde woman. Everyone got out of the car and Laila suddenly threw her arms around Rosie.

'Oh, Rosie, how can I ever thank you?' She broke down.

'Not me,' Rosie choked. 'Thank Asima here, and Ismal. They're the guys with all the courage. And of course, Omar – not forgetting poor Hasan, our guard.'

'Hello, Rosie Gilmour.' The tall silver-haired man approached with his hand stretched out. 'Welcome. I've heard a lot about you. Gerry Owens, and my wife, Deirdre.' He swept his hand across his clothes. 'Forgive our casual clothes – we had a mixed doubles match and couldn't get out of it.'

Rosie noted he said it tongue in cheek, as she shook both their hands. She felt as though she was nearly home.

He turned to Ismal.

'Good to see you, Ismal, and Asima. Come in. Let's get your man fixed up, and we can sit and you can tell me all about your drama.' He walked ahead. 'Bring him in. I have a room all set up.'

In the early morning, Gerry drove them to the airport in his Mercedes, and was waved through check-in all the way to final security. They got out and took their bags.

Ismal's phone rang and he looked grim as he listened, then hung up.

'There's trouble. They know Laila is with us and they're looking for Asima and me. They've been to our house.'

'Jesus! What now?' Rosie asked.

'You can't go back now, Ismal,' Gerry said.

'I know.' Ismal looked resigned. 'But I've left everything

at my house. And what about the people at the camp ... it's leaving people short-staffed.'

'Not your problem, you've done all you can. Time to go home now.'

'We've no passports.'

'Well, you're with the British Embassy – we'll sort that out for you. Give yourself a day or so, then we'll get the paperwork done.'

Ismal turned to his wife.

'We can't go back, Asima.'

'I know.'

'Look,' Gerry said. 'Once we get the passports, then we'll get a flight, and we'll look after you. I honestly advise you not to go back up there and to get out of the country as soon as possible. Have you got money?'

'Yes. I keep a UK bank account so I have access to money.'

'Then you should leave. I can protect you while you're here, but if you go back in, I can't.'

Rosie, Matt, Omar and Laila said their goodbyes, hugging Ismal, then Asima, who was tearful. Rosie watched as they disappeared out of the airport. The four of them were on their own now. They approached final security and handed over their passports. The guard looked at all of them, then, when he came to Laila, went off to converse with two armed guards nearby. Rosie's stomach hit the floor when she saw them making a phone call.

'Oh shit, Matt! Something's wrong,' Rosie said.

'Don't let them take me, Rosie.' Laila grabbed her arm.

'Sssh. Just stay calm. Nobody's going to take you.' She tried to convince herself that what she'd said was true.

'I'll offer them money,' Omar said. 'That's what they're after. It's all corruption.' He went into his pocket and pulled out a bunch of twenty-dollar bills as the uniformed guard came across to them.

Omar turned his back and showed them the tip of the notes in his hand. The big guard shrugged and slowly nodded. Omar handed him the wad of dollars, and he went across to the desk. The guard waved them over and handed them their passports, then jerked his head dismissively towards the departure gate. They pushed through the barrier and walked briskly. Rosie wanted to break into a run. They were safe. The notice board showed the British Airways flight to Heathrow was boarding in half an hour.

'Coffee, anyone?' Rosie said.

'Is it too early for a drink?' Matt asked as he hugged Rosie and Laila.

CHAPTER TWENTY

Nikki was only half listening to Julie explaining all the details to her. It was a bit like a sales pitch, and not unlike the one her best friend made to her a few weeks ago, when she'd convinced her she could earn a few extra quid a week as an escort. Look where that had got her, she thought, glancing down at the bandaged stump. Since they'd taken her off the morphine, Nikki was swiftly discovering why half the country was hooked on heroin. With the morphine drip, even though she'd been aware of how much shit she was in, there was a euphoric sense that she was hovering somewhere above it all, and that this was really happening to someone else. The stump was always a stiff reminder, but when they'd changed her bandages every couple of days, and the surgeon had inspected her, declaring how fast she was healing, Nikki had always managed to summon a grateful smile. At least she was alive. But the last couple of days, she'd been feeling wiped out, depressed and had hardly slept. She was still on strong painkillers, but they were nothing like the warm blanket of morphine, which had soothed away all her pain, inside and out.

'Nikki, you're not listening to me.' Julie sipped tea from a polystyrene cup.

'I am,' Nikki protested, propping herself up and picking up the cup from her bedside table. 'I'm just a bit out of it the last day or so. That morphine is the business. Makes everything a bit easier.'

'Aye,' Julie said. 'Plenty will testify to that.' She pulled her chair forward. 'But, listen, now that we know for sure what we've got on our hands . . .' She paused, biting her lip.

'Hands?' Nikki snorted. 'Aye, nice one, Julie, just don't expect me to applaud your patter.'

'Sorry, pal. You know what I mean, the rough diamonds. I went to the Mitchell Library and had a look at a book on diamonds from all over the world to see what they look like. Apparently it all depends on the colour of them. White, brownish, etc.'

'Yeah? So what does it mean?'

'Well, white ones are the most valuable. They're the ones that, once a diamond expert polishes them down and cuts them, are likely to have a decent carat or two in them. Brownish ones aren't so valuable, but still worth money.'

'So, the ones in the pouch . . .' Nikki screwed up her eyes, trying to remember. 'I can't even think straight. What colour were they?'

'White.' Julie's eyes lit up. 'The most valuable.'

Nikki gave a soft whistle.

'Christ! There were two pouches and quite a lot of them, were there not?'

'Yep. Plenty. Enough to know we'd never be poor again.'

'Yeah, but you're forgetting one thing, Julie. They're not actually ours, and I have this to prove it.' She held up her injured arm. 'How am I going to live my life like this? I haven't even thought about that.'

'I know, pal. I know. But we can work this through in time. We just have to lie low, as long as possible, and, don't worry, there's enough money in the case to keep us for a while, until the time is right. Then maybe we can start looking for a diamond dealer.'

Nikki sighed.

'Yeah. It all sounds great, Julie. But I don't know if we'll ever be able to get away with this . . . if it will ever die down. Especially now you're saying we've got really valuable stones. These guys will stop at nothing.'

'We'll just take our time. The ward sister told me when I came in earlier that you could be out of here in a couple of days, so we need to work on a plan. The cops haven't been around for a few days, so I reckon we just blow town when you get sprung from here.'

Nikki nodded slowly, trying to get her head around the next twenty-four hours, never mind the rest of her

life, with a disability, on the run with someone else's
diamonds.

Suddenly, Nikki saw the colour drain from Julie's face as
she turned her head towards the corridor. She let out a
gasp as she saw big Gordy walking towards the open door,
with Paul behind him.

'Fuck me!' Julie whispered. 'What the fuck?'

'Oh Christ, Julie. Will I press my alarm?'

'No,' Julie said quickly. 'Do nothing. He won't do any shit
in here. Let's just calm down, let me deal with it.'

Big Gordy's burly frame filled the doorway, and he stood
for a few seconds and looked at Julie, then at Nikki, his
eyes wandering down to her stump. He said nothing, and
Nikki could see he was lost for words. He looked different
from the last time she saw him in his office. Less
threatening.

'Nikki.' He took a step inside, his face full of sympathy.
'Listen, darlin', I'm sorry this had to happen. Are you
alright?'

Julie leapt to her feet.

'Is she alright? Are you having a fucking laugh, you big
prick?' She stood, hands on hips, face ashen. 'Look at her.
She's lying there with half her arm off, and you're asking
her is she alright! After you set her up, you useless fuck of
a man! Is she alright? What do you think, you cunt?'

Nikki was aghast at Julie's outburst. She knew she had a
temper and could always fight her corner. But this was big

Gordy MacLean she was ripping apart. Julie's lip twitched a little as Gordy stood there, looking too stunned to speak.

After a few beats, he stretched out his hands in a pleading gesture.

'Listen. Just give me a minute. Let me talk.'

'I can call the fucking cops right now, and you can talk all you like to them,' Julie spat, prowling the length of Nikki's bed, her face set in anger.

Gordy's lips curled a little and Nikki saw the expression of the ruthless bastard she knew he was.

'Well, why haven't you, Julie? Why have the cops not been to accuse me of setting this up? Eh?' He stepped towards her and leaned in, rasping in a loud whisper, 'Listen, you fucking tart. You are up to your arse in this. Both of you. Now, I've come here to try to make the peace, because the fact is, I'm the only one who can get you out of this. And you'd better believe that.'

'It's a bit fucking late,' Nikki said, holding her arm up, suddenly feeling Julie's bravery rubbing off on her.

'Look, Nikki.' He turned to her. 'That was a total mistake. Honest to Christ! I didn't know that was going to happen to you. I know I'm a cunt, but I had no idea they were going to do that to you.'

'So you did set her up, you arsehole?' Julie interrupted.

'Look, I was told she was going to get a bit of a slap, roughed up. A wee frightener. It was something that came from one of the big guys down south. The suitcase belongs to them. The Paki guy who died was only delivering it. He smuggled it in, I told you that before.'

'So you allowed some bastard you don't even know to come up here and do Nikki over? So much for Mr Big Baws.'

'It wasn't supposed to have been like that. I've already made my feelings clear to the big man down south . . . believe me.'

'Aw, cheers for that, Gordy. I'm well moved that you stood up for me.' Nikki shook her head. 'Because what the fuck am I going to do for the rest of my life now that I'm disabled? Can you maybe give me a wee job at the tills, or something in the club? I won't be much use as a hooker with one hand.'

Silence fell over them. Nikki watched as Gordy shifted from one foot to the other, surprised at his awkwardness.

'And what's *he* doing here?' Nikki jerked her head towards Paul, standing sheepishly behind him.

'He was staking the place out for me. Waiting for Julie to arrive. He's been here two days.' He paused. 'Look. Just give me a minute. I want to explain something to you. Plant a wee idea in your head. As I say, you're both in the shit. I know, and you know, that you've got that case, so this is not going to go away. They were up here the other day and they're going apeshit about it. So, just hear me out.'

Another silence. Nikki and Julie exchanged a long look, and she knew that between them right now they had two options. One was to go to the cops and spill everything and the other was to listen.

'Get that ratbag out of here.' Julie gestured towards Paul.

Gordy turned a little, but didn't look directly at Paul.

'Blow,' he said.

Paul backed out of the room, catching Nikki's eye as he scurried away along the corridor.

'Right.' Gordy turned to Julie. 'Sit down a minute.'

He pulled a plastic tubular chair from the stack in the corner and sat down. Nikki shifted her body a little in the bed, pulling the sheet over her pyjamas.

They sat in silence for a few seconds, then Gordy took a deep breath and cleared his throat.

'It's all about the diamonds.' He paused for effect, giving both of them a long, slow look. 'I assume by now you've been inside the case and you've seen all the shit in there. I know there was a lot of money, but nobody gives a shite about that. And passports. But it's the rough diamonds they want. Did you know that's what they were?'

Julie said nothing and glanced at Nikki, who could feel her tongue sticking to the roof of her mouth with nerves. She wanted to reach over to the bedside locker and pick up the cup, but her hand was trembling. She pushed her arm under the sheets in case Gordy could see. Julie's face was blank.

'Julie. I know you, pal. Don't tell me you haven't opened the case.'

'I'm not your fucking pal, and you don't know me. So let's get that straight.'

'Okay. Have you seen the diamonds?'

Julie glanced at Nikki, and nobody spoke for so long she thought she was going to explode.

'Gordy, what's your game here? I mean, are you suddenly riding in here on a white horse like a knight in shining armour, saving these two poor birds? What's the game? Get to the point, and get to it quick, or I'm going to ring for the nurse and it's game over for you.' She narrowed her eyes. 'And if you know me, then you know I'm fucking serious, you prick.'

Nikki bit her lip, terrified at the way Julie was speaking to Gordy. There would be payback for this, one way or another, because he was sat there getting his arse kicked by one of his tarts. Beads of sweat broke out on his top lip. Nikki wished she still had the morphine to take the edge off this.

'Right. Here's the story. I got a visit from Johnny Vanner. You don't need to know who he is—'

'I know who he is,' Julie snapped.

'Fine. Then you'll know how much of a big player he is. He comes up with some Paki bastard on the rampage because the case with his diamonds has disappeared, and the guy who was delivering them can't tell him anything because he's fucking lying in the mortuary.' He turned to Nikki. 'And believe me, I gave that Paki cunt pelters for what happened to you. I was going to cut the bastard's throat, and I might still do it. In fact, Johnny had to haul me off him. I went for him. Honestly, Nikki, I didn't know they were going to hurt you like this.'

'Aw, give me a fucking violin. I'm tearing up here,' Julie interrupted. 'Get to the point.'

'They're desperate to get the diamonds. They're putting so much pressure on me to find them.'

'So what did you tell them?'

'I told them I was all over it. I'd find you. I'd get the diamonds back to them.'

'Oh. Just like that, Columbo.'

'I've got a deal to put to you.'

Julie looked at Nikki and said nothing. The air was thick with tension.

'We're all ears.'

'I can protect you. You've got two pouches of rough diamonds that you'll never in a fucking month of Sundays be able to shift. Not tomorrow, not next year, or in the next five years. You're way out of your depth, and you don't know who you're dealing with. I can fix this for you. I can look after you. If I've got the diamonds, I can work it all out and we can split things three ways. I know a good fence in the town. Known him for years. An old pal of my da.' He turned to Nikki. 'No way in the world am I going to give them back the diamonds after what they did to you, Nikki. Listen. I know you hate me right now, but trust me on this one thing. I fucking despise them for doing that to you, and I'm going to make them pay. Because I *can* make them pay. They'll pay for it with their diamonds. Call it compensation or whatever the fuck you want. But you deserve it. Fuck them, I mean that. You have to trust me.'

They sat in silence. Then Julie spoke.

'And we're supposed to trust you, Gordy. Just like that. Because you're suddenly the straight guy? You couldn't lie straight in bed, you prick.'

Gordy put his hands up.

'I know what you're saying. Listen, Julie. I deserve a shed-load of shit dumped on me for not seeing what these bastards were capable of, but I honestly didn't expect it. Chopping women up isn't what I do. It's against everything I am. Just let me make it right for you. I can fix this. Please, just trust me. Because, believe me, you don't have a lot of options right now.'

'Like you give a fuck!' Julie spat. 'Don't give us any of your shit, Gordy. You're not doing this because you care. You didn't come here to help us out. You came here because you think we've got diamonds and you want to fuck your pals over down south and get your grubby paws on the money. At least don't treat us like fucking halfwits.'

'Okay. The money is part of it, I'll admit that.'

'So how do you propose to fuck these guys over? If they came up here and told you to hunt us down, what are you going to tell them?'

'I'll work that out. I'll give you money and you can set yourselves up somewhere out of the way, where nobody will find you. We'll keep in touch, and once it's all settled down we can get the diamonds moved on. I'll take care of that.'

'Oh, so you mean like a life insurance or something. Like a policy that will come good in a few years. We hand you the diamonds – if indeed we have the diamonds – and hope for the best? It's not as if we can go to a lawyer and make it legal, is it?'

'I hear what you're saying.'

'So it's all on trust?'

How could they trust him? It was like walking out of the lions' den and stumbling into a nest of vipers. But right now, she knew he was right. They were running out of options.

They sat in silence. Nikki could tell by the expression on Julie's face that she felt the same way.

'Right, Gordy. Disappear for ten minutes till we have a talk. Go.' She stood up.

Gordy stood up, and gave Nikki what looked like a pleading look as he left.

CHAPTER TWENTY-ONE

Rosie watched, delighted and perplexed at the same time, as Laila began running as soon as she spotted her mother and sister among the crowd at the arrivals hall in Glasgow Airport. So much for her instructions to stick together in case any of the story had leaked out and there was a media scrum. Matt sprinted after her, determined to get the reunion pictures that would make a historic splash and spread for the *Post*. Omar had told Rosie it was best if he walked off the flight on his own and disappeared into the crowd. He didn't want to run the risk of being spotted with a reporter, or with Laila, by one of his own. That way, he could pick up all the inside information discreetly. There would be some ructions in the Asian community once Rosie's story hit the front page, and it would be best if Omar was able to quietly keep his ear to the ground.

It was only once they'd flown from Islamabad to Heathrow that Laila had phoned her mother to tell her she'd done a runner, that the *Post* had come and rescued her. She'd already confided in Rosie that her mother had been totally against the marriage, and had threatened her husband with divorce if he went through with it. When he did, and Laila was taken away in the middle of the night, she'd left, taking Laila's twelve-year-old sister with her to stay with her parents. But this was never going to be an ordinary Glasgow divorce. Pakistani women didn't just walk out on their husbands. The fact was that there would be consequences that could impact on Laila and her mother. But right now, when she saw Laila and her mother in floods of tears, hugging as Matt fired off pictures that they could never in a million years have staged, she knew she had done the right thing.

A taxi from the *Post* picked them up outside and drove them to Laila's grandparents in Maryhill. They were waiting at the door of their big sandstone villa. Seeing the delight on their faces made Rosie suddenly realise that whatever she had witnessed in the name of religion in the lawless, brutal backwater of the Swat valley, this was a family who cared about each other first and foremost. No politics, no dogma. Just glad to have their granddaughter back home. Rosie smiled to herself as she told the taxi to head to the office.

'There's going to be all sorts of political shit flying around once our story hits the streets, Gilmour. But it won't half leave the rest of the papers with their mouths dropping open. I do love it when that happens.'

McGuire was in bullish mood as Rosie graphically spilled out the drama of the last few days.

'I want to use all of that, every cough and spit. The stoning of that poor bloody woman will rock the world. We hear about that kind of thing, but when do we actually ever see it? I hope Matt's pics are good.'

'They're great. Graphic – to say the least,' Rosie replied, thinking how some things never changed. No matter how gory, how shocking or cruel, McGuire's priority was what it would look like on the front page. He was right – she was too much of a bleeding heart to ever fill an editor's chair. Not that she ever wanted to.

'Perfect.' He drew imaginary layouts with a felt pen on the pages in front of him. 'The stoning of the woman will be a separate breakout. We'll have all the narrative of the journey in one long spread, let it run and run. We'll do it over two or three days. This is about the *Post's* bold journey into some hellhole in Pakistan to bring our Glasgow girl back home.' He linked his fingers in front of him on the desk, as though he was giving a party political broadcast. 'And we'll make it clear: we're not going to take any view on this – political or religious. We'll tell the story of a young girl's plight, taken against her will. Taken to a place where women are stoned to death, for fuck's sake! Once we do that as graphic as I know you'll write it, Rosie, we don't need to make a comment. People will make their minds up how barbaric this is. This is a kid from Glasgow!'

Rosie knew McGuire was right in everything he said, but the flak would still fly.

'But it will still upset a lot of Pakistanis here, who arrange marriages like this on a regular basis. Plenty of them seem to work fine.'

'Then we'll see how it pans out. See how many Pakistani people want to talk about it. You never know how many women or families might come out of the woodwork saying how their lives have been ruined. Who knows? Perhaps it's time for a UK law against children being taken out of the country to wed.' He smiled as though a light had gone off in his head. 'Now there's a campaign, Gilmour.'

'It will isolate some readers.'

'Fuck it! Whose side are you on?'

'I'm playing devil's advocate.'

'Well, forget it. Look. We can't please all of the people all of the time. We don't make this shit happen. We just write it as it unfolds. I mean, this is a big thing for us, to go out there and save one of our own kids from a hell of a life. I love this! And, hey – hats off to you and Matt for digging it out. You can treat yourselves to a Ruby Murray at my expense.' He stood up. The meeting was over. 'Now go and get it written up and get it over to me this afternoon.'

'I've got it half written. I did it on the plane. I kind of knew how you'd want to play it.' Rosie grinned.

'Aye, don't mind me.' He handed her the news schedule. 'Do you want to take the morning conference, smartarse?'

'No, I've got better things to do.'

As she turned towards the door, McGuire shouted after her.

'Oh. And any news on the diamond story? What about those girls?'

'I've been out of it for a few days, but I need to talk to them. Remember about the passports? I need to see them again. Laila was repeating the story about the passports being used by diamond smugglers. But it was just something she's overheard in conversation and I'm not sure if she has any hard evidence or much detail on the connection, but if I can get my hands on these passports, then we can check whom they belong to and see what's what.'

'You mean get your hands on the *stolen* passports,' McGuire frowned. 'Listen. I don't want to know what you're doing . . . so I won't have to perjure myself in court.' He waved her away. 'Now clear off.'

Rosie was putting the finishing touches on the main story when her mobile rang. It was Julie.

'Julie. I was going to call you in a little while. How're things?'

'It depends on where you're sitting, Rosie,' Julie said. 'If you're sitting where me and Nikki are, your arse is twitching. But tell you what, things are going to get better.' She paused. 'We need to talk to you.'

'That's why I was going to call you. I've been away in Pakistan for a few days. Just got back this morning.'

'Pakistan?'

'Yeah. I'll tell you about it when I see you. I'm working on the basis that it's all connected to your situation, but I don't want to talk about it over the phone. How's Nikki? Do you want me to come up to the hospital?'

'No. She's out. The doctors let her out yesterday morning. They've done all they can do at the moment, so it's a healing process.'

'So where are you?'

'We're holed up in a wee place outside Stirling, I took a rental – a farmhouse. We can't go too far away as Nikki's still got to get things checked every few days, but we didn't want to hang about Glasgow. Can you come over?'

'Of course,' Rosie said quickly, pushing away the thought of a long hot bath and the early night that she was planning. 'You mean now?'

'Yeah. Is that okay with you?'

'Sure.' Rosie knocked back the last mouthful of black coffee. She'd be needing more of that to keep her awake. 'Just give me the address. I'll leave here in about ten minutes. Is it easy to find?'

'It's on a farm. A cottage in the grounds. Close to Bannockburn. You got a pen?'

'I'm a reporter,' Rosie joked. 'I've always got a pen.'

She scribbled down the address and instructions in her notebook and shoved it into her handbag. She sank back in her chair and puffed out an exhausted sigh, massaging the back of her neck while re-reading all her copy. It was as good as it gets, every paragraph bursting with colour – the shocking scenes of the woman being stoned making her shudder all over again. For a moment, Rosie allowed herself to bask in the warm feeling of having nailed it, and living to tell the tale. Stuff like this is what got her out of bed in the morning. Without it, she had nowhere to go. But right now, she'd have loved to put it all on hold to sink into a long sleep and wake up to see her byline all over the front page. Chance would be a fine thing, she mumbled, as she hit the key on her laptop and sent the stories to McGuire's private email address. She briefly considered calling him to say where she was going, but decided the less he knew the better.

It was dark by the time she got close to Bannockburn. It had been raining all afternoon and the country road off the motorway was now glistening with evening frost. Rosie slowed down, careful of black ice. She glanced at her notebook on the passenger seat, reading the instructions and watching for the sign to turn into Whitlock Farm. After driving up and down the Bannockburn road twice, she finally saw it – the name painted onto a lump of wood, half hidden in a hedgerow. She turned into the pitch-black, single-track road and negotiated the potholes for half a mile. Eventually, she could see the lights of what looked like a two-storey farmhouse at the end of the road, and close by, a smaller cottage. She seemed to be in the right place, as Julie had told her it was a working farm, and the big house was where the farmer lived with his wife and son. Julie had rented the cottage after seeing it advertised in the local paper. Rosie drove up and parked outside the old cottage. It looked as though it had been white at some stage, but it was now patchy and tired-looking under her headlights. There was a glow in a crack in the curtains. She took out her mobile and rang Julie.

'I'm outside, Julie.'

'Great. That was quick.'

Rosie got out of the car and shivered as she glanced around the darkness. One thing's for sure, nobody would think to look for them in a place like this, in the middle of nowhere. She heard bolts being slid back and the door half opened, then fully, and Julie stood in the doorway, a smile on her face. She looked different. From their last meeting, she'd got the impression that Julie wasn't big on smiles.

'Could you not have picked a place a bit more secluded?' Rosie joked as she stepped inside.

Julie laughed.

'I did think about finding a flat in the centre of Stirling, but you never know who you might bump into. Nobody will find us here, I hope.'

Rosie was struck at the warmth and comfort the living room had, with a glowing gas fire in the hearth and the soft light from the kitchen. A woman lying back on the sofa sat upright and looked at her.

'This is Nikki,' Julie said.

Rosie's glance flicked to the bandaged stump, and a little punch of fear ran through her. Christ! How screwed up did your life get, when you found yourself on the run in the middle of nowhere with half your arm hacked to bits? She stepped across to her and shook her good hand.

'Hi, Nikki. Glad to meet you. Sorry it's such awful circumstances.' She shook her head as Nikki looked up. 'What a terrible thing to happen to you. How are you coping?'

Nikki tightened her lips into a grimace.

'Well. I've had to give up the juggling career, but apart from that . . .'

Rosie smiled.

'Yeah. Well. Important to keep your humour up, despite all the crap flying around.'

'Coffee?' Julie said, heading for the kitchen.

'Yes. Please. I definitely need that. It's been a long day.'

'Sorry to ask you to come at such short notice, Rosie, but there's been developments.'

'Really?'

'Yeah. Big time. You want anything to eat? I can make you a sandwich.'

'No thanks. Coffee will be fine.' Rosie had grabbed a sandwich in the canteen as she left, and wolfed it down on the motorway. Nerves always made her hungry.

Julie came in with mugs of coffee and sat them on the low table in front of the fire. Rosie sat on a chair and Julie plonked herself down on a sofa opposite Nikki.

'So,' Rosie said, slipping off her jacket. 'What's happening?'

CHAPTER TWENTY-TWO

'We got a visit,' Julie said. 'Big Gordy.'

Rosie almost spluttered her coffee everywhere at an image of him kicking the door in.

'Christ! Here?'

'No. At the hospital.'

'You're kidding!'

'Nope. Bastard came waltzing in like the hospital chaplain, all concerned about Nikki.'

'Aye. My arse!' Nikki piped up.

'So . . . what . . . he just came in to visit? You must have just about died when he appeared.'

'Actually, Rosie, the opposite. The sight of that big bastard made my blood boil, and it was all I could do not to jump across Nikki's bed and choke the life out of him.'

'You should have seen her, Rosie. I think Gordy got such a fright, it was *him* who shat it.' Nikki chortled.

'I nearly lost it,' Julie said. 'Something came over

me – call it attack is the best form of defence? I don't know. But I found all this courage and rage, and I kind of snapped. I stood up to him. I know, if he wants to he could cut my throat for that, and maybe he will one day. But right at that moment, I wanted to show him that he was dealing with the wrong people.'

Rosie said nothing, wondering for a moment if they'd been at the drink. Because she didn't look like the kind of woman who could take on a bastard like Gordy MacLean, who had slashed his way across Glasgow most of his adult life. But she'd have to listen politely, see where they went with this. She wanted a look at the passports, and a chance to interview both of them, so she really needed them onside.

'So, what did you do?'

'Well, he's obviously been getting his arse kicked by this big shot, Johnny Vanner, down in Manchester. You know him?' Julie asked.

'Can't say I do.'

'He runs just about everything out of Manchester. Heroin, coke, women, the lot. Has done for years.'

'Right.'

'Well, Gordy came to see us and make peace, he said. Put his cards on the table. All apologies and covered in shame over what happened to Nikki. Said it wasn't supposed to happen and if he'd known they were going to do what they did, he'd never have allowed it.'

'Pure shite,' Nikki said. 'But we let him talk.'

'Then he drops the bombshell,' Julie said. 'He says he knows we've got the diamonds. Christ knows how he can prove that, but he definitely knows, so there was no point in keeping up the pretence. He didn't even wait for us to confirm we have them. Suddenly he says that if we give him the diamonds, then he'll stiff Vanner for them and split the money three ways – once he can move them on to a fence.'

The deal had double-cross stamped all over it. All Rosie could see was blood on the walls, and it wasn't going to be Gordy's.

'That's never going to happen.' She looked at both of them. 'Surely you must know not to trust him.'

Julie and Nikki exchanged glances.

'Rosie, we're not buttoned up at the back. Of course we know he'll double-cross us and bump us off. That's the problem we have. I mean we can fuck right off in a few days out of here with the diamonds. Take a flight far away and hide for the rest of our lives. But we don't want to do that.'

'But surely you haven't agreed on a deal with him.'

Silence, as they looked at each other again. Rosie ran her hands through her hair and shook her head.

'You have? You've done a deal with Gordy MacLean? Christ, girls! That's like signing your own death warrant. You must know that.'

'No it's not, Rosie. Because any double-crossing that's

going to be done, it'll be *us* who'll be doing it. That big bastard is going to get done up like a kipper.' She paused. 'After what he did to Nikki, setting her up like that, he's finished, and we'll make sure of it.'

'But, how?'

'How do you think?'

'Jesus, Julie. I can hardly think at all right now. The only thing you can do is go to the cops.'

Julie and Nikki both looked triumphant.

'Precisely.'

Rosie looked at them in disbelief.

'You're going to hand yourselves in and tell them everything? About the dead guy in the Albany, the attaché case, and the diamonds?'

'Well, we're not going to hand ourselves in. Not quite. But we're going to cooperate with them so they can get Gordy, all in one go.'

'You mean work with the cops?'

Julie nodded.

'Do you think they'll go for it?'

'Oh, I'd say they will. But it's tricky, Julie, because these things are never straightforward, and you are implicated in a crime now because you stole the case.'

'We'll cross that bridge when we come to it. That's why we asked you to come through here. To see if you could set it up with the cops. That way, you get your story too.'

Rosie let out a long sigh, her mind firing off half a dozen scenarios. It was the strangest game plan she'd ever come across – two hookers trying to pull off a sting like this with one of the biggest gangsters in the country. You couldn't make it up.

'I can talk to a detective contact whom I'm quite close to. Sound him out. I know they're desperate to talk to you, Julie, and I heard they tried to talk to you, Nikki. So have you made the deal with Gordy?'

'We made a deal with him.' Julie gave a manic grin. 'He was slavering at the mouth with excitement once we said we'd go along with it. Bastard. So we drove a very hard bargain. We said we'd hand over the diamonds if he handed over his club, El Paradiso, to us. If he actually signed it over to us.'

'You have to be joking.' Rosie almost laughed.

'Nope. He was that desperate. He's obviously been told he was getting shot if he didn't get these diamonds, so he's prepared to do anything. Go to any lengths. He must be confident that once he gets the diamonds, we'll get bumped off by him or one of his arseholes, because he actually did it. He signed over the club to us.'

'You've seriously got that in writing?' Rosie couldn't believe her ears.

'Yup. I've got it here, in black and white.'

Julie went into the kitchen and brought out a black leather folder. She produced a document and handed it over. Rosie sat studying it for a moment, but saw quickly that it was a legal contract on the headed notepaper of a leading Glasgow law firm. The document had some legal jargon, naming the club, and signing ownership to them as of yesterday's date.

'Christ almighty!' Rosie said, placing the document on the table. 'Where did he sign it? Not here, I hope?'

'No. In the hospital. Yesterday morning. We told him Nikki was getting out today so he would disappear after it was signed. We wanted to make sure he wasn't following us out here.'

'And the lawyer was present?'

'Yep. Some guy he uses. Bent as hell, no doubt.'

'So when do you hand over the diamonds?'

'We said we'd call him in a couple of days and make the handover. Might even do it here, then we can disappear.'

They sat in silence for a long moment, Rosie not quite knowing what to make of it all. She knew her detective pal Don would jump at the chance of bringing these women in. All sorts of promises would be made to keep them from prosecution and to protect them, but Rosie had been down that road before. It didn't always work. A fleeting picture of Emir, the Kosovan refugee shot while in police protection, came to her mind.

'So, what do you think, Rosie? Will you help us? Can you talk to the cops? If we go phoning them out of the blue, they'll be all over us like a cheap suit, and we'll be banged up in Cornton Vale before we know where we are. Will you help?'

Rosie spread her hands out.

'Yes, of course. If that's what you want, I'll talk to them. Are you going to hand over the diamonds to the police?'

Julie and Nikki looked at each other and nodded, but said nothing. Rosie didn't want to know, so she let the question hang there. She looked at her watch. Matt would be waiting in Stirling motorway services centre for the call to ask him to come and take photographs.

'Okay. Well, if we're going to go down that road and talk to the police, then if it's okay with you, I'd like us to have a chat just now about how it all came to this.' She looked from one to the other, hoping they were sure what they were getting into. 'What we speak about now will be your own story, your interview for the paper, telling how long you've been friends, a bit about each of your lives and how you came to be involved in the escort agency. Okay? Also, if we could talk a little about your work. Just be honest with me. It's important you do, because if this is going to appear in the newspaper, then you want to be able to get your side of things across. People sometimes judge women who work in prostitution, and unfairly in a lot of respects. I like to look at the other things, the women themselves, the reasons that drove them there. So this is your platform to talk frankly. Do you know what I mean?'

Julie and Nikki glanced at each other and nodded in

agreement. So far, so good. Rosie switched to full-on reporter mode. This was her one and only shot and it had to be right, because once the police were involved, they were out of her control. And, realistically, they could be dead in a few days.

'Oh, and I have Matt standing by . . .' Rosie looked at Julie. 'Remember the photographer who came and took pictures of the diamonds that day? Well, we need some more detailed pictures of the passports. We're working on a line about where they came from and whom they belong to. It's all criminal involvement, and if we can track them back then it's useful. There's a chance the people who belong to the passports are either dead or have had them stolen. So, is that alright?'

'Yes,' Julie got up and went into the kitchen. 'I think we might have a glass of wine while we do this.'

'Sure,' Rosie said. 'Relax. But not for me, I'm driving and it would only put me in the mood for more.' She smiled, flipping her notebook open. She decided not to mention that Matt would want a picture of both of them together. Nikki's story alone would be a splash any day of the week. She could feel the familiar tingling of excitement when a story was working out like this, and all the tiredness, guilt and thoughts of tomorrow vanished while she got ready for the first question. The pop of the wine cork from the white wine made it sound like it was a girl's night in, but the reality was far from that. This was two women fighting for their lives, plotting to bring down a big shot who could wipe them out without turning a hair.

'So, Julie, if you start by telling me how long you've been friends.'

Julie came in with two glasses of wine and handed one to Nikki.

'God . . .' She gazed down at Nikki affectionately. 'Like forever, I suppose. Since we both used to get sent to the back of French class in secondary school for carrying on. We hit it off then and have been pals since.'

Rosie switched on the tape recorder and listened as Julie reeled off her story of them growing up, Nikki chiming in. She looked sad as she talked of their Glasgow youth growing up in the housing schemes, with drunken fathers and gang fights, watching as the schemes became ravaged by drugs, and families who had just been poor were now torn apart. Teenager after teenager in their streets became hooked on heroin, and how they escaped it, Julie said, was a miracle. But both got married reasonably young and stayed in the same block of flats, hoping that one day they'd have enough money to move on. Julie had a succession of dead-end jobs, and her marriage fell apart after four years when her husband left her for another woman. Years later, Nikki's teenage sweetheart, Paul, had ruined their lives by gambling away everything they had. Rosie listened, thinking that they were just a couple of years younger than her, and all of their lives were blighted by hardship and shit thrown at them. She identified with everything they spoke about: the drunkenness and the shame of poverty. She was lucky she got out early, did a runner and upped sticks to London with nothing but hope. She was more than lucky.

Matt arrived after her interview was over, and Julie brought out the attaché case. This time, Julie emptied a few of the diamonds on to the coffee table, and they all gazed at them, Matt snapping away. Rosie and Matt knew there would be all sorts of trouble over what they were doing, but they'd let the lawyers deal with it. The important thing was to have the pictures. The diamonds were white, like small, misshapen sugar cubes, but there were a lot of them. From what Rosie had gleaned from her contact, the white ones were the most valuable when cut down and polished. Who knew how much there was here in terms of cash? She wouldn't have a clue, but she could take the pictures to a contact. She considered asking to take one of the diamonds to have it assessed, but that was just too reckless, even for her.

Then they looked at the passports, and Matt took detailed pictures of each page. Rosie checked each of them to see if they were stamped, but some of the ink was blurred. She could see the dates on others, though, and they'd been presented to Customs in recent months. Three of the names of the places visited definitely looked like Sierra Leone and although she couldn't make out the rest, the stamp and crest on their pages looked the same. Whoever they belonged to, they were being used for smuggling. This was dynamite if she got lucky enough to nail this side of it down. She took a note of passport numbers, names and dates of birth, and would get them checked through her private eye contact, Mickey Kavanagh.

'So what do you think the police will do, Rosie? Will they come and see us here?'

'Yes. I think so. Once they talk to you – and it won't be tomorrow, because they will have to talk to the bosses to see how they play this – if they decide to go along with it. So you have to hold big Gordy off until we get everything set up.'

Rosie was already thinking that if there *was* to be a set-up and she was the one who had passed the information to the police, then she wanted ringside seats for her and Matt. It would be the usual banging of heels on the floor, because the cops wouldn't want her near it. She'd see how the information went down with Don first. Matt looked at Rosie inquiringly, signalling for her to ask about the pictures.

'Girls, we'll need a picture of both of you and one of each of you on your own. Obviously, Nikki, your ordeal and the way you've described it is truly harrowing. But we need a picture to go with it. Same for you, Julie. You okay with that?'

They looked at each other and grimaced.

'It's getting scarier by the minute,' Nikki said.

'I doubt it can get much scarier than what happened to you that night, Nikki,' Julie said.

Rosie nodded in agreement.

'If you're going to do this, really get these guys nailed, then you have to put yourself on the line. Before it comes out in the newspaper, we'll make sure you're well out of the way. Abroad, possibly, if that's what you want. Then you just lie low for a while.'

They exchanged glances and both nodded.

'Okay. Let's do it,' Julie said.

Matt didn't wait for a second invitation, and started re-arranging furniture and getting the girls to pose together, then afterwards took pictures of Nikki. As usual, he took too many for Rosie's liking and she could see the girls beginning to feel uneasy. Eventually, Matt was done.

'Okay. So we'll go and let you relax for the night. I'll be in touch tomorrow, by phone, once I've talked to my police contact. I'll get a fair idea of how they're likely to view the situation from him.'

CHAPTER TWENTY-THREE

The rain had stopped, but the pea-soup fog on the motorway slowed the traffic to a snail's pace. This was the last thing Rosie needed. The past few days had been so pumped up that even an adrenalin junkie like her was beginning to feel the strain. Exhaustion washed over her now that she was beginning to relax, and she had to keep opening her window to make sure she didn't drop off. She was glad when eventually the fog lifted and she could see the city lights of Glasgow twinkling in the distance as she picked up speed. Soon, she'd be home and asleep before her head hit the pillow. Her mobile rang and flashed on the passenger seat. She glanced across and her gut did a little flip. It was Adrian. She pulled into the deserted inside lane and put the phone to her ear.

'Rosie.'

Adrian. His rich, deep voice as though he was lying next to her.

'Adrian! What a surprise! How are you?'

She cursed herself. Was that the best she could come up with? 'How are you?' It would have been more accurate, if a little basic, to say, 'I'm dying here, Adrian, at the sound of your voice.' But she couldn't. Not with him.

'I am good, Rosie, thank you. I have not called you since I left – you know . . . I thought it was best after that bad business in the apartment in Glasgow that day.'

'No problem, I understand,' she lied. 'Where are you?'

'I am here. In Glasgow.'

'Really?' She felt a little catch in her voice.

'Yes. I come with a friend. She wants to find work here.'

Something resembling jealousy lashed across Rosie's insides. She *had* heard right – he definitely said 'she'.

'Oh,' was all Rosie could muster, as she swallowed her naked disappointment.

'Not my girlfriend, only a friend,' he said quickly.

'Oh.' Rosie cursed herself again for her being so tongue-tied. What the hell was happening to her here?

'She did not want to travel from Sarajevo by herself . . . you know. Sometimes it is dangerous these days. She is the sister of a good friend of mine. I remember you met him one time in Sarajevo? I have friends here who can give her a room for a few weeks. Maybe she will find a job. I hope so.'

'Okay. I understand. That was good of you to travel with her.'

'I'm here only for a few days.' He paused. 'I . . . I hope I can see you. Are you free tonight? I arrived just four hours ago.'

Rosie hesitated. She knew she was too tired to cope with Adrian on any level tonight. He would understand. But that's not what came out when she spoke.

'Yeah. Well, I've been away, Adrian, and I'm on my way home from an interview now. I'm dog tired . . . Er, but sure, I'd love to see you too. You want to come to the flat for a little while? I'll be there shortly.'

'Thank you, Rosie. I will wait for you.' He hung up.

Well done, Rosie, she muttered to herself as she reached the outskirts of the city. You could have played a little hard to get. She felt her face smile.

A few minutes later Rosie was about to turn off the motorway at Charing Cross, when Adrian called again.

'I'll be there in a couple of minutes,' she said.

'Rosie. One moment. There are two men in a car in your car park. You know who it is? I'm thinking of the other time a couple of years ago. Maybe someone is looking for you? I don't want to worry you, but it's cold here, and I think it's strange maybe people sitting in the car park.'

Rosie felt a little stab of panic.

'What do they look like? Can you see them?'

'They are like Indian or something. Not white. Maybe Pakistanis.'

'Shit.'

'Is it a problem?'

'Maybe. I was attacked outside my flat last week. I'm working on an investigation.'

'Oh.' Adrian paused. 'Don't worry. Listen to me. Just drive into the car park as normal. Trust me.'

'Jesus, Adrian. Now I am worried.'

'Nobody can see me. I'm at the edge of the car park, in the shadows. I can see everything. I'll be here.'

Rosie gripped the steering wheel as she drove along Woodlands Road, glancing up at her flat on the third floor where the timed lights were already on, so that the place would look lived in. She drove slowly towards the car park, scanning the streets for any sign of Adrian. There was none. She prayed he was somewhere. As she drove into the car park, she recognised the cars of all of her five neighbours – except one at the far side. And now it was reversing, facing the exit. She parked her car and switched the engine off, her heart pounding. She didn't look in the direction of the car, but walked the few steps towards the stairs to her entrance briskly. Then she heard a car door clunk open. Too terrified to look back, she quickly fumbled in her pocket for her key, but dropped it. Shit! She could hear heavy footsteps sprinting across the car park, and she stumbled as she got to the top step, dropping her bag.

'Bitch!' A voice behind her spat.

Rosie tried to straighten up, but her legs were like lead.

Then, suddenly, she heard the sound of a grunt and a body hitting the ground. She turned her head to see Adrian on top of someone, punching the back of his head, then grabbing his hair and thumping his forehead against the step. Every time his head came up, Rosie saw the shocked look in the Pakistani man's eyes; his nose had burst open and face was bloodied. Rosie watched, a little horrified, at Adrian's cold concentration as he bashed the man's head four or five times against the step.

'Adrian!' Rosie said.

He didn't look at her, but let the man slump down on to the stairs. Then he pulled him to his feet and dragged him towards the other man's moving car, its engine revving and main beams on. The wheels spun and the car raced towards him. Adrian lifted a brick from the ground and hurled it through the windscreen. The car screeched to a halt and Adrian yanked the passenger door open and threw the man in. Rosie got to her feet and strained her eyes against the blinding light from the headlights. Adrian reached in and took a swipe at the driver – she thought she saw the glint of a knife – then the driver put his hand to his face. He must have cut him. She could hear Adrian's voice, angry, emphatic.

'You come here again, you are dead. Both of you.' Adrian slammed the door and the car sped off, swerving and skidding as it smashed against the low brick wall on the way out.

Rosie opened the door and went inside, her back against

the wall, her whole body shaking. Adrian came in behind her, and his arms went around her. He held her tight and she could feel the hard muscles in his shoulders as he pressed her head to his chest. Then the tears came.

'Ssssh,' he said. 'Is okay now, Rosie. Come. You must get in the house.' He supported her up the stairs to her door.

Rosie hit the hall light and walked unsteadily down to the living room. Once inside, she slung her bag on the sofa and turned to see Adrian in the doorway. All six foot two of him, his face paler than the last time, tiny beads of sweat on his forehead.

'Oh my God, Adrian!' Rosie was safe now, and somewhere between hysteria and weeping. 'Welcome back to Glasgow. He could have killed me.'

'No. If he was going to kill you, he would have done. It was to frighten you.' He took a knife out of his pocket, holding it by the blade. 'This was on the steps. He must have had it in his hand. You should give it to the police for fingerprints.'

Rosie nodded.

'I thought you were going to kill him . . .'

Adrian shrugged in that way that he did that looked as though he was a little bored.

'No. Just teach him a lesson. I think he has it now. They won't come back here, but you should go to the police with the knife.'

'Yes, maybe I will. You certainly scared the pair of them. Did you do something to the driver?'

Adrian shrugged but said nothing.

'Christ! I need a drink.' Rosie shook her head.

She went into the kitchen with Adrian behind her and picked up a half-full bottle of red wine. She tried to pull the cork out, but her hands were still shaking.

'Let me.' Adrian took the bottle and popped the cork, as Rosie brought out two glasses.

He poured a little wine into each of them, and handed one to Rosie.

'I'm so glad to see you, my friend.' He clinked his glass to hers.

'Not as glad as I am to see you, pal.' She knocked back a huge gulp of wine.

'So. Tell me. Who are these people? You have made them angry enough to come to your house.'

Rosie shook her head as she crossed the room to the sofa and threw herself down.

'It's a long story, Adrian.'

Rosie began to stir, conscious of Adrian's warm body next to her. She stretched out her legs, eyes still closed, recalling the night. They'd finished the bottle of wine and flopped into bed, not lovers, but old friends, comfortable in their nakedness. By the time he leaned across and softly kissed her on the lips, she was already drifting into an exhausted slumber, incapable of responding. She couldn't recollect the details of her dream, but only that she'd been struggling and gasping for breath. Then Adrian's arms were reaching across to her, holding her close, his soothing tones telling her she was having a nightmare. Half asleep, they'd fallen into the comfort of each other, arms and legs caressing, Adrian's tender kisses on her wounded neck, then all the way down, his tongue probing and tasting her till she moaned with pleasure and pulled him on top of her.

Now, with the morning light creeping into the room, she watched the silhouette of his handsome face as he slept peacefully. She'd come to know so much about the big Bosnian since their fateful encounter in a cafe all those years ago, yet even though he had allowed her to see his darkness, in Sarajevo last year, standing at the graveside of his wife, who had been murdered by Serbian butchers; even though some of the layers had been stripped away and they'd shared nights like this before, where their passion was unstoppable, Rosie still didn't know who he was. Or even what this was between them. He was so much more than her friend. He was her occasional lover, but still it was nothing. He would leave in a couple of days and she would feel mildly bereft, but her life would go on and she wouldn't pine for him the way she still, deep down, pined for TJ in her darker moments. But what could she ever do with a man like Adrian? He had saved her life and she had watched him kill as he protected her. But there was something deep and dark about the way he'd done it, the clinical way he had shot the man in the Glasgow apartment, then went through his pockets and taken his money that day, and minutes later threw another attacker to his death from the third-floor stairwell. And last night, as she watched him pound the Pakistani attacker's head again and again on the stairs, there was something frenzied about it. Something inside him was so angry that hurting people who had hurt others was about more than protecting the victim. It was as though he was avenging everyone who had ever been hurt, because he hadn't been able to save his wife and unborn son that day when the Serbians came. She had noticed it more last night than ever before. He was angry. So angry. And he hid it well, in that pragmatic, quiet way of his that made her feel safe any time he was around. But sooner or later, he had to find a way not to be this angry, and Rosie didn't know where to begin with that, or if he was even capable of getting to that place. She took a deep breath and let it out slowly, feeling her heartbeat reduce. She picked up her phone from the bedside table. It was eight thirty. She'd slept far too long. She slipped out of bed and padded along to the bathroom.

CHAPTER TWENTY-FOUR

'You're looking a bit rough,' McGuire said, glancing briefly at Rosie, then back to his screen, as she walked into his office.

'You really need to work on your chat-up lines.' Rosie threw herself on the sofa and flipped open her notebook.

'I'm just saying . . . in a caring way.' McGuire came from behind his desk and sat on the easy chair opposite her. 'You need to get a few early nights.'

'Yeah, right. It's on my forward planning agenda.' Rosie stifled a yawn. 'What do you have to do to get a cup of coffee in here?'

'Marion!' McGuire leaned his head back and shouted at the half-open door. 'Can you bring me and our intrepid Gilmour a couple of coffees, sweetheart?'

Rosie glanced over her notes, flicking through the pages, trying to work out where to start with Julie and Nikki's story.

'So how did it go last night?' He put a hand up. 'Oh, and by the way, your copy on Pakistan is fucking awesome! I was going to phone but I got tied up with the first edition.'

'Thanks. Last night with Julie and Nikki was great, Mick. The two of them spilled everything – just about got the story of their whole lives. I was there till half nine. Matt came and took pictures, so we have everything in the bag. It's great stuff.'

Better to get the good news first, Rosie thought.

'So where are they actually hiding out?'

'In some little farmhouse outside Bannockburn. I don't think anyone will go looking for them there. It's a working pig and sheep farm, apparently. Some old guy, his wife and their disabled son live in the big house, and the girls are in a cottage next door.'

'How long are they planning on staying there? They're going to have to put their heads above the parapet sometime. What about the Nikki bird with the arm? How is she?'

'She's getting there. Really nice woman, actually. Well, on the face of it they both are. Julie is a bit of a hard case – looks like Nikki got talked into the escort-girl lark by Julie, who's her best friend from way back.'

'She must feel a bit responsible then.'

'She does, but she's a tough cookie. She's the one who's suddenly got the bravery pills to take on big Gordy MacLean.'

'What do you mean?'

'Believe it or not, this big bastard came and visited Nikki in the hospital. Julie was there too.'

'Jesus! After setting her up? Bet that went down well.'

'It didn't, at first. But he gave them all this crap that it wasn't his fault. Came across all contrite and offered them a deal.'

'A deal? They should have called the cops there and then.'

'They can't, Mick. Have you forgotten? They've got the bloody suitcase.'

'Well. Yeah, but they need to do something.'

'They are. He offered them a deal. Said that this big shot in Manchester, Johnny Vanner, is putting all the heat on him to get the diamonds back. He's told them if they go along with him and give *him* the diamonds, he plans to stiff Vanner for them, keep them, and sell them in due course and – wait for it – split the proceeds with the two of them.'

'Aye! They can trust that bastard as far as Nikki can throw him with her bad arm.'

'Exactly. And they're aware of that, but they've decided that they're going to take the piss out of him. They made a deal with him. But they have no intention of honouring it. And what a deal, by the way. You know what they did? They could see that he's is so desperate to get the diamonds that they drove a ridiculously hard bargain.'

'A bargain?'

'Yep. They got him to sign his club – that tacky shithole, El Paradiso, round in Mitchell Lane – over to them, before they agreed to give him the diamonds.'

'The lap-dancing club? That'll be right!'

'I'm telling you. I've seen it in black and white. He must be even thicker than we thought. He's only signed his club over to them, and now he's waiting, with his arse twitching, hoping they come across with the diamonds.'

'Gordy MacLean did that?'

'Shows you how desperate he is.'

'But there has to be an end to this story, so what is it?'

'They said they want to get him done. Hand he over to the cops, once they get him to admit that it was him who set Nikki up for the attack on her. They want him done for that.'

'If these women are so clever, they should be running some company, not working as hookers.'

'Well, they *are* company bosses now. On paper, anyway.'

'So let's think how we're going to play this.'

'I don't think we should get the cops involved in any way at all, Mick. I think the best thing is to get Julie and Nikki wired up and get it all on tape. Then we have our story, and then we go to the cops.'

'And where will the girls be?'

'We can get them away as soon as they finish dealing with MacLean.'

'But he'll shoot them. As soon as they hand over the

diamonds, they're history. Are they that daft they can't see that?'

Rosie sighed.

'Well, that's the problem.'

They sat quietly, Rosie turning it over in her mind, watching as McGuire did the same.

'We've also got some more detailed pictures of the passports.' She put her hands up as McGuire gave her a reproachful look. 'I know what you're going to say. But it had to be done. How are we going to find out if the passports are genuine if we don't get the passport numbers and dates of birth? I had to get a close look. I've got a contact who can trace who they belong to. I noticed that all of them have had a stamp in Sierra Leone in recent months. And one of the passports is in the name of Rabia Sahid – the same date of birth as our suicide bride from Pollokshields, though I don't know if Sahid was her maiden name. But I'll find out. That's the main one we want to trace.'

Mick's eyes widened.

'I like the sound of that. We could use that as a separate story, a stand-alone splash, if we can prove it is her passport. It would put these people in the shit if they really are behind her death.' He paused for a moment. 'Yes, let's do that. In fact, is there any way we can drop that hint to the cops without showing all our cards? The family could get their collars felt at the very least.'

'It might not be her passport, though. I mean, it's got her

date of birth and first name on it, but it's a different photograph. Probably been doctored.'

'Well, we should tell the cops anyway and get them to ask the family to see her passport.'

'Okay. I'll speak to my contact.'

'I want it as a story, Gilmour. Even if it's only a form of words that says passports may be getting stolen and used for smuggling, something like that. You can get the cops to say they're investigating. That gives us a chance to use it in the paper, and you never know who it might flush out.'

Rosie nodded in agreement. McGuire stood up and walked behind his desk.

'Right. We're running your Pakistan rescue tomorrow, all guns fucking blazing. Just the story, no opinion, no comment. But if we can throw in something about dodgy passports, it's a good fresh line in a couple of days. You never know who's gone missing, or who's missing a passport.'

'Okay. I'll make some calls to my pal now with the passport connections and see what he can come up with.'

Rosie had given her private eye contact, Mickey Kavanagh, details of the passport with Rabia's date of birth and name. She was surprised when her mobile rang at her desk and it was him.

'Hey, Rosie, I've got a result.'

'Already?'

'Yep. If you've got a few passports it might take a day or so, but let's deal with this one first, since it's the most important.'

'So what've you got?'

'The passport was issued on the date you gave me to one Rabia Sahid in Lahore. I haven't seen the picture, but I might be able to get a hold of it, though that'll take at least a day. But I've got an address, so you can check that out.'

'Brilliant. The girl's home address in Pakistan should be on the wedding certificate at the registry office in Glasgow. We can check it there.'

Mickey reeled off the address and Rosie carefully wrote it down, reading it back to him to make sure she'd got it right.

'How many more passports have you got? And are they all Pakistani?'

'There are seven in total. All Pakistani.'

'Okay. Give me the details and I'll check them out with my mate. But the problem you'll have there is that you've nothing to check against. I mean, you can authenticate the girl, Rabia, if the address is the same one she put on the wedding certificate. But the others – they'll be just random addresses across Pakistan. Unless you can find who they are, you'll never really know.'

'I know that, Mickey. We're not going to be able to track every one of them down, but if we can prove Rabia's is a fake, then that's a pretty big deal. It gives us an in. We can ask the family where her passport is. In fact, my editor wants us to get the cops to do that.' Rosie paused. 'But I'd like to find out a bit more on the background about how this happens. There are obviously criminals behind it, but I need to be able to explain it simply.'

'Well, put in simple terms, fake passports and stolen passports faked up with another picture or doctored, are quite commonplace. Gangsters are all over it, especially these days. My mate was saying that it happens a lot with Pakistani or Indian passports. People get out of the country by whatever means they can, either trafficked by gangmasters or in other ways. They turn up at UK border control and they've no passport. They just say they're seeking asylum, and without a passport they can't work, but they are given benefits. Then they disappear into the black economy. They've probably given up their passport before they left, maybe as payment for their passage here. That kind of thing.'

'All of the passports I've seen have recent Sierra Leone stamps on them. Did I mention that earlier?'

'No you didn't, darlin'. Not like you to miss out such a salient point.'

'Sorry, Mickey. I'm completely knackered. My head is all over the place. I just got back from Peshawar two days ago, and believe me it was mental over there. I'll tell you all about it when we have that dinner. But since I came back,

I've been flat out writing the rescue story I was telling you about, and now it's developing arms and legs.'

'No worries, sweetheart. I was only joking. But I'll go back to my mate re: the Sierra Leone stamp, though I think we can safely assume that the passports have been used for smuggling diamonds out of the country.'

'Excellent. I'm really grateful to have your expertise on this. We'll have to get whatever story I write past the lawyers. But the main thing is, if I can get anything on Rabia's passport – the rest is a bit of conjecture, but I'll get some official expert to comment. The editor is very keen on the passport line. He thinks it might flush something out.'

'It might well do. Good luck with it. I'll be around next week, so let's have a plate of pasta.' He paused. 'And get yourself an early night, Rosie. You can't keep going at a hundred miles an hour all your life.'

'I know. I'm going to have an early night very soon.'

'See you, darlin'.' He hung up.

CHAPTER TWENTY-FIVE

Rosie went to O'Brien's fifteen minutes before she was due to meet Don. She did it on purpose, because she wanted to sit at the bar, sip a glass of wine, and relish how the day had panned out. The dog tiredness that had threatened to overwhelm her by four in the afternoon had been replaced with that sense of elation which only came from knowing you had nailed a story. Nothing else came close to it for her. Call it an empty life. Call it obsessed, but when everything fell into place, and people were about to be unmasked for the ruthless bastards they were, this was all the life she needed. It made up for the countless blind alleys you went up every day in pursuit of the truth. And it sure as hell pushed away the melancholy musing of her mixed-up personal life. That would probably never fall into place. But when Declan had given her the thumbs up as he appeared at the top of the stairs onto the editorial floor two hours ago, she could have done a triumphant back flip.

He'd just returned from the registry office in Martha Street, where they didn't part with any details of births, marriages or deaths, unless you went there in person. Declan had gone up and bought an extract from the marriage register showing the wedding certificate of Farooq Shah and his wife Rabia. And there it was, in black and white: Rabia Sahid's address in Lahore, and the same date of birth Rosie had seen in the passport from the stolen suitcase. She still didn't know how Rabia's passport had ended up in the hands of criminals. But it had, and it had clearly been used for smuggling. At first it was euphoria that swept her away, but it was quickly followed by rage. She thought of the bedroom, the locks on the outside of the door, and the elders of the family in the living room, the whole house cloaked in menacing silence. Everything in the house had been suffocating for the poor girl who wasn't able to fight back. Whether she jumped or was pushed, Rosie would probably never know. But she had been wronged in so many ways. Maybe she too had been part of a business deal, in the way Laila was when her father punted her across to Pakistan to marry a man at least three times her age. Now, Rosie was in a position to go and knock on the door of the Shah house again. She swallowed a mouthful of wine and felt herself smiling as Don walked through the swing doors.

'Pint?' Rosie kissed him on the cheek. 'I'm only having one drink, Don, I'm totally done in. But I needed to see you. I'm going to make your night.'

'Don't say that, Rosie. You'll get me all breathless with anticipation. I think I've got a warm glow in my pants.'

Rosie chuckled.

'Not that kind of excitement. Even better.' She knew he was as driven by his work as her.

The barman put the pint on the counter and Don took a long drink. He took out a packet of cigarettes and handed one to Rosie.

'Smoking and everything,' he joked. 'You're either wrecked with stress or onto something.'

'I'm onto something. But I need to know that you won't do anything about this until I knock on the door of these people.'

'What people?'

'The Shah family. Rabia's father-in-law, the widower, all that crowd. Something is rotten in that whole set-up.'

'We've felt that since day one, but we haven't got a whisker on them.'

'Well, that's about to change.' She took a deep breath, feeling excited just repeating her story. 'I haven't said anything to you because I've had to keep things really tight, but I've been working on a story attached to this. Don't ask me, because I can't tell you a thing about that right now – I will when the time is right. But I think Rabia's death is connected to this other story I'm pursuing.'

'What other story?'

'Can't tell you right now, just trust me.'

'So what's going on? You're talking in riddles. I'm getting excited here because you're excited.' He blew smoke out and smiled through his craggy face. 'Come on. Spit it out, pal.'

'It's to do with passports, or part of it is. I've discovered that Rabia's passport has been used for smuggling. It's been doctored and faked up with another picture. But it's definitely *her* passport.'

He looked bemused.

'How in the name of fuck can you know something like that, Rosie?'

'I just do, okay? Put it this way: I've seen it. I know someone who is in possession of stolen passports, and I've seen them all. Much to my surprise, one had her name – her maiden name actually – and date of birth. But a different picture.'

'Really? Aye but there's bound to be more than one Pakistani girl with the same name and date of birth. I hope you've got more than that.'

'I've had it checked out with my connections in the passport office, and the address where the passport was issued to is the same address Rabia put on her wedding certificate.' She watched his face light up. 'And before you ask, yes I've checked the wedding certificate too. I have a copy of it.' She reached into her bag and brought out the certificate, handing it to him. 'Here. It's a present, don't say I'm not good to you.'

He glanced at it.

'Fuck me, Rosie! Are you sure? Where's the passport?'

'It's with some people I've met, but I've seen it with my own eyes and it's been photographed.'

'Christ. But if all we've got to go on is a wedding certificate—'

Rosie interrupted.

'Don. All you do is go to the house and ask to see Rabia's passport. They can't show you it, because it's not there. Just watch their expressions and how they try to get out of it. Listen, if she was married a couple of months ago, then her passport should be around the house somewhere, because she would need it for the registry office to register the marriage. So ask them where it is. Ask them to show you it. They'll shit their pants.'

'So what have they done with it? What are they getting used for? You said smuggling?'

'They can get used for anything once they get into criminal hands. A passport legitimises just about anybody, as you know.'

Don let out a long sigh, scratching his chin.

'The boss is going to want to know what's going on.'

'Well he'll have to start by asking them where the passport is. What I'm saying to you is that you have to put some heat on them. Let them know their arses are being felt, and see what happens.'

'But they could say the passport is missing, or stolen.'

'Well, just bluff it then. Come on, pal. You're the cops, don't tell me you've not bluffed your way through an investigation with a suspect, telling him you know everything so he'll confess.'

'How very dare you!' Don grinned, stubbing out his cigarette.

'But here's the catch.' Rosie finished her wine. 'You can't knock their door until I knock on it first. And I mean that. In fact, I'll have them shitting themselves, so that by the time you hit the door, they'll be just about ready to confess.'

Don smiled.

'You're making me an offer I can't refuse, Gilmour.'

'I know. That's why you love me. And if you play your cards right and keep me out of it, then something bigger might be going down in a few days.'

'To do with the Pakistani girl?'

'Don't ask. Just trust me . . . I'm a journalist.' She gently eased down her rollneck jumper to expose the scar on her neck, still red and angry.

'What the hell's that?' Don looked shocked. 'Somebody try to cut your throat?'

'Well. They threatened it. The cut is just the first bit of what's to come.'

'Christ's sake, Rosie! Who did that? Just tell me.' He was angry. 'I'll kill the bastard myself.'

'Listen, Don. I'm going to tell you something else here, about me getting attacked. But right now, I'm not making an official complaint, so have you got that?'

''Course. Who did it? Just tell me, I'll deal with it.'

'Okay. It was done as a warning because I've been digging around on the Rabia story. I spoke to a girl I saw in the house that day I went in. This young woman kind of gave me the eyes, and I thought it was worth pursuing. I met her in Queen's Park along with a cousin who's only fourteen. It turns out, the kid was getting whisked to Pakistan to marry some old bastard.'

'Christ! What is it with these people?'

'It's how they do business. It's their culture.'

'Culture, my arse. So how did this happen to you?' He reached across and touched her neck softly with the back of his hand, shaking his head. 'Makes me really fucking angry, Rosie.'

'Somebody must have rumbled that the woman and her cousin talked to me, and a few days ago, as I was going into my flat, I got attacked. He was a Pakistani, that much I know. He warned me to stay away. "Stay away from my family" is what he said.'

'Fucker!'

'It was a warning, but I was so scared, Don. I thought I was done for.'

'Your paper should be getting you protection round the clock.'

'I don't want it. I can't be arsed with bodyguards. I had them before, it's like my life isn't my own.'

'But nobody would cut your bloody throat.'

'I know, but still. Next thing is, I get a phone call from the woman that her cousin has been taken to Pakistan to get married.'

Don drained his pint and gestured to Rosie if she wanted another. She shook her head.

'Don't tell me you went there to rescue her.' He raised his eyebrows.

'Got it in one. It'll be all over the *Post* tomorrow.'

'Jesus wept! You're off your head.'

'But it's an amazing tale – we brought the kid back! Okay, nothing is perfect, but she was saved from being more or less a prisoner in a foreign land with some old bastard dragging her to bed every night.'

'So the knife man will be after you again.'

'He already was. Last night.'

'Christ almighty!'

'But luckily, I had someone there. A friend of mine who happened to be in town and was meeting me at the flat.'

'I presume it's not a lady friend.' He put his hand up. 'Not that it's any of my business.'

Rosie smiled.

'No. Someone who can handle himself.'

'He wouldn't by chance be from Bosnia?' Don gave her a playful dig in the shoulder.

'Never mind where he's from – he dealt with the bastard. And I mean a right battering. Not sure if it's the same guy from last week, but I'd say it was. He dropped the knife during the beating.'

'You've got a knife? With fingerprints?'

Rosie nodded.

'But I don't want to do anything about this right now. I *will* pursue it. I will get him done, if we can find him. But there is so much going on in this bigger picture I'm working on that I can't take my focus off that. Do you understand?'

Don puffed impatiently.

'Yeah. I do, Rosie. I won't do anything, but get me the knife and I'll find him. We'll get prints from it and see where it takes us.'

'It's obviously someone attached to that family, or the extended family.'

'Fuck them! When we hit them tomorrow about the passport, I'm going to get every fucking one of them fingerprinted, just to noise them up.' He reached across and touched Rosie's face. 'I'm going to get this bastard, Rosie. I promise you that. I'm not having this. Where's the knife?'

'In my bag. I'll give you it when we get outside. She slid off the stool. 'Now I really need to get home. So do I have your word?'

'Come on, do you really need to ask?'

'Just making sure.' They walked towards the door. 'So . . .

I'm going to knock on the door in the morning, and after that I'll call you. If I were you, I'd get in there quick, before people start disappearing and all sorts of shit hits the fan.'

They walked out into the cold, blustery night. Rosie hailed a taxi, then discreetly reached into her bag and brought out the padded envelope that held the knife.

'Don't worry. My friend picked it up cleanly. There are no other prints on it.'

'We're kind of flying by the seat of our pants – I mean, we the cops, that is. Because we haven't seen this passport you're talking about, and we only have your word, which, of course, is good enough for me. I hope the boss buys it, but I'll have to tell him about the knife attack, because we need to use this as leverage tomorrow.'

'Okay. I've met your boss. He knows me. So tell him all this is from me, that should be enough.'

Rosie gave Don a hug and blew him a kiss as she climbed into the taxi.

CHAPTER TWENTY-SIX

The raw wind slapped big Gordy flush in the face, but that wasn't what was making his eyes water. As he stood at the graveside, he sniffed and flicked the tears away, glancing over his shoulder in case anyone was around to see him. Gordy MacLean didn't do tears. Everybody knew that. Except his ma. He could speak to her here as though she was still sitting across the table from him in their kitchen, gazing at him adoringly while he polished off a massive Saturday morning fry-up. Hard to believe that it was five years ago. Five years, yet he could still feel the warmth of her peachy cheek next to his when he had hugged her. He sniffed again, recalling her final weeks in the hospital bed where he sat holding her hand, watching as she slept. Even at the funeral, when his ma's coffin was carried in a horse-drawn carriage through the Maryhill streets where he grew up, to the chapel, Gordy kept his face like flint. Every-one was there. Faces from the criminal world, legends, many of them who'd spent more time behind bars than on the streets. All of them respected among their own kind, and all who remembered Dolly MacLean from the old days, when she was the buxom beauty that his da had landed because he was the biggest fish in Glasgow. Dolly had seemed to shrink after his da got a bullet in the back that winter afternoon, on his way home from the Old Firm match fifteen years ago. It had obviously been a well-planned execution by their biggest family rival. And it worked; sent messages everywhere.

Gordy was a respected young hardman at the time, but everybody knew he was no Gavin MacLean. No matter how big his dreams were, he could never match his father's reputation. Even after a stint in jail for armed robbery, when he'd swaggered out of the gates into a waiting Rolls Royce, Gordy would always be the nipper. But all of that changed when he sorted Joe the Pole out for his father's murder, blowing up his car with him and his wife in it. Gordy's reputation across Glasgow and beyond went right off the scale. He was feared as he built up his own empire. El Paradiso, which his da had opened as a cabaret club twenty years ago, had been lying derelict, but when he renovated it and re-opened with a massive party, everyone knew the MacLean dynasty would live on. He'd never be his da, who had bumped off anyone off who'd got in his way. Gordy knew he couldn't kill them all. He had to adapt. There wasn't so much money to play with in the beginning, but there was still some, and it was Gordy's goal to make it grow. Gordy made a fortune from the club, and from investing in coke at the crucial time when it hit Glasgow. He reinvested in property, bought houses in Spain and on the Clydeside, and Dolly had proudly watched the progress of her boy. But the club was their most treasured possession, where his father had held legendary poker games for big stakes, where bare-knuckle fights in the back court were gambled on. The club was where his heart lay, and now this fucking bitch, Julie – and her pal – had made him sign it over to them.

He wished he could just shoot the two of them, but he couldn't because Vanner was on his back every fucking day and night. Where are the diamonds, Gordy? Your time is running out, he kept saying down the phone, with that bastard, irritating *Coronation Street* accent. Gordy could, if he wanted, arrange for him to be done in, but the shit would just keep on coming. In the end, he had to deal with it. But it broke his fucking heart handing those two dizzy birds the document signing over El Paradiso. His lawyer told him he must be nuts, but Gordy warned him to zip his mouth and draw up the necessary paperwork. Now he was at the graveside telling his ma the tragic news. He knew she would understand, but it would have broken her heart. He was glad she wasn't here to see it. But someone was going to pay for this, he vowed to her. Killing those birds wouldn't be enough. But right now, he had to be Mr Nice

Guy, all flowers and chocolates for that stupid one-armed tart. Fuck me. If his da could see him . . .

Gordy picked his way through the mud and puddles on the way back to where his Jag was parked, the engine softly purring. Terry kept his gaze fixed on the windscreen as he approached, and Gordy knew his trusted driver was careful not to look at him in case he witnessed any slip in his boss's steely mask. You didn't get much more loyal than Terry. Well, apart from wee Alex, who was shot by that fucker Vanner. Terry just did what he was told. He wasn't the brightest tool in the shed. A big, bumpy face, and a bottom lip you could hang your jacket on, made him look a bit like a village idiot. But he was handy with his fists and even handier with a knife. And he'd shoot anyone he was asked to and not even question it. When Gordy thought about it, part of him wished he'd sent him that night with Nikki. At least he would only have lost his driver and bodyguard. It would have been tough, but Terry wasn't his best mate. Even thinking about Alex made Gordy's insides hurt with rage.

'Take me through to Stirling, mate. I need to see these birds.'

'Sure, boss.'

They drove in silence, Gordy staring blankly out of the window as the city and suburbs gave way to countryside and rolling hills in the distance. He saw pictures of himself as a kid on trips to the Trossachs with his ma and da, where they holidayed in a caravan. They could have afforded a hotel no sweat, but the caravan was what you did, and Gordy would kick a ball in the park with Alex and other kids while his parents drank and had sing-songs, getting pissed with other families on the campsite. He remembered fighting with one of the other kids, a bigger boy than him, who had bullied him at the football. Gordy had snapped, and punched him till the others had to drag him off the kid. That was the first time Gordy knew he was capable of killing, if the circumstances were right. And that's when it started. When his da got to hear about the fight, he beamed with pride at his son. And his ma did too, but with a sad look in her eye that the time was coming when she was going to lose her wee boy.

The car turned off the motorway and up the Bannock-burn road, then into the farm lane. In the yard Gordy could see pigs in a pen and some guy in a wheelchair being pushed by an older guy. They were scattering something out of a bucket into the pigsty, while the pigs snorted and gorged themselves, pushing each other out of the way. The old guy stopped when the Jag pulled up. He pushed the wheelchair towards the cottage. Gordy got out of the car as the farmer approached.

'Can I help you?'

The silver-haired farmer eyed him suspiciously.

Gordy looked him up and down.

'No, you can't.'

Gordy closed the car door and turned as the younger man in the wheelchair came towards them.

'Who are you looking for?' the old man asked.

Gordy pushed out a bored sigh.

'Who do you think?' He looked through him, then away.

'Are you a friend of theirs?' The farmer jerked his head in the direction of the cottage.

'What are you – their fucking bodyguard?' he snarled, throwing a look of contempt at the guy in the wheelchair.

'They're very private. They don't like visitors. They like to keep themselves to themselves.' The man in the wheelchair spoke slowly, as though he was finding the words somewhere in his head.

'Aye, fine, Chief Ironside. I'll bear that in mind. Now you two just go back to feeding the pigs. The girls are friends of mine, okay? So fuck off.'

The older man's face fell and his lips hardened in rage. If his face hadn't been so red and weatherbeaten in the first place, he might have been blushing with anger. He stared at Gordy for a long moment and then went behind his son's wheelchair and turned away.

'Come on, Euan. Our dinner will be ready.'

Gordy muttered 'Fuck me' to himself as he rapped the knocker against the old door, and watched as the pair made their way to the big house. It took about a minute before the voice shouted. 'Who's there?'

'It's me. Gordy.'

Julie opened the door. Gordy went back to the back of the Jag and brought in the bag.

Julie opened the door and beckoned him in.

'I bought you girls a present. Some champagne and chocolates. You can have a wee celebration of your new business venture.'

'Very big of you,' Julie said, as he put the bag on the table. 'I hope they're not poisoned.'

Gordy's face moved to a smile.

'Nope. I'm over it. Fuck it, it's only bricks and mortar. To be honest, I'm out of the whole fucking shebang. I've decided to move over to Spain for a while, get some sun on my back. I've had enough of this shithole.'

'Aye? Well, bon voyage and all that, Gordy. But I hope you're not going to be calling in here every day now. We're not mates. We've done a deal here, that's it. Are we clear about that?'

'Aye?'

'So, are you lonely or something? Are there no sixteen-year-old Eastern European birds to suck your dick?'

Gordy spread his hands.

'Look, I'm trying to do the decent thing here.' He glanced at Nikki, who was sitting on the sofa watching the scene. 'I'll honestly never forgive myself for that. Because I played along with that bastard Vanner's game and set her up, I lost my best mate. Believe me, I *am* lonely without him. But

I'm more angry than lonely, and this Vanner fucker's getting it.'

'Nice speech, Gordy. But we're fresh out of scones and sympathy up here, and we only do absolution on Mondays after mass. So, listen. Thanks for the present, much appreciated. But will you take yourself to fuck now?'

Gordy could feel his rage rising from his stomach to his fingertips. He clenched his fists by his side. He'd love to knock some respect into her mouth right fucking now. But he bit his lip.

'Okay. Fine, have it your way. But, we have a deal. So when am I going to see the diamonds? I need to take at least one of them to get it seen by my jeweller mate.'

Julie glanced at Nikki and nobody spoke for a long moment.

'Yeah, well we knew that. We'll give you one, but that's all. You can take it and let us know what the guy says.'

She went into the kitchen and opened a drawer. Gordy wondered if the whole bag was in the drawer. He could simply cut all this shit short if he wanted and shoot the two of them right now. But no, he'd wait to see what they were worth first. What if they were shite?

Julie came back in and opened the palm of her hand.

'That it?' Gordy bent over, peering at the small stone, no bigger than a gravel chip and just as grimy.

'Yep. That's it. I don't know much about rough diamonds, but they don't come in the size of lumps of coal. This is it.

The rest of them are similar.' She put it between her thumb and forefinger and handed it to him. 'Here. Don't lose it.'

Gordy stood with the stone in the palm of his hand, moving it around with his other hand.

'Doesn't look much.' He took his silk hanky from his jacket pocket, wrapped the stone in it and folded it half a dozen times, then put it into his pocket. 'We'll see.'

They stood there in silence. Nikki flicked the TV channel and two women came on arguing over something on Sky News.

'You alright, Nikki? How's the arm?'

'Great. I'm filling in forms for the Paralympics. I'm thinking of the table tennis.'

Gordy stifled the urge to snigger and shook his head.

'Aye. Well, glad you're not letting it get you down.'

He turned towards the door.

'I'll be in touch as soon as I get this valued. Next couple of days probably, then that's it. We're done. You agreed on that?'

'Of course. We have a deal.'

He left, headed towards his waiting Jag, and got in and slammed the door.

'Table fucking tennis,' he muttered.

'Eh, boss?' Terry asked.

'Nothing. Let's go.'

CHAPTER TWENTY-SEVEN

Rosie flicked through the *Post* as Matt drove out of the office car park and headed along the Clydeside. As tabloid front pages went, it couldn't have been much more sensational. WORLD EXCLUSIVE, the coloured strapline blazed across the top, and below, a massive picture of Laila at Glasgow Airport in the arms of her mother. The banner headline screamed: TEEN BRIDE'S ESCAPE FROM PAKISTAN HELL. Underneath, a smaller strapline: I WAS PROMISED TO AN OLD MAN. Running along the foot of the page was a small graphic picture of the bloodied woman lying in the dirt. The strapline read – Inside: STONED TO DEATH.

Rosie browsed the shocking images on the spread of the stoning.

'Jesus! Still makes me feel sick, Matt, just looking at this. Amazing pictures, though. Your mates will all be jealous.'

'Yeah. Not a bad job, all said and done.' He slapped her thigh. 'And we got away with it, mate.'

'I spoke to McGuire briefly when I came in this morning, and he's already had Sky TV and the Beeb on asking for pictures. They'll go worldwide. Especially the stoning snaps.' Rosie pulled down the sun visor, examining her face in the mirror. Not too bad. She'd slept better last night – almost seven hours and no nightmares, surprising given what she'd just been through in recent days. 'Though I'm not expecting hearts and flowers when we hit this door.'

'No. They'll be going nuts. How do you want to play this?'

'I think it's best if I go in on my own. That's if I get past the doorstep. You'd be better to stay outside. You can't take pics inside anyway unless they allow it, and I definitely don't think they'll be up for posing. So if you just get one of whoever comes to the door, then be there for the moment they chuck me out . . . which might not be too long after.'

'Is it safe enough for you to go in there by yourself? You've already been attacked, probably by someone connected to them.'

'I know, but it's different now. They can't do anything because the story is all over the papers. I'll be safe enough, but if I'm any more than twenty minutes, and I don't even think I'll get that long, then phone me. And if I don't answer, come and get me.'

Rosie's tone was buoyant, but inside she was edgy. She'd

felt intimidated the first time she came here, with all the elders sitting staring at her in the living room. Now they'd be beyond furious. But it would take a crazy person to attack her on a day like today, when their culture and way of life would no doubt be scrutinised by all the media, who were probably banging on Laila's grandparents' door right now. Rosie was confident they wouldn't talk, but she hadn't heard from her this morning, and there was a little twinge of worry that they were upset by the coverage in the *Post*. People often poured out their hearts to reporters, but when they saw it in black and white blasted all over the newspapers, they sometimes got cold feet. It happened. She'd dealt with it before. She pushed the niggle away. Matt pulled up and parked outside the house. Several cars were in the driveway and a couple more bumped up on the pavement as though they'd been parked in a hurry. They might have already gathered for a family crisis talk. But Rosie had the upper hand – they wouldn't have a clue how much information she had uncovered. She took a deep breath and let it out slowly. She was ready.

'Good luck, pal.'

Rosie climbed the steps and knocked on the door as she switched on the tape recorder in her coat pocket. From the corner of her eye, she saw a curtain twitch in the bay window. No answer. She knocked the door again, three emphatic hits of the knocker and listened to hear if there was any activity inside. There was the sound of several locks being turned and the door opened fully. Shah, the father, stood in front of her. Rosie instinctively glanced beyond him in time to see a couple of young girls scurry upstairs. No sign of Sabiha. At the far end of the hall, she was sure she saw Faroq slipping into the lounge, where there was a low hum of conversation.

'What do you want?'

'I want to talk to you, Mr Shah.'

'I have seen your paper today. Rubbish! You attack our people. Our family. I have nothing to say to you.'

'I have said nothing about *your* family, specifically, Mr Shah. Not yet. There is no mention of Rabia, or you, or her apparently heartbroken husband Farooq.' Rosie knew the last words had a hint of sarcasm. She hoped he got it. She was in no mood to be pushed around.

'What is this rubbish about the girl, Laila? She is the daughter of my cousin. Her marriage was arranged in the normal way. This has nothing to do with anyone except our own community.'

'Arranged? To a forty-eight-year-old man? Laila is fourteen.'

'That has nothing to do with you or your newspaper.'

She was getting more than she expected. It was good. If he'd slammed the door in her face, it would have been difficult to take things further. But as long as he was fighting back like this, she could pull him along, before she got to the real questions.

'Look, Mr Shah. Can I come in? I'm happy to report what you're saying to me – your side of things, if that's how you want to play it. Let's not stand out here on the steps where everyone can see us.'

She stood her ground. He waited a few moments and stepped back as though he was going to close the door, then, to Rosie's surprise, he gestured with a nod for her to come in.

'Some of my family are here,' he said over his shoulder as he went along the hall. 'And I can tell you that your paper will be receiving lawyers' letters from the Pakistani community. Many people are outraged.'

When Rosie entered the room, the low murmur of voices stopped, and the men inside looked at her with disgust. One of them got up and stormed past her out of the door, muttering something in Urdu. Shah called him back, but Rosie heard his footsteps in the hall and the front door open and slam shut. She wasn't intimidated this time, not like the last; she wasn't suffocated by these men. It wasn't that she didn't respect them. She didn't know enough about their lives, and the way things had been drummed into them for generations. All she knew was that they were hiding something.

'Sit. Please.'

Shah motioned her to sit in an armchair. She felt the eyes of the eight or nine men in the room burn through her. Farooq sat on a wooden stool, leaning his back against the wall, his mouth tight in his lean face.

'Can I ask you something?' Rosie looked straight at Shah. 'Where is the girl, Sabiha? The girl who brought us tea the last time I was here?'

The question hung in the air, and the men shuffled their feet and looked at Shah.

'Why are you asking that?'

'Would it be possible to see her?'

'Of course not, don't be ridiculous. Why should you ask that? What is that to do with you?'

Rosie let the silence hang for as long as she could. Farooq shifted in his chair. Shah held her stare.

'I think you know why.' Rosie looked him in the eye.

He glanced around the room and waited several seconds.

'Sabiha is busy with her children.'

'But she lives here.'

'No. At the moment she is with the family of her husband. They are living in Paisley now.'

Rosie's heart sank a little. She knew she couldn't admit that she'd spoken to her. They would know it anyway, but she couldn't give them the proof. Nearly two weeks now and nothing from Sabiha. Shah was irritating her with his obtuseness, but it was clear she would get nowhere with questions on Sabiha.

'Okay. I'd like to ask you something else.' She paused. 'Rabia . . .' Her eyes fixed on Farooq and he tried to stare back, but dropped his gaze to the floor. Rosie went into her bag. 'Farooq, I have a copy of your wedding certificate here.' She held it up. 'It says Rabia's address is in Lahore. You see? Right here?' She pointed at the line with the address.

Farooq looked at his father but said nothing.

'Yes,' Shah said. 'That is the birthplace. We had to put that on the wedding certificate.'

'And you would need the passport for the documentation for the marriage. That right?'

Shah glanced away and nodded in agreement.

Rosie pressed on.

'Where is her passport now?'

Shah looked at Farooq.

'It will be in Farooq's possession. Why?'

'Are you sure?'

'What are you getting at with these stupid questions?' He shook his head.

Farooq squirmed.

'Farooq doesn't have the passport, Mr Shah. It's gone. I think you know that. I have seen a copy of Rabia's passport, but it has a different picture.'

Shah shook his head and tried his best to look incredulous, but Rosie could see a muscle twitch in his jaw.

'I have seen it, because the truth is that criminals had it in their possession.'

She watched him in silence, then asked:

'Did you sell it?'

'What? What is this rubbish?'

Shah stood up, doing a good impression of outrage. The other men mumbled and muttered angrily.

'Throw her out,' one of them shouted.

'You can throw me out if you like,' Rosie snapped back. She stood up. 'But you don't scare or threaten me. None of you do. I want all of you to know that. And I want you know this: we are going to expose what you have done here. To Rabia. To Sabiha.'

Shah pointed to the door.

'Get out! My lawyers will speak to your editor.'

'They can speak all they like. But you know what you've done. What really happened to Rabia, Farooq? Do you want to comment on that? Did she fall? Or was she pushed?'

The men began to get to their feet, raising their voices and shouting over each other, arguing among themselves. Some of their anger was directed at Shah, but most of it was at Rosie.

'You should go now,' Shah said.

'I'm going. What are you going to do to me? Send someone to cut my throat? Because you don't scare me. You might be able to intimidate some women into silence, but there are girls like Laila who will talk to people like me. There always will be. I'm asking you again. Where is Sabiha? What has happened to her?'

'Get out! Nothing has happened! She lives with her family. I told you. Coming here and stirring up trouble.

And . . . and you go to our country and try to make us look like bad people. That is our land of our fathers. How dare you!'

'I went to find Laila. To bring her home.'

'It's not your business!' He raised his voice.

'It is,' Rosie said calmly. 'She's a fourteen-year-old Glasgow kid and she needed our help. She *asked* for our help, you know that. That is why you and her family took her to Pakistan.'

Rosie went towards the door of the room, as several of the men closed in on her. Her heart was racing.

Shah marched her along the hall to the front door and opened it up. He put his hand on her arm as he pushed her out. Rosie could see Matt taking pictures.

'How was it?' Matt asked when she get into the car.

'Er . . . I was about as welcome as a Rabbi at a Taliban fundraiser. They're raging. Tried to intimidate me as I was leaving – all these crusty old men gathering around me.'

'Aye? Did you tell them where to go?'

'I had to keep my anger in check. I felt like punching someone out. They're playing the race card. Threatening legal action . . . claiming our story is criticising their way of life. They just don't see it as we do. In their eyes, they've done nothing wrong.'

'What about the passport?'

'I could see the husband squirming in his seat about that. They're guilty of something there, but we can't really prove what, as yet. Not sure if the old father knew. We'll just have to go with the fact that it's been used by someone else. They wouldn't show it to me.' She shook her head. 'That's because they know they haven't got it.'

'Maybe they'll be a little more forthcoming with the cops.'

Rosie punched in Don's number.

'How did you get on?' he said without preamble.

'They're not exactly happy, Don. Over to you.'

'What about the passport?'

'Didn't crack a light. But when you go there, watch out for the husband, Farooq. He definitely looked worried when I mentioned it, and when I showed them the wedding certificate. But they just denied everything, then chucked me out of the house.'

'Well. We're on our way there now. Best for us to hit them straight away. And of course, we'll be much more charming than a tabloid reporter.'

'Yeah, sure you will. Good luck. Give me a shout later.' Rosie hung up.

CHAPTER TWENTY-EIGHT

Nikki looked out of the window as the farmer and his wife were coming across the yard. The wife was carrying a plate with a tea towel over it. The son followed a few yards behind in his wheelchair.

'The O'Neills are coming,' she called over her shoulder to Julie, who was chopping vegetables in the kitchen. Julie came through to the living room and watched as they approached.

'Maybe they're bringing us some lunch,' she joked. 'A wee welcome.'

'We've been here five days. They'd have done it before now. Do you think they suspect anything?'

'Don't be paranoid. We had coffee with the son the other day and he was fine. He's a lovely guy. I wonder what happened to him that he's in a wheelchair.'

'But they must wonder about us a bit, you know, with

Gordy suddenly turning up in the big motor. Maybe they think we're hookers or something.'

Nikki turned to Julie and they both burst out laughing. There was a gentle knock on the door and Julie painted on a smile as she opened it.

'Hi. How you doing?' she said, looking surprised to see them.

'Oh, hello, Julie.' The wife smiled with her eyes and leaned her head to the side to nod. 'Nikki.'

Julie waited.

'I . . . I was baking for the WRVS,' Mrs O'Neill said. 'And I've an extra Victoria sponge here. Thought it might be nice for your tea later.' She lifted the tea towel back to reveal a perfect sponge, oozing jam and cream, icing like powdered snow on top.

Julie glanced at Nikki and they both flashed bright smiles.

'How lovely!' Nikki said.

'That looks delicious. Come in.' Julie stepped back.

'Oh no . . .' Farmer O'Neill put his hand up. 'Me and Euan are up to our ears here in work, and our own lunch is nearly ready. But thanks anyway. We just wanted to hand the wee thing in to you.' He glanced at his wife, who handed the cake to Julie.

'Well . . . what can I say?' Julie enthused, patting her stomach. 'As you can see, we've not missed too many dinners, but no doubt this will get scoffed in the next couple of days.' She turned to Nikki. 'I hope we don't get any visitors.' Nikki smiled back.

There was an awkward moment as the O'Neills stood outside, not showing any signs of moving. Then she saw O'Neill kind of brace himself.

'Ladies. Er . . . talking about visitors, before we go, I wondered if I could have a quick word.'

'Of course.' Julie looked puzzled. 'Anything wrong?'

'Well,' O'Neill shifted in his feet, the colour rising a little on his neck. 'The visitor yesterday – the bloke in the Jag . . .'

Nikki felt a little dig of tension in her stomach. She didn't dare look at Julie.

'Is he a close friend?'

'Not close as such, Mr O'Neill,' Julie answered quickly. 'But we've known him for a while. He was just dropping by.' She hesitated, a look of concern on her face. 'Is it okay to have the odd visitor? We don't expect a trail of visitors, we're enjoying the quiet here.'

'Aye, of course, but that bloke. He was quite insulting to me and my son. Quite intimidating, actually.'

Nikki cursed under her breath. Trust that big bastard to open his mouth and bully somebody. He couldn't help being a complete arsehole. She bit her lip and prayed Julie would be able to think on her feet.

'Oh him? He's a bit of a cave-dweller sometimes. Sorry about that. He wouldn't mean any harm by it. I'll have a serious word with him.' She grimaced. 'Sometimes he just comes out with things and he doesn't even engage his brain.' She looked at the son, who stared back. 'I'm sure he'll be happy to apologise. It's not as if he's going to be a regular. Though he might back in the next few days, and then that will be it. I'll make it clear to him that he can't go around insulting people – especially yourselves. I'm very sorry.'

O'Neill didn't look like he was for shifting, and Nikki was beginning to get nervous.

'Look,' he finally said. 'It's none of our business. I mean, you've rented the house and it's up to you what you do and who you have round here. But I just want to be clear. I don't want any trouble here. That big bloke looked to me like a gangster or something.'

The silence hung for two beats. Julie shifted her grip on the cake tray and raised her hand dismissively.

'Listen, Mr O'Neill. Don't worry. There will be no trouble. I promise you.' She paused. 'Are you sure you're okay with us being here? We're really happy. It's a great house. But I mean . . . if there's a problem . . .'

Nikki saw the wife jab a not very subtle elbow into her man's ribs.

'No. There's no problem,' she said. 'James was just a little annoyed at your visitor. His attitude. He was rude to Euan. But really, you're fine here, and to be honest, it suits us to rent the house as it brings a bit more money in. With Euan not able to work now to the same extent, things can get a bit tight.'

O'Neill glared at his wife.

'Martha, don't be telling people our life story, for Christ's sake.'

She looked at the ground, embarrassed.

'Anyway,' O'Neill said. 'As long as everything's alright, ladies, and you're fine here, and you're not in any trouble . . .'

Nikki detected a look in his eye. He knew something.

'No, thanks. We're all good here.'

Nikki could barely keep her face straight at Julie's performance. She was so jovial, she could have been serving tea on the WRVS stall.

'Oh well. Enjoy the cake!'

'You bet. Thanks a million!'

The two of them watched as the O'Neill's headed across the yard and up the path. When they were out of earshot, Nikki nudged Julie.

'That old bugger is suspicious. I told you. '

'Nah, don't worry. Let's get our lunch and then we can get wired into this baby.'

James O'Neill cleared his plate and pushed it away from him. He gave his mouth a wipe with the square of kitchen roll his wife had left as a napkin and pushed his chair back.

'Right. That's me fed and watered. Now I'd better go and do the same for the pigs, before they start squealing.'

'Will I help you, Da?' Euan soaked the remains of the baked beans up with a chunk of crusty bread.

'No, son. You just batter into those accounts this afternoon, so we can see where we are. I'll manage myself. I need to go and check the silage tank as well.'

'Alright.'

James grabbed his padded jacket off the hook in the back porch, but he could still see Euan sitting staring down at the table. He could read his son's mind and immediately felt a stab of guilt. Maybe he should have just told him to come out and help with feeding the pigs. But it was freezing outside, and Euan in the wheelchair was chilled to the bone within five minutes because he wasn't able to move around the way he used to. Time was when he'd have been working in the dead of winter with his shirt sleeves rolled up, and wouldn't even feel the cold because he was moving from one task to the other like a machine. It broke his heart to look at him now, a broken man and not yet thirty. He would never stride in from the fields on a Friday afternoon and head for the shower, then come back out looking like a strapping film star ready for action. A handsome and talented rugby player whose name was first on the team sheet every Saturday, Euan was the glint in the eye of every eager girl at the Young Farmers' nights. But look at him now. At least he was alive, James had to keep reminding himself in his darker moments. But it killed him to watch his brain-damaged son struggling to form certain words. One time he'd seen him in tears with frustration when he'd watched through Euan's bedroom door as he'd tried time and again to stand up, each time falling on the floor. He didn't even have the heart to go in and pick him up, because he knew it would make him feel worse.

But at least Euan had survived the awful night when the thugs nearly kicked him to death outside some club in Glasgow where he and his mates had gone while out on the town for a stag party. For three months, Martha had more or less lived at the hospital at his bedside, willing him to come out of the coma. His teammates and farmer pals all rallied round and visited every day. But in time the visits trailed off and it was just him and Martha. When their son woke up, Martha claimed it was a miracle and that her prayers to some saint or other had been answered. But what they got back was what was left of Euan. The brain damage had affected the nerves that operated his legs. He would never walk again. That was how the surgeon had put it, in stark simple terms. His son's life as he knew it was over. He had had to learn to speak again, and even now, four years on, he still had difficulty. His mind was sharp as a tack, but the communication was sometimes a problem. Any girlfriends who visited initially had come and gone, because the big lad they all fancied wasn't there any more. He was now a weaker, thinner version, losing his hair, forever dependent on his parents. And money was tighter too. James couldn't afford to take on another farmhand so he doubled his own work, but had to leave a couple of fields just for silage and cattle feed. Even the pigs, which didn't seem such hard work before, were now more difficult to deal with. The machine ground down all the waste so it was just a matter of feeding them, but it was time-consuming, as it used to be Euan who went out with the van, picking up all the discarded foodstuff and waste from various shops, restaurants and houses.

James went into the pig yard, then through into the back of the building where the machine was. The pigs followed him, bumping into him, nipping at his wellies and he jerked his feet, kicking them out of the way. He switched on the lever and collected some food, then scattered it into the troughs, watching them. When he came outside to the yard he stood gazing across at the afternoon growing greyer, the sky full of rain. He saw the girls switch on the light on the cottage. They seemed nice enough. Euan had stayed there before the attack, but it was more convenient with his disability for him to move back to the house with his parents. He pondered, not for the first time, who the women were. They didn't seem to go to work. He'd wondered at first if they were a couple of lesbians who wanted to be away from everyone. Or maybe they were shady characters in hiding? But he told himself couldn't be thinking of all sorts of crap like that. Live and let live – though he was seriously raging at that big bastard who pushed him around the other day. Who did he think he was? Some slimy fucker in a shiny suit and a big car coming onto his property and sneering at him! If Euan had been fit he'd have decked him straight away, and a few years ago James might have knocked him out himself for his cheek. But he had to stand there and take it now. Shame washed over him. That's what was burning his gut more than anything since yesterday. Then, a thought came to him. That girl Nikki with the half arm all bandaged. It must have been some kind of accident, he'd assumed when he first saw her. But something was at the back of his mind about a girl with an arm cut off, and he couldn't get it out of his mind. Now he remembered. There had been a story in the *Post* a few weeks ago about some girl found on the motorway near Glasgow with her arm cut off. She'd nearly died. Could that be her? He remembered the police saying they were trying to identify her. Perhaps it was just his vivid imagination, but with that big guy turning up yesterday . . . He walked towards his house. Maybe he should phone the cops anonymously and ask if they'd found the girl yet. Just out of curiosity.

CHAPTER TWENTY-NINE

Ezra Berkley's shop was tucked away at the far end of Glasgow's Argyle Arcade, the last in a line of jewellers whose windows sparkled with glittering promises. Diamond engagement rings – solitaires, two-and-a-twist or three-in-a-straight – twinkled under the lights alongside eternity rings declaring that love would never die. Ezra Berkley's shop wouldn't be the place where eager young girls dragged their boyfriends to savour the delights in the window, though – there were many other shopfronts that looked more attractive than his little place. But Gordy MacLean knew that Ezra's customers were not the kind who browsed for gifts. Ezra was a fence who could shift a gold Rolex watch or a diamond ring before its rightful owner even noticed it was missing. It was a family dynasty for the portly little man. They used to say that Ezra's father, Ave, had moved more stolen jewellery than any of the Nazis had plundered from Jewish homes in the bad old days. Ave

Berkley was a Holocaust survivor who saw his family per-ish in the concentration camp at Treblinka, and anyone who got close enough to call him a friend would listen respectfully as he re-lived his darkest days. He never forgot them, and he made sure his son Ezra didn't either. Gordy remembered his father taking him into the shop when he was only nine years old. Ave had told him that he was his age when the Nazis took him and his family from the ghetto where they'd been living in squalor. Gordy had sat wide-eyed, enthralled, listening along with Ezra, a couple of years older than him. Ezra used to nod gravely, proud that this was who they were, and this was why they were the chosen people. At his young age, Gordy had never quite understood that part. Gordy's father used to bring Ave the proceeds of armed robberies – rings, bracelets and watches – and he would examine them, and pay whatever sum they agreed. By the time the police had come to investigate, the place was clean as a whistle and Ave would be hunched over his table, eyeglass fixed to his face, as if he'd been born that way. Gordy's father had always told him that the old Jew would never sell him down the river at any price, but he had to remember: Ave wasn't in this to make friends. He was a fence, and a good one, and money was his only game. As long as he never forgot that.

Now as Gordy slipped into the shop, he could see through to the back office where Ezra was sitting in exactly the same way his father had. The teenage boy at the counter nodded to Gordy and disappeared into the back.

'Gordy, ma boy. Come in.' Ezra's husky, jovial voice came through from the office.

Gordy lifted the clip on the underside of the counter and went behind.

'Daniel,' Ezra said to his son, without even looking up. 'Make us some tea, boy.'

Ezra turned around, taking his eyeglass out. His heavy features crinkled into a smile. His silver hair was slicked back in waves, his widow's peak cutting into his deep furrowed forehead and leathery complexion from long holidays in Tel Aviv.

'How are you, Gordy? It's been a while.' Ezra cleared a leather chair piled with papers and boxes so he could sit down.

'I know, Ezra. I've been so busy with the club and stuff. Few wee business deals here and there – and the property stuff is building up well.'

'You'll soon be for the easy life on the Costa then, my friend.'

'Yeah. One of these fine days. If I'm honest, I'm ready for it sooner rather than later. I'm puffed out with all this shit now. Too many pricks around – Turks, Albanians and all these fuckers from Eastern Europe. They want a slice of everything nowadays.'

'Yes, I know. I've had a couple of Russians in here looking

to buy, but I won't deal with them. I don't know who these people are. I don't need to do business with men who might get me killed. I'm ready to retire too. Soon, I hope.'

Daniel came in and put the mugs of coffee on the table, along with a small jug of milk. Ezra reached up to a shelf and brought down a small white bowl of sugar.

'I'm supposed to be off it.' He put his finger to his lips. 'Rina . . . She's always at me to lose the stomach.' He patted his round belly. 'So. Tell me your story, Gordy. What you got for me? I'm looking forward to this. You were so vague on the phone.'

'I know, mate. But you never know who's listening.'

Ezra nodded.

'I hate to talk on the phone about business.'

Gordy went into his pocket and pulled out the small envelope and reached inside to bring out the handkerchief. He unfolded it and placed it on the table.

Ezra looked at the small whiteish lump, squinting, but didn't touch it. He took a sip of his coffee. Then he reached for his eyeglass, glancing across to Gordy before he put it in. He pursed his lips.

'My, my . . . What kind of people are you dancing with these days, Gordy?'

Gordy didn't answer for a moment, but Ezra waited.

'I acquired it,' he eventually said. 'There's more of them. Rough diamonds.'

Ezra gave a wry smile.

'I *know* what it is. But what I don't know, is why? Why do you have this? Or these, if, as you say, there are more.'

'There *are* more. Quite a lot more, I think.'

'Are you in the smuggling game these days?'

'No.' Gordy shifted in his seat. 'Come on, Ezra. Just look at the fucking thing. Put me out of my misery here.'

Ezra snorted, his lips curling. He leaned over his table.

'I know before I even lift it that it looks good.'

Gordy felt a little glow in his gut.

'Yeah?'

'Let me have a look.'

Ezra picked it up between his thumb and forefinger, then placed it in the palm of his hand and rolled it over a few times with his finger. Then he lifted it again and put it close to his eye. Gordy was barely breathing as he watched him in anticipation. Ezra said nothing, just kept turning it around, making little noises through his nose as he concentrated. Then he lifted a small blade next to him and scraped the stone a little, then polished it. All the time, Gordy sat like an expectant father. He fought the urge to get up and pace the room. He'd no idea really how many more of these there were, because Vanner had been vague about it, but there were obviously more than half a dozen if he was in this much of a lather to get them back.

Eventually, Ezra put the diamond back down and sat back. He let out a soft whistle.

'She's a little beauty. She will either make you happy, or put a nail in your coffin.'

Gordy looked at him, surprised.

'What you saying that for, man?'

'Because, unless you are in the smuggling business, then I can guarantee that someone is looking for this – and the others.'

'Fuck!' Gordy said shocked. 'What do you mean?'

'Word gets around. Something valuable goes missing, it's not just the cops who come here looking for it. The victim sometimes comes too, to give me a message.'

'Tell me.'

'Johnny Vanner.'

Gordy felt as though he'd been punched in the stomach. He could feel his whole body deflating. Surely he hadn't walked into a fucking trap here?

'Fuck me!'

'Oh, I think so, Gordy. But not in a good way.'

'So. How do you know? Has Vanner been in touch?'

'Not him. Not personally. That piece of shit knows better than that. But, let's just say I got the gypsy warning from one of his people. I got a phone call a few days ago, saying that some goods belonging to one of his associates had gone missing. Stolen, he said. And now there is all sorts of heat on Vanner.' He shrugged. 'Like I bloody care about him.'

Gordy felt a little relieved. Even if Ezra's life depended

on it, he would never do a deal with Johnny Vanner. Ezra hadn't forgiven him for the day he'd walked in here fifteen years ago and slapped his father up and down the room, calling him an ugly little Yid who should have been gassed by the Nazis. Vanner had been chasing some stolen jewellery then too, that had been robbed from him, even though it was he who did the initial armed robbery, leaving a man and a woman to die of dehydration after being tied up in their bedroom for two weeks. Someone must have told him that the jewels had been moved to the fence in Glasgow, and Vanner didn't even stop to ask or reason. As it happened, Ave had never even seen the haul. But Ezra had never forgotten the humiliation and how his father couldn't fight back. He had fought so long in the concentration camps that he was too tired to fight any more.

'So,' Gordy said. 'What do you think?'

'Well. I will give you my professional assessment first. You probably won't understand it, so let me explain. A rough diamond this size, as you see, looks like nothing. But a lot of it is in the colour. They come in brown, sandy-coloured and white. Like this. White is the most valuable. I have to cut and examine it to see how deep it is, look at the facets. But from what I can see here, you have at least one clean carat in here. And once I get to that and shape it, it will be worth about twenty to twenty-five thousand alone.' He raised his eyebrows. 'What do the others look like?'

'I don't know. I haven't seen them.'

'So you don't have them.'

'No. Not yet. But I'm getting them in the next couple of days.'

Ezra breathed in and sat back, clasping his hands across his stomach, steepling his two forefingers.

'Its not my business, but who has them?'

'Don't ask. It's irrelevant. I'm getting them. That's all that matters. So what was the message? I mean, what did Vanner's man say?' Gordy knew he sounded anxious.

'I was told there had been a robbery, and that maybe someone would come to me and make me an offer. He said if I touched this stuff they would cut my hands off. Those were his words. He said if anyone came, I had to call them immediately, because one day, they would find out if I had touched them, and by that time it would be too late.'

'Usual heavy duty shite.'

'Yes, in a manner of speaking.'

'So. What do you think?' Gordy scrutinised Ezra's face, his pale grey eyes, wondering if he could see betrayal anywhere in there.

'I think it is a very dangerous game to play.'

'But one that could make us very rich.'

'I'm already rich.'

'But I'm talking big rich. Listen, Ezra. If there are, say, maybe ten or even fifteen of these little beauties, that's big bucks, right?'

Ezra nodded.

'Shifting them is the issue, though.'

'Well. You're the man for that. Can you do it? Will you look at them for me, when I pick the rest of them up? I'll cut you in big time – more than just expenses and payment for the work.'

'I know you will, Gordy. I trust you on that.' He looked at the framed photograph of his father back in Poland. 'I despise Vanner. You know that.'

Gordy nodded.

'Then let's fuck him.'

They sat in silence, both of them looking at the diamond.

Gordy felt a little spring in his step as he walked out of the Argyle Arcade and along the street, turning left to where Terry was parked in the Jag. Things were looking up. He knew he'd have to pay through the nose to weigh Ezra in for moving the diamonds, and even though he didn't know the size of the pot himself yet, he got the feeling there was plenty to go around. These two tarts back in the farmhouse, pontificating like mobsters, hadn't a clue what was coming to them. But they deserved all they got. Ideas above their station, making him sign over his beloved club, talking down to him. He opened the passenger door and got inside, immediately noticing the worried frown on Terry's face.

'Boss,' Terry said, glancing up as he eased the car up

Renfield Street and stopped at the traffic lights. 'We've got a problem.'

Gordy looked at him, as Terry flicked open the glovebox and brought out a mobile phone.

'What?' Gordy asked, irritated. He wasn't in the mood for bad news.

'Paul's mobile. He must have left it here when I gave him a lift to the club this morning.' He hesitated, scrolling down the recent calls. 'It just rang. I didn't answer it.' He showed Gordy the screen. 'Johnny fucking Vanner,' Terry said, matter-of-fact.

'What? You're fucking joking!' Gordy snatched the phone from his hand, staring at the screen in disbelief. 'In the name of fuck! I don't fucking believe this! When did it ring?'

'About ten minutes ago. I was going to come and get you, but I didn't want to interrupt you.'

'Shut up a minute!' Gordy said, his mind a blur as he studied the mobile's menu and checked outgoing calls. The rage rose in his face like a fireball as he screeched, 'The scheming wee cunt! He's been phoning Vanner! Fucking twice in the last two days. I'll kill the cunt. Stone fucking dead, I'll kill him!' He wanted to smash the phone to pieces, but his walnut dashboard cost too much to damage. 'I'm going to ram this fucking phone right up his arse. Where is he?'

'I left him in the club, like you said, Gordy. He was

stocking the shelves and cleaning the floors. Brian was going down to make sure he wasn't spending any time on his own or he'd have his fingers in the till. We know what a thieving wee cunt he is.'

'Pull over here for a minute,' MacLean snapped at Terry. 'Get Brian on the phone.'

Terry stopped the car, picked up his mobile and punched in Brian's number. When it was ringing he passed it to Gordy.

'Brian. It's me. Listen, don't react to this. Don't say a word and listen good. Is that wee fucker Paul in there? Just aye or no. Right. Good. Get him to go into my office – just tell him to pick up a folder or something. Then lock him in. Understand? Then I want you to take the keys, lock every door and window and lock the door from the outside. I want that wee cunt locked in the place. I'll be down in five minutes. Just you get off your mark when you've done what I say. Okay?'

He turned to Terry. 'Right. Let's go.'

Suddenly, Paul's mobile rang, and they both sat staring at it on the dashboard. It was the number of the call box in the club. They let it ring.

'Wee bastard's obviously just discovered he's lost his phone.' Gordy's lips curled into a sneer.

'What a silly cunt!' Terry said. 'He'll be shitting himself.'

'He'll be shitting blood when I'm finished with him.'

Gordy could feel his heart thumping, a mixture of rage, anxiety and adrenalin, as minutes later Terry eased the Jag into the reserved space outside the front door of the club. He took a deep breath and tried to calm himself. He needed to deal with this coldly and clinically, without making a song and dance about it. He didn't need to ask why Paul was phoning Vanner or Vanner was phoning him. It was staring him in the face. He was double-crossing him. After everything he'd done for the wee bastard, weighing in that leech of a money-lender Paul had got up to his arse in debt with. He'd done it, not out of some big hand of generosity, but because he was a useful wee sneak to have around, and Gordy knew he'd be forever in his debt, doing his bidding at every turn. This is how he repays him. He didn't need to ask him why he'd phoned Vanner, but he as sure as fuck was going to get it from his lips before he battered the shite out of him.

Gordy got out and fumbled in his jacket pocket for the keys, unlocking the main shutter and then the heavy double doors. Terry was at his back. Inside, the club was in darkness, depressing when you saw how vibrant and busy it was at night with the lights and colours and music blaring. He walked softly across the wooden dance floor to the steps at the far side and climbed up to his office, Terry behind him. They both stood outside the locked door, Gordy breathing hard from the exertion of the stairs and the excitement. He put the key in the lock and pushed the door open, fast. Paul, his face the colour of death, was in the corner. Gordy walked in and stood for a moment, letting the silence hang, watching.

'Where's Brian?' Paul's voice sounded shaky. 'He told me to come in here and pick up a yellow folder and then the stupid bastard locked me in.'

Gordy said nothing. Paul gave him an edgy look, then looked down at the floor. He couldn't look either of them in the eye. Gordy went into his jacket pocket and pulled out the mobile. He stepped forward, slapping it on his desk so hard that Paul jumped.

'Your mobile,' he said. 'You left it in Terry's car. You've got a missed call there.'

With each word, Paul's body crumpled a bit more and Gordy could see his legs actually shaking.

'Pick it up,' Gordy said.

Paul looked at him, then Terry.

'Fucking pick it up, I said.'

Paul stretched a trembling hand across the table and picked up the phone, barely able to hold it.

'Now go into your missed calls and read the last call you didn't get.'

Paul looked at the screen, the mobile trembling in his hands. He did nothing.

'Do it, you wee prick!'

Paul scrolled down, then his legs slightly buckled and he steadied himself against the metal filing cabinet.

'Read it out!'

Paul swallowed, his Adam's apple moving up and down like a golf ball.

'Read it!'

'J-Johnny V-Vanner.'

'Louder!'

'Jo-Johnny Va-Vanner,' Paul stammered, glancing from one to the other.

'Johnny Vanner. Calling you. And as you'll see, last night you also called him. Twice.'

'I . . . I don't know, Gordy. Honest . . . Fuck me, man! I just don't know how the fuck that happened. It's not me who was calling him. Somebody must have had my phone. Or . . . Or . . . I mean, it must be a mistake. I didn't even know I had his number.' He looked at Terry. 'How did I get Johnny's number in here?' His lip quivered so much he could hardly speak.

Terry rolled his eyes to the ceiling. Gordy felt a little switch go off somewhere inside his brain. He'd heard enough. More than enough of this little shit trying to squirm his way out of it. Stupid, thick bastard thought he could play with the big boys. A coldness ran through him. He'd felt it before, that surge of adrenalin like a rush of blood to his head, so that he almost felt high and detached from what he was doing. He'd felt it the first time as a kid in the caravan site, when he would have beaten the bigger boy to death if they hadn't dragged him off. And over the years when he'd battered or shot someone – point blank in the face if that's how it happened – he was almost on automatic pilot. In total control of his movements, but unable to stop. In two strides Gordy was at his desk and into the right-hand drawer. He brought out the Glock, the weight and the metal feeling good in his sweaty palm.

'Aw fuck, Gordy! Please! I'm sorry . . . I'm so sorry. I just got into bother . . . I dropped over a grand the other night at the racing, and I owe some bad people a lot of money. They were going to do me in . . .' The words came out between sobs, saliva and snot dripping from his mouth. A dark patch spread across the front of his jeans.

'Shut the fuck up! What did you tell him, you prick?'

'Nothing! I don't *know* nothing!'

'Lying bastard! Did you tell him where the birds were staying?'

Nothing.

'You've got five seconds to answer. The truth!'

'Okay. Okay . . . I told him where they were. I'm sorry. I'm sorry. I'll make it up to you. Please—'

Gordy didn't wait for a response or a final plea. He lifted the gun and fired. Paul's chest exploded and blood splashed back onto Gordy's clothes and onto his desk. He watched as Paul slumped against the wall and then slid down to the floor, blood pumping out of his torso. Gordy had done it without thinking too hard. It was the only way. You dealt with it and you moved on.

'Fucking arsehole!' Gordy put the gun back in the drawer and closed it.

'Get Brian back in, Terry,' he said 'You guys get this shit off my floor and get rid of him once it's dark. Do it before the club opens later. Alright?'

'Sure, boss.' Terry took out his mobile and punched in a number.

CHAPTER THIRTY

It hadn't been a hugely successful confrontation, Rosie concluded, as she and Matt went through the revolving doors and into the foyer of the *Post*. Apart from the few good pictures he'd snapped of her getting manhandled out of the Shah household, there wasn't much that would take the story forward. She was hoping Don and his DCI would lean on them enough for someone in the house to burst. Right now, the first of two interviews with Laila, back home and talking about her plans for the future, would have to be good enough. She still had to put it together for the spread. The teenager's father had hot-footed it to Pakistan to sort her out when he'd heard she'd absconded. He'd probably been in mid-air at the same time as they were en route back to Glasgow. That, in particular, felt good, but Rosie wouldn't be happy until she'd nailed someone over Rabia's death.

'Hey, Rosie, you've not half upset our Asian brothers.'

Jean the receptionist greeted them with an indignant face. 'These phones have been red-hot with complaints.'

'Really?' Rosie grimaced. 'Sorry, Jean.'

'Great story, though. Actually one or two of the phone-ins were in support. I fielded all the calls up to Editorial.'

'Great, thanks. I'll see what's happening in a minute.'

As she and Matt stepped onto the editorial floor, at least three reporters looked up from their desks, where they had been furiously taking notes. Judging by their frustrated expressions, they'd been getting pelters all morning. It happened sometimes, if a front page had been controversial or ruffled a few feathers. Some would predictably be spitting rage, but in Rosie's experience, plenty more callers backed the *Post* for having the balls to tackle the big issues. She went across to her desk and dumped her bag, fishing out her notebook.

'I hear it's been a bit busy,' she said to Declan as he put the phone down.

'Aye. Just a bit, Rosie. I've taken about twenty calls myself. I don't think we're too popular out in Little Karachi this morning . . . or even the real Karachi.' He grinned. 'You might need to go into hiding, like Salman Rushdie.'

'Oh dear,' Rosie said, half joking. 'Are they all angry, or is there anyone, I mean of a Pakistani type, who thinks the story was good?'

'Oh yeah. Quite a few actually. Women. No men. None of the callers would be identified, but I've got some good lines, and a few women talking about their own experiences. Some good stuff.'

'Hmm. But without names, it's not great. We'll just be accused of making it up. I'll have to speak to McGuire and see how he wants to play it.'

As she said it, her desk phone rang.

'Hi, Marion.'

'I've been watching for you. Mick says to come straight through.'

She made a here-we-go face at Declan as she picked up her notebook and pen.

'Showtime!'

Rosie knocked once on the door and walked in. She wasn't that surprised to see the managing editor, Jack Weaver, sitting on a chair opposite McGuire. It was clearly not a social visit, because the paper's lawyer, Tommy Hanlon, was sitting on the sofa, throwing her the kind of mischievous look he did when they were all in the shit.

'Do I sense a little problem, chaps?' Rosie raised her eyebrows, half smiling.

'Just a bit. Sit down, Rosie.' McGuire gestured her to the sofa.

'We expected a bit of aggro,' Weaver said. 'But it's a bit more than that, so we're having a chat on how we respond.'

'So what's happened? The troops say there's been a lot of phone calls.'

'Yeah. To Editorial, to here, and to the MD's office.'

'Why are people phoning him?'

'It's through the Pakistani Association. I think he was at a dinner there last year, so he made a lot of contacts.'

'Aye. Well, he'll not be asked back this year, then,' Hanlon quipped.

Rosie tried to keep her face straight.

'Declan tells me a few calls were also supportive,' she said. 'Mostly women saying they agree with the story and the girl's plight. Some telling their own stories. No names though . . . Well, they're hardly going to be posing for pictures if they're in an unhappy situation.'

'True. But it's good that we're getting both sides. We'll pick the best of them today and do some kind of story to go with the main Laila-back-home interview. We've got to stand our ground.' He gave the managing editor a look that was bordering on defiance.

'Of course we do, Mick,' the managing editor replied. 'But we also need to put some balance on tomorrow. We—'

'The story was balanced today, Jack,' Rosie interrupted. 'We didn't even do a leader on it. All I did was tell the story the way it unfolded.'

'Well, it's caused outrage.'

'That's tough shit. People don't like it when their way of life is questioned.' Rosie spread her hands. 'But we were a hundred per cent right.' She gave McGuire a pleading look. 'Guys, we're not going to start backtracking here, are we? Not after the kind of stuff we had about the stoning in

Swat, and the more-or-less kidnapping of a wee girl to get married to some old geezer in the middle of nowhere. We're in the clear here.'

'No, no,' McGuire waved his hand. 'But we've had a lawyer's letter from the Pakistani Association. They're taking it to the Press Complaints Commission.'

'Big deal.' Rosie snorted.

'It still needs to be dealt with, Rosie. So I'll need you to write your account,' Hanlon said.

'My account was all over the paper today,' Rosie replied, more belligerent than she meant to be.

Hanlon sat forward, more businesslike than friendly now.

'I mean, how you got the story. How you pursued it. What the leads were. We have to be seen to be totally clean here, or they'll accuse us of harassment.'

'Harassment? That's good coming from them. Tell that to Laila. If it weren't for us, she'd have woken up this morning with some old bastard grunting on top of her – if you'll excuse the graphic image. If anyone was harassed, it was her. Come on, for Christ's sake, lads!'

Hanlon chortled under his breath.

'Look. What we'll do is defend this rigorously. You know that, Rosie. Once you write your account, I'll fire a letter back to them. We'll wait to see what the PCC says. We can't react until they contact us, but I want to be ready.'

'And that's not all,' the managing editor said.

He had the kind of hangdog face that was made for

delivering bad news. 'We've had a call from over a dozen newsagents across the country saying they're stopping taking the *Post*. That'll spread.'

'Well, that's just stupid if they do that. They'll lose money,' Rosie said.

'They've threatened it anyway.'

'Have Distribution got contingency plans?' Rosie looked from McGuire to Weaver.

'Yes. We've still got plenty of retailers onside at the moment. But we're going to put some vendors on the street,' Weaver said.

'Plus, this will get plenty of publicity,' McGuire said. 'It already has. Breakfast TV was holding up our front page this morning, and all the papers will follow it today. We're clean on this. Aren't we, Rosie?'

'Of course. I'm not even worried.' She shrugged.

What she wanted to say was that the angry mob would soon be silenced when she officially reported to the police that she was attacked outside her flat by some headcase who threatened to cut her throat just because she was trying to do her job. She didn't want to mention it right now because it had only been between her and McGuire. The managing editor would explode if he knew that the editor had sent Rosie to Pakistan on a dangerous mission, after she'd already been attacked investigating the same story. He was always covering his back in case a reporter came back at any stage, claiming they weren't given proper help or counselling by the newspaper after some traumatic experience. But Rosie knew the moment she went public with the information it would have a serious impact. If they wanted a fight, the gloves were off.

Rosie was running late for her meeting with Don in the coffee shop at the bottom of Great Western Road. Her sit-down interview with Laila and her mum and grandparents had been more of a human story than an explosive one. But she hoped it would quell a lot of the anger in the Pakistani community over this morning's revelations. She was surprised when Laila's grandfather, an orthopaedic surgeon at the city's Western Infirmary, shook her hand and congratulated her for exposing what he called a 'sham' marriage when she'd arrived at their home. His own parents, he told her, had also come from the Swat Valley a generation ago and moved to Karachi before the family emigrated to the UK when he was six years old. He had been brought up at a time when Swat was a beautiful part of Pakistan and tourists flocked to it. Now, he said, it was a hotbed of Islamist fanatics. Much of the community in Glasgow had turned their backs on his part of the family long before Laila's arranged marriage, and he was prepared to keep it that way. Plenty of other Muslims in Glasgow and Scotland felt the same way as him about throwing their children into a marriage they didn't want. The interview had gone well, and with the other calls to the *Post* from women telling their own stories on both sides, Rosie was satisfied she had a balanced spread for tomorrow's paper.

Don was already waiting for her at the cafe when she arrived. He looked up and smiled when she walked in.

'Sorry I'm late. I had a big interview to write up, and it took longer than I expected.'

'No problem. Great story today, pal. But you are definitely not popular. Remind me never to go for a curry with you again.'

Rosie chuckled as she sat down and slipped off her coat. The waitress came up and she ordered a decaff white coffee. Don ordered another black.

'So how did it go?'

Don sat back and smiled broadly.

'I'm about to make your day, sunshine.'

'Really? I can't wait. Did they buckle under the stiff questioning of Strathclyde's finest detectives?'

'Not quite. But we did we get lucky.' He paused. 'And I'm going to need your full cooperation on this – sooner rather than later.'

Rosie shot him a puzzled look.

'Cooperation? What do you mean?'

'I need you to make a formal complaint about the knife attack at your house.'

Rosie raised her eyebrows, still not sure.

'How come?'

'Well. Here's the situation. We were at the Shah household and everyone was getting a little hot under the collar. But of course, as you know, we didn't have a whole lot to go on – much the same as yourself, except we had more documentation. I could sense unease around the room – a few of the guys were beginning to argue amongst themselves and I got the feeling they were trying to blame each other. We didn't get all that far, but I do know they're beginning to feel the pressure. So, softly softly, as they say. We're making our way to the door, telling them we'll be back, when suddenly we spot some guy coming out of a car and up the path. His face is showing all the signs of having been recently battered to a pulp.' A playful grin on his face. 'You get my drift?'

'I do.' Rosie smiled.

'So, me and the gaffer look at each other, and we're both thinking the same thing. Then over our shoulder Mr Shah shouts something in Urdu, and the guy with the bashed face shits himself, and about turns, back to his car.'

'Jesus. It must be him.'

'Yep. So we had to fuck with the rules a bit. And this is the part where the old-fashioned police work takes precedence over protocol.'

'Meaning what?'

'Meaning that we went in hot pursuit of this bastard – as you know, all evidence is pointing to him being the main suspect in your knife attack. But, of course, as you also know, we don't have an official complaint yet from the victim.'

Rosie nodded.

'I see.'

'So we shouldn't have been chasing him. But that's not how we do business. This had to be the suspect, so we chased him, all the way out of the Southside and into Rutherglen towards Whitlawburn, and forced him off the road.'

'Oh Christ!'

'Then my gaffer, who isn't known for his political correctness, drags him out of the car by the scruff of the neck.'

'So did he burst?'

'I'm coming to it, Gilmour. Don't waste my story!'

'So what happened?'

'The boss tells him in no uncertain terms that he's nicked. That we have him on CCTV from your attack, which of course we don't, but he doesn't know that. And he gets told we're taking him in for fingerprinting. We need to see if his prints match the knife.'

'So you took him in your car?'

'Yeah. He was screaming for a lawyer all the way in, but we told him he was looking at five years in the pokey as he was facing attempted murder and resisting arrest . . . Okay we gilded it a bit.'

'Just a bit.'

'Anyway, we took him in. Got his prints. And, hey presto, they match the knife.'

'Oh, you beauty!'

'Thank you. But, therein lies the problem.'

'What did he say?'

'He said nothing. Demanded a lawyer. We were in a bit of a sticky situation about that, so we had to let him go. We can't have a lawyer coming in and asking to see the official complaint, because there isn't one.'

Rosie let out a sigh.

'I see. So what do we do now?'

'We'll find a way round it. We can say you couldn't make the official complaint as you were leaving the country, but that you told me about it. A good lawyer will drive a horse and cart through it if it comes to court, but we've got to give it a try. Plus, even if it goes nowhere, it will give us the leverage we need just now, because the mob back at Shah's house were clearly shitting themselves. And if they really did send him out to do you over, then they'll all be worried that he grasses them up.'

Rosie nodded.

'It's brilliant, Don. Just getting his prints to match . . . I'm sure you'll be able to build a case.' Rosie smiled. 'It won't be the first time I've interviewed a crook who claims he was fitted up by the cops!'

'We would never do that, Miss Gilmour.'

'Of course not.'

'So I'll talk to my boss and we'll work out a way to get the complaint done. But you need to come along today as soon as possible and make it official. Can you do that?'

'Sure. I'll come this afternoon.'

'Rosie. I'm glad it's given us leverage, but I really want this bastard done for attacking you. I felt like doing him myself when I saw his wee rat face. I gave him a few more bruises about his face for good measure.'

Rosie laughed.

'Of course, he'll scream self-defence when you hit him with the knife charge.'

'Sure he will. But by the time we're finished with him, I'm hoping he'll have grassed everyone up and there's more than him in the shit.'

Rosie grinned.

'Got to love a bit of make-it-up-as-you-go-along police work.'

'Has to be done sometimes.' Don stood up. 'Right, I'd better move. Give me a buzz later on when you're coming in and I'll walk you through it.'

Rosie watched as he left the cafe, buttoning her coat up as a gust of icy wind blasted in when he opened the door.

CHAPTER THIRTY-ONE

It was almost dark by the time Rosie left the police station and stepped into Matt's car.

'You'd been in there so long, I was half expecting you to come out with sergeant's stripes on your arm.' He switched on the engine and drove towards the motorway.

'I know. I thought the questions were never going to end. But that's it done now, so the cops can pick this bastard up and charge him.'

Let's keep it simple, Rosie told herself. She didn't want to tell him that she'd just made a statement to police that could get her into all sorts of trouble if the case went to trial. It wasn't that she'd had lied – not really. Only a small white lie about a minor detail. She and Don had agreed that she would say in her statement that she didn't make an official complaint at the time of the attack, but had told him as a friend. She had pleaded with him not to report it officially at that stage. Most of that was true, but when it got to the nitty-gritty of details of the second attack and how she came about having the knife in her possession, the waters began to muddy. She told them that a friend of hers had saved her, but when they asked who it was, she couldn't tell them it was Adrian. The officer taking the notes kept looking up, from Don to his boss. The DCI asked for the friend's name. Rosie told him she couldn't say. He was just a contact. The DCI told her in no uncertain terms that a defence lawyer would piss all over that if she were in the witness box. Why couldn't she name him, he asked again? She just couldn't, she told them. Don and his boss both knew that she had some mysterious Bosnian contact who'd been responsible for the two dead bodies in the Glasgow flat in her last brush with the cops. But if they dragged that up, all sorts of shit would hit the fan. Let sleeping dogs lie, she told them. Her attacker wouldn't go to trial, she assured them. He'd be off his head. What if he pleads self-defence, claiming your friend was going to kill him? the DCI insisted. Rosie knew he was playing devil's advocate. Let's cross that bridge when we come to it, she'd told them, with more bravado than she actually felt.

The cottage appeared to be in darkness as they drove up the single-track road and into the courtyard. The farmer's house looked dark too, but smoke swirled from the chimney. Rosie was relieved when she saw Julie's car parked outside. They got out of the car and knocked on the door. No answer. She looked at Matt, as she tried again. Still no answer.

'Maybe they've done a runner.'

'Don't think so,' Rosie said, more in hope than conviction.

'Who is it?' said Julie's voice.

Rosie shot Matt a relieved glance.

'It's me, Rosie.'

'Right. Hold on.'

The door was unlocked and opened and Julie stood there, looking a bit paler and more tired than she had before.

'Come in.'

Rosie stepped inside, followed by Matt.

'Anything wrong, Julie? You look worried.'

Julie puffed her cheeks out and her confident look reappeared.

'What could possibly go wrong, Rosie? We're holed up in the middle of nowhere with a dead man's stash of smuggled diamonds, a load of passports and a few grand. All going great here.' She went into the kitchen. 'We've just eaten. You want some tea or coffee?'

'Tea would be great,' Rosie said. 'Black. No sugar.'

'Tea for me. The same,' Matt said.

Rosie glanced at Nikki on the sofa, who turned the TV down with the remote. She looked exhausted.

'You okay, Nikki?'

'Aye, well . . . Just a bit worried and stuff.' She brushed

her hand over her bandaged stump. 'I'm shitting myself, to be honest. About tomorrow . . . I . . . I wish we could just bugger off before big Gordy comes. I don't think we can trust him.'

'We can't do a runner. He'd hunt us down for the rest of our lives.' Julie came in carrying a tray. 'We can't, Nikki. We've got to go through with it now. If we do it this way, he'll be in the pokey before tomorrow night and we'll be long gone.' Julie looked at Rosie. 'Is that still all on for us, Rosie. The car. The hotel and stuff?'

'Sure,' Rosie said. 'You just drive down to Manchester and stay over for a couple of nights, then get on a plane to Malaga. I've squared it all with my boss.'

'Christ,' Nikki said. 'I'm still freaking out a bit, though.'

'What's changed?' Rosie had a sense that things might be slipping away from her. 'Has something happened?'

'We've been a bit nervy the last couple of days. We thought we heard someone outside last night. A bit of noise.'

'Really?' Rosie asked. 'A car?'

'No. Not a car. Like someone was prowling around.'

'That could have been the farmer,' Matt said, lifting a mug of tea. 'You know what these guys are like – always checking on animals and stuff before they turn in for the night. Or even a fox.'

'Did you actually see anything?' Rosie asked.

'No,' Nikki said. 'We were scared to open the curtains.'

'It was probably the farmer,' Rosie said. 'Nobody knows you're here apart from Gordy.'

'Aye. He's a right prick, him,' Julie said. 'He came up here yesterday to make arrangements to come tomorrow and pick up the diamonds. He took one with him. Said he was going to some dodgy jeweller he knows to get a value on it. But he just can't keep his big mouth shut. The farmer's son, Euan, is in a wheelchair. He's a nice guy and he's been over for a coffee a couple of times. But big Gordy insulted the poor bloke, so the farmer was raging. He came over here after Gordy went away and was asking a few questions of us.'

'What kind of questions?'

'Just who the guy was in the big motor, and he told us Gordy insulted his son. But I get a niggly feeling he's a bit suspicious. I think he knows something. I wouldn't be surprised if he's talked to the cops. Maybe that's what the noise was last night.' There was a note of panic in Nikki's voice.

'But why would he phone the cops? He doesn't know anything,' Rosie said.

'She thinks maybe he remembered the story about the girl with the arm hacked off that was in the papers, and has put two and two together. The cops will still be looking for us, because we just fucked off out of the hospital without leaving any details.'

'But you said you told them what you knew.' Rosie turned to Nikki.

'Yeah, but they didn't believe me. They'll be looking for me. I know it.'

Rosie knew the cops were looking for them, big time. But she couldn't say or they'd be out of here before she was. Part of her wanted to tell them, but it wasn't just the story that she would lose if the women went. Gordy would hunt them down and kill both of them, and if not Gordy, then this Vanner guy. The only way to get anything out of this was to do it her way. Get them on tape and away from the scene, and then pass the tape to the police. That way they'd get time to be long gone. They all sat for a few moments, the room silent except for the log fire crackling and the low murmur of the television.

'It's entirely up to you, girls.' Rosie eventually looked from one to the other. If she was going to lose the story, then so be it. She wasn't about to tell them any fairy story of how perfect it would be, but her gut told her they'd be dead meat within a week if they didn't do it her way. 'Look.' She put her mug of tea on the table. 'If you really feel this is too much for you, then I swear, we can just forget it and let you do whatever you think is best. No hard feelings. Honest. But I don't think it's a good idea to be on your own, and I'm not just saying it for the story. I'm thinking of where you go next. You can't just keep on running. Sooner or later they'll catch up with you. But if it all goes to my plan, then the cops will be on them in the next couple of days, and you'll be well away from it by then. Of course, that's not without its risks. But it's less risky than just bug-gering off with a case full of diamonds.'

'But are you sure you can organise this with the police?'

'Yes,' Rosie said. She'd talked to Don about it on the phone last night, and he was hooked in. 'I have some good contacts in the cops. They trust me and I trust them. When I give them the story and the tapes – if you get wired up and we tape it all tomorrow – you two will be the last people they want to make trouble for. You might have to be available at some stage to make a statement, but you can do that from anywhere. The police can come to you.'

She didn't want to tell them that Don had already sounded out the DCI and he was up for the plan.

'I don't trust cops,' Julie said.

'I know how you feel, Julie. Believe me.' Rosie remem-bered Emir, the Kosovan refugee who was murdered while under police protection. 'But sometimes you don't have an alternative. I honestly think your options are limited.'

Julie pushed out a long sigh and looked at Nikki.

'Okay. Well, let's get this underway. Go ahead and show us how this tech stuff works, then we can get the hell out of here tomorrow. For good.'

Matt opened his case and unpacked the box of tricks for surveillance. It had improved over the years and was now more discreet than ever before, after Rosie had convinced McGuire they had to invest in some decent equipment.

*

'Do you think they'll still be there tomorrow when we turn up?' Matt glanced back at the farm from the corner of his eye as they drove out of the farm's lane and onto the road towards the motorway.

'Well, if they're not, we can't do much about it,' Rosie replied. 'But my gut instinct tells me they'll go through with it. Bloody hope so or there'll be hell to pay from Don.'

'Yeah, well *my* gut instinct hopes that if they do bugger off, they leave my surveillance equipment, or I'll get my arse kicked.'

'You and me both, pal.'

Rosie's mobile rang and she could see Adrian's name on the screen.

'Rosie.'

'How you doing, Adrian?' Rosie could sense Matt's eyebrows going up, even though she wasn't looking at him.

'Can I see you?'

'I'm just heading back to Glasgow. Sure. We can have a bite to eat. How about that bistro at the bottom of West Regent Street? We were there before. I can be there in an hour.'

'Okay. I see you.'

He hung up. Man of few words, was Adrian. Rosie felt a little glow inside, part desire and part happiness that she didn't have to spend the evening alone in her flat.

'Is that me blown out then?' Matt made a hurt face. 'I was going to invite you for dinner. I didn't know Adrian was in town. You kept that quiet.'

'It's only a flying visit – he was travelling with a friend and helping them to get settled,' Rosie said, a little defensively. 'You know how he likes to fly below the radar . . . Why don't you join us for a drink?'

'Nah, I'll leave you to it, I think. Just in case there's a posse of Pakistanis hunting you both down. I don't want to get lynched.'

Rosie chuckled. She hadn't thought about that.

Adrian was already sitting at the table and Rosie stood for a few seconds to look at him through the half-glass door. He had a bottle of red wine in front of him and was smoking a cigarette, lost in thought. The warm air of the bistro hit her as she opened the door. He looked up, but didn't quite smile. His eyes softened as he stood up and took a step towards her. He kissed her on the lips briefly, and hugged her.

'I got some wine. I'm thinking you might need it if you had a long day.' They sat down and he half filled her glass. 'I saw your story in the paper this morning. Last one on the shelf at the newsagent next to my friend's house. It was very good.' He shook his head. 'The poor woman attack by the stones . . . And the young girl. This is not right.'

'I know.' Rosie clinked his glass. 'Cheers, Adrian. Here's to . . .' She caught his eye and for a moment they held each other's gaze. Rosie felt heat rising in her chest. 'Here's to getting out of another scrape and living to tell the tale.'

She quickly composed herself, aware that he was watching her. 'At least I didn't put you in any danger this time.'

'I would have come if you told me. To Pakistan.'

'I know. I did consider it, but Pakistan is different from a lot of other places, and anything could have happened. Best you lie low for a while anyway, after all that business here the last time.'

Adrian nodded and sipped his wine. Rosie felt a little awkward in the silence, and she picked up the menu.

'I'm leaving tomorrow, Rosie.' Adrian broke the moment, his voice low and deep.

Rosie heard it as she swallowed a mouthful of wine, and hoped, when she looked up from the menu, that her face didn't show the slap of disappointment she felt.

'Oh. So soon? Is your friend settled?'

'Yes. She is fine. She has some part time work. Not legal, but she is doing some small cleaning jobs for a woman in the city.' He paused, fiddling with the menu. 'I have some work I must do back in Sarajevo. In the importing business I told you I am in just now. My friend called me last night and said the people he wants to make a deal with want to talk to me. They were not supposed to come until next week, but now is urgent. We are trying to build things up.'

'I see,' Rosie said. 'Oh, well. It was lovely to spend some time with you, Adrian. Really.' She locked eyes with him again, and felt for his hand across the table.

'Me too. I like you . . . I think about you a lot when I go back home. I hope you know that.'

'Yes, I think I do.' Rosie caressed the back of his hand.

'I . . . What I'm saying . . . is I don't want you to think that I am only here just to sleep with you. I want that, yes. But you are my friend . . . I do think about you.'

Rosie didn't know what he was trying to say, or even what she should say to him.

'I know that, Adrian. You're a good person . . .' She paused as the waiter came up. 'Can you give us a minute?' she asked him and he backed off.

'I . . . I know you're not here to sleep with me, Adrian. I suppose what I'm saying is that we're friends first and most importantly, and we probably shouldn't have got involved the way we did, but it was one of those things.'

He nodded.

'You have regrets?'

'No. But I don't think we should get too hung up about it.'

Adrian's face stayed its usual deadpan, but something else flashed across his eyes. Disappointment, sadness? It was always so hard to tell with him because there was something much deeper behind those soft grey eyes.

Listen to yourself, Rosie thought. You're sounding as if it didn't matter a damn. You'd think you'd hardly given this man a thought, when the truth is he was never far away from your mind, and right now you want nothing more but to lean across the table and feel the softness of his kiss. Rosie took a long breath and looked him in the eye.

'What I'm trying to say is, Adrian. We're both in a situation where we don't think we can go anywhere with this . . . I mean, we're not really sure what it is. Am I right so far?'

'I suppose.' He nodded, looking at her, then away.

'Do you want it to go anywhere?' she asked.

'I . . . I don't know, Rosie. All I know is you are on my mind and I would do anything for you. But I don't think I can make you happy.'

There was a little sting in that, and she wondered if Adrian would have known that when he said it. Her heart sank a little. Her life was okay if she didn't address that single question – could anyone make her happy? Yesterday in O'Brien's, she was the happiest she'd been in a long time – but it was because of work and the success of nailing the story. This? This reminded her of sitting with TJ, and him questioning her closely on her feelings. Look where that got her. Eventually, after a long silence she answered, swallowing the emotion.

'I . . . I don't know Adrian. It's a very difficult thought, if I was to accept that nobody can make me happy.'

He put his hand up apologetically, then touched her face.

'No. Please. I don't mean to hurt you. I never do that, Rosie. I just know that you are . . . I don't know the word . . . Comp . . . comp–'

'Complicated.' Rosie half smiled and shrugged.

'Yes. I think that is the word. Like your life is already too full.'

'But what about your life, Adrian?' Rosie paused, choosing her words. 'Sometimes I look at you and I know you will always be somewhere else. Like your heart is always in a . . . well, in a dark place.'

Adrian said nothing and stared at the table for a long moment. She could see a muscle in his jaw twitch. She had crossed a line. When he looked up she could see the pain in his eyes.

'I don't think I can be a whole person again – like other people. I am different. I am living the life I have, the life I have been left with. The truth is, I don't even know if I want to be a whole person, you know, with the normal things . . . a wife, a family.' He swallowed hard.

They sat in silence, the door opening and closing as people came and went. Rosie wanted to ask him about his anger inside, to ask him to talk about why he was so violent. The truth was that if Adrian hadn't been prepared to kill, then she would have been murdered the first night he had saved her life on the Clydeside, when Jake Cox's henchmen had been about to throw her into the river. Time and again, it was his quickness to violence and his instinctive action that had saved both of them. But the other night, watching his attack on the Pakistani, there was something in his eyes that told her he wanted to hurt and hurt. Rosie waved to the waiter for the bill, and reached across and squeezed Adrian's arm as he went to go into his pocket for money.

'No. You don't buy the wine when you come to my city.'

Adrian held her hand and they sat looking at each other as the waiter placed the bill on the table.

'Let's go home.' Rosie said.

They paid the bill and left.

Rosie's dreams had been peaceful when she drifted off after they'd made love. Now, as she was beginning to wake up, she reflected on how gentle, yet fierce and passionate it had been. It suddenly came back to her that Adrian had said 'I love you' when they were in the throes of passion. She hadn't said it back. Had he been waiting? She pondered the moment as her eyes opened slowly and she got used to the light. She reached across the bed. It was empty. She didn't need to get up and look through the house. She knew he wasn't in the shower or making coffee. Adrian was gone, without a word. Her heart sank.

CHAPTER THIRTY-TWO

McGuire already had his shirtsleeves rolled up, and it wasn't even time for the morning editorial conference. He usually began his day at the *Post* striding out of the lift, impeccably dressed, slipping out of his suit jacket as soon as he got into his office, where Marion was ready with his first coffee of the day. But the sleeves were always down at this point, usually cufflinked with something monogramed or with a ruby – depending on how he felt of a morning. The rolling up of the sleeves was part of a ritual, like a ringmaster preparing for showtime. Once they were up, they stayed that way all day, as he fought and jostled with his subs and executives on all corners of the room. Today, he was ready for anything. Rosie was glad. He was sitting with her splash and spread on his desk. It was Laila's story of her escape and her plans for the future, alongside some other Pakistani women's accounts. He was taking no nonsense today. He'd said that to Rosie last night after her meeting with Don, when she'd told him about the knife and how they'd nicked her attacker. 'We have plenty of ammo now, if they come for us. Wagons in a circle,' were his parting words. 'Boots and saddles . . . we're ready.' Any melancholy thoughts she'd had about Adrian's exit from her bed were quickly banished by his infectious dynamism.

'Right, Gilmour. Great stuff this morning, but where exactly are we on this now? This is the big day, isn't it?'

'Yep. All set. I went across to Stirling with Matt and saw the girls last night, so they're all wired up.'

'How confident are you that their bottle won't crash if things get a bit hairy out there?'

'As confident as I can be.'

McGuire shot her a glance.

'I think I want to hear more than that.'

'Come on, Mick. You know how these things are.'

'Yeah. If it goes tits up, are the cops on hand?'

'No. Not yet. We agreed not to.'

He ran a hand through his hair.

'What if this bastard Gordy shoots them and there's some kind of bloodbath on the farm? I don't want this all over us.'

'Don't worry. You can just blame me.'

He chuckled.

'I bloody will.'

'I know.'

'So, what's the plan?'

Rosie laid it out for him, how she and Matt would go to a back road at the edge of the farm that they'd already recced and wait there for the signal from Julie that the diamonds had been handed over. Then Julie and Nikki would make themselves scarce. They'd all meet up later on a location on the M74 as the girls drove south. Only when she had the tape in her hand and the story ready for the paper, would they tell the cops – in time for the first edition to bang onto the streets.

'I'm edgy about it. How do we know Gordy's not going to turn up armed to the teeth?'

'We don't. We'll just have to go with the flow.'

'I worry about you. In case anything happens to you.'

'Stop it, Mick. You'll have me greetin'.'

He sat back, clicking on his keyboard, looking at the screen, gnawing the inside of his cheek.

'Right. Okay. Off you go. But keep in touch with me, every half hour. You hear me?'

'I hear you.'

Rosie picked up her bag and left.

The rain was horizontal, sweeping across the fields and lashing onto the motorway. Matt kept to a steady sixty, which was unusual for him, because so many cars had slowed down amid flashing overhead warnings of black ice. For all its rain and snow, Scotland never really seemed to cope well when a hard winter struck. As Matt took the slip road and drove into the slush-filled back road towards Bannockburn, Rosie felt the familiar mix of excitement and dread, as she always did on the verge of a big story coming together. Julie had sounded relaxed when she called Rosie earlier, as arranged, to say that Gordy had phoned and everything was going to plan. Nikki was nervous, she'd said, but she was wired up with the camera and was also wearing the recording device discreetly in the waistband of her trousers. They'd packed everything into the car last night and all they had in the house were the attaché case and the diamonds. They were ready. Matt took the first lane before the farm road leading up to the house. Previously, he'd established that the lane was part of the farm's land and if you followed the narrow path long enough, it brought you in at the back of the farmer's house. The road was, as they expected, deserted. The snow in the fields was disappearing fast under the rain, and the thaw was definitely on. Matt pulled the car into the layby and switched off the engine.

'So. Now we just wait.' He eased his seat back a little, then stretched over to the back seat for his camera bag.

'Yep. Could be an hour or so, by the time it's all sorted and we get the call from Julie. It might get cold here, so we'll have to put the engine on from time to time.' Rosie took out her mobile. 'I said I'd give Julie a text once we were in place.' She pulled off her gloves and punched out a text.

*

Rosie gazed out of the windscreen. The rain had stopped, but the sky was dark and threatening. She checked her mobile again to see if there were any missed calls or texts from Adrian, even though she knew there wouldn't be.

'So, where's the big man?' Matt said, without looking up from the camera as he attached a long lens.

She turned to him, a little embarrassed that he seemed to be reading her mind.

'You mean Adrian?' She said it as if she'd already forgotten about his visit.

'Yeah. Is he still here? I wouldn't mind a pint with him. Talk about old times. He's some guy!'

Rosie felt her face moving to a smile, a flurry of memories of Spain and Morocco and their narrow escapes. She remembered Javier, and the easiness of how they all threw themselves into the venture to get the missing kid. And Sarajevo, and their long, emotional trip back through Kosovo. It seemed such a long time ago, and now it had developed into something that, no matter how much she pushed it away, still gave her a dull ache, which would come in waves whenever she thought of him. Why hadn't he woken her before he left, to say goodbye? He shouldn't have done that. She wasn't angry – she was big enough to know that things like this didn't last – but she wanted him to be her friend. The passion of that hot night in Sarajevo should never have happened. When would she ever learn?

'I haven't heard from Adrian. Maybe we'll try phoning him later.' Rosie knew that he was probably already on a plane to Belgrade.

She glanced at her phone again, a bit surprised that Julie hadn't replied to her text.

Nikki pulled on a heavy jumper over her long-sleeved T-shirt. She was surprised at how easily she'd adapted to working with only one hand. Simple things like buttoning a blouse or doing up her jeans had reduced her to a frustrated wreck in the beginning, but if she took her time, it was all workable. You adjust to your life and what you've been left with. Julie had told her that two years ago when she'd found her in bed in a stupor, a bottle of paracetamol and a half bottle of gin by her side. She hadn't wanted to live any more. The darkness she woke up with every morning had grown heavier and she'd become less and less attached to the world. She'd be better off dead, she'd pleaded with Julie, who'd dragged her into a cold shower. Then, Julie had told her that when you lose someone you love, what you get back is what is left of you. You're never the same person again, but you hold onto what is left and make the best of it. She told her to do it for the baby who didn't get a chance, and for all the people in their lives who had gone – their mothers, both dead in their sixties from heart attacks. Hold onto what you've got, she told herself as she looked in the mirror and smoothed her jumper over the recording device. She felt a little flurry of nerves, but she was determined to make it through this day.

There was a gentle knock on the front door and Nikki went into Julie's bedroom, where she was dressed and ready, applying the final stages of her make up. There was something of the girls-on-holiday feel about this, Nikki thought . . . if only that's how it was.

'The door,' Nikki said. 'Someone's at the door.'

Julie looked at her watch.

'It'll not be Gordy. He's not due for another half hour. Go and answer it. Maybe it's Euan.'

'What will I do if it is?'

Julie made eyes at her.

'Make him a coffee, for God's sake. Just be normal. Relax. We don't want to arouse any suspicion.'

Nikki went out the bedroom and crossed the hall to the front door. Euan smiled and held up a plate as though it were a trophy.

'Wee chocolate sponge Mum's made for you. Honestly! You'll not be able to resist it.'

Nikki opened the door wide and smiled back at him. He was lovely, all sparkling eyes with a hint of mischief in them. She wondered what he must have been like before he was stuck in this wheelchair, relying on his parents.

'Come on in. We'll have some coffee. I'll never say no to a chocolate cake.'

She went into the kitchen and filled the kettle as Euan made his way inside.

Julie dabbed some perfume on her wrists and glanced at herself in the mirror. She was looking well, considering all the shit that had been flying around, The fact that this was coming to an end had given her a new lease of life. By this evening, she and Nikki would be in a hotel in Manchester, sinking a bottle of wine and gearing up for their flight to Malaga in the morning. They'd be free. And they'd be rich. There was as much chance of her parting with all the diamonds to that bastard Gordy as her flying in the fucking air, she told herself. He was such a stupid prick, he'd even told her how this Jew fence had described the difference between a good rough diamond and a bad one. Well, there was probably no such thing as a bad rough diamond, but a good one from a not-so-good one, was how he'd described it. Last night, once Nikki had fallen asleep, she'd gone into the pouches and taken a closer look at every one of them. There was a fortune in this stuff. Plenty of white ones, and good sizes too. She didn't know how valuable the other ones were, but she concentrated on the white ones. She took out three white ones from each pouch and stashed them away in her zipped bag. No need to get greedy. She could have taken more. Gordy or this Vanner guy didn't really know exactly how many diamonds there were anyway. But she decided she'd take just enough to give her and Nikki the chance of a decent start in whatever new lives they were about to embark on. She also took the rest of the money and hid it. Stuff them! Gordy would be so grateful to get the diamonds, he wouldn't be hanging about counting – especially if he was planning to stiff Vanner. She could hear Nikki and Euan chatting as she headed for the living room.

'Are you eating *again*?' she said to Nikki.

'You need to taste this cake, Julie. It's magic. I've made you a coffee.'

Euan gave her a thumbs up, a mouthful of cake preventing him from talking. She brought her coffee and sat on the sofa opposite Euan in his wheelchair. She was about to ask him how he was when she heard the click of the back door. Her head swam when she saw the figure appear in the kitchen. She opened her mouth to speak, but nothing came out.

'Morning, ladies.'

The Manchester accent sent a chill through her and she glanced at Nikki, whose face had turned white. The big, well-dressed figure with a shock of greying hair stood in the kitchen in his black Crombie coat and red scarf, icy blue eyes staring down at them. Behind him was a shaven haired minder in a padded anorak, with a slash mark from his cheekbone which spread to a wide dent in his neck that looked as though someone had taken the bolts out.

'What the fuck!' Julie stood up. Nikki also got to her feet.

'Hey. That's no way to treat a guest who's paid an unexpected call on you . . . It *is* unexpected, is it not?'

'Who the fuck are you? What are you doing in our house?'

The big man's mouth snarled to a smile, but he kept his icy stare on her.

'I'll give you two guesses, love. In fact, I'll give you one guess, and if you don't get it right, then my boy here will break your nose.' He raised his eyebrows, waiting for an answer.

Julie looked at Nikki.

'I . . . I think I'm going to faint.' Nikki faltered back and sat on the arm of the chair.

The minder moved forward.

'Fucking leave her.' Julie stepped between them. 'I know who you are. You're Johnny Vanner.'

'Got it in one. You've wasted my boy's morning. He likes hurting people.'

'What the hell are you doing here?'

He sniggered.

'Like you don't know?'

'Gordy will be here in a minute.'

'Well that'll be nice and cosy then. He'll get a surprise too.'

'What's going on? He said he was giving the case to you. He said it was all arranged. What are you doing here?'

Vanner tugged off his leather gloves, one finger at a time, revealing tattoos on each knuckle. He took a step forward, then suddenly grabbed Julie by the hair.

'Listen, you arrogant cow. Never mind what I'm doing here. Never mind about that cunt Gordy. I'm here for the case, then I'm off. So let's not fuck around here for any longer than is necessary.' He pulled Julie's hair tight. 'So if you want to stay alive, just give me the fucking case and I'm off.'

Julie looked at Nikki, and there was a flash of recognition between them that they both knew the game was up. There *would* be no other life, no jobs abroad where they would reinvent themselves. This bastard would kill them. He wasn't going to take the case and walk away. How the hell did he even know they were here? He'd obviously been planning to stiff Gordy the way Gordy planned to stiff him. Except that Vanner was smarter. He let go of her hair.

Julie went into the kitchen and knelt on the floor, rummaging in the cupboard until she got to the little place at the back where she'd stashed the case. She brought it out and handed it over.

He placed it on the worktop and opened it, while his minder kept his eyes on Julie and Nikki. Vanner took out the pouch of diamonds and sprinkled them onto his hand. He caressed them, weighed in his palm, then brought out the other pouch. He went across to her.

'You'd better not have taken any of these.'

'I'm not fucking stupid! Just take them and go.'

He slapped Julie hard on the face and she tasted blood.

'Stop! Leave her.' Nikki burst into tears.

'Shut the fuck up, you, or you'll get your other arm torn off.' He gestured to his minder, who took a rope out of his jacket pocket.

'Sit on the chairs and shut your fucking mouths. The two of you. If you stay that way, I might even let you live.'

Nikki stumbled as she crossed the room to sit on the kitchen chair next to Julie. The minder grabbed Julie and tied her hands behind her back, then pressed Nikki's good arm against her side and wound rope around her.

'Who's the cripple?' Vanner gave Euan a long look. 'Are you turning tricks for him?'

CHAPTER THIRTY-THREE

It wasn't so cold now that he'd been walking and work-ing in the field, but James O'Neill decided he'd go back to the house and make sure the fire was well stoked for Euan. His wife was out for the morning for a hospital appoint-ment, then she was going for lunch with his sister. He enjoyed the days when it was just the two of them, talking about the farm and the rugby. Deep down, his heart bled for his son, still the same boy in so many ways, trying hard not to show the frustration and disappointment he must feel every morning he woke up and saw his wheelchair at the side of his bed. But that was where they were now. Nothing they could do about it.

It was the car at the back of the cottage that James noticed. He'd not seen many visitors in the time those girls had stayed there. That big bastard who insulted Euan was the only car he'd seen before, and from this distance he could see it wasn't that Jag. He crossed the field where he'd been checking on sheep in case the heavy rain turned the place like a swamp. Last year, after heavy snow, then the big thaw, one of his sheep drowned in a pit of mud, so he had to make the mile-long trek twice a day when the weather was like this.

The narrow pathway from the field took him out at the back of the rented house, and now he had a clear view of the car. He crept around the back of the house, familiar with every nook and cranny, knowing where to move so nobody would see him. He felt as though he was spying on the girls, but there was a niggle that something wasn't right. He didn't want to knock on the door after the last time, but wanted to peek in the window and see what was going on. He walked carefully around the house, and with his back to the wall, made his way toward the kitchen window. In the second he looked in, he saw enough to make him feel physically sick. Someone was tying up his son, and his face was bloodied and battered. Jesus wept! A sudden image flashed up of Euan's head like a football on the morning he and his wife had gone into hospital after the beating that had left him paralysed. A surge of rage almost knocked James off his feet and he gripped the wall for support. He chanced another glance. The girls were already tied up on kitchen chairs, and the Julie girl had blood on her face. A big guy in a black overcoat was pointing a gun, waving it at the girls, then at Euan. James could hear his heart thumping and his mouth was dry as a stick. He slunk away, slowly at first, then ran as fast as his legs would carry him to his house. But as he did, he suddenly remembered the car he'd spotted in the layby up by the field he'd just been in. He'd seen it for the first time in the distance as he was walking in the field yesterday. He was sure it was there again today, but had thought nothing of it and assumed someone was taking a shortcut. But now, he realized that this meant there could be more of these bastards. He threw open the door of his farmhouse, his hands trembling as he grabbed the key to the old pantry.

Big Gordy was feeling buoyant as Terry drove the Jag out of Glasgow and onto the motorway. He'd have a pocket full of diamonds on his way back, and he planned to take the big driver for lunch on the way home as a bit of a celebration. A pocket full of diamonds. Christ! You could nearly get a song out of that. He thought of his ma and how she'd be egging him on, especially now that his mind was made up that he was chucking Glasgow and moving to Spain. But first, he'd have to deal with these two bitches who thought they'd made a tit of him. Making him sign over the club. He'd just shoot the fuckers and be done with it. Who gave a fuck how long their bodies lay there festering? The old farmer would find them eventually, but he'd be long gone by then.

Terry drove up to the front of the cottage and switched off the engine.

'Will I come in, boss?'

'Yeah, you might as well. We'll not be too long, though. Just pick up the case and then sort these birds.'

They both got out of the car and went up to the door. Instinctively, Gordy took a furtive glance around to make sure there was nobody stupid enough to phone the cops. You never knew with those two nutters inside, and he'd already seen that the farmer could be a bit of a meddling bastard. So if he came anywhere near, poking his nose in, he was getting it too. He wasn't in the mood to piss around. He knocked on the door. Nothing. He shrugged, then rapped on it harder. He winked at Terry when he heard the lock being turned, then the door opened, and his jaw dropped to the ground. It was the barrel of the gun he saw first. And some baldy, scar-faced bastard behind it.

'What the fuck!'

'Shut it and get in here.'

Gordy recognised the voice coming from inside the house, and a chill ran through him. Johnny Vanner. In the name of fuck!

They both stepped inside slowly, the gun pointing at them all the time. He knew Terry was tooled up, and so was he, but a lot of good it was going to do them now. Fucking Vanner! That wee Paul had done this. Bastard! He was choking with rage and could feel sweat inside his shirt, and the hairs on his neck standing up. Get a grip, he told himself. Think fast. There has to be a way out of this.

'Johnny! What the fuck is *this*, man?'

'*This*, my friend, is why I'm the kingpin down south and you're just a pile of steaming shite from Glasgow.'

'What the fuck are you talking about? We have a deal here! I was getting the stuff for you. Did you think I was going to do you over?'

Vanner shot him a sardonic smile.

'Aw, don't insult my fucking intelligence, mate. I know exactly what you were going to do, even before that little cunt Paul told me.'

Nikki looked at Julie, shocked.

'Paul's a fucking wee grass, Johnny,' Gordy protested. 'I knew he'd done something and was going behind my back. I knew he'd phoned you. That's why I plugged the cunt the other day. But I did it to protect us all. I was going to tell you about it. He was a loose cannon. Couldn't be trusted.'

'Paul? You killed Paul?' Nikki's voice trembled.

'He was her husband,' Julie said.

'I know he was,' Gordy spat. 'Who gives a fuck! He's a wee troublemaker. A wee rat's bastard . . . Hey, come on, Johnny. Let's just calm the fuck down here. Put the heavy metal down and let's sort this.' He glanced at the case. 'Come on. You've got the stuff. We've got a deal, pal.'

'I'm not your fucking pal.'

'So what you going to do here? Eh? Bump the fucking lot of us off? Even the bastard cripple in the wheelchair?'

'Shut it!'

'Get off my fucking land.'

Rosie's eyes were closed and for a second she imagined she'd dropped into a dream when she'd rested her head back to break the monotony of waiting for Julie's text. But no, this was really happening. There was a single barrel shotgun pointed at her window.

'Oh fuck!' Matt said. 'Where the hell did he come from? I nodded off.'

'Sssh. Jesus Christ! It's the farmer!' Rosie turned her body towards the window, a pleading look on her face as she raised her hands in surrender.

'Get off my fucking land.'

'Look, mister! Listen! Let me just roll the window down a second. Please. We . . . We're not here to do you any harm. Sorry. We got lost.'

'Liar. Who the fuck are you?' He took a step back as Rosie slowly lowered the window.

'Rosie. Just tell him, for fuck's sake. He might use that thing,' Matt muttered.

She heard it, but ignored him. She couldn't tell him who they were. Not right now. Who knows what he would do? It was too hard to explain. Too long a story when you're looking down the barrel of a gun. But she'd better say something – and fast – because the click of the gun being cocked made her heart miss a beat. Jesus! This silver-haired, middle-aged man, who wouldn't have been out of place selling his homegrown produce at a farm shop, had a deranged look in his eye.

'Okay.' She glanced at Matt and muttered at him to start the engine. 'We're going. We're nobody, honest. We don't want any trouble. We're going right now.'

'You've got three seconds to tell me who you are.'

His finger wavered over the trigger, ready to squeeze.

'Look. Actually . . . Er . . . We're journalists. We . . . We're from the *Post*. We're on an investigation. The girls in your house—' Rosie hated herself for saying it, but right now she had no choice.

'Them girls have got a gun pointed at them right now in my house. But my son's in there. What the fuck is going on? Who are these bastards?'

'I . . . I don't know. And that's the truth. But if you've seen someone with a gun in the house, then I think we should call the cops.' She showed him her mobile.

He pushed the gun into the space on the window almost touching Rosie's head.

'No! No cops! Someone's got a gun pointed at my son. No fucking cops! I'm dealing with this, you just get off my fucking land! Now!'

'Okay. No cops. We're going. We're going right now. Come on, Matt. Let's move.'

Matt reversed the car a fraction so he could get back onto the tight road and the farmer stood back.

'I'm sorry. Really. Sorry. We're going. We won't phone the cops. I promise.'

Matt's wheels kicked up mud at the farmer as they spun and he tried to control the car as they took off.

'Christ! There's mud all over him. I hope he doesn't shoot,' Matt said, looking in his rear-view mirror.

'Just drive, Matt. Let's get as far away from here as we can.'

'You going to phone the cops?'

'Shit! I don't know. Something's gone seriously tits-up in that house, but if I involve the cops right now, they'll all get done – Julie and Nikki as well.'

'But if someone's already got a gun pointed at them, they might all get *killed*, Rosie.'

Rosie bit her lip and looked out of the side window, trying to peer across the field to where the two farmhouses stood side by side. She could see the big black Jag that she knew belonged to Gordy MacLean. What the hell had gone wrong?

'Matt. Listen. I think we should park the car somewhere and go on foot.'

'What? Into the fucking line of fire? Are you serious? How many guns do you need pointing at you, Rosie, to tell you the fucking game's up?'

'I know, I know. But if we could get close enough to see,

but far enough to be hidden. You know what I mean? That wee outhouse at the bottom of the road. We could park there and nobody can see us from the house. We just have to cross a bit of the field and then we can see.'

'Then what, Rosie?'

'We might be able to witness it. You might get a great picture. Come on.'

'Fuck! This is fucking reckless! Totally crazy. We might get killed.'

'We won't. They won't be able to see us. We were even thinking about parking down there when we did the recce, if you remember, but thought it was too close to the main road up to the house. But we could make it on foot. The farmer won't come back now. Let's just dump the car down there.'

Matt shook his head and gritted his teeth as he made his way down the bumpy road. He pulled in and picked up a camera – the lightest one he had.

'Right. Come on. But when this is over, I might actually punch you right in the face, Gilmour.'

Rosie said nothing. She opened the door and stepped into the road. They went towards a fence and climbed over into the field, their feet immediately sinking into the mud and slush.

'Fuck me, go gently,' Matt said. 'We could get swallowed up by a bog.'

'Come on, we'll be fine. We've only fifty yards to go till

we get to the outhouse. We can hide there.' Rosie's feet squelched and sank in the mud as she struggled to walk.

James was at the back of the house, sliding along the wall towards the porch. He'd considered just going to the front door and blasting it off with the shotgun. If Euan hadn't been in there, he would have. But who knew what would happen if he did that? It was risky now trying to creep in like this, but he knew every corner of this house like the back of his hand. He could get in quietly, slip down the back hall and just appear from the kitchen. That's where he needed to be. Slowly, he eased open the handle of the porch door and he was in. He stood for a second next to the washing machine and chest freezer, barely breathing. He could hear shouting and arguing. One voice had a Glasgow accent and the other one was from somewhere in the north of England. Whoever these guys were, they were arguing over money, and he thought he heard someone say diamonds. What the hell had he done renting his house to these two women? They'd looked like ordinary girls to him, and his wife had thought maybe they had been beaten by their husbands and were getting away. He never should have allowed them in. And he should have phoned the cops. But he couldn't. Only *he* knew why he could never do that, and he would take that secret to his grave. Just save Euan, he told himself. The rest are scum. Like the bastards who left his son for dead that night. They got their comeuppance and these bastards would too. Just a few more steps. Then he was in, silently standing in the kitchen. He clicked on the gun and everyone in the room froze. They looked at him as though he were a ghost. Euan's face was grey and bloody, and the sight of him sent such a shock through him he had trouble stopping himself from firing the gun.

'Get fucking out! All of you! Get out of my house, and off my land!' He raised the gun and pointed it.

Then suddenly a gun went off. Not his, but immediately the big guy in front of him with the shaven head slumped to the floor. Another rapid shot and the man next to him in the Crombie coat hit the ground, blood spreading across his chest. It was happening so fast it was almost a blur, but he was able to see the shooter. It was the driver of the bastard who had insulted Euan the other day. He raised the shotgun to his shoulder and pointed it at the man, but the driver was aiming a pistol straight at him. I should blow your head off right now, James told himself. But suddenly, the driver's boss pulled a handgun out of his coat and pressed it against Euan's head.

'Thanks for that, Terry,' the big man said. 'I couldn't have dropped that pair of cunts better myself.' He turned to James. 'Now, listen, you old prick . . . You either get to fuck back to the farm and sit on your hands, or this fucking retard gets it right now.'

'Stop!' He lowered his shotgun. 'Leave him!'

'Put the fucking gun down and get out.'

'I'm taking my boy with me.'

'No you're not. He's staying right here until we're gone, and if you move a fucking muscle, I'll blow his head off.'

James felt his legs shaking, his whole body trembling, even the muscles in his face twitching. He saw the anger and desperation in Euan's eyes, and right now he'd have taken a bullet for him. He put his hands up.

'Okay. I'm going.' He began to back away slowly, placing the gun on the worktop. He glanced at the two women as he was leaving. Nikki's eyes were swollen and tear-stained, but Julie's were blazing with rage.

'Just keep doing that and you might survive,' the big man said.

James kept walking back slowly until he was out of the back door. Then he heard a heavy thud and a painful scream from Euan.

'What the fuck you doing, Gordy?' It sounded like Julie. 'Leave the poor guy alone. He's got nothing to do with this. Come on, let's just get to fuck out of here.'

James could barely walk as he made his way to the barn. He was heading to get his other shotgun, the double-barrelled one he'd bought at an auction last year, in case of emergencies.

Rosie flinched and looked at Matt when they heard the bang.

'That's a gunshot. I'm sure of it,' Matt said.

'Christ! I know. What the hell's going on up there? Can you see anything through your long lens?'

'No . . . Nothing. It's all happening inside. But they'll come out, that's all we can hope for. Because before you suggest it, we're not going to go up there and announce ourselves.'

'Don't be daft. I wasn't going to suggest *we*, pal. You're the one who takes the pix.'

'Aye. That'll be right.'

'Only joking. We'll just sit tight. I hope to Christ Julie and Nikki are alright.'

James stayed in the barn, trying to breathe deeply to calm himself down as his trembling fingers loaded two cartridges into the shotgun chambers. He had to do this. Just hold your nerve, he whispered to himself. They would come out the front door towards the Jag. He knew exactly where to go. He was ready. He crept round to the front of the house and hid behind the big stone coal bunker. He waited, his heart thudding against his ribs. Then after a few moments, he saw the driver come out of the house, carrying an aluminium attaché case. He put it in the back seat of the car, started up the engine and went back inside the house. James watched as the door opened again, and someone pushed Euan outside in the wheelchair. It was the driver again. Then the big bastard they'd called Gordy came out behind them. James waited, held his breath. What about the girls? Surely they were all part of the same gang. Maybe they'd double-crossed them and that's why they were on the run? None of that mattered now. James felt his hands begin to steady as he gripped the shotgun. He controlled his breath. The driver went towards the car, pushing the wheelchair, then let go of it, and it rolled down the small incline and came to a halt just behind the car. There was a space of about six feet or so between the wheelchair and the car. Were they going to take Euan with them? Stuff him in the boot? If they did, he was totally powerless. He watched as the driver got into the car. He had to get the direction of the shot right. If he got it wrong, Euan would be hit with buckshot. Then he saw Gordy, looking all around him, suddenly aiming his gun at Euan's head. James bit the inside of his cheek till it bled, trying to keep from shouting. He watched Gordy's face break into a grin as he opened the passenger door and backed in, sitting down, half hanging out, his gun still pointed at Euan. They weren't taking him, but they might shoot him just for sheer badness. James stood up and took aim in one seamless movement. Then he fired. The windscreen shattered into a million shards, and Euan was hit with flying glass as he threw himself out of the wheelchair on to the ground behind the car. James rushed forward. He could see what was left of the two bastards – not much. But he fired the second barrel, then threw down the shotgun and broke down.

CHAPTER THIRTY-FOUR

As the second shot was fired, Nikki and Julie closed their eyes tight, bracing themselves for the next blast. This is it, Nikki thought. If big Gordy walked in that door, they'd be next. If it was the farmer who'd been shooting, they could still be next.

'Dad! Dad!'

Julie opened her eyes, straining her neck to see if she could get a glimpse out of the window. But the rope cutting into her wrists was too tight for her to move.

'I'm alright, son.'

Nikki opened her eyes.

'Oh Christ, Julie. Is he going to kill *us* now?'

'Sssh. No,' Julie whispered. 'I don't think he's a psycho. He only shot them to protect his son. Let me handle this.'

'Christ, Julie. It's because "I let you handle this" that we're in this mess.'

'Listen. Just trust me. I think the farmer's a good man.'

'What if he phones the cops?'

'With four dead bodies? No chance. If he'd been going to get the cops, he'd have done it before he started shooting people.'

They both froze as the farmer suddenly appeared in the doorway. His eyes were glassy, as though he was in another world.

'Mr O'Neill . . . Er . . . James.'

Silence. He went across to the worktop and lifted his shotgun.

'James, could you please listen to me for a minute?'

He put down the gun.

'Don't worry, I'm not going to shoot you. There's been enough killing for one day. Those bastards deserved to die. They'd have killed my boy.'

'You're right, James,' Nikki gushed, too enthusiastically.

'James. Look. Can we explain?'

He nodded, said nothing. To their surprise, he took out a knife from the kitchen drawer and began to free them. Euan appeared in the doorway in his wheelchair.

'Are you going to get the police?' Julie asked.

He shook his head.

'No police.'

'What about the bodies?'

He said nothing.

Nikki glanced at Julie; both of them were wondering if he was out of his mind.

Julie took a breath.

'Can you please just let us go?'

'Tell me what this is about.'

'It's a long story. Too long. Please just let us go. Is it okay if I get up? I want to get that case out of their car.'

He stood to the side and let her pass.

Nikki got to her feet, but her legs were weak and she supported herself on the worktop. She started to cry.

'I'm sorry,' she sniffled.

The farmer looked at her for a long moment.

'You're that girl, aren't you?'

'What?'

'The one who got her arm cut. The one who was in the paper.' He glanced at her stump.

She sniffed and nodded.

'It's all part of this, isn't it? You were on the run from them. Is that right?'

Nikki nodded.

'I'm sorry. We brought you all this trouble.'

'They were going to use my son. Maybe take him hostage or something. They'd have killed him.'

'I'm so sorry, Mr O'Neill.'

He said nothing, looked away.

'I know about bastards like them. What they do to people. I don't know what you did to get them to cut your arm off, but my son did nothing, except be in the wrong place at the wrong time. It was bastards like them who left him with brain damage.'

Euan looked at the floor. Silence. Julie came into the room carrying attaché case. The farmer turned to her. She went into her handbag and rummaged around.

'James. We'd just like to get into our car and drive away and you will never see us again. I promise you, we will never talk to anyone about what went on today. We are going far away from here and nobody will know a thing.'

His gaze moved beyond her, as though he was bewildered. Julie went across to him and opened her hand. Two rough diamonds were in the palm.

'Please take these.'

He looked at her, then at Nikki and finally at Euan.

'What are they?'

'Rough diamonds.'

James glanced at Euan, who wheeled across the room.

'Is that what this is all about? Did you steal them?'

'As I said, its a long story.' She paused and glanced at Nikki. 'Look, James. We took the case during something we were involved in. It was stupid. We didn't even know what was inside. Honest. By the time we did, it was too late, they were going to kill us anyway. Gordy was going to kill us, and so was Vanner, after he killed Gordy.' She swallowed. 'You saved our lives . . . I want you to have them.'

He shook his head.

'What am I supposed to do with them?'

'Just keep them for a while. Then go somewhere and get a good jeweller who knows about stuff like this. It might take a while, but you'll find someone who will help. But you have to be careful – don't do it till all this dies down.' She looked at Euan. 'They're worth a lot of money. I know that for sure.'

James shook his head.

'I can't. I don't want to be involved.'

'Please. You must. What difference does it make now? You're already involved.' Julie gestured at the bodies on the floor and outside. 'Just take them. I know you need the money . . . If you didn't, you wouldn't be renting out your house. Get the place fixed up so that Euan can live independently. Or take him abroad where he'll get better treatment. You can pay for it with these.'

Nikki turned to Euan. 'We're so sorry, Euan.'

Julie took James' hand and opened it. She placed the diamonds in it and closed it. He said nothing and turned to Euan, who slowly nodded.

Julie glanced at Nikki and they both made for the door.

'Good luck. And . . . thanks,' Julie said as they walked out and got into the car.

Rosie and Matt struggled through the mud to get back to the car.

'Did you get anything?'

'I got some images, but don't know how good they are.'

'Could you see Julie and Nikki anywhere?'

'No. They're definitely not in any picture. They must be in the house.'

'Do you think they've been shot?'

'I don't know, but before you suggest it, I'm not going up there to find out.'

'No. I know. Let's just get on the road and get out of here.'

'You going to phone the cops?'

'I can't. Not until I get in touch with Julie. Let's just get to the car first, then I'll phone.'

They got the car, feet thick with mud, and Rosie threw herself onto the passenger seat. Her hands shook as she punched in Julie's number again.

'Rosie!'

Relief flooded through her.

'Nikki? Are you okay?'

'Yes. We're on the road. Jesus, Rosie! It was totally mental up there.'

'Is Julie alright?'

'Yeah. She's driving. We left about ten minutes ago. We're hammering it on the motorway.'

'Okay. So you're not hurt?'

'Julie got a punch in the face from that big Vanner guy.'

'Vanner? He was there? Christ!'

'I know. He must have been coming up to do Gordy.

Turned out they were all there. Like a convention of arseholes.'

Rosie could feel herself smiling.

'So what the hell happened? We could hear gunshots.'

'Gunshots? It was like *Pulp Fiction*!'

'So what happened?'

'The farmer shot Gordy and his driver.'

'The farmer? The old guy? You're joking.'

'No. They were going to kill his son, or take him with them as a hostage or something. We didn't see it as we were tied up to chairs in the kitchen, next to Vanner and his minder's dead bodies on the floor.'

'Christ! Who killed them?'

'Gordy's driver.'

'Shit! So there are four dead bodies?'

'Yep. Two in the house and Gordy and his driver in the car. The farmer just blasted them to fuck.'

'Unbelievable! How the hell did the son get involved? He's in a wheelchair.'

'I know. He happened to call over to the house as we were preparing for big Gordy to arrive, then suddenly, out of nowhere, Johnny Vanner appeared in the back door. We nearly shat ourselves.'

'I'll bet. So has the farmer phoned the cops?'

'No.'

'No?'

'He said no cops. He'll deal with it.'

'What the Christ? He's a farmer, not a hitman.'

'I don't know, Rosie. We didn't stay long enough to ask questions. We just got the hell out of it. We're heading south, as planned.'

'Did you get anything on tape?'

'Yeah. A lot.'

'The shootings?'

'Probably the noise, but not on the camera. Vanner tied us up to chairs, so we'd maybe be too low down to record faces.'

'Okay. Just keep driving. We'll catch up with you later.'

Rosie hung up and slumped back in her seat, rolling down the window for some air.

'What's happened?' Matt said.

Rosie shook her head.

'I can't believe what I'm hearing. Jesus Christ, Matt! It sounds like a bloodbath up there. But the girls are out and on their way south.'

'Who's dead?'

'Four. Vanner, his minder, Gordy and his driver.'

'Fuck me! Who shot who?'

'Believe it or not, the farmer shot Gordy and his driver. Apparently Gordy's driver shot Vanner and his minder in the house.'

'So the farmer shot two people. Mind you, he was in that kind of mood.' Matt smiled. 'He looked like one of those mad bastards that is all mild-mannered until you push him over the edge.'

'I guess that's what happened.'

'What about cops?'

'No cops. Not yet. Let's just get to the cafe up off the motorway before we head south. I feel shaky. I need to eat something.'

In the driving rain and sleet, it was nearly two hours by the time Rosie and Matt pulled into the roadside cafe outside Abbington, close to the Scottish border. Nikki had phoned to say they'd stopped there, but were planning to hit the road to Manchester before it got dark. The cafe car park wasn't busy and Rosie scanned the cars as they drove in.

'That's Julie's car,' she said to Matt as he parked.

'I don't suppose there's any chance they were followed? I hope we're not walking into something.'

'Don't even think that way.'

Rosie's mobile rang and she pulled it out of her coat pocket. It was McGuire.

'What's happening, Gilmour?'

Rosie made impatient eyes at Matt.

'Er . . . Can't talk right now, Mick. But I'll be back on the road in half an hour and I'll call you back.'

'What the fuck's happening?'

'A lot, Mick. A lot has happened. I'm going to meet Julie and Nikki now.'

'So they got away?'

'Yeah.'

'What about Gordy?'

'I'll tell you when I phone you.'

'That means he's fucking dead.'

'Mick, I need to go. Don't worry. I'll call you soon.'

'Christ al-fucking-mighty, Gilmour!'

Rosie hung up.

'He's not happy,' she said to Matt.

Matt chuckled.

'He's going to go mental when you tell him what happened.'

'Well. Let's see what we've got here first.'

Matt held open the swing door and Rosie walked in. Nikki spotted her and waved her good arm.

'So,' Rosie said as she slid into the booth. 'You made it.' She shook her head. 'I can't quite believe you got out of there alive. All we could hear was gunshots.'

'*You* can't believe it,' Julie piped up, taking a mouthful of her sandwich. 'You should have seen it from where we were sitting, tied to chairs, waiting for someone to blow our heads off. Honest to Christ, Rosie! I don't even know how I drove down here. It's a complete blur – I just kept driving on nerves and fear. When I got in here, I nearly passed out in the car park.'

Rosie looked at both of them. The waitress arrived and both her and Matt ordered tea. Matt asked for a pastry.

'Are you okay now? The two of you?'

They nodded, but Rosie could see Nikki had been crying, her face blotchy and eyes red. She began to fill up again.

'I . . . I was so scared, Rosie. Still am. It's all just getting on top of me.' Tears spilled over. 'They killed Paul, my husband.'

'Paul? Who killed him?'

Julie made a slightly frustrated face.

'Big Gordy killed him. So he said anyway.' She put her arm over Nikki's shoulder. 'Listen, Nikki. It was Paul who grassed us up to Gordy. Don't shed any bloody tears over him.'

Nikki sniffed.

'I used to love him. I've known him all my life.'

'Aye. But he *ruined* your life. It's because of that wee gambling, cheating bastard that we're in this mess at all. If he hadn't done in all your money, you wouldn't have ended up as an escort and none of this shit would have happened. Don't start looking at it with rosy specs now, Nikki. You were well shot of him. And the point is, he grassed us for money, knowing he would get us killed. That's the kind of bastard he was.' She dabbed at Nikki's wet cheeks with a napkin. 'Come on. You're better than this. Your new life starts here.'

Nikki nodded, swallowing hard. Rosie glanced at Matt. She was dying to see what they had on tape, but had to allow them a moment. She resisted the urge to look at her watch. The tea arrived and Matt scoffed the pastry as if he was on a day out in the country.

Eventually Julie produced the tape and the camera from her bag and handed it to Matt. He immediately put it onto his laptop and began running it through.

'Okay, before we listen to the tape,' Rosie looked at both women, 'can you just walk me through what happened?'

Julie began from the moment they were in the bedroom getting ready to meet big Gordy. Rosie listened, took notes, used her own tape recorder to get it down. Right now, she didn't know what she was going to do with it all. It was explosive stuff, but there were bodies piling up with every sentence, and sooner or later, the cops would have to be involved. The farmer sounded like a decent guy – albeit with some kind of crazed vigilante streak – but at the moment he was looking at two killings. Even if he claimed self-defence, it did look a bit over the top. Matt turned his laptop around and they looked at the footage. At first, Vanner was on the tape and he had some gorilla with him. They could hear his conversation clearly. Brilliant. They could see Euan on it, in his wheelchair, his face a mix of fear, anger and frustration that he could do nothing. Then they heard the front door being opened. By that time the girls must have been tied to the chairs, because everything was only visible from waist height and below. They could clearly hear Gordy's voice and the argument. Then the shotgun fire.

'It's all pretty stunning stuff,' Rosie said, delighted, but still not sure how this would pan out. They'd have to take it to the cops. McGuire would never touch this in a million years, but it was so good. Better to have it than not have it. And if they did hand the tape to the police, they would look like responsible journalists keen to do the right thing.

'So,' Julie said, glancing out of the wide window at the fading light. 'We need to get moving soon. It's getting dark. I want to be into the hotel as soon as possible and on this flight out first thing in the morning. Nobody is looking for us – well, that we know of. Now that all the major players have been bumped off, we've got a clear run . . . I think.'

'What about the diamonds?' Rosie asked, glancing from one to the other.

Julie looked at Nikki.

'I've got them. I took the case.'

This was tricky, Rosie thought. They could go off now and never be seen again. A stash of rough diamonds would see them alright, maybe for the rest of their lives, if they ever found a place to shift them for the kind of money they were worth.

'So what are you going to do?'

Julie seemed uneasy.

'Well, what about the cops?' she asked. 'Are you going to get the cops?

'I think I'm going to have to, Julie. At some stage. There's so much going on here, I'm just not sure yet where we take this. But if we're going to write a story for the paper, I need to talk to the editor to see where he wants to go with it. There are four dead bodies at O'Neill's farm and police will have to be involved eventually. The only witnesses to what happened, apart from him and his son, are you two, so you'll be crucial to this investigation, once the cops get a hold of it.'

'Might we end up in the jail?'

'Why? You haven't done anything. The police don't want you for that dead guy from the hotel. You stole some crook's diamonds, but they were the proceeds of a crime anyway. And you didn't know there were smuggled diamonds in it when you took the case.' Rosie paused, spread her hands. 'Look . . . I think you need to talk to the cops. Not right now, and maybe not till you're out of the country. But I think you do.'

'What, and give you the case to give over to them?'

'Well, it's an option. But handing over the case and telling the full story to the cops involves me too, so I'm not sure how I'm fixed on that. I need to talk to people back at the office. But if you're getting a plane out of here in the morning, then you don't want to deal with a haul of smuggled diamonds. Where are you going to put them, for a start?'

'Never really thought about that,' Julie admitted.

'You could put them somewhere . . . Like, in a safety locker or deposit box in the airport, and then we could tell the cops – if that's what's decided. But I think to clear yourselves, you don't want to be going out of the country with a stolen case. That in itself incriminates you. I mean, you could admit to the police you took the case from the hotel room, and they might think you look well dodgy. But leaving the country with the case actually confirms it.'

Julie nodded.

'Okay. You might be right.' Her mouth curled a little in a wry smile. 'Of course, nobody actually knows how many diamonds were in each of these pouches . . .'

Rosie shook her head and put her hands over her ears.

'I never heard that.'

Rosie and Matt finished their tea and she went up to the counter to pay the bill. Julie, Nikki and Matt were already heading for the door. She joined them as they walked towards Julie's car. She opened the boot and alongside two holdalls was the aluminium attaché case. She clicked it open and Rosie could see the passports and pouches inside. They all stood staring at them in silence.

'So,' Julie eventually said. 'That's us ready to roll then. When will we know about the story?'

'We have to talk to the editor first to see what we do. What about the case?'

'I'd rather leave it with you.'

Rosie looked at Matt, who gave her an oh-shit! look. McGuire would go nuts, but having the actual case to hand over the cops would be a major coup, even if she had to be economical with the truth.

'Okay. I'll take it.' She'd work out what she would do later.

Matt rolled his eyes, and Rosie looked at him and shrugged. Julie pulled the case out and handed it to her.

'We'd best get moving. Rosie, please don't do anything till we're on that flight tomorrow.'

'Don't worry. The editor has some decisions to make. Just let me know tonight how you are, and call me tomorrow from the airport. You need to keep in touch with me. I need to know where you are. Can I trust you on that?' She gave the pair of them a stern look.

They nodded.

'We've trusted you all along. So it goes both ways.'

'Both ways,' Rosie replied.

Julie stepped forward and hugged her and she hugged her back, feeling more emotional than she meant to. It had been a long day. Nikki hugged her too. She swallowed. Poor bastards. God knows where they would end up. The kind of company they had noised up, they could be hunted down and dead within a week. Rosie promised herself that before she handed over anything to anyone, she needed clarity from McGuire and from the cops. These girls weren't gangsters – just half-daft, naive women who'd got in way too deep.

Julie and Nikki gave Matt a hug, then they got into their

car. Julie reversed out of the parking space and turned towards the exit.

She blew a kiss, and it brought a smile to Rosie's face as she waved back. She watched as the car drove out and round the bend onto the motorway.

'Come on,' said Matt. 'Let's go.'

As Matt drove the car up towards the roundabout and onto the motorway, Rosie's mobile rang. It would be McGuire again. She took it out of her jacket. It was Laila's name that came up on the screen.

'Rosie . . .' Laila's voice trailed off.

'Laila! You alright? Something wrong?'

'Oh, Rosie . . .' she sobbed. 'It's Sabiha.'

'Sabiha? What's happened?'

'She's dead, Rosie. Burned to death in her house this morning.'

'Oh Christ, Laila! Jesus! What . . . What happened?'

'They . . . they said it was a fire in the house . . . But it wasn't. Rosie, I know it wasn't. Sabiha was found in the living room. She . . . she was on fire.'

'Who's told you this?'

'The police. They told my grandfather. They are saying it might have been suicide. That she set herself on fire.'

'Aw Jesus, Laila!' Rosie choked, recalling the first day her eyes met Sabiha's and the angry welts on her wrists.

'I . . . I know Sabiha wouldn't do that. She has three children, Rosie. They did it. I know they did.'

'Laila. Listen. I'm not in Glasgow at the moment, but I'll be there by tonight. I'll come and see you.'

'Okay. Thanks . . . But they did it, Rosie, I know.'

'I'll see you later. Just . . . Just talk to your mum and grandparents. Stay with them . . . Take care. Don't go out of the house.'

The line went dead.

CHAPTER THIRTY-FIVE

McGuire was working with his executives on the *Post*'s first edition when Rosie appeared at the top of the stairs. There were only a couple of late-shift reporters around, both on the phone, and the hub of activity that was normal around the area was eerily quiet. Rosie dumped her bag on her desk and sat down for a moment, a polystyrene cup of tea in her hand. She was done in with exhaustion, and she still had McGuire to face. He happened to look over his shoulder and clocked her at her desk. It took all of two minutes before he was striding her way, his expression a mix of concentration and frustration.

'In you come, Gilmour.'

Rosie got up and trotted behind him, bracing herself for a row, not in the mood to take any shit.

As he passed Marion's empty desk, he picked up a piece of paper, crushed it into a ball and drop-kicked it.

'What the fuck, Rosie? It's half seven. Not even a phone call. Fuck all!'

'I know, Mick. But listen . . . Let me speak. I've got a lot to tell you.'

'The last time I talked to you, I had this feeling there were dead bodies at the farm. So then I don't hear from you, and I'm wondering who's shot who, if maybe someone's followed these daft birds on the motorway and you've been shot.' He shook his head and stared at the ceiling. 'What do I have to do to stress the fucking word "communication" to you? I mean how hard can it fucking be?'

'Everything happened so fast. Honestly, it was just crazy. I met the girls in the cafe at Abbington and then got caught up in the interview with them, then it was a case of trying to hammer up the road in the fog. I couldn't get a phone signal on the motorway.'

He pushed out a beleaguered sigh.

'Oh, forget it. Sit down and talk to me.' He pointed a finger. 'Everything.'

Rosie began with the moment she and Matt were confronted by the farmer brandishing a loaded shotgun as they sat in the layby. She told him everything that had happened, and relayed what Julie and Nikki had told her.

'The farmer shot two people? Christ!'

'I know. I haven't seen the bodies with my own eyes, because we didn't go up to the farm. It wasn't safe. But Julie told us what'd happened to Vanner and his minder. Then as big Gordy was getting away, he got it too, from the farmer. He was doing it to save his son, because Gordy looked like he was going to take him hostage. The guy's in a wheelchair.'

'What's wrong with him?'

'Julie said that the lad – Euan's his name – told her it was some brutal kicking he got four years ago in Glasgow. Brain damage. He was a promising rugby star, apparently. Doesn't ring a bell with me, though.'

'Get it checked out. Might be interesting.' He loosened his tie. 'So . . . two things. First, what about the cops? And two, what about the case with the diamonds? Where is it?'

'Well. As you know, Julie and Nikki are flying out to Malaga from Manchester in the morning. So they couldn't take it with them.'

McGuire closed his eyes for a second, then opened them.

'Don't tell me you've got it.'

Rosie put her hands up in surrender.

'What else could I do, Mick? We couldn't just leave it in the boot of the car. And we couldn't get the cops – I didn't want to do anything till I talked to you. Until we work out how we're going to play this.'

'I'll tell you how we're going to play this, sweetheart. We're going to phone the cops right now and tell them chapter and verse. I'm not sitting here on a fucking case full of smuggled diamonds stolen from some stiff in the Albany Hotel. Enough of that shite. And as for the farmer? I mean, who does he think he is? Charles fucking Bronson?'

Rosie stifled a laugh. McGuire was funny when he was bordering on hysterical.

'I know. Of course we'll have to get the cops. But I think we need to sleep on it tonight and decide what we do. I don't want to get suddenly banged up by some earnest detective because I've got this suitcase. Plus, I want to go and see the farmer myself.'

'What? Charles Bronson? Listen, if he's in that kind of mood again, you might be next on his hit list.'

'No. Julie gets the impression he's a good man.'

'Yeah. And Julie's a bright spark. Was it not her who talked her pal into all this that night at the hotel?'

'Yes. But she is pretty smart. They were wired up with our recording gear during all this.'

Rosie knew it would do the trick, and McGuire's eyes widened.

'What? You've got the shooting on camera?'

'Well. Not quite. But we've got clear, identifiable images of Vanner when he appeared in the house, and Gordy coming in. Then the girls were tied up, so they were too low down to capture any proper images, but you hear the shotgun going off. It's good stuff.'

'Where is it?'

'Matt's got it. He's in the canteen.'

'Get him up here. I want to see it.' He phoned the picture editor. 'Bob. Can you pop in?'

Rosie phoned Matt and told him to come upstairs.

'Something else, Mick. Before we start going over all these tapes.' Rosie swallowed. 'I got a phone call from Laila. She was hysterical. Her cousin Sabiha is dead. Burned to death in her house.'

'Oh Christ! Where?'

'Somewhere out in the Paisley direction. She was living with the in-laws. Laila swears they set fire to her.'

'Christ!' He shook his head, genuinely upset. 'Poor bastard. What . . . they set fire to her for speaking out?'

'For talking to me. Maybe some kind of honour killing – by speaking to us, she's brought shame on the family.' She paused, feeling a lump in her throat. 'I feel like shit, Mick. I . . . I . . .'

'Listen! There's no such fucking thing as honour killing! What a pile of shite that is. If they've done this to her, in the name of honour, then we'll hound the fuck out of them, I promise you that.' He gave her a sympathetic look. 'Listen. I know how you must be feeling. I know how you get involved. But it's not your fault, Rosie.'

'I know . . . But it feels like it is.'

There was a knock on the door.

'We'll discuss this more in the morning. Come in, lads.'

*

It was almost nine by the time Rosie arrived at Laila's grandparents' house. She'd phoned them first to make sure they would see her this late. She didn't want to impose. As if she hadn't imposed enough, she chastised herself, guilt twisting her gut as she climbed the stairs to their house and rang the bell.

Laila opened the door, her face flushed and eyes swollen from crying. She burst into tears and threw herself into Rosie's arms. She held the girl, sobbing, on her shoulder. Her mother and grandparents appeared in the hallway, their faces grim and pale.

'Come in,' the mother said, and she eased Laila out of Rosie's arms.

'I'm so, so sorry,' Rosie choked. 'I . . . I just don't know what to say.'

'Come inside,' the grandfather said. 'We will have some tea.'

In the living room Rosie sat in the armchair next to the glowing gas fire, opposite Laila and her mother on the sofa, who were clutching each other's hands. Laila's grandmother disappeared into the kitchen. In the heavy silence, Rosie didn't quite know where to start. But she had to start somewhere.

'So . . . So, what happened? When did you find out?'

'We only heard today – I phoned you immediately. I think it happened last night, around teatime. We still don't know the details.'

'A lot of people in our community are not talking to us Because of . . . Well, because we went against their wishes, and protected our granddaughter.'

'I was so close to Sabiha,' Laila said. 'I was with her all the time with the children, before all this happened. I used to go to the house with Rabia and listen to them both talking about their lives. That's why I know so much . . .' Her voice trailed off and she glanced at her grandfather.

He took a breath and let it out slowly.

'Rosie.' His voice was soft. 'Laila wants to talk to the police. I . . . I'm worried about it. But I think it is the right thing to do. She has heard things about Rabia, and she didn't even tell us until she came home from Pakistan.'

'Do you mean you have evidence that they harmed Rabia?'

Rosie looked at Laila, then at the grandfather.

'Not evidence, as such. Just what Rabia told her about being ill-treated. And that wouldn't mean much now, because it's too late . . . she's already buried,' Laila's grandfather said. 'But what Laila heard from Sabiha and Rabia about the passports, and how Rabia's husband Farooq was involved in it, that's important. I don't know how much his father knew, but if Rashid did know, even if he wasn't involved, then he turned a blind eye. That is wrong. They are all guilty. If Rabia was pushed out of the window, or was so depressed because of how they ill-treated her that she jumped, then they all deserve to be punished. They should face justice.'

Rosie nodded. This would be a tall order without evidence. The police had already noised the Shahs up sufficiently, though, so they would be on edge. Probably already starting to blame each other for the passport scam. Laila's grandmother appeared with a tray with tea glasses on it. She handed Rosie one which was so sweet she could feel it punch its way straight into her bloodstream.

'Well, I can talk to the police. I have some good contacts, and I know that they have already been to the house, so I know the detectives would welcome more evidence – even if it is only what Sabiha and Rabia told you. Sadly, these poor girls aren't here to back it up now, but with everything that's gone on in the past couple of days, I think the case is ripe for the police to move in. Your evidence would definitely be good for them to have, Laila.'

Rosie hesitated. She hated taking her notebook out, but she was going to have to. She wasn't a police officer; she had a story to tell, and if Laila wanted to fill in the blanks, then she wasn't going to wait until the police arrived to decide whether or not they would pass the information on to her sometime later.

'Do you mind if we just have a chat now about what you, Sabiha and Rabia talked about?'

'No – I want to talk,' Laila said.

'Are you sure you're okay with it? We can do it tomorrow if you'd rather?'

'No. I want to do it now. I want to tell the truth. We have

to.' She glanced at her mother, who clasped her hand tighter, then her grandfather. He blinked slowly and nodded.

Rosie's heart went out to them. It was impossible for her to understand what it was like to live in this kind of close-knit community. You had to be a part of it to know. Her dealings with Pakistanis and Asians was very limited, but she had always found them polite and hard-working. What she'd seen in recent weeks had opened up a different world to her. She'd been shocked to the core by what she'd witnessed in Pakistan, but the notion that an entire community, right here on her own doorstep, could keep up a cloak of secrecy about a young girl's death, was a different issue. She opened her notebook and asked Laila to start at the beginning.

CHAPTER THIRTY-SIX

Sleep just wouldn't come for Rosie. She'd wrestled around the bed, a mix of too much tea and being just too exhausted to relax keeping her awake. Eventually she drifted off, but the last time she'd looked at the clock it was four in the morning. When she awoke three hours later, she just lay in the darkness, staring at the ceiling, listening to the rain batter on her bedroom windows. Her face was wet from her nightmare, and she didn't even attempt to make sense of it. All she could remember was a blaze and someone screaming. She felt her throat tighten, and the urge to cry was almost overwhelming. If she didn't get out of this bed right now, anything could happen. She threw back the duvet, grateful that the central heating had clicked on and the room was warm. She padded naked into the living room and clicked on the television, then pulled open the curtains. It was still dark outside and the lights twinkled from cars making their way to work, the slow line of commuters from Charing Cross snaking its way into the city. She stuck the kettle on, then went for a shower and stood there till she was almost sleeping again. She finished it off with a blast of icy water to shock her into her day. By the time Matt's text sounded on her mobile, she was dressed, caffeined up, and as ready as she would ever be.

The drive to Stirling was a crawl in the semi-darkness, but at least the rain had stopped. She and Matt didn't speak too much on the journey, both exhausted. He hadn't slept much either. Eventually, they took the slip road and went along the Bannockburn road towards the farm. On the way up there, they could see the farmer's pickup was outside the house, and the lights were on. As they drove into the courtyard, they exchanged glances when they saw the Jaguar with the shattered windscreen. Rosie noticed one of the window curtains in the farmer's house was pulled back a little. She was relieved to see there were no bodies lying around on the ground. By the time they got out of the car, the front door was open and Euan sat in in the doorway in his wheelchair. He looked tired, his eyes were swollen and bruised, and there was a graze on his forehead. He manoeuvred his wheels until he was outside, pulling up the zip on his fleecy jacket against the wind.

'What do you want?'

'Sorry. It's Euan, isn't it?'

'Who are you?'

'We're looking for your dad. Is he around?'

Euan shook his head, biting his lips together as though he was about to crumple.

'Are you the people my dad met up at the field yesterday? You said you were journalists?'

'Yes. We're from the *Post*. Is your mum here?'

Euan shook his head.

'She stayed with her sister last night.'

'Look, Euan. I'm really sorry about this, but we talked to Julie and Nikki. We were with them last night when they left here. We've been working with them on an investigation for a few weeks now.' Rosie paused, waiting for a reaction. When there was none, she continued. 'They told us what happened here.'

Euan said nothing. He wheeled past them. 'Why can't you just go away and leave us alone! Why can't everyone leave us alone?'

They followed him as he went across the yard to where the pig pen was. Rosie looked at Matt, not really sure how to handle this. They stood behind him as he stared down at the pig pen, his face ashen.

'Where's your father, Euan?'

'Why?'

'Because we want to talk to him. Bad things happened here yesterday. We know all about it. Four people died. We know you were in danger.'

'Bad things happened because bad people came here.

The same kind of bad bastards who did this to me.' He reached up to his face to wipe away a tear.

'I know. I understand. But your dad is in trouble and he needs to talk to someone.'

Rosie gazed as the thin light of morning crept across the landscape, beginning to lift the darkness. She shivered in the wind as her eyes took in the outbuildings and fences in need of repair. Euan shook his head and stared into space. Then he put his hands to his face as he began to weep.

'Dad's gone. He took the shotgun . . . Oh, Dad! Oh God! Can somebody help us . . .?' He looked up to the sky, pleading, tears streaming down his cheeks.

Rosie shot Matt a worried glance.

'Where? Where did he go?'

No answer. She went forward and stood in front of Euan, reaching out to touch his shoulder.

'Euan. Tell us where he is. We can go and look for him.'

'He wants to die. He said we'd all be better off.'

'That's not true. Listen, where do you think he is?'

Silence. Then Euan's lip trembled.

'He'll be down by the graveside. My wee sister died when she was only four, and my mum and dad wanted her buried on our land. He might be there. I don't know . . .' His voice trailed off.

Rosie and Matt exchanged looks. Matt shrugged and sighed.

'Come on, let's go. Where is it exactly?' she asked.

'Over there.' He pointed towards an area beyond the garden that was walled off with trees and bushes. 'Behind that clump of trees. That's where the grave is. He might be there, I don't know. Please . . . Can you go and find him? I . . . I feel helpless here. Useless.'

Rosie and Matt turned and walked quickly in the direction he'd pointed to.

'This is dangerous, Rosie,' Matt said. 'Should we not phone for help? If he's in a mad state of mind, who knows what he'll do? He's got nothing to lose by shooting us.'

'He won't shoot us. Why would he do that?'

'How do you know?'

'I just don't believe he will.'

'Christ almighty,' Matt muttered as they quickened their step.

Across the garden they dipped down to a path through the thicket and as they walked further on, they could see a shape sitting on a bench in front of what looked like a headstone. A conifer stood on each side, and white pebbles surrounded the area.

'What're we going to do?' Matt whispered.

'You stay here. I'll go. In case we spook him.'

'You'll spook him just as much with one as two.'

'Maybe not. Look, Matt, just wait here. I won't do anything daft.'

'Christ. Like this isn't anything daft.'

'Sssh. Don't say a word.'

Rosie walked slowly along the path through the wet grass, picking her steps carefully in case she stood on a twig that would snap and cause a sudden noise. Then she went on in a semi-circle so she would be in his sight, hoping she was far enough away that if he did instinctively fire, it might just be buckshot she'd get, instead of the full force of the shotgun at close range. This was madness, she knew it. But every fibre of her told her to keep going. When she was in what she hoped was his line of sight, she could see him clearly, head bowed. The gun in his hand.

'James. Mr O'Neill,' Rosie said loud enough for him to hear, but not loud enough to be threatening. At least she hoped not.

His head came up and he looked startled. He grasped the gun.

Shit! Please don't let him shoot me. Rosie stood rigid, her hands up as though she was under arrest.

'James, please. A moment. Don't shoot! I met you yesterday. At the field? You remember?'

He raised the shotgun to his shoulder.

'Please, Mr O'Neill. Don't shoot. I . . . I want to see if we can help you. Listen, you need help. You're not a bad man.'

He shook his head.

'I am a bad man.'

'You're not, James. Everyone will see that. You were trying to protect your son, that's what they'll see. That's *all* they'll see.' She paused, watching him, ready to dive to the ground if he pointed the gun at her. 'If anything, you're a hero. Those bastards you shot yesterday were the scum of the earth. They murdered and robbed and built their whole lives on power, and were rotten to the core. You did the world a favour. People will see that.'

He shook his head, but looked up at her.

'What good will I be if I'm in jail? How am I going to help my son and my wife? Tell me that. I failed them. I failed them all. Just go away. Let me do this.'

He lowered the shotgun, then turned it around, so that the barrel was below his chin and his thumb was on the trigger. Christ! He was going to blow his own head off.

Rosie took a step forward, her heart in her mouth. Anything could happen, and she was getting too close to protect herself. What the hell was she doing? She could get herself killed. But she took another step, her eyes fixed on his.

'I won't let you do it, James. I won't let you kill yourself and leave your family. I've seen too much killing in my life as a journalist. Needless killing. I know you're angry and bitter at what happened to Euan, but please, believe me, people need you. I know you are a good man. Julie and Nikki told me you saved their lives.'

He was silent and Rosie watched as he seemed to process the information. She prayed she was getting through to him. But she also knew that people bent on suicide could just flip at the last minute. She could feel her knees knocking and her face raw in the biting wind.

'James. Please listen a minute. Let me get you help. Let me get the police and they will look at your case. I promise you, I know how they work. You won't get done for murder. You were protecting your disabled son, for God's sake. You did what any father would do. And even if you do go to court, they'll never send you to jail. The whole country will be behind you. My newspaper will get behind you. I promise you. Please. Put the gun down. Your family need you.'

He pulled back the safety catch, and Rosie braced herself for his head blowing off. She closed her eyes and looked away. Then, suddenly she heard the clatter. She opened her eyes to see that he'd thrown the gun away from himself, onto the pebbles at the graveside. He slumped forward, sobbing into his hands. She stood watching him for a second, her instincts telling her to go forward and comfort him. She took a step closer, then another, the sound of his wailing carrying in the wind.

'Why . . . Why did they do this to my son? Look what they did to my family . . . Oh God! Somebody help me. Please!'

Rosie went within touching distance.

'Come on, James. Stand up. Let's go back to the house. We'll get the police. You know we need to do that.'

He sat for a moment, sniffing, his big hands wiping his tears away. Then he stood up, shaky on his feet, and walked towards her. He allowed her to take his arm and walk him back up the path.

When they got to the top she spotted Euan in the distance and then heard his cries.

'Dad! Dad! Oh, God, Dad! I thought we'd lost you!' He frantically pushed his wheelchair forward.

The farmer walked towards his son, tears streaming down his face.

Rosie went up to Matt and puffed out a relieved sigh.

'Christ! That was close.'

'Jesus, Rosie! You took a chance. You did good.'

He hugged her and she buried her head in his shoulder.

'Sorry . . . God almighty! That's twice I've blubbed with you. You'd better not tell anyone, or I'll cut your throat.'

'No chance, Rosie. I love you too much.' He held her tight while she composed herself.

They went inside the house, where a small fire flickered in the hearth. The farmer wheeled his son close to the fire, then sat in the armchair, as Rosie went to the kitchen and put on the kettle. Tea, she thought, sweet tea for the shock. Hers as much as theirs. Matt was still outside.

'I'm going to call a police contact I know, James,' Rosie said. 'He's with Strathclyde, and I know it's a different area, but they have contacts over here and they'll liaise. Just stay strong. I know that if it comes to it, Julie and Nikki will back your story up, so just hang on.'

Rosie could see bloodstains on the carpet, but no bodies. She didn't want to ask. Matt appeared at the door and gave her a look, beckoning her outside.

'What?' Rosie asked as they walked into the yard.

'Over here.' He walked towards the pig pen.

'What is it?'

They walked close to where the pigs were sloshing around in the mud, grunting and pushing each other around, slavering.

'What?'

'On the ground. Look. In the mud.' He pointed into a puddle.

Rosie peered and stepped forward. Then she saw the gold ring shining in the puddle. A big G on the ring. She looked at Matt, her eyes wide.

'Oh Christ!'

'Shit, Rosie. Do you think he's already fed them to the pigs?'

'Shit! That doesn't bear thinking about.'

'How else can you explain a big gold ring with the letter G lying on the ground, and a lot of well-fed pigs farting and squelching about?'

'Stop it, Matt.' Rosie felt queasy.

'Where are the bodies? There were four of them. Did you ask him?'

'Put it this way, I don't think the atmosphere is right yet to start asking questions like that. I'm phoning the cops. Let them ask.' She paused. 'Did you get a picture of that ring?'

'Is the Pope a Catholic?'

Rosie punched in Don's number.

'Don. I need your help. Right now.'

Rosie waited outside the barn, trying to stay far away from the DCI and his team, who had arrived from Central Scotland Police. Don had come through from Glasgow, to liaise, but when he'd introduced Rosie to the youngish DCI from the Central Scotland police force, he'd given her short shrift. He'd asked why she didn't dial 999. What kind of game was she playing here? he'd badgered her. Did she think she was in some kind of television drama? Rosie had said nothing. This belligerent bastard was clearly the kind of detective who hated journalists. In his pinstriped suit and raincoat, he looked like some city financier rather than your run-of-the-mill detective. Don had told her in an aside (while the DCI was busy dishing out orders) that he was one of the new fast-track university graduates who'd probably not spent much time on the street before they pushed him up the ladder. He'd told her it was best to keep her mouth zipped and not to give him any smartarse comments, because this guy looked like he was in the mood to arrest her.

Rosie watched as a team of officers in white overalls went into the barn. Matt had tried to coax Rosie to go inside for a look before the police arrived, but she didn't know what they would find. She was relieved when an officer came out and signalled for a stretcher. Don was on the end of the DCI's conversation, and he came over to tell Rosie that there were four bodies on the floor of the barn. They showed signs that they'd been moved there. Rosie was relieved. At least O'Neill hadn't turned them into pig feed – presumably he'd realised the ring would help identify the bodies and had tried to dispose of it in his half-crazed state. After half an hour standing freezing in the cold, she'd told the DCI she would have to get back to Glasgow as she had a deadline. He reluctantly let her go. He would be in touch and officers would come through to Glasgow to interview her, he said. He reminded her, unnecessarily, that she was part of a murder investigation. Rosie walked Don to his car and told him about Sabiha, and everything else Laila had said last night, and that she was willing to make a statement. He was already on the phone to HQ as he was getting into his car, arranging for officers to be at Laila's grandparents' house in the next couple of hours.

As she went towards Matt's waiting car, Rosie wanted to put her head into the farmhouse before she left, but there was a police officer on the door and the area was taped off as a crime scene. Through the window, she could see O'Neill sitting on an armchair, staring down at the floor. Euan was in the wheelchair by his side, and he looked up and raised his chin slightly to acknowledge her. She got into the car and they drove off.

CHAPTER THIRTY-SEVEN

McGuire had phoned for Tom Hanlon, the *Post*'s lawyer, to come in to advise on how far they could go with the story of the shoot-out at the farm. As usual, Hanlon would push it as far as it could go without the paper being on a contempt of court charge. If O'Neill wasn't charged with murder, or anything else, by the time the first edition went to bed that night, they could run with a form of the story on the splash of the bloodbath at the Bannockburn farm. They would probably get pelters from the Crown Office tomorrow for using anything at all, given the likelihood of a trial in the near future. But Hanlon had told Rosie to work on a form of words that he could legally justify. He advised McGuire to exercise major restraint on the pictures. The editor wasn't happy, but knew that, come any kind of trial, they would be in possession of material nobody should have been anywhere near. It was a win-win situation, he declared. Not if your name was

Johnny Vanner or Gordy MacLean, Rosie reminded him. Fuck them, McGuire said. He was already thinking of BLOODY BATTLE OF BANNOCKBURN as a headline. Some things never changed.

It was now gone six and Rosie sat back, re-reading her story once again. It was as good as it got. She hadn't even written up Laila's story about the fake passports and her claims that Rabia's husband was involved yet. One day at a time, she told herself. Her mobile rang on her desk and she saw Don's number.

'What's happening, Don?'

She could hear the background noise of a bar.

'What's happening, Rosie, is that it's all happening.'

Rosie detected a two- or three-pint swagger to his voice.

'You've started early,' she said.

'I'm celebrating. We're celebrating. Come on up. I'm going round to O'Brien's once I leave the boys.'

'What's going on? Celebration?'

'We've nailed that fucking Pakistani husband. Nailed the bastard to the wall.'

'Get away!'

'Nope. Straight up. We got a couple of officers to go up and interview the kid, Laila, after I spoke to you – by the way, thanks for that. The DCI says he owes you.'

'I hope he remembers,' Rosie said.

'The kid was brilliant. Of course, none of it is provable,

but we got enough. So we went down to see the Shah family again. I knew they'd burst if we had enough on them.'

'So tell me.'

'Actually, I don't think the father knew all that much, but he was definitely shielding that bastard son of his. So we go in there and give him chapter and verse, how they're all getting done, and that it was only a matter of time. We were pretty heavy on them.'

'How unlike the police!' Rosie knew he would enjoy the sarcasm.

'Anyway, he seemed shocked that we were in possession of so much evidence. Okay, we gilded the lily a bit.'

'Of course.'

'But we went away, empty-handed.'

'So what's to celebrate?'

'Because less than two hours later, this Shah character appeared at the HQ with his son in tow. He asked to see the DCI, and the son spilled the whole fucking lot.'

'You're kidding. A confession?'

'Yep. And we didn't even need to pull anyone's finger-nails off.'

'Confessed to what? Not to killing Rabia, surely?'

'Not quite. But we're going to get him on that. Well, we're going to try. He confessed to the passports, to using her passport after she was dead, and said he'd been getting paid off by contacts down in Manchester to be part of the fake passport game. He told us all that. That'll get him five years, anyway.'

'What about old Shah?'

'He actually handed his son over and told us that he had known nothing about it, and it was only after Rabia died that he became suspicious.'

'So why didn't he come forward?'

'Protecting his son. Protecting his community.'

'So why the change of heart?'

'I think he just knew that we were onto them. That this won't go away, and it could bring shame on all of them. Most Asians wouldn't even know anything about this scam. But there are plenty of crooks among them – same as there are among anyone else, anywhere else.'

'What a result!' Rosie knew she didn't sound as enthusiastic as she actually was. This *was* a real result, and she had played a critical part in it. She should be heading for O'Brien's and sinking at least two gin and tonics for starters. But tiredness was kicking in. So much had happened today, her mind was beginning to melt down.

'Come up for a drink.'

'I can't, Don. I'm tired. Totally done in. Let's do it tomorrow, after work.'

'Okay, darlin'. It's a date. I'll give you a shout. And, Rosie . . . Thanks.'

'All part of the service, pal. Just make sure the DCI sends me a Valentine's card.'

Rosie hung up.

On the editorial floor she was taking her jacket from the back of her chair when Declan signalled that he was coming off the phone in a second and wanted to talk to her. She waited.

'Rosie. I wanted to show you this before you go.' He handed her a newspaper cutting.

Her eyes scanned over it, but were drawn to the picture of the strapping young man in the rugby strip. It was Euan. Smiling triumphantly, he was holding a trophy aloft, surrounded by his team. The story highlighted the court case, in which the man charged with stamping on his head was cleared of attempted murder. There was a photograph at the bottom of a grinning, crop-haired thug on the steps of the High Court in Glasgow. There was a quote from James O'Neill, saying that there was no justice.

'And this.' Declan handed her another clipping.

Rosie looked it over. The headline was: MISSING. She read it quickly. It told how the man cleared of causing brain damage to a young farmer had gone missing. He hadn't been seen since leaving the building site where he'd worked in Stepps, near Glasgow. The story was over a year old. Rosie couldn't remember it, so she must have been abroad when it was published. Missing. She thought of O'Neill and his anger at the thug walking free from court. Could he have done something to him? Dished out his own justice? She pictured the pig pen and the big machine they'd seen inside the barn. It could probably grind down just about anything into pig feed. Would O'Neill really be capable of that, and of living with it?

'Thanks, Declan. I'll have a word with McGuire about it.'

Rosie left the floor and went down the steps, folding the cutting and putting it in her bag. She wondered if the cops would now look into the case of the missing thug, or even if O'Neill, in his present state, would suddenly confess it all to them if he was guilty. What if the farm held a grisly secret? It sent a shiver through her. She stepped out and swallowed a lungful of the biting wind. Stuff it, she thought. This was one story she wouldn't attempt to unravel. If the missing thug really had become pig feed, then that was good enough for him.

Her mobile rang as she was driving out of the car park. She could see from the corner of her eye that it was Adrian. There was a little twist in her gut. She stopped the car at the exit and stared at the screen. It rang and rang, but she didn't answer. Maybe it was time to cut loose. She felt deeply for Adrian, but even now she wasn't sure if it was lust, friendship or the fact that he had saved her life so many times. Let it go. Deep down, she knew there might be other times when she'd call on his help. But, right now, she needed to let go of whatever it was between them. The phone stopped ringing, and there was no message.

Rosie parked her car at the edge of Renfield Street and

strolled across to the Buchanan Street precinct, aimlessly gazing in shop windows, her mind beginning to clear and relax for the first time in weeks. She toyed with the idea of going for a drink, but didn't want to go into O'Brien's because Don would be there by now, all euphoric and six beers ahead of her. Somehow she didn't feel like celebrating. Unwinding with a coffee was what she needed right now, in the quietness of the cafe close to O'Brien's where she could feel detached from the world. Then she'd go home, have a long bath and sink into bed. Tomorrow would be a good day. There were good days to come. She turned into the side street where the cafe windows were steaming up from condensation, but it looked reasonably quiet. A blast of hot air and the aroma of fresh coffee hit her as she walked in. Then, as she scanned around for a quiet corner, the room suddenly swam − like one of her vivid dreams on nights when she'd wake up crying, reaching for the image as it melted before her. He looked up, as though he felt her presence. TJ smiled and stood up.

'Rosie.'

ACKNOWLEDGEMENTS

Writing takes up most of my time these days, and I'm privileged to lose myself in characters and create stories. In many ways I'm living the dream – even if it gets a little lonely sometimes. But when I'm not in Rosie Gilmour mode, I have a raft of people who mean the world to me, even if I don't say it too often. So this a word of thanks to them.

My sister Sadie is my biggest fan and has supported me even when my childhood dreams seemed far fetched. Also my brothers Des, Arthur and Hugh, who are always there for me.

Talented nephew Matthew Costello, who's building my new website, and Paul Smith who brings calm to techno chaos. Thanks to Christopher Costello, who's always bursting with ideas, and to Katrina Campbell, my fashion and and PR guru.

It's a joy to see the children of nephews and nieces grow,

so, welcome to our world, the delightful Jude Campbell, who's finding his feet.

My research on the rough diamond trade was made easier thanks to Dave O'Brien's invaluable advice.

I'm blessed with true friends I can count on, even if we don't see each other all the time: Eileen, Liz, Mag, Annie, Mary, Phil, Betty, Kathleen and Geraldine, Anne Sharpe, Ann Marie Newall, Helen and Irene Timmons, Sarah Hendrie, Alice Cowan and Debbie Bailey.

And here's to my old newspaper pals, Helen, Barbara, Donna, Jan, Si, Lynn, Annie, Maureen, Keith, Mark, Thomas, Ross, Gordon and Janetta, Jimmy, Brian and Peter.

To Cathy, and all the Motherwell Smiths – particular thanks to Maureen and Jimmy Martin, Clare and Paul McMurray, and Mairi Timmons for the golden times on our Camino de Santiago this year.

In Dingle – thanks to Mary, Paud, Siobhan, Martin, Cristin, and Sean Brendain.

And on the Costa del Sol, valued friends who have been constant with their support – Lisa, Lillias, Nat, Mara, Yvonne, Wendy, Jean, Sally, Sarah, Fran, Jean and Dave, Davina and Billy.

And, of course, my friends on Facebook who support my shameless self-promotion, and make me laugh with their posts.

Special thanks to Jane Wood, my publisher at Quercus, for her belief in me and continued encouragement and advice, and my editor Katie Gordon who picks up all my slapdashery. Thanks also to the super efficient Therese Keating, who misses nothing, and all the terrific team at Quercus who promote my books.

And a big thanks my agent, Euan Thorneycroft, for his frank and honest advice.